GW01454053

ALTERNATIVE
OUTCOME

where fact and fiction collide

PETER ROWLANDS

Topham
PUBLISHING

Alternative Outcome
© Peter Rowlands 2016. All rights reserved.
Topham Publishing, London
www.tophampublishing.com

Peter Rowlands has asserted his right under the Design and Patents Act 1988 to be identified as the author of this work.

ISBN: 978 0 9957224 0 8

To Fleur,
who never doubted that it would be worthwhile

Prologue

Stepping off the train at Euston was never inspiring. However smart the trains or swift the journey, the dimly-lit platforms were always an anticlimax.

I negotiated the obstacle course of pillars, impelled as always to outpace the dozens of other travellers heading the same way. Why? Was it a race?

Up the long ramp and into the thronging station concourse, I threaded my way over to the sliding glass doors leading out to the forecourt.

As I approached them I nearly collided with someone coming the other way: a woman in her thirties. About my height, straight shoulder-length dark hair, attractive face.

We both side-stepped in the same direction, then again the other way. The woman smiled briefly in acknowledgement, then stopped abruptly, looking at me.

We stared at each other for a long moment. Did we know each other? I was on the brink of asking, but I felt sure the answer was no. Yet her look was so intense, the exchange so protracted, that we seemed bound to speak. So what else were we going to say? What conceivable subject would match up to the moment?

Finally she seemed to give a little shrug – almost as if to say, "Well, I gave it my best shot." Then she was moving again, she was gone. I watched her disappear amongst the mass of people crossing the concourse.

It was nothing, yet immediately I felt a sense of loss. I should have spoken up, and now the opportunity had passed.

Had I known her after all? This puzzle nagged at me as I walked across the forecourt. She'd stirred some distant memory in me, but I couldn't tap into it.

Then it came to me. She reminded me of a girl I'd met on holiday as a child. At the time I couldn't have been more than eleven or twelve years old.

Surely not. Would she still be recognisable after all these years? It seemed ridiculous. More to the point, would I? That was even harder to believe.

I tried to conjure up the face I remembered from the past. Was there really any correspondence? I couldn't tell. I hadn't thought about the girl from my childhood for years. Yet I couldn't altogether dismiss the idea.

Unsettling memories now trickled to the front of my mind. The girl I'd known in the past wasn't just any girl, she was someone who had fed my adolescent romantic aspirations long after our encounter, and at the same time had helped define my sense of the fragility of expectation.

The notion that I'd actually known her was largely wishful thinking. I'd wanted to know her, that was for sure, but I'd been too shy to follow through. Our brief and inconclusive encounter, and others like it, had blighted my adolescent years. No wonder I'd shunted this one to the back of my mind.

I headed on towards Euston Road.

PART ONE

Chapter 1

Two years later

"Here's to your first million – and ten weeks at the top of the best-seller list." Joanna lifted her glass and clinked it against mine, smiling encouragingly.

"Here's to it." My smile was a little more forced than hers, but her enthusiasm was infectious. "But maybe ten weeks is a bit optimistic. Let's agree on eight."

She settled into a corner of the sofa without being asked and held out her glass for a top-up. "But just a small one. I don't want to be reeling when I pick Jeremy up." She studied the diminutive glass I'd given her. "Unlikely, I should think." She looked up again. "John sends his regards."

John, her husband, was a friend of mine from college days, but since they'd married a few years back I seemed to have seen more of her than him. By coincidence they'd ended up living just a few streets away from me in south London, and she'd taken to making unannounced visits like this in the middle of the afternoon, usually on her way to collect her young son from school. Since I worked from home, I was usually here when she called.

I wondered idly, at moments like this, whether Joanna sought out my company because I was now single and she was attracted to me, or for the opposite reason – because she regarded me as safe enough not to make any moves on her. At such times I was also uncomfortably conscious that if I'd been having this discussion with her, she would have been chiding me for such cynical, self-doubting thoughts. "Can't I just be a friend?" she would have said.

I looked down at her now, considering her dark hair, her warm brown eyes and her slight tendency to excess weight – held in check by endless dieting, or so she often told me. The truth was that Joanna wasn't my type, though I couldn't easily have said what *was* my type. If we'd been discussing the matter, she would have made me itemise my must-have features, whereas to me, attractiveness usually hung on some indefinable aura.

I did value her friendship, though – probably a lot more highly than I realised.

Belatedly I answered her, "Give John and Jeremy my best."

"Remind me, Mike – is it Amazon you've published your book on?"

I sat down beside her. "No, it's on Endpaper – one of the other online publishers. They seem to offer the best deal for authors – the ones who actually sell any copies, that is."

"Sorry, yes, you did tell me." She sipped her wine. "Well, I think your book is great. You ought to sell loads of copies."

I smiled at this positivity. "Well, it's a crowded market. Many are called, few are chosen – all that. I'm not exactly holding my breath. At least it's out there now."

"You need to promote it. Why don't you get all your friends to buy it and write glowing reviews? I can be the first. I know I've already read it, but I haven't paid for it yet."

"You are too kind." I smiled at her. "Actually a couple of other friends have promised to look out for it, and they say they'll pay real money to buy it. But I don't really want fake reviews. It's like shouting out 'I'm self-published.' It devalues the whole process."

"All the more reason to get those reviews written, though. At least it means you'll be starting on a level playing field with everyone else."

I sighed. She was probably right, but I didn't want to think in that way. The whole idea of writing a book had been to step away from the rat race of commercial journalism, but it had dawned on me long ago that in its own way the literary world was just as cut-throat.

She wasn't done yet. "You could have a web site for the book as well, and a blog."

"I've got a basic web site. Didn't I tell you? And I've got my Facebook and LinkedIn pages set up."

"One of those bastard literary agents should have picked up your book and run with it." She said this with real feeling. I had reported on my progress with them last year, though I now rather regretted doing this. Joanna seemed to feel she had taken a stake in the project, and I wasn't sure I was quite comfortable with this.

"There's a lot of competition. They need to be confident that the publisher will get their investment back. Only outstanding books actually get published in the real world."

"Who says yours isn't outstanding?"

"Your support is greatly appreciated, even if your judgement is clouded."

She reached over and punched me in the arm. "Bollocks! Stop being so bloody self-deprecating. You should have more confidence."

"Perhaps."

She raised her glass to me again. "Well, today is still a red-letter day, so here's to you and your book. May it have many grateful readers."

I raised mine again in return.

* * *

My mobile phone buzzed on the dining table. I apologised and stood up quickly. Freelance writers can't afford to let any call go unanswered.

The voice on the other end was economical to a fault. "Mike. Jason. Rick Ashton. Lunch. Tomorrow."

I couldn't resist holding the phone away from my ear melodramatically and mouthing obscenities at it. Joanna raised her eyebrows. I knew exactly what the caller, Jason Bright, was talking about, and it annoyed me. He was the deputy editor of a logistics magazine, and he was telling me he wanted me to interview the head of a national parcels company over lunch.

I had no complaint about the commission itself, which should earn me a useful few hundred pounds. What grated was that these things were never arranged at such short notice, as he was well aware. Some other journalist must have cried off, and now he was asking me to step in at the last minute. Everyone's mop-up guy – that was me.

Perhaps I should have taken it as a tribute to our long-standing familiarity that we could talk in shorthand like this, but to me it merely summed up the imbalance in our relationship. He demanded, I complied.

I drew breath, mainly to avoid seeming in too much of a hurry. "Should be OK, yes."

"Excellent." He hesitated. "And you're all right with this, are you?"

Now he was off the script. I wasn't sure what he meant.

"All right? Yes – why wouldn't I be?"

"It's just … never mind, if you're on it that's fine." He started to reel off the place and time for the meeting.

Joanna stood up and gave me an exaggerated wave, pointing at her wristwatch and then towards the front door. She whispered, "What are you doing on Thursday?"

I held the phone away from my ear. "Let me see." I pretended to think. "Nothing."

"Come and have a meal with us. John should be back from his trip, and he'd love to hear about the book."

She slipped quietly out of the room, and I lifted the phone back to my ear. "So you're definitely all right with this, are you?" Jason was saying again. "Sixteen hundred words by the end of the month?"

* * *

I returned the half-empty wine bottle to the fridge and poured myself a whisky instead. A bit early in the day, but so what? I opened the sliding door on to my diminutive patio and stood there a moment, breathing in the unseasonably warm March air. The achievement of getting my book online and on sale had given me a brief buzz, but it wasn't going to earn me my first million any time soon; and meanwhile I still had to work. Unfortunately, that meant dealing with people like Jason.

What made matters worse was that two years ago I'd occupied his role – deputy editor of a long-established transport and logistics magazine. Our specialisation: trucks, vans, warehouses, home deliveries – everything to do with getting goods from A to B.

In an era when print publishing seemed on the way out, the publication still had a respectable circulation, not to mention a lively and popular web site. I'd had a reasonably free rein to call the shots when it came to choosing which articles to write, and I could contact freelances and dump work on them to my heart's content.

But I'd badly messed up. Not in any specific way, just in general. It didn't help when I came back from an interview one day with barely enough material for ten lines of copy, but the malaise ran deeper than that. Somewhere along the line I'd lost my sense of the point of it all, and my discontent must have communicated itself to my employers.

They were very gentlemanly, of course. They simply explained that they were rationalising, and my role was no longer needed. The press was under fire from the internet, and they had to watch their costs. They would keep me on as a freelance, but I could also work for other publications. I might even end up better off.

I hadn't. Two thirds of my work was still for them, and to compound the indignity, a year ago they'd appointed Jason to what had been essentially my role.

Meanwhile, any other work I picked up seemed to involve articles on increasingly outlandish subjects. It was almost as if my clients were defying me to say no. Then they could cut me loose with a clear conscience.

To hell with them all. I poured myself another whisky.

Chapter 2

"Michael," Rick Ashton greeted me, his strong Australian accent immediately evident. "Always a pleasure."

I tended to be wary of this sort of instant cheeriness. Usually you had to jump through hoops to get interviews with top people like Ashton; then the great man or woman would wave away all the hassle as though it were merely an irritant. It was a game with an established set of rules.

Today, though, I was simply grateful for his goodwill. I'd woken with a hangover, then wasted far too much time finishing an overdue article. In the end I'd left home almost too late to make it to this meeting, which was being conducted in a discreetly upmarket West End hotel.

Ashton beamed at me – a well-groomed figure in his late forties or early fifties with a full head of dark hair and an expression of perpetual amusement. He was perhaps a shade heavier than he should have been, but if so it was a close call, and I always felt there was a natural elegance about him. Although no taller than me, he still somehow managed to tower over me. Today he was wearing a pinstripe suit and a tie.

"What do you think of the wide tube stock?"

I stared at him blankly for a moment, glancing for help at Darren McLeish, his young PR man, who was sitting discreetly to one side. He gave an almost imperceptible shrug.

"On the District line. The latest trains."

Enlightenment dawned. I'd known Ashton slightly for at least five years, and for some reason he had gained the mistaken impression early in our relationship that I was a railway enthusiast. Ever since then his ice-breaker had been some sort of observation about trains.

I prepared to improvise a reply, but then felt a sudden desire to press the metaphorical reset button. Surely we could find something more relevant to pass the time over? "Actually, the big thing with me at the moment is that I've just published my first novel. Online, that is."

He stopped mid-stream. "You're a dark horse." He looked at me with what appeared to be genuine interest. "What kind of book is it?"

"A mystery thriller."

"Just my kind of thing. Where can I get a copy?" To prove he meant this he immediately pulled a tiny leather-bound notebook from an inside pocket and made a show of holding his pen poised. I couldn't help smiling inwardly. Even his selection of leisure reading evidently had to be approached as an executive decision.

I told him the publisher's web address and he wrote it down carefully, asking, "What's it about?"

I hesitated. I hadn't intended to talk about the book to anyone I knew through my job, and I was also wary of giving away too much of the plot. I felt it should speak for itself. However, clearly I'd committed myself now, so I tried summarising the story in a few sentences.

He listened carefully and nodded, apparently satisfied. "Good stuff." He looked at me inscrutably for a moment, then abruptly unclicked his pen, put the notebook away and sat forward in his chair. The formal interview had begun.

*   *   *

As always with Ashton, the session went well. You couldn't help feeling beguiled by his plain-talking charm. He made it seem that running a major parcels company was something anyone with a modicum of intelligence could do – and if you had any suggestions about how he could do it better, he was more than happy to hear them.

He was also good value. His company was currently under fire in the press and the Twittersphere for poor service levels and frequent mis-deliveries, but he was ready to acknowledge all these problems before boasting about solutions. He understood the goodwill value. It meant I could write what looked like a frank, informed interview, even though we both understood that it was largely choreographed by him and his people, and my ultimate message would be broadly the one he wanted to convey.

After fifty minutes the three of us adjourned to the hotel's elegant restaurant: small and even cosy, though it had been made to seem spacious through judicious use of mirrors, white walls, brushed steel pillars and soft grey accents.

I'd wondered if Ashton would skip this bit, given that I was a stand-in today, but he seemed committed to going the whole nine yards. Before long we were sipping Sauvignon Blanc and putting the world to rights.

As we chatted, a man in a grey suit materialised by our table.

"Richard," he said, addressing Ashton, "what a pleasant surprise to see you here today." But he didn't seem especially pleased; his expression was difficult to read, but his tone suggested heavy irony. His accent was hard to place: not British, not discernibly from anywhere specific. I couldn't glean much from his appearance either. He was a tallish, well-toned white man in his mid to late forties, perhaps with middle European features. He had immaculate slicked-back black hair and an open-neck shirt.

Ashton looked up at him, apparently undaunted. "Janni, good to see you." He turned to me. "Mike, this is Janni Noble." He pronounced Janni with a soft J, like "Yanni". He added, "Our folks up in the North West have been doing some business with him."

Of course. Janni Noble. I knew the name, though I'd only ever seen him in photographs until now. Peripherally, he'd been involved in an article I'd written several years before, though we'd never met.

The man looked at me enquiringly. Ashton said, "Janni, this is Mike Stanhope, an associate of mine from the business press. We're just putting the world to rights."

I reached out my hand. He hesitated for a moment, regarding me coolly, then gave me a light, almost reluctant handshake. "I know you from somewhere." It was a neutral comment, yet somehow from this man's lips it also sounded like a threat. "It will come to me."

He turned back to Ashton and they exchanged a few more words. Then he turned back and gave me another long look. I could see a flicker of recognition dawning in his eyes. "So you are Michael Stanhope, and you are a journalist?"

"Correct."

He nodded to himself. "This is interesting."

I raised my eyebrows, but he declined to elaborate. He turned instead to rejoin his colleagues at another table, glancing back at me a final time as he walked away.

"A powerful presence," I commented to Ashton.

"You think so?" He glanced after the man. "A useful colleague. He came to our rescue up in the north last year when we needed some extra fleet resources."

I marvelled to myself at the way powerful men like Ashton could seem so unimpressed when they encountered others like them. To me, it felt as if a chill had just passed over our table. Without being invited, I poured myself another glass of wine.

Chapter 3

"What's your book about?" John grinned at me amiably over Joanna's improvised goulash.

He was a happy soul; with his florid complexion, upstanding red hair and thickset build, he looked exactly like the rugby player he had been until recently, and he radiated a rugby player's confident goodwill. He had just returned from a trip that involved trying to sell British-designed hand dryers on the Continent, which I didn't envy him; but his lifestyle seemed to suit him well enough.

I said, "It's a mystery story based round a robbery from a security van. Most of the gang are caught, but one of them escapes and disappears off the face of the earth. The main part of the story is about a man who tries to track him down many years later."

John looked at me expectantly, so I added, "I based it vaguely on a real robbery back in the nineteen eighties."

"Right." He pondered this a moment. "And will it be published in print as well as online?"

"Huh! I doubt it. There's too much competition."

He nodded, perhaps searching for something else to ask. "So in real life, were all the thieves caught?"

I'd had this same reaction from one or two other people who'd asked about the book. For some reason they seemed more interested in the real story than in what I'd made of it in my novel.

Barely swallowing my frustration, I said, "Well, no one really knows. According to folklore one of them did get away, but there's no definitive evidence. I've simply hypothesised that he did." I paused, then said with exaggerated patience, "It was the underlying idea that interested me, not the real-life specifics."

I caught Joanna giving John a warning glance, and immediately felt guilty. These were good friends. I shouldn't be allowing my jaded attitude to upset them.

John merely said, "Ah, OK. So what happens in your story then?"

I was tempted to say "Read the book", but this time I managed to bite my tongue. I'd already reached the conclusion he was never going to, so what was the point?

When I'd embarked on the book, I had naively assumed that all my friends and acquaintances would be pressing me for sight of it as soon as it was ready, but I'd soon found that many of them seemed resoundingly underwhelmed by the idea. I hadn't decided yet whether this was simply because they weren't interested in mystery thrillers, or because they couldn't conceive of a world in which I would be capable of writing one that they would want to read.

I took a deep breath and made an effort. "Well, the book follows the fortunes of the man who escaped, and his family." I hesitated. "I based the family on real life too, but the people I had in mind had nothing to do with the actual robbery. It was a family I came across on holiday when I was young. I tried to contact them years later, but no one knew what happened to them. They seemed to have disappeared. It seemed like a cue for a mystery story."

Joanna shot me an accusing look. "You never told me about that."

"I don't tell you everything."

*   *   *

Later, helping Joanna to stack the dishes in the kitchen, I said, "Sorry I was a bit defensive earlier." I glanced over at the door to make sure we were alone. John had gone upstairs to check his emails. "Sometimes people don't seem to get the idea of this book. They focus on the wrong things. I should be more patient."

"John doesn't mean any harm, but he can be a bit of a philistine. I wouldn't take any notice if I were you."

I smiled. Joanna had supported my idea of writing a book from the start. I knew she saw it as therapy for me. She thought I'd taken too long to get used to my ex-wife Sandy's departure, and needed a distraction. She was probably right.

She said, "So who were these people you modelled your fictitious family on, and why were they such a big secret?"

I considered this for a moment, trying to decide how to shuffle my thoughts into a coherent form. Finally I said, "To be honest, the whole idea for this book came from a tiny incident a couple of years ago. I'd just got off a train at Euston station, and I bumped into a woman I thought I knew. Afterwards I fantasised that she might be a girl I used to fancy from afar when I was a kid, when we were on holiday in Falmouth."

"How sweet."

I ignored this. "I had a look to see if I could track down her family, but I couldn't find any trace of them. Then it occurred to me that there must be a story in it, and I realised the robbery theme fitted in rather well with it."

She leaned back against the sink, absorbing this and smiling at me reflectively. "So these people that you knew as a child – how far did you get with tracking them down?"

"I didn't get anywhere. I tried to contact the hotel where we all stayed, but it went out of business years ago. I didn't know the family's name, just that the girl was called Trina. Maybe Catrina? With a C or a K. Something like that. So the trail went cold straight away."

"Couldn't you have pushed it a bit further? People don't really just disappear. They must be out there somewhere."

I shrugged. "I wasn't really that bothered. I was concentrating on the book. I was more interested in the narrative possibilities than the actual people."

"Narrative possibilities." She smiled mockingly at me. "You're beginning to sound like the *Times Literary Supplement*."

"Very funny."

She looked at me speculatively. "You ought to try looking for them again. See if you really can track them down. I can definitely see the makings of something here."

"Huh! Bit late now. My novel is already finished and self-published, in case you'd forgotten."

"Maybe you'll get some ideas for the follow-up. You could develop this into a series."

I scowled at her. "Stop making fun of me."

"Not at all!"

She started preparing the coffee, then turned to me again. "That woman you saw at Euston station – do you think she really was the same person you knew as a child?"

I shrugged. "I very much doubt it. It seems a bit unlikely, don't you think?"

"I suppose so. But just imagine if it really was her!"

"What – you reckon we would fall gratefully into each other's arms? I don't think so."

She laughed. "OK, fair enough." She clattered three coffee mugs on to a tray. "But you could do with shaking up your love life a bit, Mike. It's too long now since Sandy."

Ah, we had to get round to my marriage break-up in the end. I said, "Thanks for reminding me."

She wouldn't let it go. "You're not a bad looking guy, Mike. Plenty of my girl friends would be more than happy to step up to the plate."

"Huh. Flattery will get you nowhere. Anyway, I suspect I'm a bit ragged round the edges these days." I made for the kitchen door. "Can we talk about something else please?"

* * *

As I walked home I wondered again about John's question: would my book ever be published in print? I had strong memories of an abortive visit I'd paid to a literary agency a few months before.

It was one of two dozen who had already rejected the book, and by chance I happened to spot their street address in central London. I managed to talk my way in, only to find there was no one around except the office administrator, a slim woman in her mid-forties with severely-cut greying hair and an aura of nervous energy. She knew nothing about my book, but proved unexpectedly willing to talk about the company in a general way.

"To be honest, hardly any speculative submissions are accepted," she admitted confidentially. "It might be different at other agencies, but that's how it is here." He lowered her voice. "You probably know it's sometimes called the slush pile." A brittle laugh. "Not very flattering."

I left my response hanging in the air, and after a moment she added, "It's not as if we *want* to reject people's work. We *want* to discover great new literature. That's what we're here for."

I nodded. "But there isn't a lot of it about."

"Exactly. People think they know how to write a best seller, but they don't."

I asked how the firm handled unsolicited submissions. She said, "Our readers work through them when they get the opportunity."

"Who are the readers?"

"Experienced specialists." She declined to elaborate.

"Do you ever reject any books and then find they've been taken up by another agent or publisher, and they've become big sellers?"

"Certainly. That's why we usually tell writers to keep trying. Some of them do, and in the end it sometimes pays off." She pushed her chair back from her desk and stretched. "But not often."

CONCISE TREATMENT

1988

The white waterfront houses of Polperro gleamed in the sun. From my clifftop vantage point I gazed down at the picturebook town, nestling in the cove like some artist's dreamscape.

Mixed emotions surged through me. Polperro looked simply splendid, and seemed to underpin the simmering joy I felt. She was in the world, and what's more she was in my world. That knowledge gave me an inner glow, and Polperro itself seemed to feel it.

But she was leaving tomorrow. Her second week had overlapped our first – I was certain of that. Six days wasted, only one more left. Too little time to step forward, to become an active player in her story, not just an onlooker.

Polperro mocked me. The joy it radiated was not mine. It was a joy other people felt; I seemed condemned to remain always the outsider. Her presence was a constant reproach for my inaction. I would be glad when she was gone.

I picked myself up and started back to rejoin my parents at the car, but I misjudged the narrow path. Nettles brushed my bare legs, an angry rebuke, and instant tears stabbed at the back of my eyes: not just from the stinging, but also from my inner turmoil. I blinked them away angrily.

Never mind; at least I would see her over dinner tonight, across the restaurant or somewhere out in the grounds. She would remind me of a world of infinite possibilities.

Chapter 4

There was something wrong with my web site.

I didn't notice at first. I was examining the site a couple of mornings after seeing John and Joanna – trying to view it as a stranger might. Did it make my book sound irresistible? Did it convey the right balance of readability, intrigue and menace? Would I want to read the book myself if I saw a description like this? Joanna had reminded me the other day that I needed to get this kind of thing right if I really wanted to ratchet up my sales.

Then I noticed a curious black panel at the very top of the browser window, obscuring part of the page and pushing other parts slightly out of position. This certainly wasn't part of the intended design.

There was some tiny, nearly-illegible grey text on the panel. I leaned forward and zoomed in. It looked like some sort of computer code. I clicked through to some of the other pages, and realised that the intrusive black panel appeared on all of them.

What the hell? I logged into the administration site – the place where I normally changed the page contents or uploaded text to my blog. There was something wrong here, too. There was no black panel this time, but some of the normal sections of the page had been nudged slightly out of position.

I sat back abruptly and let go of the mouse as if it was too hot to handle. I felt as if the site was tainted, and I shouldn't be touching it. Had it been hacked? Or was Kevin, my web designer, simply playing around with it?

I grabbed my phone and scrolled down to his number. Kevin, a freelancer, had once worked for the magazine publisher where I'd been assistant editor, and had completely rebuilt my old, simplistic web site for next to nothing to help me promote my book. He owed me the favour from a time I'd helped him rewrite the text of a site for one of his customers. The downside of our arrangement was that I never knew quite how much support he was prepared to throw in as part of the deal.

Fortunately he answered my call immediately.

"Kevin, it's Mike Stanhope. About my web site."

"What's up, mate?" He had that classic techie's tone – apparently helpful, but at the same time guarded.

"Have a look. There's a weird panel at the top of all the pages. I wondered if you were doing some more development work on it or something."

"Not guilty. As far as I'm concerned the site is finished." His tone said it all; the debt was repaid, and he had no further obligation to me.

"Fair enough. But the fact is that something's gone wrong with the site."

"Let me have a look."

There was a pause, then he said, "OK, I'm looking at the home page now. That doesn't look right, does it?"

"Exactly."

"And you haven't been uploading some bizarre content to the site, have you? Custom Javascript or something like that?"

"You must be joking. I wouldn't know how to."

"OK, well I'll need to get into the site and have a look round. Leave it with me. I'll ring you back in a few minutes."

* * *

He was as good as his word.

"You've been hacked, mate. Have you been handing out your password and username or something?"

I swallowed, trying to keep my patience. "Of course not. Why would I do that?"

"I dunno. It's just that this kind of attack is quite simplistic. It usually starts when spammers or hackers get hold of your FTP logins. That allows them to put anything they want on your site, basically."

"Well I can't see how it could be down to me." I paused. "What have they actually done, anyway?"

He hesitated, perhaps trying to reduce the message to simple terms. "It's an iframe injection attack, so far as I can see. Basically a bit of some other web site gets incorporated into your pages. It means that if someone clicks something on your site, it might send information back to the attacker's web server instead of yours."

"So they could intercept messages sent to me – that kind of thing?"

"Probably, yes. But this is a bit of a bodged job. You shouldn't be able to see the iframe really – unless it's meant to look like an advert or something. Otherwise it's a clue that something's wrong."

"Well let's not be sorry that they're bodgers."

He gave an ironic laugh. "True enough."

"So can you put it right?"

"Yeah, no problem. It might take a while, though. I'll need to go through everything to see how much damage has been done, and then change the username and password. I'll have to get back to you."

It was clear from his tone that he rather resented the work involved, but couldn't think of a way to duck out of it. I thought it was probably time to end the conversation, but he now commented, "That's strange."

"What is?"

"Well, these iframe attacks can be quite automated. Once there's a security breach, the injection process just kicks in." He paused, perhaps peering at his screen. "This looks like more of a manual attack."

"How can you tell?"

"Well …" He drew breath to answer, then seemed to think the better of it. "It's complicated to explain. It's just my gut feeling."

"OK, so what does it mean?"

"I suppose it suggests that someone was specifically targeting you – trying to capture your passwords and other stuff about you, that kind of thing."

"Charming."

"I can improve the site's security and use stronger passwords. I can tighten things up generally. But if you use the same passwords for other things, I would definitely consider changing them. You never know what else these people might get up to."

I put the phone down reflectively. Web sites got hacked all the time. I shouldn't read any special significance into this. Yet it had never happened to me before in all the years that I'd had a basic web site and blog, and the thought that I'd been targeted intentionally was unsettling. It felt like an intrusion into my personal space, and I didn't like it.

Chapter 5

An unexpected phone call put thoughts of my web site out of my mind.

"Mr Michael Stanhope?" The accent was foreign, the voice distantly familiar.

"That's me."

The speaker seemed uncertain how to continue. He said nothing for a moment, then, "This is Tommy Noble."

Of course. It was three or four years since we'd spoken, but the occasion was hard to forget. I'd written an investigative article for the magazine I was then working for – an exposé about international people trafficking and its impact on the haulage industry – and Tommy Noble was the key to it: Tommy, the brother of Janni Noble, the man I'd met in the restaurant with Rick Ashton.

The article came long before the subsequent international crisis over migrants from the Middle East and Africa. My piece was much more specific. It was about the trickle of people who had been entering Britain for many years, aided by a small band of specialist smugglers. They targeted individuals or small groups of people from eastern Europe and beyond, bringing them all the way from the source country to Britain in customised freight containers. The haulage industry was nervous, and my article focused on how these schemes actually worked.

I'd amazed myself by arranging an interview with Tommy Noble, a whistle-blower who was actually involved in this trade himself. That said, I couldn't exactly claim the credit for making the contact. Originally it was he who had approached me. Seemingly he'd asked around discreetly, on the lookout for a writer who would keep his identity secret, and eventually he'd obtained my name from a driver I'd once written about – a man who was being exploited by his employer.

All the same, at the time it felt like a coup. I had vivid memories of the shivering transport café outside Luton where I'd met Tommy, and the drab yard where he'd nervously taken me to show me the custom container: empty, but still bearing clear evidence of recent occupants. All this seemed very much in keeping with the reputation I seemed to have created for myself among the fellow-journalists on my magazine.

However, I'd never spoken to Tommy since the article was published; so how come he was telephoning me two days after I'd bumped into his brother? Surely this had to be more than a coincidence?

I said, "What can I do for you?"

"Ah, well, you will remember that you took some photographs. Pictures of me ..."

I did remember. When I'd interviewed him, I'd persuaded him to let me photograph him and his container on the promise that his face would be concealed. It had seemed to me that including him in the pictures, even disguised, would make the whole article seem more real, more credible. Remarkably enough he'd agreed – on condition that I would email the images to him to prove he couldn't be recognised.

However, in the event I'd never used the pictures. Tommy had rung me from a call-box a few days later and begged me not to. He thought – no doubt rightly – that his co-offenders would be able to identify him from the actual container, whether he himself was concealed or not.

In a way I'd been relieved. I'd already come to the conclusion that using the pictures would be pushing things too far. I didn't want to risk his anonymity. Or perhaps more likely, I'd had a failure of nerve about the whole thing. Pictures made it all seem that bit too real.

I now said, "I do remember."

"Good. So, what I wondered ..." He hesitated again. "I had the impression that there were more pictures. Pictures that you did not show me at the time. Is that correct?"

Were there? I thought not. I only took a few, and I was pretty sure I'd sent him all of them. "No, you saw everything there was."

"Surely there were alternative shots, different angles, this kind of thing?" A pause. "I should very much like to see these other pictures."

I said, "I'm sorry, but I don't think so."

"This is unfortunate." The disappointment was evident in his voice.

"I don't know what else to tell you."

"Very well." There was a long pause, then a click as he disconnected.

* * *

What did this mean? Had Janni Noble asked Tommy to phone me? If so, why? And if not, what was Tommy after?

I'd never fully understood Tommy's motivation for talking to me in the first place. From what he'd told me, his brother Janni was the moving force behind the smuggling operation, so it was hard to make out why Tommy wanted to undermine it.

In the end I'd concluded that his attitude stemmed not from principled opposition to the smuggling, rather from simple sibling rivalry. Janni actually ran the company, whereas Tommy seemed to have a relatively insignificant role in it. I suspected that he was aggrieved at being sidelined, and had decided to demonstrate how vulnerable the smuggling operation made it. In effect it was an act of rather reckless vengefulness.

At the time, his reasons for speaking out hadn't mattered to me. Nor, it now struck me, had the surprising fact that his brother – the head of an apparently thriving company – would want to be involved in this kind of activity in the first place. What mattered to me at the time was that I was able to write an interesting and topical inside story based on Tommy's revelations.

Looking back, I could see that my shallow attitude and failure to ask obvious questions didn't do me much credit. And to make matters worse, I'd never followed up from a journalistic point of view. I'd been side-tracked by other stories, and by events in my own life.

So what in fact did happen to the brothers after my article was published? I vaguely remembered that the whole smuggling enterprise had come to an abrupt end, but I was no longer sure of the chronology.

I opened a browser window on my laptop and flicked through press reports from the time I wrote the article. As I thought, soon afterwards the police had raided the company's headquarters outside Oldham, near Manchester. They had arrested some of its staff, including Tommy himself, though Janni had been released without charge.

In theory, Tommy might have formed the view that I'd had something to do with this turn of events. So might Janni, though only if Tommy had revealed his own part in the article, which seemed unlikely. But logically speaking, one or both of them might consider that I'd betrayed them.

Yet I knew I'd been careful. I hadn't named anyone in my article; hadn't revealed where in Britain they were working from; hadn't said which eastern European countries they were targeting. In short, I'd made the article as bland as I dared without robbing the whole thing of any substance. And no police had ever come calling on me, demanding the names of my informants. I felt sure the article had played no role in their investigation.

In any case, the whole thing had quickly died a death. Within days of the police moving in, it had been announced that the case had been dropped. I couldn't remember now why this had happened, but browsing further, I saw that it was basically down to lack of hard evidence. Clearly the container that I'd photographed had never been found, and there had been a resolute silence among peripheral participants who had been expected to blow the whistle. Whether Janni had achieved this by cajoling or coercion wasn't clear. The fact was that apparently no one involved wanted to see the prime suspects going down.

In theory, this meant that neither of the brothers had any real reason to be harbouring a grudge against me. Yet I couldn't altogether dismiss the thought that one of them might be. Such concerns came with the territory.

*   *   *

The irony was that I'd never written any further articles in this vein, and these days I wondered if I even could. I knew that some of my colleagues from that period still regarded me as a relentless investigative terrier, but in my own mind that image had never seemed to fit. I'd had to wind myself up to researching every probing piece, and eventually it had all seemed like too much effort. Other writers were being paid the same as me for turning in predictable ring-around articles or routine interviews like the one I'd conducted with Rick Ashton, so why was I putting myself through such stress?

It was around this time that my wife Sandy informed me she'd had enough of our marriage. I was never at home, I was always too serious, I wouldn't relax, I didn't know how to have a good time, it was all a mistake, bla bla.

I hadn't been able to decide at the time whether my behaviour was the result of work-induced stress, or was just my natural state. Either way, her departure seemed to kick away my resolution to do battle for every article. Six months later I was writing anodyne feature articles about cryogenic chemical tankers and airfield crash tenders, and within a year I was out of a full-time job.

Somehow, I doubted that Sandy would have found me much more congenial now than before.

Chapter 6

I stared at the nearly-blank page of my notebook. Two days had passed since Tommy Noble's call, and I was trying to force myself to catch up with neglected work. I wasn't getting very far.

My self-imposed task this morning was to construct an article about trends in refrigerated transport. In a determined burst of activity I'd looked up and written down the telephone numbers of five companies that built truck and van bodies, but that was the sum total of my progress so far. My plan was to telephone them all, find someone at each of them who was willing to talk to me, and ask them about their latest product developments.

I tossed my pen down. "What's new? What's bleeding new?" I swivelled round in my office chair and stared out of the window. "Nothing's bleeding new sir. Fuck all is new. We are building the same old same old. Kindly sod off and leave us to do it in peace."

They wouldn't take that line, of course; they would be polite and would try to be helpful. At the end of the day, they knew they would get publicity out of it. But I felt sure they'd like to.

What could I do instead? Eighteen months ago I would have been breaking off at this point to write a bit more of my novel, which had provided an ever-available distraction from proper work. Even when it was finished, I'd spent hours fine-tuning it and then preparing extracts for potential agents. It had seemed like a project with no end, yet inevitably the end had come when I'd uploaded it to the web. It had left a void.

Should I be working on a follow-up? No, not at this precise point in time. I had no ideas for one, and anyway I wanted to see how the first one fared before committing myself to a second. I needed something else, and playing games on my PC or phone wasn't going to do it for me.

So what else? I swivelled back to my desk and sat up straighter. Well, I could get on with promoting my book online – uploading extracts to reading groups, submitting the title to review sites, tweeting about it, blogging about it. This was, after all, what I'd planned. I no longer had the excuse that my web site had been compromised. Kevin had emailed me a couple of days ago to confirm that it was now secure again and working normally.

Perversely, though, all this activity seemed too much like "real" work. What I craved was some single-minded project, whether writing a book or investigating someone or something. Even though I was fed up with doing this kind of thing for my job, it seemed I didn't mind doing it for myself.

And that's when I knew what I would do. That girl I'd known in Falmouth – I really would try to find out what had happened to her. For my book I'd built a mystery around the character I based on her; but what had happened to the real girl and her parents? Was it anything like the outcome I'd conjectured?

I stared out of the window again into a grey suburban morning. I hadn't thought properly about the real girl for years – not even when I was writing the book. I'd simply grabbed the memory and translated it into a new character who fitted my plot. She immediately took on a separate, objective existence, insulating me from thoughts of the actual person I had in mind.

Now I found myself drawn back to those distant days from my childhood, and I allowed myself to remember the yearning that the real girl had aroused in me: to be part of the adult world, to have a proper relationship with another person – an attractive, exuberant person like her. My trouble was that I didn't know how to make it happen. In my imagination it had seemed incredibly simple, but in the real world I felt invisible. I simply lacked the wherewithal to break through some impenetrable barrier between us.

Finally, incredibly, when it had seemed all hope was lost, we'd actually spoken, and she'd told me she would write to me when we both got home. But she never did. It was the first genuine relationship trauma of my life.

Objectively I wasn't surprised when I heard nothing from her. I was already adult enough not to invest high expectations in such a promise, especially when given so lightly. Yet subjectively, the disappointment had festered. For maybe six weeks I'd clung to the hope that a letter might still arrive. Daily I'd watched for the postman, hoping against hope to see her missive drop through the letterbox. Nothing came.

Eventually I'd reconciled myself to the fact that it never would. The episode had turned into an object lesson in the way life can sometimes let you down. And although at the time I would have considered myself above such sensitivities, I knew that for years afterwards the disappointment had blighted my subsequent attempts at adolescent relationships. Either I'd approached them too intensely and frightened them away, or I'd avoided any kind of commitment from the outset, convinced that it wouldn't work. My sense of isolation had grown from year to year.

So was I now finally seeking closure, half a lifetime later? Hardly. It had all happened so long ago. But thinking back, I found it impossible not to wonder what had become of the girl herself. Presumably she was alive at this moment, about my own age and living her adult life somewhere. Where? Under what circumstances? Were her parents still around?

And I couldn't deny it – I wondered if she'd ever thought about me. Had she meant to write, but been distracted? Had she had second thoughts? Or had she never intended to keep her promise in the first place? Realistically, I could see that even if I actually found her, it was years too late now for me to be asking her any of these questions. But if I did find her, maybe the answers would be self-evident.

I glanced back at my computer screen. An entirely separate question was whether her life could possibly have followed a similar pattern to that of her counterpart in my story. The thought seemed extremely far-fetched; yet I now felt a sudden urge to find out.

And even if you discounted all the above, could she be that woman I saw at Euston? This idea seemed about as unlikely as any other, but I couldn't entirely discount it. My emotional reaction to that woman had been too intense to dismiss; she really had drawn me back to those distant days, and I could now see that in a corner of my mind it still mattered.

* * *

I opened a browser window on my laptop. Was this it then – the start of my search? No, for a moment I held back. I felt that if I was to conduct a search, it also required some more practical imperative. I needed to be able to tell myself there was a tangible objective, not just a will o' the wisp ambition to resolve some issue from my childhood.

Well, it was undeniably intriguing that the hotel in Falmouth had closed down soon after we were there. It was a ready-made scenario for a mystery. Two years ago, when I'd started work on my book, I'd done a perfunctory web search on the place, but come up with very few results, and nothing to identify the girl or her family. So I would be starting with a blank canvas.

I thought about this for a moment. I didn't know these people's surname, so their subsequent lives were bound to be a mystery to me. That didn't mean they were a mystery to the world at large. I simply didn't know where to look for them.

But if I followed up and still had difficulty tracking them down, that would validate the endeavour, wouldn't it? The harder they proved to find, the more profound would be the mystery behind their disappearance, and the more worthwhile it would seem to look for them. I could feel my latent journalistic instincts stirring.

I picked up my mobile phone to check my calendar app, and found to my joy that the article on refrigeration wasn't needed for nearly three weeks. Ha! So I didn't actually have to work on it today at all.

Immediately I felt a sense of guilt. No wonder I was writing so many of my articles at the last minute these days, and doing it in a blind panic. I needed to get a grip. I couldn't afford to let customers down, and there was a mortgage to pay on this house – far higher since Sandy had left, and only just within my current means.

Yet three weeks was three weeks. The thought of doing something more interesting suddenly seemed irresistible.

* * *

A new thought occurred to me. I wandered out on to the landing, opened the hatch to the loft and climbed the ladder. The air was dry and dusty. I hadn't been up here in several years – not since Sandy left. But I knew that somewhere there lurked a large collection of photographs inherited from my parents, and no doubt from *their* parents and grandparents, and it didn't take me long to find it, stashed in a bulging cardboard packing case.

It was hard to find any order amongst the contents. I pulled out battered albums, manila envelopes with large prints stuffed in them, yellow and pink paper sleeves with prints tucked into one side and negatives in the other. For a long time I rummaged fruitlessly.

Then, almost by chance, I realised with a jolt that I'd found it – the picture I'd almost unconsciously held in my mind all these years, looking suprisingly similar to my memory of it: a dark-haired girl of roughly my age, captured in front of an expanse of bright green foliage and smiling cryptically at the camera.

Was that a look of surprise? Coyness? Guile? Well, I thought I knew the answer to that. It was good spirits tempered with puzzlement. My family didn't actually know her, and up to the day this picture was taken I'd scarcely even spoken to her. Despite this, she seemed quite willing to be photographed, though she must have been wondering why we would want to photograph *her*.

My father, of course, would have assumed in his innocence that we young people must automatically be socialising with each other – joining in with whatever holiday activities were on offer. He could never have comprehended the shyness and self-doubt that almost prevented me from even speaking to this girl, let alone getting to know her. He simply pointed the camera and clicked – and there she was, printed into our family history book, but not into our lives.

Back in my office I brushed the loft dust off my clothes and looked at the picture again. The colours were a bit faded, but the girl's white top and blue shorts still stood out against the greenery.

I stared at that cryptic smile. Could she have grown into the woman I saw at Euston? The hair colour was about right, but that didn't necessarily signify anything. The shape of the face also seemed to fit, but

I could have been fooling myself about that. I was probably making connections where there simply weren't any – hoping to inject a bit of intrigue into my currently barren love life.

Yet the photograph had already intensified my memories of that time. This was the face that sparked so much in terms of my adolescent emotional life. And rightly or wrongly, that woman at Euston had unquestionably reminded me of her.

Experimentally I placed the picture on the mantelpiece, leaning it on the carriage clock that didn't work. That would do for now. See if I still wanted to track her down tomorrow.

See if I still thought this could possibly be the woman I'd seen at the station.

1988

It felt like a dream, Hawkins reflected: Simon leaning over the map, stabbing at different locations and looking up for acknowledgement; Frank gazing unseeing across the room and drumming his fingers on the corner of the table; Joey pacing back and forth, interrupting frequently; Darren staring pensively into his mug of tea. Did they all think this was really going to happen?

Hawkins leaned on the windowsill, watching in disbelief. It felt like a scene from a film. The Lavender Hill Mob? The Italian Job? The Great Train Robbery? *Hadn't these people ever watched those films, and noticed what happened in the end? The bad guys always got caught, that's what happened. And someone usually got killed. Why did they think this would end any differently?*

Simon wanted something from him. He was gesturing indignantly – "Aren't you listening to this, you pillock? You're the one who has to do the driving." *He nodded. Of course he was bloody well listening. He needed every last detail to be etched clearly on his brain.*

He glanced out through the window, across the grey stone wall at the edge of the farmyard and up the sweep of land beyond it. Rain was drizzling down relentlessly. It never seemed to stop raining here. Maybe that was a good sign – a reminder that life had to offer more than this. Wendy said it was raining in the West Country too. Well, with luck it wouldn't be raining where they were going.

He turned back to the room. Simon was still running through the plan. "We have to make sure they know we mean business from the start," *he was saying. Abruptly Target stepped forward from the back of the room and thrust both arms in front if him. All eyes turned to him, and with a dramatic flourish he racked the slide of an automatic pistol.*

The metallic clicking sound hung in the silence. He grinned at the assembled company. "These should make the point."

Chapter 7

My report on my interview with Rick Ashton was due, and I hadn't even started writing it yet. I'd postponed that refrigeration article yesterday, but this one wouldn't wait.

I pulled out my notes and read them through about five times. The longer I left it to work on tasks like this, the less I remembered about the actual occasion I was reporting on, and the more reliant I became on what I'd written down. I'd learned that lesson long ago, but too often failed to take account of it.

Grasping for inspiration, I opened Rick's company web site. An item in the *Latest* panel on the home page immediately caught my attention: "Vantage Express to negotiate new funding." It sounded important, yet the story itself had little substance. Clearly Vantage didn't want to reveal the details.

I tried Googling the company instead, and quickly came up with various recent bits of industry analysis. Basically they all said the same thing: the company could be facing a cash flow crisis, and was trying to secure new capital investment.

I stared sourly at the screen. A few years ago I would have been turning up stories like that myself, not reading them secondhand on other people's web sites: evidence if any were needed that I was losing the plot.

To make matters worse, it was now plain that Ashton had skated round this issue when I interviewed him the other day. He must have been rubbing his hands in glee when he realised I knew nothing about it.

I reached for my phone and rang Ashton's PR man, Darren McLeish.

"What can you tell me about this new funding? Has the deal gone through yet?"

"No, we've got several irons in the fire, and the press picked up on it. That's why we went public with it. Normally we wouldn't have announced anything until it was a done deal."

"I should have raised it with Rick the other day."

There was a pause. I could imagine him trying to keep the smile out of his voice. "Yes, we did wonder why you didn't." Quickly he added, "But you covered a lot of other ground between you, so I'm sure you'll have got a good article out of it."

"Hopefully."

I disconnected, irritated by his transparently patronising attitude, and rang Jason Bright at the magazine.

"I just wanted to check what sort of news coverage you're giving to this restructuring deal at Vantage. I don't want my interview piece to conflict with your information."

"No need to mention it in your article, except in passing. I got a statement from Rick Ashton myself this morning, and we'll run a separate news item when the time comes. They're nearly ready to go public, but probably not before we go to press." He hesitated. "Rick said you didn't discuss it with him when you met up."

"No, well there were loads of other things going on at his company. It didn't seem a priority."

This sounded so weak that I was cringing before I'd even finished saying it. Jason evidently thought so too, and said nothing for a moment. My excuse hung limply in the air. Finally he said, "OK, well it sounds as if you've got plenty of other stuff to write about. Bang your article over and we'll see what we can make of it."

* * *

I gazed at my laptop screen, feeling dejected. I couldn't keep messing Jason Bright around like this. Pretty soon he would lose patience with me – and I would lose a large part of my income. What was the matter with me?

I should start on the article immediately, but I also needed to cheer myself up. I opened Google on my laptop and typed in "Fairmile Hotel

Falmouth". This was the place where those events in my childhood had played out.

It came up with twenty finds. There were references to the place in articles and blogs, and there was even a postcard of the building for sale on an auction site. However, I couldn't find anything of any substance that had been written directly about it. It had closed twenty-three years ago and been demolished two years later, and somehow all this seemed to have happened in a time frame that search engines found uninteresting.

I sat back, faintly disappointed. There was virtually nothing here that I hadn't seen two years ago. I'd been hoping that new information might have materialised since then, but it appeared not.

I looked again at the list of finds, and focused on the Facebook references. What if I tried contacting people who might have stayed at the hotel around the time we did?

At first sight this didn't look very promising. There were three finds, but they were just scene-setting comments in the person's profile. However, one mention was moderately interesting. "Fond memories of Fairmile – launch pad for lifelong friendships". Nicely resonant, I thought to myself. The woman who had posted this, one Linda Dysart, didn't appear to be my woman, but she might be someone who knew her.

So this could be it: the start of my campaign to find Trina and her parents. Up to now I'd merely been thinking about it; if I reached out and tried to contact this woman, I would be making the pursuit a reality.

I glanced around the screen, wondering if there was any way to find an email address or other contact details for Linda Dysart. Apparently not – but I could send her a friend request. I hesitated a moment, then typed a short message to her. Might as well find out first if she'd accept the request. I clicked the button. I was on my way.

There was a possible shortcut to all this, of course. I could tweet my enquiry, and see what that culled. My Twitter account still had a following of sorts, though interest had lapsed since my investigative articles had tailed off. But something held me back – perhaps a sense that such a solution would be almost too direct, too much of a frontal assault. What if I found these people? How would they feel about having their name and history plastered across the Twittersphere?

No, I preferred to pursue the search on my own terms.

I looked back down at my Rick Ashton notes. Reluctantly I closed the browser window and opened a new Word file. Time to get to work.

*   *   *

Twenty-four hours later, my article was finished and on its way to Jason Bright, and I'd received a friend request from the woman I'd contacted on Facebook.

I accepted immediately and uploaded a post. "I had a couple of holidays at the Fairmile Hotel outside Falmouth in the late 1980s," I wrote. "You said you used to stay there. Did we ever meet? I'm trying to hook up with some of the other people who were guests at the same time."

I wondered how long she would take to react to this. It could be days. However, I should have realised from her extremely busy and active online presence that she would be more responsive than that. Within an hour a reply had appeared.

"Hello Mike. I think I must have stayed there a few years before you. Did you ever meet Sabrina, Marie M, Danny Boy or Suzi K? I've stayed in touch with some of them ever since."

I replied, "None of the above, I don't think. How about a girl called Trina?"

After a while she came back with, "Afraid not. Must have been after our time. Does anyone else know the name?"

For the time being no one did. Our asynchronous exchange faltered to a halt. I was wondering what else I could do to advance the search when my phone rang. It was Jason Bright.

"Mike, I just wanted to say thanks for the Rick Ashton interview. It reads well."

He sounded sincere, but after my omission of the new funding development I was nervous. Guardedly I said, "Good."

"Yes, useful bit of background to this financial stuff. Fits in well."

I sensed that he had something else on his mind, so I waited.

"The thing is, I wondered if you would fancy a trip to the West Country? I don't really want to send any of my own guys all that way."

He was actually offering me more work. Trying not to sound over-eager I said, "Sounds good to me. What's the deal?"

"I need a feature article on those people near St Austell. Latimer Logistics? Take a camera with you."

"Expenses paid?"

"The usual." He hesitated. "Nice rounded piece? Lots of detail? No stone unturned?"

"You've got it."

I disconnected and tossed my phone on to the desk. I couldn't really blame Jason for telling me to do a good job, even though it rankled. In his shoes I probably wouldn't have offered me this article in the first place. He'd given me a chance to redeem myself, and I should be grateful.

However, my chagrin over this was easily outweighed by my amazement at the coincidence of this commission. Just as I was obsessing over events that had played out in Cornwall, I was actually being asked to go there. In my world, paid visits to the West Country were few and far between, so this was a remarkable piece of luck.

I opened a map on my screen. St Austell was about fifteen miles short of Truro, the regional capital, and Falmouth was only a few miles further on from there. If I planned things right, I could pay a visit to the Fairmile, or what was left of it.

I phoned the logistics company and made arrangements to see them the following week, then booked myself into a hotel in Truro for two nights. I sat back, feeling pleased with myself. I might not learn anything significant from going there, but at least it would make a change from my normal routine.

As it turned out, I picked up my first clue about my missing family during the trip.

Chapter 8

Cornwall was further away from London than I remembered. The distance to St Austell turned out to be 270 miles via the motorway route – nearly as far as from London to Newcastle, which had always struck me as a seriously long way. To make matters worse, there were road works on the M4, and it took me well over two hours in my ageing Nissan to complete the first hundred miles past Bristol. At least I'd made an early start.

Traffic on the M5 was much lighter once I'd cleared Weston, and the A30 dual carriageway across the moors from Exeter was eerily and gloriously empty. The holiday season was still a couple of months away, which no doubt helped. The broad undulating wooded vistas lifted my spirits. It was too long since I'd come back to this part of the country.

Latimer Logistics had made its name working for the china clay trade, but had long since switched to general logistics, and now had a massive modern warehouse full of consumer goods.

The Latimer team were friendly and cooperative. They showed me around their extensive site, and allowed me to photograph some of their lime green and blue trucks at the loading bay.

Then they gave me a whistle-stop tour of their modern office complex. I was introduced in passing to various people in different departments without actually picking up their names – unsure as always in this situation whether to act like a visiting celebrity or a diffident guest.

The only person I remembered even vaguely afterwards was an attractive young woman in the marketing department. I warmed instantly to her wry smile. In another life, I thought to myself, I might have tried to find a reason to go back and seek her out.

Eventually I sat down in the boardroom with a couple of the directors to talk, and by the end of the afternoon I had enough notes for an article of twice the length required.

Finally I was able to slip away and drive on to Truro. The hotel radiated olde worlde charm, from its apparently genuine oak beams to the ingrained but not unpleasant smell of cooking – that sense of a million meals past. Its other-worldliness was strangely cheering. I felt almost as if I was on holiday.

* * *

I'd allowed myself the next day off, and after breakfast I drove the fifteen miles from Truro down to Falmouth. My plan was to find the site of the Fairmile Hotel, though this proved harder than I expected. I vaguely remembered the road to the hotel out of Falmouth, but when I found it, nothing about the landscape was even remotely familiar.

After driving around fruitlessly for twenty minutes or so I pulled up outside a small suburban convenience store, and here I immediately struck lucky. The man at the checkout looked more than old enough to remember the hotel, and remarkably enough, did remember it. He took me over to the shop doorway and pointed along the road. "See that new housing estate up there? That's where it was."

"Did you know the people who ran it?"

"The Armitages? I knew them vaguely. Mrs Armitage sometimes came into the shop I used to own." He shrugged philosophically. "That's gone now too."

"Do you know what happened to them?"

"Old Teddy Armitage died a long time before they closed down. Mrs Armitage ran it on her own after that. She had the staff to help her, of course."

"What happened in the end?"

"She died too, and there was no one to take over. The developers moved in."

I looked towards the new houses that were just in view down the road. "We used to have our holidays there. For a couple of years, anyway."

He smiled. "Very nice spot. Lovely gardens. All gone now, of course."

"Do you still see any of the staff? Do you know if any of them live around here?"

"I doubt it. They were mostly young people – students doing holiday jobs, young people here for the surfing up at Newquay. Not many locals." He looked thoughtful for a moment. "I used to know the head chef. He was a local man. But he died years ago."

I thanked him for his help, and was walking away towards my car when he called me back. "I tell you who might remember more about the place – Elizabeth Alderley. I think she used to do book-keeping for Mrs Armitage – something like that. She still lives in the big house up the road."

* * *

The large double-fronted Victorian property was quite close to the new housing estate. I found it easily, but knocked on the front door without any high expectations. However, a woman of about eighty with unruly grey hair and wiry build answered promptly. She was wearing faded jeans and a woollen jacket, and was holding a trowel. I gave her what I hoped was a friendly and unchallenging smile.

"I'm sorry to bother you. Vic at the shop suggested I speak to you. I used to have holidays with my parents at the Fairmile Hotel, and I'm trying to track down some guests we met there. I'm not having much luck."

"Good gracious. That's going back." Her expression relaxed into a smile as she gave me a slightly mischievous once-over. She glanced down at her muddy hands and wiped her forehead with the back of her sleeve. "I'm not sure I should be giving out that sort of information to a complete stranger, assuming I even knew it." She blew a stray strand of hair out of her eyes.

"Ah, well, I can understand that. I don't want you to break any confidences."

I left that remark hanging, and after a moment she said, "Oh, what does it matter? It was all so long ago. What were your friends' names?"

"That's the problem. I'm afraid I don't know. Except for the daughter. She was called Trina, I think. This was about two years before the hotel closed down."

She seemed to reflect for a moment, but simply shook her head and smiled. "I'm really sorry, that doesn't ring any bells. It's a long time ago now." She looked at me more carefully. "Why do you suddenly want to find them now?"

"It's a whim really. I'm trying to fill in some gaps in my childhood memories." I shrugged. "I was visiting the area anyway, so I thought I'd see what was left of the place."

She smiled wryly at me. "As you can see, the answer is not much."

"Do you think the hotel records still exist somewhere?"

"Oh no, that's one thing I do know. There was a fire at the place not long after it closed, and everything went up in flames. I know that, because I intended to go back and sort it out, but the office wing was destroyed."

I asked if there were any suspicious circumstances.

"Oh, no, it was caused by an electrical fault."

One way or another, it looked as though I would find little help here in tracking down the missing family.

* * *

I left the woman and drove in towards the town centre, leaving my car in a peripheral car park. The narrow lanes of the old town seemed a world away from the London suburb I'd left yesterday. The gulls' cries echoed round the whitewashed walls, and a few early-season tourists hovered in front of artisan shop windows. A pall of dampness was drifting in from the sea.

I emerged into the harbour area and leaned over a railing, looking out at the mix of dinghies, yachts and a few fishing boats. Much bigger naval vessels lowered in the distance. The rigging of the nearby vessels clattered in the light breeze. I'd come down here with my parents once or twice during our holidays; the intense scent of sea air mingled with chip fat took me straight back to that time.

Despite being thwarted in my search for clues about the missing family, I felt strangely revived. The weight of work done or not done seemed to have been lifted temporarily from my shoulders. For the first time, I was starting to understand the depression that had been descending on me for what seemed like years, largely unrecognised and unchecked. Here, it was as if I'd stepped out from under the cloud. I could empty my head of day-to-day concerns, and just drink in the sights and sounds.

I headed for a pub and a lunch of fish and chips.

Chapter 9

Back in Truro that evening, I considered my options for a meal. I could go out and look for a restaurant in the town, or eat in at the hotel for a second time. In the end I opted for the latter. Its olde worlde charm prevailed.

A party of eight or ten were sitting at a long table opposite me. I had the impression they were a family group, and it was someone's birthday. As my meal progressed I gradually realised my eye was being drawn repeatedly to one of the party – a girl with shoulder-length dark hair, perhaps in her late twenties. She was pretty and animated, and was facing my way. I fancied that occasionally she caught me looking at her, though she didn't seem too discomfited by my attention – perhaps just mildly curious.

Eventually the waiter came over to ask me to sign my bill, and as I was doing so a female voice said, "Hello again." It was the girl from opposite, smiling down at me tentatively. "We met yesterday afternoon at Latimer's. I work in their marketing department."

She had even features, greenish-blue eyes, and a tendency to small dimples when her face creased in a smile, as it had now.

I said, "My god – I'm so sorry. I thought you seemed familiar, but I couldn't think where from." I hoped this sounded plausible.

"You probably see so many transport offices, in the end they all look the same."

"No, no. Not at all. Well, yes." I attempted a smile and lifted my arms in submission. "I didn't recognise you out of context."

She looked down at her loose multi-coloured top and red skirt. "Not my normal workwear, I suppose."

I held out my hand. "Mike Stanhope."

She shook it briefly. "I know. Sally Meadows introduced you to us all."

Sally was personal assistant to Bob Latimer, the managing director, and also seemed to have the unofficial role of head of press liaison.

I said, "Oh god." Inwardly, though, I was still marvelling at the fact that this girl had actually materialised here in front of me tonight.

Her smile widened. "Don't worry, I'm taking advantage. You can tell from the way I'm standing over you while you're sitting down. Gives me the upper hand."

I smiled back at her for a moment. Then a well-built man in his thirties detached himself from her table and walked over. He put his arm casually round her shoulders. "Are you going to introduce us?"

She looked round at him amiably. "Ah, Jack, this is Mike Stanhope, a journalist from London. We met yesterday afternoon. He's doing a feature about Latimer's. Mike, this is Jack, my fiancé."

Of course he was. Had I imagined for one second that she would be single and available? My brain went into overdrive as I struggled to unwind the fantasy relationship I'd already constructed: irrepressible fool.

Her party was in the course of standing up and shuffling their chairs back. She said, "You'll have to excuse us," and they returned to their table. I pushed back my own chair. My two options were the hotel bar or a film on the TV in my room. Neither seemed to hold much appeal.

Then the couple were in front of me again. "Some of us are hanging on for a while in the bar," the girl said. "Would you care to join us?"

"Are you sure? I wouldn't want to intrude."

She smiled. "You're in Cornwall now. Time to experience a bit of Cornish hospitality."

* * *

Five of her party came through to the bar and gathered at the counter. I made a weak attempt to pay for the first round, but it turned out they had already started a tab.

It was her father's birthday, and he smiled benignly at the assembled company, sipping his brandy. I felt sure he would have been waving a cigar if it had been permitted. He was around sixty-five with a reddish complexion, slightly heavy features and thinning brushed-back hair.

The girl turned to me. "Mike, let me introduce you. Gordon Renwick, my father. Mary, my mother. Ben, my uncle. And you already know Jack."

"I'm ashamed to admit I don't know your own name."

"No shame in it. You wouldn't remember such intimacies from yesterday. I'm Ashley."

"Pleased to meet you, Ashley." I held my hand out and she shook it for a second time. Her hand was warm, her grip brief but confident.

For a while I found myself chatting to Uncle Ben, a retired sales manager. Then it was the turn of fiancé Jack, who managed a sports equipment shop in the town. Next on my list would have been Ashley's mother, who was currently deep in conversation with Ben. She had a carrying voice, and I had the impression she could be quite intimidating.

However, Ashley now turned to me. "What have you been up to today, Mike? Sampling the joys of life in the duchy of Cornwall?"

"Well, I went down to Falmouth this morning."

"Ha! We used to live there. What were you doing? Another interview for your paper?"

"No ..." I broke off, wondering what to tell them, then decided the truth wouldn't hurt. "I went there on a whim, actually. I was trying to track down a place where I spent a couple of holidays in my childhood." I paused. "But it was pulled down and replaced by a housing estate, so there wasn't much to see."

"You must mean the Fairmile. Was that it?"

I nodded.

"That's amazing!" Over her shoulder she said, "Mike used to stay at the Fairmile!" She turned back to me. "But what on earth made you go there now?"

"It probably sounds daft. I just had a fancy to track down some people we used to see when we were staying there."

She seemed intrigued. "Who? We might know them. Me and my brother Patrick used to play there sometimes. My dad knew the owner, Peggy Armitage."

I was still recovering from my astonishment that these people actually knew some of the near-mythological characters from my childhood – were trotting out names as though there were nothing remotely remarkable about them. But what should I tell them about my search for the missing family? I decided I'd keep it simple.

"To be honest, I was trying to track down a girl who stayed there. It probably sounds a bit weird now, but obviously we were both about the same age. I just wondered what became of her."

A beam spread over Ashley's face. "So what was this girl's name? No need to be coy."

"Trina. I think that's what it was."

Amazingly, she immediately said, "Yes! I remember Trina." She looked upward, scanning her memory bank. "Tall girl. Dark hair. Bubbly personality. Mind you, I was only about six. Everybody seemed tall to me then."

I stood there marvelling. Apart from that single photograph, this was my first evidence that the mystery girl and her family had ever even existed.

"You've got a good memory, if you were as young as that."

"She made an impression on me. I liked her, so I always remembered her."

"Did you know her surname?"

"Marsh? Something like that?" She turned to her father. "Do you remember a girl at the Fairmile called Trina? Very lively personality. What was her surname? Was it Marsh?"

"Unusual first name." He squinted for a moment. "Trina Markham. Daughter of Desmond Markham. Must be her."

I turned my attention to him. "Do you know where they were from?"

He shook his head. "Sorry, no idea. Peggy Armitage used to introduce us to guests at the hotel sometimes, but it was all very fleeting. I'm amazed that I even remember Desmond." He drained his brandy glass and placed it with emphasis on the bar, then turned away and engaged Jack in conversation. Evidently the conversation was closed.

I turned back to Ashley. "Well, I think that's truly remarkable. This is practically the first concrete evidence I've found that she existed at all."

"So you didn't keep in touch with her at the time?"

I shook my head. "I was a tongue-tied youth. We only knew each other slightly. Keeping in touch wasn't on the agenda."

I heard myself hesitate as I said this. Keeping in touch had certainly been on my agenda, for a while at least, but evidently it hadn't been on hers. It seemed inappropriate to mention it now.

She looked at me questioningly. I said, "OK, so why am I chasing her up in that case? Well, it's a long story. I'll happily tell it to you some time, but this probably isn't the right occasion."

She gave me a teasing smile. "So you think you and I going to stay in touch, do you?"

Chapter 10

Someone had broken into my house.

I didn't notice as I opened the front gate. I was feeling battered after the return trip from Cornwall – my second three hundred-mile drive in three days. How truck drivers dealt with such stress every day I'd never understood. I'd almost reached the front door before I realised it was slightly open. I felt an instant kick of adrenaline. I had certainly locked it when I left the day before yesterday. Then came a further shock of realisation; the intruder could still be inside.

I hesitated a moment, unsure what to do, then shrugged, stepped forward and thrust the door wide open.

It swung back and banged loudly against the interior wall. If there was anyone inside, they would certainly know they were about to be discovered. I paused and listened. No sound. I pushed the door fully open and stepped inside.

In the main room the flat-screen TV had been wrenched off the wall and lay face down on the token hearth, presumably now dead. The old fireplace was exposed behind it like a toothless mouth. Many of the books and CDs on the bookshelf had been half-pulled out or completely removed and dropped on the floor, ornaments had been moved from shelves, the coffee table had been kicked over, and a glass vase was lying in pieces on the floorboards in the centre of a drying puddle of murky water.

I contemplated the mess with horror. It was like a personal assault. Finally I stepped back into the hallway and headed warily up the stairs. Bedclothes had been stripped from my bed and garments from drawers lay strewn on the floor. In the office, papers were scattered all over the desk and the floor – notes from interviews, old article drafts, bills and receipts. Yet a pile of pound coins on a shelf had miraculously survived intact.

In the kitchen, crockery and utensils had been pulled out from drawers and cupboards, and several mugs were lying shattered on the floor. I returned to the lounge and slid open the patio door. Nothing in the tiny garden looked amiss.

Back indoors, I remembered my computer archives. I kept backups of recent work on an assortment of CDs, thumb drives and hard disks, and I stored these underneath the stash of plastic bags in the cupboard under the stairs. It seemed a disorganised approach, but I'd always felt this made it more secure. I lifted the plastic bag nervously, but there they all were, safe and sound.

Relieved, I returned to the main room and surveyed the damage. It was hard to understand the objective of the intruder. Was this theft, wanton vandalism or the outcome of a frenzied search for something? All these possibilities seemed to fit.

Whatever the answer, I felt an immense sense of violation. It was the same feeling I'd had when my web site was hacked, but magnified massively. On that occasion strangers had invaded my virtual space; now they'd intruded into my physical space. Contempt radiated from the chaos they'd left behind. It was like a violent slap in the face.

I sat down shakily on the sofa, pulled out my phone and called the police, and then I phoned Joanna. I felt guilty about taking advantage of her good nature, but I needed a friendly word from someone, and I knew she would provide it.

"Bastards!" was her summing-up, and her earnest fury immediately made me feel better.

*   *   *

Two uniformed officers came round surprisingly quickly, but told me no one would be available to process the scene until next day. Processing, one of them explained, meant taking fingerprints round the front door, where the intruders had clearly broken in, and possibly checking for any other forensic evidence.

Having said this, he made it clear that he thought it unlikely that his colleagues would have much time to spend on the case. "They're already fully stretched as it is." But this break-in might provide evidence of a pattern, he added. "They'll definitely want to know about it."

Looking around at the chaos, he asked, "What do you think has actually been stolen?"

I glanced around myself. Was anything missing? Well, the ugly silver dish I inherited from my parents still sat in its proper place on the bookcase, the coins upstairs hadn't been disturbed, and the TV had been trashed, not taken.

"Nothing that I've noticed, but I'll need to check."

"What about computers, tablets, that kind of thing?"

"I was away, so I had those with me."

He nodded. "Lucky for you."

He reminded me to bolt the front door after they left, since the lock was now shattered and the jamb was hanging in ragged splinters.

Once the police had left I poured myself a large whisky, savouring the instant buzz it gave me. I slumped down heavily on the sofa. What a bloody day. What a fucking day. All that endless driving, now this. Just when I'd felt unusually cheerful.

Sandy and I had bought this house together, and in seven years there had never been any trouble of this kind. The house was in a terrace with limited rear access, and had always felt pretty secure. But not, I reflected, if you took a sledgehammer to the front door. I wondered why no neighbours had been roused. Perhaps a single well-judged blow had been all it had taken: enough to wake people up, not enough to prompt them to action.

I wanted to believe this was a random intrusion, but something about it didn't ring true. If you were inclined to break into any old house, surely you would look for a weak point, you wouldn't just barge in through a locked front door – almost indifferent to possible detection, and presumably not even certain that the door would yield? It felt as though someone had singled me out, and was determined to make a show of the intrusion.

I had no idea who that someone might be, yet somewhere in a corner of my mind, my memory of the Noble brothers wouldn't let go of me.

1988

"I've come for my passports."

The short man looked back at Hawkins. "Sorry mate – passports? This is a hardware store, not the passport office."

Hawkins sighed. "Milo arranged it. Ask him if you want. I've got the money."

The man glanced nervously around the shop, even though they were the only two people in it. "Show me."

He unfolded a roll of notes and fanned them out.

"OK, OK, no need to advertise." The man crossed to the door, flipped the lock and rotated the sign to "Closed", then turned to Hawkins. "Follow me."

The back room was confined and damp. Ancient stock in limp cardboard boxes exuded mould from the shelves. A single table lamp cast a pool of light on a wooden work surface topped in brownish linoleum. On it were three UK passports.

"The price has gone up. Did Milo mention it? It's double now."

"The fuck it is."

"Take it or leave it. Either way, we keep the deposit."

A tube train rumbled past on the District line, nearly overhead. The lamp shook slightly.

"It's a fucking rip-off." But he reached into his pocket and pulled out a second wad of money. Somehow he'd expected nothing less.

"Nice doing business with you."

Chapter 11

My house phone rang next morning while the police were dusting down the front door for fingerprints. Most people used my mobile, so I picked up the receiver cautiously.

"Mike, it's Sandy. How are you doing?"

What in the world did my ex-wife want? We hadn't spoken for more than a year, and the last occasion hadn't been particularly amicable.

I'd never entirely understood where our marriage went wrong. We'd lived together for four years, then been married for eleven, and in the beginning things had seemed fine.

Looking back, I could see that the spark had disappeared much too soon. It was as if we'd been searching for something when we met, and had both been deceived into thinking we'd found it. She'd kept on jumping from job to job, unable to settle to anything but unwilling to think of starting a family, while I'd immersed myself in my journalistic life. We'd ended up on different trajectories.

Still, it took us a long time to admit we'd reached that point, and even after we did, I carried on trying to make the best of it. Sandy, however, had become increasingly restless and unhappy, and finally we decided the only solution was a complete break.

Uncharitably, I now felt I needed to head off some kind of reproach. I couldn't stop myself from replying a little curtly, "I'm very well, thank you very much. How are you?"

There was a pause, then: "Mike, don't be nasty. I'm just ringing to be friendly. If we can't even start off on a decent footing I don't see the point."

"Sorry, sorry. It's just that your timing is unfortunate. I've been burgled, and the place is in chaos. I'm not in the best of moods."

"My god! What happened?"

"I don't know. I was away. When I got back last night the front door was open and somebody had turned the place over."

"God. What did they take?"

I looked around. "I haven't worked that out yet. Nothing obvious. They just made a mess of everything. I haven't got round to clearing it all up yet."

"How horrible. You poor thing." She was silent for a moment. "Did you say they came in through the front door? How come? Did they have a key?"

"No, they just bashed it in. It's a miracle the neighbours didn't hear."

"Bloody hell. Is that kind of thing common in your area now?"

"I hope not! I've never heard of anything like this before."

"Perhaps it's revenge by someone you upset in one of your campaigning articles. A kind of retribution."

Immediately I thought again of Janni and Tommy Noble and that article of mine. The menace in Janni Noble's look wouldn't leave me. But this was much too involved to raise with Sandy. I merely said, "I doubt it."

She said nothing for a moment, then, "Would you like me to come round and help you clean things up?"

This was a surprise. So far as I knew she lived with her new partner in west London, miles from here. More to the point, we hadn't actually met for several years, and it was much longer since we'd found ourselves together in a domestic setting.

Actually the idea of her help was unexpectedly tempting, but I couldn't really imagine how it would work. I said, "No, it's very good of you to suggest it, but I've got things under control."

"Well, the offer's there."

"Thanks. I appreciate it." I cleared my throat. "So why were you calling?"

Now she seemed to hesitate. "Well, I bumped into Joanna Miles the other day, and I asked her how you were doing." She paused.

"And?"

"Well …" I could tell she was searching for the right words. "She seemed to think your fridge was always full of booze, but never had any food in it."

I gave her a silent burst of ironic applause for this. She was telling me delicately that Joanna thought I was drinking too much – one of the bones of contention when Sandy finally left. Thank you Joanna.

"I get what you're saying, Sandy."

"Do you?" A pause. "I still worry."

"You shouldn't."

"You need to move on with your life. You need to find someone. It's been too long."

"Please, no lectures this morning. I've got enough to deal with here."

"OK OK. Well let me know if there's anything I can do about this break-in."

* * *

I'd left the house more or less as I found it last night, so everything was still in chaos. After the police had finished their work I started half-heartedly picking things up and putting them back where they belonged.

I didn't need Sandy's pity, that was for sure, but her comments had struck a chord; it would have been nice to be sharing this chore, not confronting it on my own. I knew things could never have worked between us, but I'd never quite got over her departure, or recovered the confidence to strike out with someone new.

One of the last items I replaced was the picture of the girl in Falmouth, which had fallen on the floor and lay half-concealed under a chair. I propped it back on the mantelpiece. "See what you've done to me," I mouthed at it. "If I hadn't taken that extra day off to chase down to Falmouth, maybe none of this would have happened."

Or it would have happened anyway, and I might have had to confront the intruders in person. I wondered how I would have dealt with that.

Wearily I picked up my *Yellow Pages* and started searching for locksmiths and joiners. I would need to have the front door repaired before I could spend another night away – and keep my computers where I could see them.

* * *

I needed something to cheer myself up, and it was a bit early for a drink, even by my standards. Instead, I called up the web site where I'd published my book. Eleven copies had now been sold – several more than the last time I looked. Was that good? Or was it just more of my friends and acquaintances rallying to the cause?

Frankly I didn't think I had enough willing friends to account for all these sales, but how else did anybody know about the book? My plans for blanket promotion on the internet had somehow slipped on to the back burner, and I wasn't sure how else the word could have got out.

I closed the browser tab and wondered what else I could do. Well, how about picking up the threads of my search for Trina and her parents? I now knew their surname, so I could do a web search – something that had been more or less out of the question before.

I typed "Desmond" and "Markham" and "Trina" into Google, and got 145,000 hits: not terribly promising. Did this mean they were indubitably out there to be found, or that even looking for them was a lost cause?

I homed in on just Desmond Markham (after all, Trina might have married and changed her surname), and that reduced the number of finds dramatically. I could actually work with the list I got. I tried following some of them up – looking at Facebook pages, LinkedIn profiles and other mentions.

Most of these Desmond Markhams seemed to be the wrong age or to have the wrong family, and I couldn't find any cross-references to Trina or the Fairmile. After a while I drew to a halt, wondering where to take this next.

If I'd been determined enough I could have tried tracking down all these Desmond Markhams and eliminated them one by one; and if I'd been a private detective on a case, presumably I would have. But I wasn't, and I felt unsure of the boundaries and constraints on this project. At the end of the day, just how important was it? The answer was not very.

As a temporising measure I called up Linda Dysart's Facebook page, checking without much hope to see if anyone had added anything to our short exchange about the Markhams. Immediately I sat up to attention. A new contributor, evidently one of Linda's other friends, had made a posting.

"I knew Trina slightly from the Fairmile, and I might have a small clue for you. She lived in a house called West End Lodge. I remember that because our own house was The Lodge, but it was in a completely different town. I wrote it in my diary, which I still have."

West End Lodge: how many of those were there in the country? Was there a database anywhere listing house names as distinct from addresses? On the whole I suspected not.

But as she'd implied, it might be a clue.

Chapter 12

"Mike. Nice piece on Latimer Logistics. We gave it an extra page. Shame to waste all that good stuff. Nice pics too."

This was an unfamiliar Jason Bright. The positive note was back in his voice. Until lately his phone calls seemed to have started much more ominously, casting doubt over my future work for his magazine. I said nothing for a moment, then tried a cautious, "Glad you liked it."

"I got the sense that you really enjoyed talking to them."

"Well, yes, I suppose I did." I was waiting for the catch.

He paused. "The Logistics Fair. I wondered if you'd like to cover it for us. Barry has twisted his ankle, stupid sod. Can't take on any job that involves walking."

Not a catch, then; another commission. Not my favourite kind of job, but under the circumstances I couldn't afford to be fussy. I adopted what I hope was an upbeat tone. "Of course, more than happy to step in."

"A nice full report? Plenty of detail?" Back to that slightly carping, admonitory note. How hard did I have to work before I could dismiss it?

"Will do."

Trade shows were grist to the mill for the business press. They meant dozens of suppliers all grouped together in one place: an ideal opportunity to quiz them about their latest products and services and get their views on the state of the universe. The only problem was that their priority was to sell to potential customers, not chew the fat with journalists. You had to pick your moment, and hope you would find someone on each stand who was willing to talk to you. It was hard work.

I sat back. What was the matter with me? I worried when I didn't get enough work, especially from Jason, then grumbled when jobs did materialise. I couldn't have it both ways, could I?

* * *

Two days later I arrived at the west London exhibition centre with a
familiar sense of trepidation. So many people to see – so much
information to gather. After fumbling through the complex registration
process I was released into the central arena, and I stood for a moment
getting my bearings.

Glitzy show stands stretched away in every direction, and a buzz of
suppressed energy pervaded the space. Visitors strode importantly past
along grey-carpeted aisles, stabbing at their smartphones or chatting
animatedly to colleagues. Stand lights glowed, music trickled from a
myriad sources. If you ever thought logistics was a boring subject, this
event was calculated to convince you otherwise.

I headed off in search of the press room. At least that would give me
some thinking space before the onslaught.

The tried and tested technique for reporting on these events was to
get a rhythm going. Find a relevant stand that didn't look overrun with
visitors, winkle out someone who seemed ready to talk to the press, find
out if they had anything remotely interesting to report, then feed on the
adrenaline to brace you for the next encounter. And make notes; without
them you'd never remember anything. The trick was not to stop, or your
energy levels would collapse. Exhausting, but it was the only way.

I was on my seventh or eighth stand, chatting to an earnest PR
woman, when a voice accosted me from the other side of the stand.
"Mike, isn't it? Mike Stanhope?" It was one of the sales staff for the
company, a logistics contractor based in Stoke-on-Trent.

He threaded his way across the stand and shook my hand amiably –
a short, wiry man of Asian descent with a Yorkshire accent and an
infectious grin. "It's Freddie. I met you when I worked with the Stobart
group. After that I moved over to Allied Northern in Oldham as their
warehouse manager."

Allied was Janni Noble's now-defunct company. "You've moved on
again, presumably," I said somewhat redundantly.

He ratcheted up the grin. "Alas, Allied is no more. I had to seek
pastures new."

"Well, I'm glad you've fallen on your feet."

The PR lady retreated to talk to another journalist, and I chatted on for a while with Freddie. "Janni Noble is doing OK for himself these days," he commented. "He's a partner in a truck and van rental business in Trafford Park now. Did you know that?"

I didn't, but immediately I connected this information with the conversation I'd had with Janni when I first met him over lunch with Rick Ashton. The business Ashton was doing with him must involve rental trucks.

"Is he here today?"

"I haven't seen him. I don't think they have a stand here. But the way they're growing, they will next year."

* * *

By four o'clock my reserves of energy were more or less exhausted. I stood in the middle of an aisle, scanning my notes. I'd visited thirty-one stands, and had enough material to write news items about seventeen of them. Surely that was enough?

Then, with a sinking feeling, I saw ahead of me a section of the show area that I'd somehow managed to miss until now, packed with stands I should have visited: mostly logistics companies. With an inward groan I headed towards them. Maybe I could drop in on a sample selection, and leave it at that?

Half an hour and three conversations later, I was standing in front of yet another stand, probably looking dazed, when a female voice addressed me.

"Mr Stanhope! Are you going to write a nice glowing piece about us?"

Ashley Renwick was smiling at me from the edge of the stand. I glanced up at the illuminated red fascia, which read "Latimer Logistics. We deliver."

I smiled at her. "What's the matter? Not satisfied with my last effort?"

"More than satisfied, actually. Very happy. Look."

I followed her gaze, and on one of the stand walls was a giant extract from my article, juxtaposed with a grainy black and white blow-up of one of my photographs, showing a warehouse interior. All very arty.

"And we had a batch of reprints produced. Here, have one." She wandered over to a table, and I followed her on to the floorboards of the stand.

"I'm flattered."

"Very old school, having physical reprints." She handed me a copy. "But they work well at events like this. It's nice to have something tactile to give people."

I looked down at the reprint. She said, "Can I offer you some refreshment?"

A quadruple gin would have gone down well, but I accepted a coffee, and I sat on a stool at the stand's own bar counter while she poured it. The show had quietened down, and there were just a couple of sales staff on the stand. One was busying himself with racks of sale literature while the other sat at a low table, tapping something into a laptop computer.

"I don't know if you wanted to speak to Bob Latimer? He's around today, but I'm afraid he and the other top brass have gone off to a reception somewhere."

"That's fine. I'm happy to talk to you." I smiled at Ashley. She was wearing a dark T-shirt with "Latimer Logistics" and the company logo embroidered in red across the chest. "It hadn't occurred to me that you would be here."

"I keep popping up like a bad penny." She gestured round at the stand. "I spend quite a lot of time organising this kind of thing. Feels like it, anyway. Off to the NEC in a couple of weeks' time. No rest for the wicked."

"Do these shows pay off for you?"

"Usually. We get solid sales leads. That's the bottom line."

We sat in silence for a moment, then she asked, "Have you had any more success finding your mystery lady?"

"Not really. Someone thought she might have lived in the north of England, but it was pretty vague."

"Aha! Well I might be able to flesh that out a bit more for you."

She called over to one of her colleagues, "Dan – are we still on for that curry later?"

"Certainly are."

She turned to me. "A bunch of us are going out for a meal when they release us from this place. If you're free, maybe you'd like to join us?" She paused, then more tentatively added, "Or … no, you probably have something to get home to, do you?"

"No, nothing. That sounds great."

"OK. Well, you'll have to twiddle your thumbs for a while till they close the exhibition, but then we'll be all set. We'll be meeting up at the White Hart at six thirty – that's the pub down the road. I can update you about our friend Trina."

Chapter 13

"Cheers to you Mike. Thanks for an excellent article. You set us up nicely for this show."

This was Tony, Latimer's sales manager – a genial man of about forty, and the first of Ashley's five colleagues to arrive in the pub from their nearby hotel.

"Glad to know it helped."

"Ashley was over the moon with it."

This seemed unlikely, but these were all sales and marketing people, accustomed to putting a positive spin on everything. I accepted the praise and watched as the others arrived together – three men and a woman in their twenties or early thirties, plus Ashley herself.

She was the last to walk in, and as I briefly caught her gaze I felt a sudden jolt of awareness between us. Or had I imagined it? She was wearing jeans and a blue top with a cinched black waistcoat, and looked stunning.

"Thank god that's over," she announced as she picked up the beer Tony had lined up for her. "One day down, one to go."

I commented, "I don't envy you spending the whole day on the stand."

She turned to me. "You're well out of it, Mike. Be glad you can swan around the show the way you do, just chatting to people."

I found myself admiring the way her expression seemed to settle so readily into a look that was at once a question and a challenge. She was even-featured, yet at the same time she was distinctively herself and no one else.

I felt her jibe needed some sort of riposte. "You wouldn't say that if you had to do it yourself. It's hard work."

"I'd forgotten – you're interviewing everybody." She turned to her colleagues. "Remember, Mike's a journalist. You're all on the record." She gave me a barely detectable wink.

"Bollocks." I scowled at her, then put my beer down and held up my hands. "Look! No notebook. No pen. No microphone. Not listening."

"Not to worry, Mike." Tony slapped me rather too hard on the back. "We're all off duty here."

* * *

We progressed to an Indian restaurant down the street. I ended up sitting diagonally opposite Ashley, facing a Londoner called Joe who proceeded to spend an inordinately long time telling me about the delights of surfing. "That's why I moved to Cornwall," he told me. "Fantastic to have it all there on tap. Lovely lifestyle, too. I'd never come back here now."

The meal ran its course. I couldn't easily converse with Ashley on her own, but I was strongly aware of her voice and personality, and this evening she seemed more animated than I remembered. I was aware of her colleagues teasing her from time to time, but I could tell it was teasing borne out of respect, and she parried it with self-deprecating grace.

Eventually Joe disappeared to the men's room, and Ashley shuffled into his place opposite me and leaned forward. Though we'd had so little direct conversation, in a strange way it felt as if we'd spent the entire evening in unspoken dialogue.

"Michael."

"Ashley."

She grinned at me. "Is that what people call you? Michael?"

"Not really. When I'm good I'm just Mike."

She nodded to herself several times.

"Michael, I have intelligence for you. Brought to you courtesy of Patrick." Unthinking, she took a sip of Joe's beer. "Fuck! What's this stuff?" She thrust it down, reached over for her own glass and took a sip from that. "Patrick is my older brother."

"OK."

"Thing is, I was telling him about you." She broke off. "Not that I want you to get the impression that I was thinking about you. No way."

"Right."

"But somehow you came up in conversation. And he remembered Trina Markham quite well. I think he probably fancied her, stupid twat. He always fancied all the girls at the Fairmile."

"Ah."

"Yes, and he says she was from Altrincham. Her father was an accountant or something, and they had a posh house up there." She looked at me in triumph. "What do you think of that?"

"Is that it?"

She smiled at me with her eyes. "That's gold-plated information there! Normally I charge for this kind of thing."

"It's greatly valued, I assure you."

"Yes, I believe you."

We continued to smile at each other for a moment, perhaps unsure where to take the conversation next.

"How's Jack?" I asked finally. I hated myself for bringing him into the conversation, but somehow couldn't help myself.

"Jack is fine, thank you." She looked away from me for a moment, then back. "We've known each other forever." She took another sip of beer.

"When are you planning on getting married?"

"Oh, no date yet. Probably next year." An airy shake of the head. "It's a moveable feast." She pondered this for a moment. "It's a virtual engagement – that's what it is. Virtual."

* * *

The meal finally came to an end, and our little group gathered outside the restaurant. Joe and Laurie, the other girl, announced that they were going clubbing in the West End, and a couple of the others were talking about reconvening in their hotel bar, but Ashley demurred. "Long day tomorrow. I need my beauty sleep. You should all take a leaf out of my book."

The rest of them started to drift away, and we were on our own, facing each other.

"Michael," she said.

"Ashley." I paused. "Thank you for a lovely evening."

"My pleasure."

"I'm really glad I chanced on your stand."

"So am I."

We stood there for a moment, smiling at each other. The engaged girl, the divorced man. I had an extraordinarily strong instinct to reach out and touch her. Instead, I found myself asking in a slightly choked voice, "What now?"

She gave me a wry look and shrugged slightly, shaking her head. "I don't know." Then she pulled her jacket tighter. "I'd better go."

We looked at each other a moment longer, then she executed a pantomime swivel and started off in the same direction as the others. But after a few paces she turned and looked back at me. "So we did stay in touch with each other. I knew we would."

Chapter 14

That night I slept the sleep of the dead, but when I woke in the morning, Ashley slammed straight into my consciousness. I felt as if she'd been injected into my bloodstream. It had been too long since I'd felt this kind of connection with anyone at all, let alone anyone as appealing as she was. I was unprepared.

The only trouble was, I couldn't visualise our relationship having any good outcome. She was engaged to someone else and lived hundreds of miles away, and I was a disenchanted hack. If she really knew me she would soon discover that. In any case, events like that logistics show were notorious for creating unlikely pairings. People were inclined to let their hair down when far from home.

Yet I couldn't shake her out of my mind. A vague yearning seemed to have settled on me, and it stayed with me as I attempted to catch up on an article I was preparing on international trade. Ashley was attractive, bright and funny – and for some reason she seemed to like me. It was a combination I'd seldom encountered before. I kept thinking about that roguish grin.

I glanced at the clock. Eleven thirty. I could picture her now, back on the Latimer stand at the Logistics Fair, conscientiously attending to visitors. She was still in London for the whole day, yet I had no legitimate excuse to see her, and the minutes were ticking away. It was a kind of torture.

My office phone jarred me out of my reverie.

"Is that Mike? Mike Stanhope?" Amazingly, it was her.

"The same."

"Oh, brilliant. I've had a hell of a run-around getting your number. I ended up talking to someone called Don, and he didn't want to give it to me."

Don was Jason's assistant at the magazine – a jobsworth with no imagination.

"They have a policy of not giving out numbers if they think the call is from a PR person."

"Huh."

She said nothing for a moment, then we both started speaking at once. I said, "Sorry, you first."

"Oh, it's just that I remembered something basic that I forgot to tell you yesterday. About your friend Trina. That's why I'm calling. My brother thought he knew the name of the street in Altrincham where she lived. It was something like Eyebrow. He always remembered because it was so strange." She seemed to reflect on this for a moment. "Don't ask me why they were exchanging address details in the first place. I'm sure they weren't that pally. In fact I doubt if she would have given him the time of day."

"Anyway, that's brilliant. Much better than just a town name." I hesitated. "Er, I don't suppose he had the house number? No, course he didn't. Stupid question."

"Reality check on that one."

But then I remembered that Facebook posting: West End Lodge. It might not be a house number, but it was almost as good as one. Surely I should be able to find the address from that?

There was another pause, then Ashley said, "I hope I didn't disgrace myself too much last night. I know I tend to get carried away at these events. Too much unwinding – too fast."

"Not as far as I could see."

"Well, that's good to know."

A longer pause, then I heard myself saying, "Funnily enough, I was thinking about you just now." I winced as I said it: too much information.

She said nothing for a second, then quietly, "You shouldn't."

I couldn't think of any suitable response to this, so I just let it hang in the air. Finally I said, "Well, thanks for the extra information. I really might be able to do something with that."

"I hope so." She cleared her throat. "I'd love to hear if anything comes of it."

"You will. Definitely."

"I've got to go. People on the stand. Take care." And she was gone.

* * *

I struggled on with the article for another hour, trying to flush Ashley from my mind. Finally I'd had enough. By way of distraction I opened my browser and did a web search on Altrincham. Like many people, no doubt, I'd heard of it, even professed to know what it was like. Actually my knowledge of it was minimal.

"A market town in Greater Manchester," I was informed. I opened a web map and typed the street name into the search box, but nothing came up. Frustrated, I zoomed in over Altrincham and pored over the street names. Eyebrow seemed a somewhat implausible name for a street, and indeed there was no sign of such a name anywhere. Had Ashley's brother been winding her up?

However, I then spotted an Eyebrook Road in a district called Bowden, and when I zoomed out, I could see that this was adjacent to, or possibly part of, Altrincham. Could this be it? From a bit of quick research I found that this was a famously affluent area. I wasn't sure quite where it got me, but it was something.

Over a lunchtime sandwich I sat mulling over all this. Was there a mystery here or not? All I knew so far was that I'd failed to track down these people, but that might be because I wasn't being very organised about looking for them.

And yet … something was nagging at my investigative instincts. Since first doing a web search for the Markhams I'd made a couple more attempts, but again without luck. Why was there apparently no trace of them on the internet, no hint of their existence in the present day? Had they in fact disappeared off the face of the earth? I didn't actually know, but the harder they proved to track down, the more I felt inclined to keep looking on for them.

It was quite possible, of course, that I was missing the obvious. They could for instance have emigrated, or been killed in a catastrophic motorway pile-up. I had to be realistic; all kinds of explanation were possible. Whatever the case, there must be documentary evidence somewhere; I just wasn't looking in the right place.

What I wasn't so clear about was what I would do if I found them. Was there really another book in this? Was there a magazine article? If so, who would publish it? It was hardly a logistics story.

Or was I simply playing into Joanna's hands, living out her "let's rehabilitate Mike" campaign?

I decided I'd worry about my intentions later. For the next stage, I felt I should visit Eyebrook Road, Altrincham – to see what it suggested to me in the flesh. However, even in my current somewhat obsessive frame of mind I wasn't inclined to fund such a long, time-consuming and potentially fruitless journey out of my own pocket. I needed some excuse to make the trip.

I rang Jason Bright to see if he had scheduled any articles involving a trip to the North West. He hadn't, so I tried a materials handling magazine I sometimes wrote for.

"The answer to my prayer," said the editor, a hard-pressed man called Phil Connor who seemed to run the publication virtually single-handedly. "I need someone to go and see a plant hire company in Ashton under Lyne the week after next. It's all set up. I was going myself, but I've just realised I'm double-booked. How does that suit you?"

1988

"Police are looking for members of an armed gang this evening, following the attempted theft of a large consignment of valuables that has left a security guard dead and one of the thieves critically injured.

"The armoured truck was held up at gunpoint at an intersection outside Newbury in Berkshire, and the thieves are thought to have transferred the stolen goods to a waiting van, then made off. In the course of the theft, one of the guards was fatally injured.

"Early reports suggest that the thieves subsequently switched the haul to a further vehicle at a prearranged point. However, police tracked this vehicle down to a farm not far away. An armed response team was called in and a gun battle followed, during which one of the thieves was wounded and most of the others were arrested.

"However, it is thought that at least one gang member may have fled under cover of darkness. Police are warning that anyone connected to the robbery is armed and dangerous, and should not on any account be approached.

"The vehicle was in the process of transferring the contents of a safety deposit vault from Newbury to new premises in Reading.

"The value of the haul has not been disclosed, but informal estimates suggest that cash and securities thought to be worth at least eleven million pounds may have been recovered at the scene."

Chapter 15

The M25 was hardly my favourite place, but for once it seemed a glorious release from the confines of my home office. That trip to the West Country a month ago had reminded me of the pleasures of travel, which these days seemed all too infrequent. Today the motorway was my friend. The sun was even shining. My trip to the North West had started well.

Three and a half hours later I was feeling slightly less sprightly as I pulled up outside the plant hire firm in Ashton under Lyne, a satellite town east of Manchester. It wasn't far from the M60 motorway, which encircled the Manchester conurbation, but there'd been a snarl-up on the M56, and the last part of the journey had taken an age.

However, the people at the firm were open and friendly, and once I'd thought myself into the world of hydraulic cranes, bulldozers and JCBs, we were on a roll. Clouds floated across the sun as I emerged into the yard to do some photography, but then they receded, leaving a brilliant sun staring out of a dramatic grey sky. Against that backdrop, even yellow cranes looked breathtaking.

By mid-afternoon I was free, and I headed back westwards along the M60, then forked off through Timperley to Altrincham.

The town's bustling central area seemed unremarkable. Its mix of styles – red-brick and grey-brick Victorian alongside ultra-modern – bespoke a solid middle class.

Eyebrook Road was something else. The street itself was narrow, but grass verges separated the pavements from walls and hedgerows, opening out the aspect, and the houses were calculated to impress: palatial, some of them, and even the more modest were large detached structures, mostly surrounded by trees and shrubs. This was more than aspirational; this was where you lived when you'd well and truly arrived.

I drove slowly down the road and round a dog-leg half-way along it, trying to make out house names. Some were in view, some weren't. Many of the properties probably just had a street number.

I felt slightly thwarted. I hadn't visualised somewhere quite as prosperous, as *dispersed*, as this. I'd imagined maybe picking a house at random and knocking on the door. "Sorry, I thought the Markhams lived here. Do you happen to know them?" That wasn't going to cut any ice in this environment. If anybody even answered the door to me, it would probably be a nannie or retainer of some kind, with no knowledge of the street's history and no inclination to pass the time of day with me.

I stopped and parked the car. I had a distinct feeling that if I appeared to be cruising without any purpose I might be pulled over and asked what I was up to. Maybe my car had already been flagged by hidden cameras.

I stared round me. There was no consistent architectural style to these houses; mock-Tudor sat cheek by jowl with Edwardian, post-war and post-modern. One of the puzzles was that many of the houses looked quite recent, and probably hadn't even existed when the Markhams supposedly lived here.

Well, I had one clue. "West End Lodge" suggested that perhaps the house was, well, at the west end of the street. The problem was that because of the dog-leg it didn't really have a west end – more of a north end and an east end. Without much confidence I decided to try the north end first.

As it turned out, the street didn't actually have a conspicuous end at all – it just ceased to be at a crossroads. I turned and started to work my way back, and then not far along I noticed a double-fronted brick-built house that I'd managed to miss before. It certainly looked old enough to fit the bill. I pulled over and got out, scanning the gateway and frontage for a nameplate.

Yes! There it was on the gatepost – a wooden plaque with the name engraved on it: West End Lodge. So it really did exist! A little nervously I walked up the driveway and pressed an elaborate brass bell-push set into the wall.

Nothing happened. No sound; no response. I looked around. The driveway was empty and the black timber doors of the free-standing double garage were closed.

I started to turn away, then heard the front door being unbolted. An elderly woman, possibly somewhere in her mid-eighties, was standing on the top step, staring down at me with a hostile look on her face.

"What do you want?"

I switched on what I hoped was my most reassuring smile. "I'm sorry to trouble you – I'm trying to track down some people who used to live in this house in the 1980s. The Markhams. Do you by any chance know what happened to them – where they moved to when they left?"

"In this house?" She squinted as if the idea was beyond comprehension. "What name did you say?"

"Markham. Desmond Markham."

"Never heard of them. Markham? Markham? No idea what you're talking about."

I stood there at a loss. Evidently this conversation was going nowhere. I decided discretion was the better part of valour, and started to retreat down the driveway. "Well, thank you anyway. I'm sorry to have bothered you."

She was still standing on the doorstep as a reached the gateway, clutching the door. I had a fancy that she was still muttering, "Markham? Markham?"

I stood by my car, wondering what to do next. Possibly the woman had younger relatives who could tell me more, but who were currently out at work; or possibly not. Should I come back later? Then I noticed movement in front of the house opposite, a sprawling structure with a large lawn and a low hedge. A woman was playing with a small child on a swing.

I wandered over. She was close enough to hear me from the verge, so I called out, "Hello!"

She turned her head and gave me a pleasant smile. "Good afternoon." She looked somewhere in her mid-forties, and had shortish blond hair. She was dressed mostly in white.

"I was trying to track down some people who used to live across the road a long time ago. I couldn't get much sense from the lady who lives there now."

"Oh, you won't get a lot out of Betty. Sharp as a knife, but not the most communicative soul." She finished straightening her child's jersey and patted him away. "Who was it you were looking for?"

"Their surname was Markham. This was back in the 1980s. Desmond Markham."

"Doesn't ring a bell with me, but my father-in-law might know – this is his house." She turned towards the building and shouted, "David!"

A man in his sixties emerged from a glasshouse adjoining the main building.

"Do you remember some people called Markham across the road? This gentleman is looking for them. Betty couldn't help him."

He strolled over. "Heavens, that's going back." Like his daughter-in-law, he gave me a pleasant smile. "Yes, I do remember the Markhams. Desmond and Shirley. And they had a daughter. Was it Tina? Something like that." He scratched his head. "They suddenly left. Never told anyone where they were going. One day here, the next day gone forever. The house stood empty for a couple of years, then Ron and Sally moved in. They're away for a month, but Betty is their live-in housekeeper." He smiled. "She's Ron's mother."

"That's really helpful."

"D'you mind me asking why you're interested? It seems rather a long time ago for you to be a debt collector." His eyes twinkled.

"No, I knew them slightly on holiday in the West Country when I was a boy, and I've taken it into my head to find out what happened to them." I smiled. "I've tracked them down this far, but I seem to be twenty-five years behind. It probably sounds a bit daft."

"So you're doing a bit of under-cover detective work, are you? Well, they should make good subjects. The word was that they had some dubious connections." He smiled conspiratorially.

"Really?"

"Oh, I never gave it much credence myself. There were just a few mutterings about how they came by their money, that kind of thing. You know what people are like. But I must say they didn't help their own case much – they were quite secretive. Didn't mix with the neighbours, never came to any of our parties or held any of their own." He straightened his back. "Not that they had any obligation to."

"How long did they live here?"

"Only two or three years. Here today, gone tomorrow. That pretty well sums them up."

Chapter 16

I could have driven back to London that night, but I had other plans. I stayed the night at a motel near Northenden, a suburb to the west of Manchester, then in the morning I drove over to Trafford Park.

This part of Greater Manchester was mixed – the modern Salford Quays development, with its TV studios and its trendy shopping; the famous cricket and football clubs; and a sprawling hinterland of light industry stretching out to the M60 motorway and beyond.

I finally found what I was looking for. Ray Noble Rental occupied a broad yard fronting a main road in the industrial district. A row of sparkling blue and white vans and light trucks faced out towards the road as if eager for action, and pennants fluttered from white poles along the boundary.

I pulled into a layby opposite and studied the plot. At the back was a single-storey brick structure, presumably containing offices. The premises were clearly not new, but looked bright and appealing. This was unmistakably a business going places.

So this was the company Janni Noble now co-owned, and had possibly funded at least in part from the proceeds of the people-smuggling enterprise – the one for which his brother had been arrested. It was hardly any surprise if Tommy felt resentful. I wondered who the Ray was in Ray Noble Rental. Maybe it was just a brand name. "Janni Noble Rental" wouldn't have had quite the same ring to it.

Nobody went in or came out while I watched. I didn't know sure quite what I'd learned from this, but it felt useful to have a first-hand sense of the place.

* * *

I'd expected to feel nervous scoping out Janni's business, but in fact my next landfall made me much more apprehensive. I drove straight down the M6 past Birmingham, then turned off at the exit for the National Exhibition Centre. There was a logistics show in progress here, and I'd decided to drop in.

I'd forgotten the sheer size of the NEC site, but visitor management was as good as ever, and in a surprisingly short time I'd parked my car in the right place and was walking over to the exhibition complex. The show I wanted was being held in one of the smaller halls, but it still seemed vast when I walked inside. I registered myself as a journalist, and before long I'd been let loose among the stands.

Prior to leaving London I'd rung Phil, the editor of the materials handling magazine, to ask if he would accept some copy about the event for his next issue. "It's not quite our thing, but yes, see what you can pick up that would fit in with us." At least my report would help cover my costs, and the commission made me feel I had a purpose here.

I wandered for a while among stands showing fork trucks and roller conveyors, noting down the things the exhibitors said were new. Eventually I gravitated to the logistics section. On a couple of the stands I was greeted by people I knew, and I paused to chat. However, I'd seen the Latimer Logistics stand looming further down the aisle, and I kept moving steadily towards it.

"Mike! Good to see you again." Bob Latimer, the managing director and grandson of the founder, was standing on a currently empty stand, smiling with what looked like genuine goodwill. He was a slim, gangly man in his early forties with flopping dark hair, and he radiated energy and focus. I'd met him when I visited the company. I shook hands with him, noticing the blow-up of my article once again displayed on the wall behind him.

"How's it going?"

"We've been very busy. A good show. Lots of the right kind of visitors. It's important to us to show we're a national concern – we're not just cut off in the far west."

We chatted for a while, then I asked diffidently, "Is Ashley around today?"

He looked around the stand. "Yes, she was here five minutes ago. I think she's gone off to lunch somewhere. She should be back later."

A party of Chinese visitors walked up, and Latimer went over to greet them. I slipped away and headed for a self-service restaurant on the other side of the hall.

I immediately spotted Ashley standing next to a table and talking to a bald man in a grey suit and an open-neck shirt. I paused for a moment, watching her gesticulating as she underlined some point she was making. She was just as pretty as I remembered – and presumably also just as engaged.

I moved into her field of vision, and instantly her face broke into a smile.

"Mike! What are you doing here? No, scrub that. Stupid question. You're a reporter, and you're reporting."

"I don't want to interrupt."

She waved away my concern. "Andrew is a stand designer. We were just talking about our stand. He reckons his people could do a better job than ours did."

I looked at the man. I'd interrupted him making a sales pitch to Ashley, but he was putting a brave face on it.

To Ashley I said, "Will you still be here if I go and get myself some lunch?"

"I might be." A quick smile.

So I left them to it and queued for a cold platter, then wandered back. Ashley was now seated at the table and the bald man had gone.

"Jesus! He was a nice guy, but he didn't know when to stop." She broke off and smiled. "You're a long way from home."

"Not as far as you." I pulled up a chair and sat down. "Anyway, have notebook, will travel."

We chatted for a while about the show and the business, and I ate my salad. Part of my brain was telling me that spending time with her was a lost cause, and rather dishonourable to boot. Another part was telling me an altogether different story.

However, the small talk gradually seemed to peter out. I was probably just looking at her and marvelling instead of listening to what she was actually saying. Finally, in a tone of amused frustration, she said, "Sorry, am I boring you?"

"God, no way!" I looked her directly in the eyes. "You don't think that, do you?"

She appeared to consider for a moment. "Look ... I don't know how long you're planning on being here. I've got to go back to the stand now, and I have to go to some dinner tonight, but if you're still here when they close the halls, maybe you'd like to meet up for a quick drink?" She looked suddenly hesitant. "If you want to, that is."

Chapter 17

I spent the first part of the afternoon wandering among the stands in the materials handling section to make sure I hadn't missed anything important. When I ran out of enthusiasm for that I looked at some of the other stands out of sheer curiosity. Then I sat in a café for a long time, checking my emails and reading the BBC news.

When the show finally closed for the day I collected my car and drove the short distance to the hotel where the Latimer team were staying. It seemed to have been taken over by the show, and the bar was buzzing with post-event chatter. People were standing in small groups or lounging in clusters of modern olive green armchairs.

Ashley was already there, seated among colleagues. She was wearing a green top and dark business trousers, and had brushed her hair back behind her ears, accentuating a pair of iridescent green earrings. I waved acknowledgement to her party, but she stood up to intercept me and ushered me away towards the bar. "They can manage without me for a while."

We sat at a table for two – still partly in sight of the others, but not within hearing distance. It struck me that I'd hardly spent any time with Ashley out of the company of her actual family or her extended business family. She always had a chaperone on hand.

We sat back for a moment, looking a little warily at each other. Then, as if some impostor had taken over my powers of speech, I heard myself saying, "In case you wondered, I'm thirty-eight, divorced, boring according to my wife, tidy in my personal habits, kind to animals, but sometimes disenchanted with my job." I leaned back. "Just by way of background."

As I spoke, a voice in my head announced that what I'd just said was tantamount to a proposal of marriage. Had I completely taken leave of my senses? I watched nervously for her reaction.

She looked at me for a moment without saying anything, then smiled inscrutably. "Well thank you for sharing that, Mr Stanhope. I don't recall asking for this fascinating information, but I never reject details willingly vouchsafed."

I laughed, relieved.

She smiled back at me. "For the record, I'm twenty-nine – I'm *never* boring, and I kick the dog frequently." She sipped her gin and tonic and frowned. "And I'm engaged."

"Right."

She sat back and twisted the stem of her glass round with her fingers, watching me. For a while neither of us spoke.

I cleared my throat. "I've just been to Altrincham."

She raised her eyebrows. "Altrincham, as in … ?"

"Yup. I found the house where Trina Markham lived. Extremely posh. Her parents were Desmond and Shirley Markham. They lived there for a couple of years, but then left without telling anyone where they were going, and were never seen again. And get this – the neighbours considered them altogether shady."

"Wow! You really are a journalist, aren't you?"

"Sometimes."

"So what happens now?"

"I don't know. I feel as if I'm on the trail of something, but I don't know what."

"Your life doesn't sound boring to me."

"You're just getting the edited highlights."

We sat for a while in silence, then she said, "You were going to tell me how come you were suddenly looking for this girl. You said it was a long story, but you'd tell me one of these days."

"Ah. So is this that day?"

"Could be."

I thought for a moment. Keep it simple. "I've written a novel – a mystery. No big deal. No formal publisher. Nothing like that. I just stuck it online."

She was looking at me with raised eyebrows, but offered no comment.

"Anyway, I got some ideas for the plot from the holidays we spent at Falmouth. I invented a fictitious place like the Fairmile, and some of my characters are based on the real people I met there. Or at least, on an imagined version of them. And I thought now I would try to find out what happened to those real people."

"Is your book any good? Could I buy it?"

"Hah! You're welcome, if you're interested."

"Don't put yourself down, Mr Stanhope. Why not go with the flow?"

I looked at her. "I thought I was."

*   *   *

We continued to chat amiably. I asked her whether she enjoyed this kind of event.

"Gets me out and about." An ironic grin. "I enjoy the travel and the people. It can sometimes get a bit wearing, but you never know who you'll bump into." Her eyes twinkled.

"You seem very competent at your job."

"God knows how. I've never done any formal training in marketing. I just pick things up as I go along. The Latimer team are great. It really helps."

"Have you always lived in the West Country?"

"Pretty much – although I went to college in Bristol." Another ironic smile. "It seemed a long way away at the time." She picked up her glass and peered at me over it. "What about you, Mike? How did you get into logistics journalism?"

"Luck, really. Probably the same as you in your job. Events just seemed to take over, somehow."

"You seem very resourceful. You were probably born to it."

I shrugged. "A lot of the work is just daily grind."

She nodded. "So you'd rather be a novelist?"

"If only." I smiled at her reflectively. "The grass on the other side is always greener, isn't it?"

"Ah, how right you are." I sensed that she was talking about more than just my job.

We shared a long look. She shook her hair back and the light glinted in her earrings. She seemed to have none of the overt self-awareness that I remembered from other beautiful women I'd briefly known. The thought that she actually seemed to be attracted to me still filled me with amazement.

My thoughts seem to take control of my speech again. I found myself saying, "I'm glad you were able to make time for this."

"Sometimes I surprise myself."

* * *

In due course several of Ashley's colleagues rose, preparing to head off to whatever function they were attending, but she seemed in no hurry to usher me away. The throng in the bar gradually thinned around us.

Eventually I glanced at my watch. "I suppose I ought to think about heading back to London. God knows what the traffic will be like on the motorway."

"Have another drink. Have a tonic water."

I laughed. "I wish you didn't live in Cornwall."

"I'm very glad I do." She grinned indignantly at me.

"Ha! Not quite what I meant."

"I know what you meant, Mr Stanhope." Abruptly she leaned forward. "Don't take too much notice of what I say, Mike. I don't really know what the fuck I'm doing, to be honest. I think I've slipped a cog somewhere here."

I leaned forward myself, and accidentally brushed her hand on the table. It was like an electric shock, and we both recoiled slightly, looking at each other with surprise.

I said, "You seem to me like someone who usually knows her own mind."

She looked uncertainly at me. "That's what I thought, too."

We sat in silence for a moment, then I stood up. "It was nice to see you."

"Thank you for dropping by, Mr Stanhope." She stood up to rejoin a couple of her colleagues who were still there, then more quietly said, "Drive safely."

1988

Hawkins adjusted his field glasses to focus on the farmhouse. Rain pattered relentlessly on the grass around him: more rain, endless rain.

Striped police cars stood clustered in the farmyard, their blue lights flashing. Officers in high-visibility jackets moved cautiously about the scene – talking, huddling, evaluating. Some were busy erecting an exclusion fence round the farm. The white-clad forensics team went cautiously about their business.

The van, a rusty long-wheelbase Transit, stood in the middle of the farmyard, already with its own inner cordon around it. The fluorescent tape hung limply in the rain.

He wondered who was injured. The radio reports hadn't given out a name. He hoped it was Target, the stupid fucker. That foolish, needless bullet had turned them all from robbers into murderers. But he himself had been long gone by the time shots were fired at the farm. While the others had been arguing about the dispersal of the loot, he'd simply driven off in his rented car, empty-handed. It had been laughably easy.

Someone had talked. It was the only explanation. Ten minutes after he left, the police had swooped. He'd narrowly missed passing them on the farm road. What that someone didn't know, or hadn't mentioned to the police, was where they'd switched vehicles. That was what he'd counted on. Seven miles away, their original van stood intact in a deserted barn – along with the boxes he'd hidden at the front of the body. Perks of being the driver.

It had taken him under five minutes to transfer them to the boot of his car, then he drove into a new housing estate a mile away and parked at the end of an unfinished road: out of sight, and out of reach of any road blocks or other surveillance. And waited.

In the morning he'd joined a gaggle of press and mawkish onlookers at the nearest high point in sight of the farm. If you were hiding, the best place to do it was in plain sight. He looked at his watch. All he had to do now was collect Wendy and Sasha. And hide the spoils.

Chapter 18

Back at my desk, I tried to focus on work, but my mind kept drifting back to the previous evening in Birmingham. Clearly there was a spark between Ashley and me, but how could I engineer another meeting with her? Even if I could, where would it lead? I couldn't imagine. Yet the tantalising promise of our exchange was drowning out all other thoughts.

As a distraction, I reviewed my limited progress with the search for the Markham family. My visit to Altrincham hadn't really yielded much, though it did seem to confirm that they had vanished overnight. What I needed now was a more organised strategy for discovering why.

I was aware of various web sites offering advice on finding missing persons, but the options were so diverse that it was hard to know where to begin. Then I remembered the Park Writing Group. They'd assembled a bundle of what they called *Writers' resource goodies*, but I'd never asked for a copy. I felt sure it would help.

I'd signed up to the group while I was writing my book, hoping for helpful feedback. They met periodically in a flat in one of the Victorian mansion blocks overlooking Battersea Park. I hadn't attended a meeting for months, but according to their web site, one was scheduled for later this week. I clicked the link to attend.

* * *

The writing group session proved challenging. There was a prolonged conversation about self-publishing, which most members regarded as an admission of defeat, and I skated round my decision to go down that route myself. "I'm thinking about it," I said cautiously.

I knew that Eric, who owned the flat and ran the group, would be against it. He was a slim man in his fifties with a vigorous head of pepper-and-salt grey hair, a prematurely lined face and a world-weary aura. He regarded himself as an expert on the book trade, and now commented, "You realise that once you do self-publish, no real-world publisher will look at your book?"

However, Amelia, a round woman in her fifties with long, slightly unkempt blond hair, put in, "That's not strictly true, Eric. If an online book goes viral, a big publisher will sometimes pick it up."

"But how often does that happen? No, the traditional route still has to be the best way to go."

I asked about the *Writers' resource goodies*, and Eric pulled a photocopied pamphlet from a drawer. "This should be your bible," he said.

Thankfully, the meeting broke up earlier than usual, and by 9.30 I found myself out on the street.

"Fancy a quick drink?" It was Amelia, who had followed me down.

This was a first. I glanced curiously at her. "Why not? I can never understand why Eric insists on these dry sessions."

"I think at one time one of the group members was an alcoholic, so he introduced that rule."

She led the way to an unglamorous pub on the edge of a high-rise estate just off Battersea Park Road. She looked around the bar critically. "Always wondered what this place was like. Now I know." I had the impression she wasn't planning an imminent return visit.

Over a double gin and tonic she observed, "You shouldn't be put off by Eric's view of self-publishing. You could wait forever to get an agent to pick up the bait. Ask yourself which is better: a dozen sales online today, or zero sales in two years' time, and a sense of your own worthiness?"

"Maybe you're right."

"Trust me, you're speaking to one who knows. I've published three novels online, and sold several hundred copies so far. It won't make me rich, but at least I know there are a few people out there who want to read what I've written." She hesitated. "People who don't spew self-satisfied claptrap about them."

I laughed. It wasn't all claptrap; I'd learned a lot from the reading group members, most of whom were simply doing their best with a difficult pursuit. But I could see her point.

"But you've never told the group about it?"

"Obviously not. You can imagine what they would say."

"But you've proved them wrong. Self-publishing *can* work."

She shook her head. "Conventional publishers would be crying into their beer if they only sold a few hundred copies of their books. Eric knows that. I haven't proved they're wrong – I've just demonstrated that there's another way."

I looked at her with new curiosity. "So what are your books about? Are they the same as the stuff you've read out to the group?"

"No, they're fantasy romance. Can't see the group taking to that, can you? But they're rooted in the real world."

I smiled at her. "I wouldn't have put you down for that genre."

"Well, there you go."

We chatted about this for a while, then the conversation ranged over the other members of the group. She commented, "Harry and Fran wouldn't have any problem with self-publishing, I bet you."

Harry was about twenty-five, and all I knew about him was that he came from Chadwell Heath. In some ways he seemed the group's unlikeliest member, but his occasional observations were usually astute. Fran was a brisk mother of three (she liked to characterise herself in exactly those terms) who lived in Putney, and was an unashamed fan of "chick lit".

I demurred, but Amelia leaned forward confidentially. "Harry has already bought your book online. A few weeks ago he told me he'd downloaded it."

I looked at her in surprise. "So you knew I'd self-published it?"

She grinned. "Well, I wasn't going to broadcast the fact unless you did."

I smiled broadly at her. "I appreciate that." Then I thought about it for a moment. "Harry didn't mention it this evening either."

"We're all terrified of what Eric's going to say."

We parted company around 10.30 and I headed for home. Unfortunately, another unpleasant shock awaited me there. When I reached the kitchen I found the back door swinging open on its hinges and the lock completely smashed. Christ – what now?

What now, I soon found, was that my laptop computer and tablet had been stolen. I felt like crying. I'd been carefully taking them with me everywhere I went, but this evening's excursion had seemed too trivial to require this measure, and I'd let down my guard.

I seemed to be in the middle of an unrelenting onslaught, and I didn't know how to stop it.

Chapter 19

"Dave? It's Mike Stanhope." I spoke hesitantly. I wasn't sure how he would react to my call.

"Stanhope – there's a name to conjure with. I thought you must be dead."

Immediately I felt a stab of guilt. This man was supposed to be my friend, yet I had no idea when I had last contacted him. Trying to strike a matching note of levity, I said, "Nice to speak to you too."

I'd met DI Dave Matthews years ago in connection with a story I was covering, and unexpectedly we'd hit it off. Over the next few years we'd spent more than a few boozy evenings in the pub, and occasionally, when I needed off-the-record updates, he had proved surprisingly forthcoming. I never really understood why.

Yet once I'd stopped writing investigative articles, I'd also stopped contacting him. How cynical did that make me? Cautiously I said, "Dave, d'you fancy a drink?"

Initially he sounded surprised, but then he said, "Yeah, why not? That place in Norbury?"

It was our old drinking haunt, and he was already sitting at the bar counter when I walked in – a thickset man in his early forties with light coloured hair, heavy jowls and a ruddy complexion. He looked more or less unchanged from the last time I'd seen him, and he gave me a quizzical smile. He gestured to the adjacent bar stool, sliding a pint over to me. "I didn't think we'd be doing this again somehow."

I smiled at him in turn. I felt unexpectedly pleased to see him. It was hard to explain the chemistry that could work between people as different as we were, but I now realised I'd missed our evenings together. He seemed to relish talking to someone outside the force, and I'd found it fascinating to hear his surprisingly frank accounts of some of the cases he worked on.

I said, "I enjoyed working with you back then, but I don't know." I took a sip of beer. "I'm not sure I was cut out to be an undercover hack."

"You underrate yourself, my friend. You were very focused." He paused, perhaps searching for a better term. "Very driven."

"Huh. I don't know about driven. All I know is there was too much stress."

"You don't need to tell me about stress, mate. It's what I do every day. Stress is my middle name."

"Sorry, what I said probably sounded tactless." I took a deep breath. "I really valued your help when I needed it."

He gave me an appraising look. "Something tells me you want more help now."

"Ha. I didn't mean to be so transparent."

"So long as we know the rest of the drinks are on you."

I paused, working out where to begin. "It's about Allied Northern Stockholders. I'm sure you remember them."

"I could hardly forget, could I? Biggest fuck-up in many a long day. I worked with the northern task force for weeks on that case. We were trying to nail those two brothers, Janni and Tommy Noble. But what did we get out of it in the end? Fuck all."

"Right. Well, the other day I bumped into Janni Noble by chance. I'd never met him before. Then a day or two later Tommy phoned me up out of the blue. Bit of a coincidence, I thought. And since then I've had two break-ins at my house. The latest one was last night. My computer has been stolen."

He was watching me closely. "And there's more?"

"Well, you might think this is a bit of a stretch, but a week or two back my web site was hacked. My web man says someone might have been trying to steal information about me, or from me."

"I'm sorry to hear all this, mate. But you surely don't think these three things are all connected?"

I shrugged. "I wouldn't have, but the break-ins seem so methodical, so intentional. It's more like being targeted than being burgled. I wondered if these guys think I have something they want from me – some kind of evidence against them or something." I paused. "And I got to thinking that maybe the web site hack was the same people attacking me from a different angle. It does fit, in a way."

I could almost hear Dave processing this for a moment. Finally he said, "But you published that article anonymously, didn't you?"

"That's right." This hadn't been my choice; it was magazine policy to use pen names on anything controversial. It was a layer of protection for the writer – or so they reasoned it.

I added, "Obviously Tommy Noble knows who I am, but Janni Noble isn't supposed to. I'm just wondering if he somehow found out."

"So you think either or both of them could be gunning for you?"

"Well possibly, though I don't see what good it would do them."

Dave cleared his throat. "Look, I don't know whether this will make you feel better or worse, but people on my team went through that article of yours at the time. To be honest, they couldn't really find anything in it to contribute to our case. It was background information, that's all. Hearsay and conjecture, but no real substance."

I was silent for a moment, reflecting on this easy dismissal of my work. But then again, wasn't this exactly what I hoped he would say? I couldn't have it both ways.

I said, "Huh. Well, might as well tell it like it is."

At the end of the evening Dave agreed to try to find out the latest on the Noble brothers, and let me know if anything he discovered seemed to fit in with my theory. "But I have to say I doubt it," he added.

* * *

My next task was to replace my laptop computer. Somehow I felt I'd said goodbye forever to the one that had been stolen, and the police seemed to concur with that view. I needed a new one, and I could only hope my home insurance would pay for it.

I headed for the computer superstore on Purley Way in Croydon, where I was dismayed to find that few modern laptops seemed to have a DVD drive built in. I ended up paying more than I could afford for the laptop itself, and more again for a separate DVD drive. I bought a new tablet, too – the cheapest I could find.

All I had to do now was find and load all my software and data, then sort out my passwords and get things back to something like normality: a dispiriting task that seemed to take hours.

It was two days later when Dave rang me back.

"Got a minute? I might as well fill you in on what I've picked up about the Nobles."

"Brilliant."

"This is how it looks to me. We were more or less certain that they were in the trafficking scheme together, but we could never find any real evidence against Janni."

"OK, I'm with you so far."

"Tommy was a different case. We had evidence that he was involved in the scheme hands-on, so we arrested him. But it all started to come unstuck, and the next thing we know, he's skipped bail and disappeared. We found out later that he'd managed to make his way back to Albania. He simply hung out there and kept his head down."

I waited.

"Well, basically the case fell apart. People who we thought would start talking suddenly clammed up, and in the end we had to drop it. So the warrant on Tommy was rescinded, and the bad guys lived happily ever after."

"Do you think Janni put the frighteners on the witnesses?"

"No, that was an odd thing. I was told they genuinely didn't seem to want to see him go down."

I thought through the implications of this. "But you reckon there might be something more recent that could have stirred up the brothers? Something that would get them taking an interest in me?"

"Well, I'm hearing that Tommy is back in the country, with an almighty grudge against his brother. That could possibly be relevant."

"How come?"

"Well Tommy's been working all this time on the family farm in Albania, or whatever he does over there, while Janni has been building up a big new business empire in the North West. So now Tommy wants to muscle in on it. But apparently he was always a bit of a loose cannon, and Janni was more than happy to get shot of him. Now he'd prefer to let him stew in his own juice."

"You've got good information."

"Just the kind of stuff we pick up all the time by keeping our ears open."

"So …?"

"OK, well let's suppose that Tommy reckons he could still put his hands on some sort of evidence that would implicate Janni in the trafficking. That would be a bit of leverage, wouldn't it? A way of prising his way into the new business."

"But surely he couldn't give up Janni without also implicating himself?"

"Well, I can't read his mind."

"Anyway, what do you mean by evidence? What sort of evidence?"

"No idea, but we wondered if it could be photographs. Something like that?"

My mind immediately jumped to those photographs I'd taken of Tommy and his freight container. Tommy already had copies, so he had no reason to steal them from me, but Janni didn't. Was he trying to get sight of them – hoping to meet Tommy's blackmail head on, and perhaps to unearth some counter-evidence that implicated Tommy?

That made a kind of sense, though I didn't really see how Dave could know about the pictures. Maybe they'd been mentioned when the brothers were under suspicion, or maybe he was just guessing. I thought I'd better play dumb, and simply said, "Photographs of what?"

"You tell me." He paused. "So *are* there any pictures, or is it all a figment of Tommy's fertile imagination?"

"To be totally honest, I'm not sure."

"Meaning that there are."

"Meaning that I need to think about it. I promise I'll get back to you if there's anything to report."

"I'll hold you to that."

The problem was that I didn't have the pictures myself. They were on a CD, and I happened to know that this was in the possession of Sandy, my ex-wife. When she left me she'd laid claim to a whole bundle of disks containing photographs we'd taken over the years. Later I'd realised that some of the pictures I'd taken for magazine articles had been muddled up among them.

I sat with my hand poised on my phone for several minutes, then pressed the code for Sandy. "It's me. How would you feel if I dropped in?"

Chapter 20

Sandy was living in a neat suburban terrace house in Ealing, west London. I drove over on a breezy spring morning. It didn't exactly conjure up the exciting lifestyle she'd implied that she wanted, but it certainly eclipsed my rather drab house in Thornton Heath. The frontage was finished in white pebbledash that gleamed in the sun, and flowers were springing up in the neat garden.

She opened the door holding her mobile phone and looking distracted. She was smartly dressed in a skirt and jacket. "I didn't think you were going to make it in time. I've got to go out."

"I thought you worked from home." She'd set up some kind of practice in alternative therapies.

"Yes, but I do have customers to see." She waved me in and shut the door, ushering me through to a sunny lounge. "So how are you, Mike?"

"I'm good. I'm fine. You're looking well." She'd let her naturally blond hair grow longer than when we were together, and currently it was tied in a loose pony tail. I still found her attractive, despite everything.

"Alan says that too, but I've put on pounds this year." She didn't explain who Alan was and I decided not to ask. Instead, I said truthfully. "I don't see it myself."

She looked at me appraisingly. "I must say you look better than I got from Joanna."

"A good friend she is."

She laughed. "You should be grateful that people are looking out for you – even me."

"I am."

We said nothing for a moment, then she said. "Hey, I like your book. I haven't finished it yet, but it's a good read."

"My god. I can't believe you bought it."

"Well, J talked it up, so I thought why not? It's quite revealing, actually."

"How so?"

"All that stuff about that girl you were pining for. I can see now that I was just a stop-gap all along. I should have realised."

I opened my mouth to protest, but she held up her hands defensively and gave me an ironic smile. "Just joking."

"The leading character isn't me. He's fictional."

"If you say so."

"I do." I wandered over and looked through the glazed double doors on to an extensive lawn, then turned back to her. "I think I'll keep my next novel secret."

"You won't sell many copies then."

Another silence, then she said, "Look, I really do have to go. I'm not just trying to avoid you. Why don't you come round again another time, when there's more time to talk? I do want us to be friends. Life's too short."

"I'd like that."

"Anyway, you want those pictures." She crossed to a pine wall cabinet and opened the door, revealing an array of CD cases. "All our old stuff is in here. Knock yourself out."

"Ha."

"Can I leave you to lock up? I really am running late. Just pull the front door after you."

* * *

Back at home, I shoved the CD into my new drive unit. There were about a dozen pictures in all, taken in that scruffy yard in the suburbs of Luton. They all showed more or less the same thing – Tommy Noble standing in front of or near the back doors of a twenty-foot freight container.

He was wearing a hoodie that hid any significant detail of his face, so he was unrecognisable even without any doctoring of the image. The doors of the container were open, revealing a small compartment to one side, complete with a wooden chair and some old carpet on the floor. Luxury travel for the upmarket asylum-seeker. Tommy had shown me how this was built to resemble a wooden crate, and had been transported alongside genuine crates.

I worked my way through the images several times, looking for something that Tommy might think Janni would find incriminating about them. Beyond the container was a nondescript wooden fence, and immediately to the right of the container, some of the shots showed the back of a big car – a sports utility vehicle. We had carefully leaned an old wooden board against the bumper so that the registration number wouldn't be visible.

It was during my third or fourth pass that I spotted something reflected in the rear window of the SUV: a man leaning on the corner of another container behind us – outside our field of vision, except in that reflection.

From the angular shape of his face I was immediately convinced it was Janni. He must have been there during the entire session, but whether with Tommy's knowledge or not I had no idea. Either way, this looked like proof that Janni was aware of the trafficking scam. It also showed that he knew Tommy had talked to me.

The figure only appeared in four of images. I applied various filters to lighten and sharpen the image, but the main features of the face remained obstinately absent, and only the outline shape was clear.

So were these pictures what my intruder had been looking for? It seemed possible. But would they give Tommy the hold over Janni that he was evidently expecting? I couldn't tell.

My first priority was to secure them. I carefully uploaded copies of the full set to two different cloud computing servers that I used. As for the original, I hid it in plain sight among the CDs on my shelf. The intruder had already checked those.

All I needed to do now was decide what to do with this new information.

Chapter 21

Desmond Markham had been born in Ashby-de-la-Zouch in 1938, and had married Shirley Hedges, also of Ashby, in 1960. He had studied accounting, and joined an accountancy practice in Burton-on-Trent in 1966. Evidently he had become increasingly interested in the property market, and by 1974 was working for a firm of property investors in Manchester.

I'd learned most of this by following internet leads suggested by the *Writers' resource goodies*. My search was now much more structured and methodical than before. Web sites that I'd never found in the past were proving unexpectedly fruitful. It was amazing what a lot you could learn about people from freely available public internet sources. You just had to persevere.

I'd discovered that in 1983 Markham left the investment firm to become a partner in a new company, HGRC Properties (1983). He was managing director and there were two other directors – Shirley Markham and Robert Stainer, whoever he was. I couldn't discover what the initials HGRC stood for, but they evidently pre-dated Markham's arrival on the scene.

HGRC had grown rapidly into a multi-million pound business, and the Markhams had moved into their expensive house in Bowden in 1987. But in 1990 Markham appeared to have resigned, and after that he and his wife evidently ceased to exist.

Catrina Markham had been born in 1979, and had attended a school in south Manchester. She too had ceased to exist in 1990.

So far I'd found no reference to the family being involved in an accident of any sort, and no press reports about them. They had simply evaporated.

On top of that information, I knew that they had spent at least one holiday in Cornwall in 1990, and I had a vague sense that they might have visited the Fairmile on at least one previous occasion. But soon after the time when I knew them, they had disappeared forever.

I wrote down a short list of possible explanations for their disappearance.

* Murdered, and bodies never found.
* Killed in some kind of accident (as yet unknown).
* Emigrated.
* Changed their name.
* Went into witness protection.

Those last three items could all apply simultaneously, or in any combination.

I decided that murder was unlikely. If a whole family had disappeared in mysterious circumstances, surely there would have been press reports over a fairly long period? Yet I'd found nothing.

Emigration was a simple explanation, and was the one I'd adopted for the fictitious family in my book. But tracking down the real family if that were the case would be an almost insurmountable challenge. I couldn't possibly access records for every country where they might conceivably have gone; the very idea was absurd. And if they'd changed their name it would be a lost cause anyway.

The idea of witness protection was interesting. Maybe Markham had blown the whistle on some financial scam and had to go into hiding. Or the family might have changed their name and gone into hiding on their own initiative. That would make them equally difficult to track down.

I pushed my chair away from my desk and swivelled all the way round. I could see a problem looming, and it might prevent me taking this pursuit much further. If the family had indeed gone into hiding, whether enforced or self-imposed, the last thing I should be doing was trying to winkle them out of it. Although many years had passed since they'd vanished, they could still be under threat from whatever had driven them away in the first place. Who did I think I was to be putting them in danger?

The Catch 22 was, how would I know? I would need to find out if they were in hiding in order to know whether I should be looking for them.

* * *

I paced around my small office trying to think this through. Maybe this was where the search ended. Joanna had shoved me off on this trajectory, and I'd kept going because it had been a diversion from proper work, but it simply wasn't necessary or significant in the wider scheme of things.

I tried to itemise the reasons for carrying on. Was there an article in this somewhere? An exposé? If so, of what? Maybe there was some potential here, but it was pretty nebulous.

Was it research for another novel? No, I'd already hijacked my memory of these people for my existing novel. I couldn't very well use the same theme a second time.

Or was I still trying to lay the ghosts of my adolescent romantic fantasies? Well, possibly; but I wasn't getting very far with that either. And now that I'd met Ashley, maybe the exercise had already fulfilled an alternative purpose. I might not have tracked down Trina Markham, but apparently I'd become involved with another girl whom I'd actually encountered at the same time. This was little short of astonishing, and serendipity if ever I saw it.

I smiled sourly to myself. I hadn't really become involved with Ashley – I just wanted to be, or wished I could be. But whatever the reality of our relationship, it didn't depend on this search.

Chapter 22

"Mike, are you up for a trip to Amsterdam?" It was Phil Connor from the materials handling magazine – by no means a regular caller.

Cautiously I answered, "I could be."

"There's a mechanical handling show coming up. Normally we would cover this one in-house – it's a big event in our calendar – but I've got unexpected family commitments and Adrian is otherwise engaged, and my usual regulars are already covering it for other people. You'll really be doing me a favour if you take this on."

I did some fast thinking. Reporting on handling systems in the context of a general logistics show was one thing – it just required some intelligently applied business knowledge. Covering a specialised technical show was a rather different proposition. My knowledge of hydraulic cranes and forklift trucks was strictly superficial, and experts would soon peg me as a total impostor.

Yet I couldn't afford to turn away good work, and I felt I should cultivate Phil. How difficult would it be to busk my way through this? I asked him how much he would be paying, and his answer clinched it. The rate was unexpectedly generous, and included the flight and a hotel.

"I'll put it in my diary."

* * *

I soon found myself regretting that decision. That afternoon my email system pinged, and I saw a message from ashley@latimerlogistics.com. It was headed "We meet again!", and there was no text in it – just a photographic attachment. I opened the image and stared at it with fascination.

I could see immediately that it was a picture taken on one of the lawns at the Fairmile Hotel. Slightly to the right of centre stood Trina, dressed in her familiar white top and blue shorts. She had her hands on the shoulders of a younger boy, perhaps pretending to strangle him; but her eye had been caught by something to the left of the image, and she was glancing over there rather than looking at the boy.

My eyes followed her gaze, and on the far left of the picture stood a much younger version of myself, on a narrow path that ran alongside the lawn. I was dressed in khaki shorts and a grey T-shirt, and I was bending over, handing an object to a small child who had presumably dropped it.

I zoomed in closer. Was this child Ashley? Had we in fact met each other all those years ago? I smiled to myself. "Met" was perhaps an exaggeration; "encountered" might be closer. The child was in part-profile, and I couldn't see anything of Ashley in that small face. But she would know.

I leaned back in my chair, staring at the picture. It must be her. Smiling to myself, I picked up my mobile and scrolled down to the number for Latimer Logistics.

"Mr Stanhope! What d'you reckon?"

"I can't believe it!"

"My brother dug it out. I scanned it this morning." She paused. "So we've known each other nearly all our lives. What do you think of that?"

"Amazing! So do you remember me now that you've seen this?"

She laughed. "Not really, sorry! I bet you don't remember me either."

"Er, no."

"Well, there you go. Anyway, Trina looks just the way I remember her."

I couldn't decide what to say next. I hadn't been able to think of any appropriate way to follow up our meeting in the Midlands, so I'd done nothing. This was the first time we'd been in contact since then.

She said hesitantly, "How's life in London?"

"Oh, you know. The usual. You?"

"Likewise."

She paused. I sensed that she was working up to some separate point. "Um, since you're on, I'm going to be in London in a couple of weeks' time. With Jack. I was going to call you anyway. We're going to a do with some of his old college mates. It's an annual thing. I was thinking that maybe you might fancy meeting for lunch while I'm there." A pause. "If you're free."

"With you and Jack?"

"Well, no." Another pause, then a little too quickly, "It's on a Monday, and he's coming straight back to Truro on the Tuesday, but I'm going up to see a girl friend in Bishops Stortford. I'll be coming back on the Wednesday. I thought maybe we could meet up at lunchtime, when I'm on my way back through London." She broke off. "I suppose it sounds a bit half-baked …"

I jumped in quickly. "It's an excellent idea. Let's do it. Consider it agreed."

We fixed a time and place, then a sudden thought struck me. The day in question was my second day at the handling show in Holland. I'd been booked on an afternoon flight back to Gatwick.

"Fuck, I'm supposed to be in Amsterdam on that day."

"Oh, look, it doesn't matter, honestly. It was just a thought."

"It does matter. There must be some way round this." My mind was racing. I'd told Phil I wanted that extra half-day at the show in case I needed to catch up on things I'd missed the previous day. Maybe I could do without it.

"Let me see if I can re-schedule. I might be able to get back to London by lunchtime Wednesday."

"Well, if you're sure …"

"I'm sure." I probably spoke a bit too vehemently, but I wanted to sound reassuring and definite. To lighten the tone, I added, "In the meantime, let me know if you find any more photos like the one you sent."

"I will." Then, "I've got Patrick on the case."

*   *   *

I put the phone down and sat there for a while, replaying the conversation we'd just had.

I'd just made a date. With Ashley. There was no other way of looking at it. We weren't old friends planning a reunion; we were scarcely friends at all. And we weren't meeting because we happened to have been thrown together in the same environment. Quite the opposite; we were going out of our way to meet up under an arrangement that could prove quite tricky to pull off.

Basically, we'd just tacitly agreed to move our relationship forward. If this wasn't a date, I couldn't think what was.

I still couldn't quite believe she was interested in me. After Sandy, my confidence had taken a battering, and I knew some women found my manner off-putting. Either I was too keen or I was too cynical – I'd heard it all. In a way I suppose I'd reverted to type. For some reason, Ashley apparently hadn't been put off. Not yet, anyway.

Where it was leading was quite another matter. Ashley was engaged, and seemed comfortable and at ease with her fiancé. At any rate, that was my memory from Truro. Yet clearly there was a real spark between us, and apparently she wasn't afraid to explore it. How was I supposed to feel about this? I'd never before found myself in the role of "other man", so I'd never bothered to work out the bounds of my moral compass.

It was clearly time I did.

I logged on to the airline web site, and after trawling around it for far too long, came to the conclusion that I couldn't change my airline booking to an earlier flight – I could only forfeit the existing return ticket and buy a new one at my own cost.

Well, sod it; that's what I'd have to do. I booked a return flight out of Schiphol that would necessitate a ridiculously early start, logged off, then sat back and allowed myself a grin of anticipation.

I opened an email window to send Ashley confirmation of our date.

1988

Sasha crouched by her windowsill, peering down into the hotel garden. The main lawn was illuminated faintly by the night light in the hall, but the trees were lost in darkness. Finally she was satisfied. She slipped out of her room and tiptoed along the corridor, then up a flight of stairs, along more corridors, and finally down the back stairs to the games room. As she expected, the door out to the garden was not locked, merely jammed shut as it always seemed to be. She eased it open as quietly as she could and stepped cautiously outside.

She had worked this out earlier, roaming the garden in the twilight, but she'd needed to be careful. She could feel the eyes of that boy on her as he sat on the terrace with his parents. Why did he never have anything to say for himself?

It didn't matter now. After tomorrow she would be gone, and would never see him or any of these people again. Or England, come to that. A new name and a new life: an adventure to end all adventures, her father called it. Such unutterable fucking crap.

She rounded the corner and glanced warily around. No one in sight. Cautiously she pulled up the grating as she'd seen her father do it last night, peering dubiously into the darkness. A shiver of trepidation ran through her, but she forced herself to ignore it as she shone her torch into the gloom. At least the faint light was reassuring. She edged her way down the ancient stone steps and pushed open a warped, decaying door at the bottom.

She sensed rather than saw the spiders and crawly things as she shone her light round various indeterminate shapes, but her anger overrode her instinctive fear. Her greater worry was how she would ever find anything down here. All she knew was that her father had gone down laden with heavy bags, and come up again with nothing.

In the end she found them under the ancient wine rack, in a brick cavity hidden by an upturned flagstone. She edged them out. They rattled slightly.

What was in them? She didn't want to know. She dragged them to the steps, and somehow managed to manhandle them to the top.

And then across the lawn and through the trees to the secret place: a much better place than her father's, she reflected with private pleasure. He should have consulted her about it. Well, fuck him, he could come to her if he ever wanted this stuff back.

That was assuming he or any of them was ever in the country again.

Chapter 23

Visits to foreign trade shows were an assault on all the senses. The different language, the unfamiliar architecture and street signs, the strange snack foods, the hassle of understanding arcane public transport rituals – everything contributed to the overall sense of displacement.

I made my way from the airport to the centre of Amsterdam by train, then took a tram out to the convention centre. After a horrendously early start that morning, I was already feeling dazed when I walked into the show arena.

Hydraulic cranes in reds, greens and yellows thrust their necks out from the stands like foraging animals from some alien planet; conveyors shuttled empty cardboard boxes pointlessly back and forth; giant lift trucks held full-sized freight containers precariously aloft. Visitors chatted to each other in a dozen languages as they paced along broad red-carpeted aisles, and everywhere the air was laden with the unique scent of machine oil and fresh paint.

At least now I was on familiar ground; shows like this transcended borders, and this one could have been taking place anywhere in the world. All I had to do was find enough news to justify the trip.

The last time I'd visited an event of this kind I'd gathered together an enormous sheaf of news releases from the press room, then written up half my report from those: the lazy man's approach, but I wasn't out to conquer the world. These days printed press releases were few and far between. If you were lucky, the people on the stands would hand you their latest news on a USB memory dongle; if you weren't, you would have to look up the information on their web site later, and hope they'd bothered to post it there.

Alternatively, of course, you could actually take the trouble to engage people on the stands in conversation. Wasn't that in fact why I'd come?

Summoning up vague memories of tonne-metres, bending moment and mechanical advantage, I braced myself to go and talk about cranes.

* * *

Some indeterminate number of hours later I was gratefully drinking a glass of white wine on a crane manufacturer's stand when I caught sight of a figure who looked vaguely familiar. It was Janni Noble, hovering a few feet away from the stand and surveying the hardware on display. A man from the crane company was standing beside him, following his gaze and perhaps wondering how best to embark on a sales pitch.

What should I do? Confront him? Avoid him? Wait to see what he would do? I sat there indecisively for a moment. I'd been speculating for weeks that he'd been orchestrating the break-ins at my house, but I had no actual evidence of it. I finally decided the best I could achieve here was to make myself known to him, and try to gauge his response. Making my apologies to my host, I left the bar warily and walked over to him.

"Mr Stanhope," he greeted me. "We meet again. What brings you to this event?" His tone was neither friendly nor unfriendly.

I stepped off the stand and held my hand out to him. "Plenty to report here for the trade press."

He shook my hand briefly and perfunctorily. "I did not know you were an expert in these matters."

"I'm not. Jack of all trades, that's me."

"I see." He gave me an emotionless stare, then turned his gaze beyond me towards the stand.

"What brings you here?" I asked him.

He focused on me again. "We are adding a batch of crane carriers to our rental fleet. I want to buy the right product for our market at the right price. This is the top show, so it is the best place to look."

It was impossible to gauge his attitude to me, but on the strength of this slender evidence he seemed supremely uninterested – almost bored.

I tried, "You must let me know if there's anything I can help you with."

He looked at me a little more closely. "And what kind of help do you think might you be able to offer?"

Once again I was struck by the force of his personality. This was someone I would not want to cross. Deciding to make light of my comment, I said, "Oh, the background to the logistics business, anything in that vein."

"I will be sure to read your report on this show."

He didn't ask what paper to look in, and I didn't volunteer it. Already he was looking back towards the exhibits. I took my leave and slid away, gratefully rounding the corner of the stand and moving out of his line of sight. I headed off down the aisle.

* * *

By six o'clock I was exhausted. Unfortunately I somehow had to find the energy to attend an evening function hosted by one of the conveyor manufacturers. Phil Connor had insisted I go to this in order to fly the flag for his magazine. However, events were about to take a different turn.

I spotted a fellow-journalist, Ade Lumsden, as we were both making our way towards the exit. "Are you going to this Armstrong function tonight?" I asked him.

"Didn't they tell you? It's been cancelled. Some kind of problem with the booking. Don't ask me."

I stopped in my tracks. "Fuck. I wish I'd known."

I'd kept my booking at the hotel that night because I couldn't have made it back to the UK after the dinner. If I'd known it would be cancelled I would have booked an evening flight home – and been sure of making it to the lunch with Ashley the next day. But I was in no mood to unpick my travel plans now.

Ade stopped and turned back. "A night on the town, then?"

I caught up with him. "Sounds a reasonable idea."

Mercifully, Ade's idea of a night on the town meant nothing more demanding than a leisurely meal in a restaurant just off Dam Square in the city centre. Two other British journalists joined us, and we sat downing local beers and discussing the state of the world, doing battle with enormous platefuls of pneumatic *rookworst*, mashed potato and sauerkraut.

Ade, a man with a rotund face and a permanently jovial expression, always seemed to know everything about everyone in our business, and took conspicuous delight in sharing the latest salacious information about mutual acquaintances. Suddenly I realised he'd turned his focus on me.

"What's this I hear about Jason Bright downrating you?"

Downrating was a term exclusive to Bright's magazine, and meant exactly what it said: moving writers off the list of priority contributors. Had he done this to me? It didn't seem to fit with his positive attitude the last time we spoke, but it would certainly account for his hesitant manner on all the other occasions he'd contacted me in recent months.

Temporising, I said, "What gave you that idea?"

"I heard there were issues. Mistakes being made. Late copy." He smiled cheerfully. "Too many nights on the razz?" He tore a chunk off his bread roll. "Only what I'm told."

I marvelled at his extraordinarily thick skin. When you wanted to know something, Ade was a useful source of information, but he seemed to have no allegiances or loyalties, and no compunction about sharing information with anyone who would listen – even if that someone was the target of the gossip.

All I could manage to mutter was, "Charming."

"Not true then? All hot air?"

I looked at him. "For god's sake Ade, what do you expect me to say?"

To his credit he looked almost contrite. "No offence intended. All I'm saying is that it's a small world, and the word gets round." He chuckled. "And I don't mean because I spread it."

I thought for a moment. "I tell you what – let's just say I was in a bad place, but now I'm in a good place again. How would you like to put that about?"

"Message received and understood." He nodded emphatically, then launched into a conversation with the journalist sitting the other side of him.

I spent a long while in moody silence. What Ade said had made uncomfortable listening, whether true or not. I thought I'd moved out of the black period I'd been in, but from his comments, that view wasn't necessarily shared by my peers. I felt all the more aware of the need to write a convincing report of this event.

* * *

It was a little later, as I returned from the men's room, that I spotted Janni Noble sitting at a table with a smaller man in a corner alcove. Janni had his back to me, and just as I was approaching I saw the other man draw a large bundle of cash from his side pocket and pass it discreetly to Janni. I only saw this because of the unusual angle.

I slowed down, trying to watch unobtrusively. I recognised the outer note as a yellow 200 euro bill. If the whole wad was made up of the same denomination, it must run to many thousands of euros.

What did it mean? Anything or nothing? If I hadn't known about Janni's history I would have dismissed it as insignificant. As it was, I was immediately speculating that it must be some sort of illicit pay-off. Could Janni still be involved in the people smuggling business?

The place was crowded, and people were constantly getting up and moving around, so I was able to hover a moment while I took all this in. However, eventually the smaller man glanced my way, and I fancied he fleetingly caught my eye. He showed no sign of recognition, but I decided I'd lingered long enough.

My party were still engaged in earnest conversation when I returned to my table. I hung on for a while, trying to summon up an appropriate level of jollity, but eventually I decide it was a lost cause. I gave them the right money to pay for my meal and headed off.

* * *

As I started down the street in the direction of my hotel two figures stepped out in front of me – Janni Noble and the other man. They must have left just before I did, but had now turned back to confront me. The

Koninklijk Paleis loomed behind them, illuminated by floodlights in soft dappled browns.

"Mr Stanhope." Noble was conspicuously blocking my way.

"Hello again."

He turned to the other man. "This is the person you saw?"

His companion, a stout figure with a round face and a dark moustache, looked carefully at me and then nodded vigorously. "Yes it is. Yes."

Noble turned to me again. "Mr Stanhope, you seem to be taking a surprising interest in my affairs. Some people might find such interference insulting." He took a step forward, no doubt intending to intimidate me by his height and his sheer presence.

I was unsure what to say. Presumably these two were not about to assault me in one of Amsterdam's main tourist areas, but what else did they want?

"Mr Stanhope, you gave me the impression earlier today that you had some agenda in what you were saying to me. Now you are spying on me and my colleagues. I find your behaviour unpleasant and offensive."

There was no point in antagonising this man. I decided the best policy was to calm the situation. "Please accept my apologies if I have given you the wrong impression. I don't mean to offend anyone."

He stared at me for a moment without replying, then said, "Mr Stanhope, please do not treat me like an idiot. You think you are a campaigning journalist. You think you are confronting the hard world out there, and doing good work. You are not. You are a minor player with no insight and no influence, but a propensity for meddling."

He turned to his colleague as if for endorsement, then back to me. "Take my advice – stick to writing articles about trucks and cranes, and do not interfere in affairs you do not understand."

He allowed his words to hang in the air for a moment, then he and his colleague stepped apart, leaving me room to walk on between them. "I wish you a good night."

Chapter 24

A good night is not what I had. I was worried I would sleep through my alarm, and I finally fell into a troubled slumber at about 3am. Then I almost did miss the alarm, and had to grab my few belongings and check out of my hotel in a panic. I more or less ran half-way to Amsterdam's main railway station before succeeding in catching one of the city's modern trams. Having negotiated the airport's check-in and security system, I then found that the plane had been delayed by three quarters of an hour. I sat in the departure lounge feeling hot, resentful and hung over.

Finally we were under way, and as the flight progressed I kept reassessing my timetable. I would just have time to catch a train home from Gatwick, shower and change, then catch another to central London and meet Ashley at Kings Cross.

It all went more or less to plan. At Gatwick I caught a stopping train to East Croydon, then from there I took a bus to Thornton Heath. Finally I was walking the last leg to my house. Should I call Ashley to confirm that I was on track? I took out my phone, then it occurred to me that I didn't have her mobile number, only the main number for the Latimer Logistics switchboard. I stopped for a moment, debating whether to ring them and ask for it.

Which is when it all went wrong. I paid no attention to the car that pulled up beside me or the two men who climbed out, and before I knew it they'd grabbed me roughly by the arms and bundled me inside. My phone clattered to the ground.

Looking back later, I found the whole episode almost unreal. I'd seen this scenario played out in countless films, read it in countless book, but never once envisaged it happening to me in reality. The sheer audacity of it amazed me – these people's practised confidence, their apparent disregard for witnesses and possible surveillance cameras.

At the time, I was simply stunned. It all seemed to happen in a blink. One moment I was on the street, the next I was pinned down in the middle of the back seat, struggling wildly and yelling, "What the FUCK are you doing? What the FUCK?"

To no avail. It was an upmarket car with a plush interior lining and lightly tinted windows. No one outside could see me, and the sound of my voice seemed ridiculously muted. Any hope I had of being heard outside was dashed when the driver, a short man in a light grey hoodie, reached out and turned up the radio, and ear-shattering dance music immediately flooded the car.

We pulled away, and were soon travelling north along London Road. For a while I continued to thrash about, yelling at the same time, but the two men were immensely strong, and conveyed an effortless commitment to keeping me in place. They seemed to know exactly how much pressure to apply without exerting themselves unnecessarily. Eventually I stopped resisting and forced myself to calm down, waiting to see what was going to happen next.

We continued north through the extended suburb of Norbury and into Streatham. It was hard to make out whether we were heading somewhere specific or just driving at random. Periodically I tried shouting "Where are we going?", but nobody answered. Eventually I gave up and risked glancing at my captors. They all seemed to be in their twenties or early thirties, and were wearing unremarkable casual clothes with woollen hats or hoodies. I couldn't easily have described any of them if asked.

Finally the man on my left, who seemed to be in charge, turned to me and shouted over the radio in a London accent, "We've got one question for you, mate. Where are they?"

The driver turned the radio down a few notches, and I said, "Where are what?" It came out as a strangled croak, so I cleared my throat and repeated it.

It was clearly not the kind of response they wanted. The other man abruptly reached out, grabbed a handful of my hair from behind and yanked my head sharply back. "Christ! Christ almighty!" The surprising and almost childlike assault was astoundingly painful. He grinned malevolently.

"Don't fuck about," the first man said, and I turned quickly back to him. "Where are they? All you have to do us tell us."

"*What*, for god's sake?" My eyes were watering from the sudden assault, and perhaps also in a reflection of my rising sense of indignation. What was the point of speaking to me in this childish code? Did they *want* an excuse to hurt me? Speaking as rapidly as I could, I said, "I can't tell you anything if I don't know what you mean. Where are *what*?"

Calmly he said, "You know perfectly well. The location. We just want the location. It's a simple question."

Location? I'd already assumed that these must be emissaries of Janni Noble, still trying to track down those photographs, but the word "location" was a strange choice.

I didn't know how to answer, or what the outcome of a correct reply would be. Would they let me go, or would I be putting myself in line for some much more sinister fate? The whole situation was terrifyingly unreal.

The man on my right lunged towards me again, threatening a repeat of the hair trick. "They're dispersed!" I gasped quickly. It sounded appropriate, and might give me moments more to think. "They're in various places. No single location."

"OK, where?"

I drew breath to offer some improvised answer, but at that point this strange episode took an even stranger turn. A police car shot up alongside us from behind, siren briefly whooping and blue light flashing. We all watched as it passed our car and pulled in ahead of the car in front of us. The traffic queue, already moving at a slow crawl, came to a standstill. I glanced out at the surroundings. We were heading up Streatham High Road, a busy suburban centre lined with small shops set in tall Victorian terraces.

The police car wasn't here for us; that was immediately evident. It was probably just stopping someone for a traffic offence. Nevertheless, it had disturbed my captors' rhythm, and the two men who were holding me spontaneously relaxed their grip.

Seizing the opportunity, I launched myself forward between the front seats and lunged with my right arm for the middle of the steering wheel.

I managed to sound a prolonged blast on the horn before the driver swiped me aside and the man to my right pulled me back.

I had no idea if the police were paying the slightest attention to this, but the men in my car evidently weren't in the mood to risk it. The driver reversed our car a foot or two, then seemed to realise there was no escape; several more cars were queuing immediately behind us, and there was now solid traffic to our right. "Fuck this," he muttered, and he started to open his door. There was a fractional pause as others flashed their mutual assent, then all three climbed out and calmly walked away, leaving the doors wide open.

I could scarcely believe my luck. From being threatened with who knew what further violence, I was suddenly and quite unexpectedly free. I simply sat there for a moment, aware for the first time that I was trembling from head to toe.

I was too slow. A voice in my head told me I needed to make myself scarce too, before the police noticed me. If I got caught up here, I would never make the lunch with Ashley. I slid cautiously over to the nearside door and climbed out of the car, but I was out of luck. One of the two officers from the police car happened to turn my way at that point, and looked me squarely in the face.

Cursing inwardly, I did the only thing that seemed plausible. I walked towards him, and as I approached him I said, "I've just been kidnapped."

* * *

I was made to wait while the police summoned a second patrol car, then I was asked to explain how come I'd just been spotted walking away from a stolen vehicle.

My explanation – that I had been abducted – seemed to strike them as mildly interesting, but they gave no indication of whether they gave any credence to it. They weren't hostile, but they weren't especially sympathetic either, which I felt I deserved.

I had to wait around for what seemed an age, still trembling inside if not outwardly, while they conferred with each other and with someone on the radio. The blue light on their car kept on flashing, and the minutes ticked away steadily.

Finally I was driven to a police station, where I had to give my account all over again to two different sets of officers. What did the men in the car look like? (Dark clothes, headgear partly covering their faces.) Ethnicity? (White.) Did I know who they were? (No.) What did they want? (I wasn't sure.)

I kept checking my watch. One o'clock came and went, then one thirty. I asked if I could make a call. They kept saying in a minute, but the minute gradually turned into an hour. Finally I was pointed to a public phone on a wall, but there were two people queuing for it, and the man currently using it was clearly in no mood to hurry.

The police still seemed bemused by my story. On one hand they seemed inclined to treat me as a car thief who has been caught red-handed, but on the other they clearly weren't ready to dismiss the idea that I was a genuine kidnap victim.

For a while I kept my Dave Matthews trump card in reserve, but finally I suggested that if they telephoned his police station he would vouch for me. To my surprise, one of the officers did. Dave wasn't there, but the person who answered the call knew my name, and whatever was said, it worked for me. At half past two I was finally allowed to leave. Ashley would already be on a train out of Paddington.

Chapter 25

I telephoned Latimer Logistics as soon as I got home and persuaded them to give me Ashley's mobile number. Then I tried calling it three times. Each time it was engaged. How many failed attempts did I want showing up in her call log? Three might look keen; six would probably seem borderline obsessive. She was presumably still on the train, so maybe she was catching up with missed work.

I had no mobile phone now, of course. I'd dropped it when my abductors grabbed me. Warily I opened my front door, scanning the scene for lurking kidnappers. Satisfied there were none, I walked back along the street and round the corner to the point where they had picked me up. Predictably there was no sign of the phone. The thought of dealing with the phone company filled me with depression. Would I need a new phone number? How many more of my electronic devices would I have to replace before this onslaught was done?

Back at the house I found that my whisky bottle was empty. There was half a bottle of gin but no tonic water, and I was just debating the merits of a neat gin when there was a knock at my front door. Now what? However, through the frosted glass window in the front door I recognised Dave Matthews.

"I hear you've been having an exciting time," he greeted me from the doorstep.

"Tell me about it." I beckoned him into the lounge, reflecting that despite the length of time we'd known each other, this was his first ever visit to my house – and he'd come uninvited, presumably on a mission.

He looked around curiously and took a seat in my leather armchair – the only piece of furniture I'd bought since Sandy's departure. I found myself apologising for the drab state of everything else.

"You haven't seen *my* house," he responded. "And don't worry, you won't be getting an invite any time soon."

I laughed dryly. "I think I owe you and your colleagues a vote of thanks for digging me out of a hole."

"I heard about that. Those people up at Streatham can't seem to tell a victim from a villain."

"I suppose it was a rather strange situation."

"D'you want to go through it for me again now?"

I recounted the events as I remembered them, throwing in my conjecture about Janni Noble's possible involvement, and adding the cash hand-over I'd witnessed in Amsterdam. Dave listened without comment, then observed, "The thing is, Janni Noble seems to have broken all ties with his connections down this end, and the people in Manchester say he's been going straight since his brother was jailed. He's not really on their radar any more."

"So you don't think he could be behind this?"

"Well, he could be, but let's say the evidence is thin. I appreciate that he might be after those pictures we talked about, but if so I don't know how he's orchestrating it."

"But who else could it be?"

"Good question."

We chatted on for a while, and then I made some tea. The unfamiliar domesticity of it seemed a stark contrast to the more blokeish nature of our past encounters. I asked him about his wife. "Since you ask, she buggered off two years ago," he said philosophically. "Comes with the territory. So you and I are in the same boat, my friend."

As he prepared to leave, Dave said, "I've asked for the cops at your local nick to keep a bit of an eye on your house. There's not much they can do really, but at least they can be aware." We moved to the front door. "To be fair, they're already trying to join the dots on your break-ins, but they haven't got much to go on."

He was already on the path when he turned abruptly. "I nearly forgot – you'll be wanting this."

He reached into a pocket and held out my mobile phone.

"You're a star!" I took it from him. The glass had a hairline crack in it, presumably from being dropped, but apparently the phone itself still worked.

"I checked up, and someone was good enough to hand it in."

"Thanks, Dave. Appreciated.

He paused at the gate. "Keep your eyes open for strangers when you're out and about. OK?"

* * *

I still couldn't decide how to contact Ashley. By the time her train had arrived in Truro it would have been after office hours, so presumably she would have gone straight home. But where was home? With a surprise I realised that I had no conception of her living arrangements. Did she share a place with her fiancé Jack? Did she still live with her parents? Or did she have some pied à terre of her own somewhere?

I now had her mobile number, but I was reluctant to ring it. She might be with Jack. I wanted her to ring *me*, but a call from her after hours would be yet another step into the unknown. I wasn't holding my breath. Seven o'clock passed, then eight o'clock, then nine. By then I'd heated and eaten a cheap frozen meal and was into my fourth neat gin.

At nine thirty she rang.

"I was there! Where were you?"

"Ashley."

"That's me. What happened to you? Was your plane delayed?"

"No, it all worked fine. I was sodding well abducted in Thornton Heath."

"What, spirited away by aliens?"

"No!" But I couldn't help laughing. "Very funny. No. I was genuinely abducted. Kidnapped. Bundled into a car by two heavies – the whole nine yards. It was horrendous."

"My god!"

I gave her an abbreviated account of the whole event, and then pitched in a summary of my recent burglaries.

"My god, you lead a dangerous life up there in the big city." She chuckled. "I'm not sure I want to be associated with you, Mr Stanhope."

"Well, you're pretty safe in Cornwall, I should think."

She said nothing to that, and was silent for a moment. Then she asked, "So do you have any idea who is doing all this to you?"

"The best I've come up with so far is that it could be some people I wrote about in an article a few years ago. They might be after revenge, or they might want to steal some pictures I took of them."

"Can't the police do something to stop them?"

"Well, it's all a bit vague. There's no actual evidence."

"It must be awful to be persecuted in your own home like this."

"Tell me about it."

I asked tentatively where she lived herself.

"Didn't I tell you? I've got this flat. Very bijou, but it's minute. Property around here isn't cheap."

"You live on your own then?"

"Yes Mr Stanhope, I live on my own."

I let that one filter into my brain. "So when do we get the chance for a re-match? I don't suppose you get to London all that often."

"Not really, no. I'll have to give it some thought."

The conversation had reached its natural end, but I wasn't quite ready to break off. I felt a sudden recklessness, probably prompted by the three neat gins. I said, "Can I just say something?"

"Go on."

I cleared my throat. "Um, I would really like to see you."

She waited a second. "Thank you, Mr Stanhope. We'll need to get back to you on that."

1998

"What the fuck do you mean, it's been built over?" Hawkins wiped his forehead with the back of his hand and turned up the air conditioning of his pickup. He clamped the phone closer to his ear.

"It's what I'm saying. You told me there was a lawn, but there isn't a lawn, it's a glasshouse thing. They call it a function suite."

"You should have taken a photo."

"Well pardon me for living, Terry. I'll remember next time."

"For Christ's sake, don't call me Terry. How many times do I have to tell you?"

"Stanley. Sorry." He waited a beat. "But it's still a function suite."

Hawkins swatted away a fly and stared along the broad avenue. Downtown Rockhampton, Queensland looked as it always looked – wide open, brilliant and sunny. This was unbelievable. He wiped the screen of his mobile phone on his shirt.

"What about a basement?"

"What, you want me to go and ask for a look at their architectural drawings?"

"I just meant what did it look like? Would there be any access to a lower level?"

"Only with a pneumatic drill. It's based on concrete foundation. Even I could see that."

He thought for a minute. "So do you think the builders must have found it? Or could they have just built over it?"

"Well I never saw the site in the first place, did I? But I would say they must have dug down quite a few feet over the whole area, preparing for piling and laying the substrate and whatnot. Looks as if they knocked down part of the old building as well, to join the new bit on. Your disused cellar will have been filled with concrete and rubble, if you ask me."

Hawkins ran his hand over his forehead again. "So we're saying the builders must have found it? Who were they? You can bet your life they sodding well never went to the police with it."

"Well for Christ's sake, Terry, how would I know? This was ten years ago. More likely they just covered it over."

"For the last time, it's Stanley for god's sake!" He took a deep breath. "Give me strength."

Chapter 26

"You are cordially invited to the official opening of Vantage Express's new sortation hub at Rugby. RSVP."

I scrutinised the email carefully. Had this been forwarded to me by one of the magazines I wrote for? No, it was addressed to me personally, and had come from the office of Rick Ashton, the chief executive of the company: the man I'd interviewed in that London hotel. It was flattering in a way; it showed that Ashton still thought me influential enough to cultivate. But it meant I had no commission to report on the event. As things stood, I would be going at my own expense.

I rang Jason Bright at the magazine, but he told me he was attending the event himself. Then I tried Phil Connor, the editor of the handling magazine, but he'd already commissioned one of his regular freelances to go. Finally I persuaded a warehousing magazine to accept a short news report on the event. It wasn't much, but it gave my visit some legitimacy. Frankly I would happily have ducked out of it altogether, but this was part of my new regime of forcing myself to take a more positive approach to my work.

Four days later I was on my way. Vantage had arranged to pick up visitors arriving by train at Rugby station, and the journey from south London took me through Euston station. Emerging from the escalator, I found myself scanning the concourse for my mystery woman. The chances of seeing her again must have been infinitesimal, but I couldn't stop myself from looking. Needless to say, there was no sign of her.

A small group of us were picked up from the station at Rugby and whisked over to the sortation centre in a hired minibus, then given a guided tour of the sparkling new facility.

A sortation hub was a central location where parcels were sent from depots all over the country for sorting and onward despatch. At the hub they were offloaded from large trunk vehicles, sorted according to destination, then put on other vehicles and despatched to the appropriate delivery depot.

Recent sortation hubs like this one were highly automated. At their heart was a vast conveyor or "carousel", from which parcels were nudged down chutes to the relevant loading bay. It was a big investment, involving a lot of advanced engineering and clever computer management.

I marvelled at the vast assemblage of chutes and conveyors, unerringly directing packages along the correct route to dozens of waiting trucks. It was a cross between a giant toy train set and a Meccano construction project run riot. We were shown the control room, the computer room, the operations room, the loading bays. Even a cynic could hardly fail to be impressed.

During a short address in the adjoining offices afterwards, Rick Ashton was forced to explain to journalists how his company could afford this kind of expenditure when they were in the midst of a cash flow crisis. He acquitted himself well, explaining that the funding for this project had already been allocated before the market dipped; but I still felt he left some questions unanswered.

As often, I had mixed feelings about this. I could see a story in it, but I couldn't help also feeling some sympathy for Ashton. I liked him, and had no personal wish to see him in trouble. It was one of the reasons why I doubted my commitment to my trade; I no longer had that instinct to go for the jugular.

Over cocktails and canapés he collared me in person. "I liked your book." His strong Australian accent was as striking as ever, and despite the grilling from the other journalists, he exuded confident goodwill. He chewed a vol au vent and gave me an amused smile.

"You bought it then!"

"Absolutely. Glad you tipped me the wink." He took a sip of his mineral water. "You must have done a lot of research to know so much about that robbery."

"Well, enough to get by, anyway."

"I liked the way the daughter played a vital role. Did you actually get to meet her?"

In truth I hadn't bothered to research the real story in any detail, and certainly hadn't met any of the characters involved. As far as I was concerned that hadn't been the point. But I had the sense that this might now seem a weakness, so I merely shrugged and gave Rick what I hoped was a conspiratorial smile. "I'm sworn to secrecy."

He beamed mischievously at me. "So did you really find out what happened to the missing valuables?"

"Aha. That's for me to know and for you to find out."

"You planning on digging them up one day for your retirement fund?"

"You've guessed my guilty secret."

He glanced round at the assembled journalists. "We could do with some of that loot around here, to be honest. Nice to get this rabble off my back."

"You'll turn things round. You always do." I didn't know why I felt it was my role to reassure him, but it seemed a natural comment.

"That's what I like about you, Michael. You see the bigger picture. You're not always looking for a scoop."

"Some people would call it a fault."

*　*　*

Should I arm myself with better knowledge of the real robbery? It might help me fend of further enquiries in the vein of Rick's. Back at home that evening I trawled the internet for information. News stories about the theft were still few and far between, but my original impression was confirmed; most of the gang had been arrested within days of the robbery, but one suspect, Liam Stone, had never been caught.

Then my eye was caught by a link I hadn't seen before. Years later, Australian police had arrested someone they thought at first was him. He was apparently living near Cairns in Queensland under an assumed name. However, he had somehow slipped the net before they had gathered any conclusive evidence, and apparently he had never been seen since.

While I was on the internet I thought I'd check on my latest book sales. How was the world receiving my fictionalised version of events? I was disappointed to find that my total sales had increased by just one unit since the last time I'd looked. The honeymoon period was apparently drawing to a close.

I was about to log off when I noticed that no fewer than three people had written reviews of the book. This I had to see.

The first was by "JM", which I immediately took to be Joanna Miles. She'd said she would write a review, and evidently she had. "Elegant, transparent prose," it said. Yeah yeah. "It really had me turning the pages." I wished I'd asked her to avoid clichés if she could. "Believable characters, and a clever interweaving of two apparently unconnected plot lines." That bit I liked. She'd given it five stars out of five.

Good on Joanna, I thought, and scrolled down. The next reviewer had given the book only three stars, "and it just scrapes that rating because of its moderately interesting subject matter." I looked for a reviewer's name, but didn't recognise the nom de plume.

"There are simply too many clichés," the reviewer complained. "You'll find set-piece scenes that you've watched in a thousand films, dialogue you've read in a thousand novels. The characters can seem deceptively real until you ask yourself where you've met them before. The answer is everywhere, and often."

Charming. A reviewer with attitude. I knew there'd be negative comment, but I wasn't expecting such a comprehensive hatchet job so soon. Unfortunately, self-publishing meant setting yourself up to be shot down, and there was nothing you could do about it.

What about the third review? I scrolled down further, and found that it consisted of just one line: "So what happened to the loot?"

I smiled to myself. At least this reviewer was getting into the spirit of the thing.

Chapter 27

Next day I rang Dave Matthews and suggested meeting for a curry. We'd never had a meal together before, but he'd been helpful and supportive over the past few weeks, and it seemed a natural step.

I did, however, have an ulterior motive. I wanted to show him those pictures of Janni Noble, and see if he thought they amounted to significant new evidence against him. I was aware that once he knew about the pictures I couldn't pretend they didn't exist, but I'd decided I had to do something to move matters forward. I printed out the clearest shots on photographic paper and took them with me to the restaurant.

"Blimey, Mike, I should be doing you for withholding evidence."

"But for god's sake, I told you – I never even realised I had these. I mean I knew I had them, but I didn't know Janni Noble was in them. I only found that out the other day when I started looking closely at them. If you factor him out, there's nothing here that your people didn't know already."

"Calm down, I'm only winding you up. You're too sensitive."

"So would you be."

He shuffled through the photographs. "Not exactly David Bailey, are we?"

"Photography is not my first skill set."

"Or your second, to judge from these." He squinted for a long time at the shadowy figure of Janni Noble, then looked up again.

"I don't think these are much use, to be honest."

Eagerly I said, "Really?" I felt an instant sense of relief.

"You know and I know that it must be him, but it's completely circumstantial. It could be anybody."

"So you don't think you could do anything with them?"

He screwed his face into an exaggerated show of thought – a characteristic gesture I'd seen many times in the past – then relaxed again. "I honestly doubt it. It's too long ago, and if this is all we have, it's nothing." He let the prints drop on the tablecloth. "Course, I ought to let our photographic team loose on the original digital files, just to see what they can rescue."

"I had a go, and I don't think they'd get much."

"They're very clever these days …" He broke off as our meal arrived, then picked up the prints. He looked briefly at them again, then seemed to come to a decision. He handed them to me, leaning forward. "Tell you what, why don't you take these away. I've never seen them. As far as I know they never existed."

I raised my eyebrows. "Really?"

"Hurry up, before I think again."

So I pocketed the prints, nodding my acknowledgement to him. I asked, "Do you think Janni Noble might be after these? Does it make sense to you that he could be the one behind these break-ins at my house, and that kidnapping fiasco the other day?"

He shrugged. "Well, he must have known you were there with a camera. He was there himself. But he wouldn't know his face was in those reflections. How could he?" He hesitated. "You never published them anywhere, did you?"

I shook my head. "No, but his brother could have shown them to him."

He looked up quickly. "What? You let Tommy Noble have these pictures? What were you thinking?"

I shrugged. "It was part of the deal, Dave. He wouldn't have let me take them otherwise."

He shook his head. "Amateurs," he muttered.

"So you agree that he could be trying to get hold of the originals."

"I don't know, mate. You're telling me Tommy has copies, so he might think they amount to evidence against his brother. That's exactly what I told you before."

"And?"

"Well, in theory I suppose Janni might be trying to get in ahead of him. He might be hoping that some of the pictures you took show Tommy's face as well as his own. If they did, and he could get hold of them, that would make the two of them even."

I sensed doubt in his words, and raised my eyes.

He said, "It just sounds altogether too far-fetched to me. Too much guesswork – too many assumptions. I'm not at all convinced."

I asked if there had been any progress with establishing who was behind the kidnapping. He said no. "Bit of a weird one, that. Your locals don't know what to make of it, and I don't see any way of connecting it to Noble." He looked at me, assessing. "How about other people you've rubbed up the wrong way with your articles? Any thoughts about someone else who could be behind this?"

I shook my head. Nothing else that I'd ever written had seemed close enough to the edge to provoke this kind of reaction, and my other probing articles had been written years ago. But perhaps I hadn't given it enough thought.

"I'll let you know if anything comes to mind."

"And meanwhile, if I were you I'd keep my guard up."

"What d'you think I'm doing? I hardly dare walk to the corner shop for a paper these days, in case there's someone hiding behind the phone box, waiting to nab me."

He gave a low chuckle. I said, "You can laugh, but it's really stressful. I've never experienced anything like it. Everything out there in the world seems a potential threat."

"I know." He looked at me thoughtfully. "All I meant was be watchful. Sounds as if you're doing that already. Hopefully the police presence will have frightened these people off."

"It would be nice to think so."

*   *   *

There was something I was missing in this whole Noble affair – an element that I'd failed to slot into place. I sat at my desk next morning, trying to think it through. It seemed evident to me that Janni Noble had been involved in the people trafficking operation – but why? That was the crux of it. He was running an apparently successful up-and-coming transport business, so why did he need to break the law in this elaborate and risk-prone way?

To make sure I was on the right lines, I did some internet trawling. Sure enough, his company, Allied Northern, had been trading well within its means when the police moved in, and had had a sound balance sheet. Janni didn't need extra money to keep it afloat.

In any case, surely he would have needed to be running a smuggling operation of grand proportions to earn enough from it to sustain a failing business of this size?

Afterwards his company had faltered, but only because of the adverse publicity surrounding the case. Janni had disposed of the assets piecemeal, rather than selling it on as a going concern, but had evidently recouped enough to set him up on a new career path.

I felt I needed a better insight into the company, and I had an idea who could help me: Freddie, the man I'd bumped into at the logistics event in west London. He'd told me he now worked in Stoke-on-Trent, but he'd been a lynchpin at Allied before the company went bust. I picked up my phone and called directory enquiries.

"Freddie, it's Mike Stanhope, the journalist from London. I wondered if you'd mind if I dropped in on you? It's not for an article – I just wondered if you'd be willing to have a private word?"

* * *

What I needed now was an excuse to drive north again. I phoned Jason Bright. "I know it's a cheek, but I'm looking for a job to do in the north. Something to pay my fare, anyway. Have you got anything coming up?"

I could hear him rummaging on his desk. "Something came in yesterday. Let me have a look." Another pause. "Yeah, here it is. Next Thursday a truck body manufacturer in Blackburn is celebrating twenty five years in the biz. Try to contain your excitement."

"So you want me to cover it."

"Well, I can't justify the travel cost for such a small story, but if you can come up with a half-decent report I'll pay you the going rate for it."

"Can't say fairer than that. Thanks."

"Happy to oblige."

I was on the point of disconnecting when a thought struck me. "Jason, do you mind if I ask you a question?"

"Fire away."

"Well, I know I've cocked up on a few things lately. I wondered if you'd shunted me off your favoured freelance list? I meant to ask you the other day at the Vantage event, but I never go the chance."

He didn't answer at first, which seemed ominous, but then said, "I might as well be honest, Mike – we nearly did. But in the end we didn't. You've done some decent stuff for us lately, and we have a history with you. Basically we still know we'll get a good result from you." He hesitated. "We will, won't we?"

"Course you will. I appreciate it, Jason."

I sat back, not knowing whether to be pleased that my livelihood wasn't currently under threat, or worried to think it so nearly had been. Some things are better not known.

Chapter 28

The traffic on the M6 was kind – which was just as well. I'd made a ridiculously early start. I had three visits to fit into this trip.

The first was to the logistics company in Stoke-on-Trent, a city whose geography always left me baffled. It appeared to have no formal centre, being made of a collection of smaller towns clustered together. However, my satnav guided me to the sprawling site of the company on the outskirts of Hanley, and I walked in at half past nine.

Freddie took the trouble to meet me in the foyer. He was wearing a dark jacket and an open-neck white shirt. He led me to his upstairs office – a pleasant space with flowers on the window sill and pictures of his family on the wall: his wife in a headscarf, plus two girls and a boy, all under ten. He sat down behind his desk and looked at me expectantly.

"You've landed on your feet," I commented.

"I suppose so, but to be honest I'd have been just as happy if I could have stayed at Allied."

I raised my eyebrows. He'd started to answer my main question before I even asked. I said, "As it happens, that's really why I've come today. I realise I've probably got a nerve, but I'm hoping you can tell me a bit about Janni Noble."

"How do you mean?"

"Well, you know and I know that he was implicated in that people trafficking scam, but nothing came of it. I'm just trying to get a sense of how the people on the ground saw it all. What did you make of it yourself?"

"What's it to you, if you don't mind me asking?" He sounded not hostile, just cautious.

"Well, the police wanted to make him out as an arch-villain, but I can't find anyone else who sees him that way. According to reports at the time, no one at the company had a bad word to say about him. I'm trying to get a balanced picture in my head."

He hesitated a moment, then seemed to come to a conclusion. "OK. Right. I can probably tell you what you want to know."

I waited while he marshalled his thoughts. Finally he said, "What you say is pretty much true. I always thought Janni Noble was a good guy. Tough – a real taskmaster. Expected results. But he was fair. He thanked you if you delivered for him. He was the kind of guy you wanted to work for. Everyone else there thought more or less the same thing – except the slackers, and who needs them anyway?"

I nodded, then said cautiously, "Obviously you didn't know anything about this trafficking stuff?"

"Obviously not." He frowned.

"Did it surprise you when you heard about it?"

He thought about that for a while. "Well yes, it surprised me that he would be into something like that. But if anyone was going to make a good job of it, Janni would have been your man. Very efficient, whatever he turned his hand to."

"But why would he have done it?"

"You'd have to ask him that yourself. Not for the money, I'm sure."

"What do you think, then?"

He shrugged. "I always wondered if maybe he was on some kind of mission."

"How do you mean?"

"No idea, but he's an earnest man. If he had a cause, he would be hard to stop. That's why everyone liked him. He was committed, and people identify with that."

I paused to absorb all this, then asked, "How about Tommy Noble?"

"Tommy? Complete waste of space. Janni only employed him as a favour. He blundered around, acting like one of the bosses, but most of the time he was completely out of his depth. He was in sales and marketing, but he didn't know one end of a truck from the other."

"But he was in the front line when the police were investigating the trafficking allegations."

"I wouldn't know about that, but if he was involved, he probably thought he would score with Janni by showing how smart he was. Or more likely, Janni was just looking for an excuse to get him away from the customers before he offended too many of them."

"Ha! I suppose that makes sense."

"Not that it would have mattered in the end. By the time the police came in and started interviewing everybody, Tommy was on notice."

"Really?" I didn't think anyone had ever mentioned this to me.

"That's what we heard. I think Janni had finally had enough of him. We all thought good riddance."

As I drove away from the depot I thought over this last piece of information. Here was yet another reason why Tommy Noble might have blown the whistle on his brother. He'd probably known by then that his time at the company was limited, and decided to go out with a bang.

* * *

It was well after midday by the time I reached Blackburn. The truck body factory I was visiting for Jason lay outside the town in a modern industrial estate flanked by low green hills. An array of gleaming trucks and trailers stood in the yard awaiting admiration, and flags fluttered in the sun.

The guests were mostly truck operators – confident middle-aged men with goodwill in their words and a look behind their eyes that said "prove it". Our hosts had little time for the press, and I seemed to be the only journalist present. I had to work hard to win their time and assemble anything like a story.

Over a buffet lunch I found myself chatting to the head of a haulage company from Wigan. On a whim I asked if he'd ever come across Janni Noble.

"You mean that guy who used to run Allied Northern, over in Oldham?"

"Yes, him and his brother Tommy."

"They got caught up in some kind of smuggling mess, didn't they? I always thought that was a shame. He was a very straight guy, Janni. Whatever he said, that's what he would do. Pity there aren't more like him in this business."

"He's running an outfit called Ray Noble Rental now, down in Manchester."

He raised his eyebrows. "That's him, is it? I've seen his vans around. Well, good luck to him."

So now I'd met yet another Janni Noble fan – this time the head of a company. In a way, his comments were more or less what I was expecting. The likelihood that Janni was behind the break-ins and the kidnapping seemed increasingly remote.

It meant a subtle change in the task I'd set myself today. I'd thought originally that if I made Janni aware that those photographs were no threat to him, it might get him off my back. It now seemed that he might not have been on my back in the first place.

If so, it seemed my mission might be to do him a favour.

Chapter 29

I reached Trafford Park around half past three. I'd checked by phone to make sure Janni was there, but decided not to ask for an appointment. I walked in unannounced and crossed an immaculate reception area to a white and blue desk, where a uniformed woman in her forties with blond curls was tapping something into a laptop computer.

"Could I see Mr Noble please?"

She looked up brightly. "Is he expecting you?"

"No, but perhaps you could tell him it's Mike Stanhope."

She reached for her phone, frowned briefly as she spoke, then pointed to a white door behind her. "Through there, last door on the left."

Janni's office was long and thin, and his desk was positioned right at the end of it. The long walk over to it seemed calculated to intimidate. Behind him was a picture window partly overlooking the yard. The brick walls were painted plain white, and the overall effect was one of almost clinical austerity. I made my way to the single hard chair in front of his desk, feeling I was shrinking with every step.

He was sitting squarely behind his desk with his hands folded in front of him, wearing a white open-neck shirt and no jacket. He didn't invite me to sit so I remained standing. He said, "Mr Stanhope, an unexpected pleasure." His look belied his words. He glanced at his watch. "I can give you five minutes."

I sat down gingerly and cleared my throat. "I won't waste your time, Mr Noble. I might be in a position to do you a favour. I might have something you want."

He stared at me. "I do not understand."

His gaze was intimidating. His staff might have loved him, but I wouldn't have wanted to find myself on the wrong side of him.

I swallowed. "Your brother …"

"What has my brother to do with this? He does not work for this company."

"I know, I know. Can I please explain?"

He frowned.

"I wrote an article about illegal immigrants and their impact on the haulage industry, and your firm was the one I was investigating."

At this Janni glanced warily about the office, checking perhaps that the door was closed. Then he turned back to me, glowering. "This is old information. I do not wish to discuss this matter. I would like you to leave now please." He adopted his most penetrating stare.

I forced myself not to feel intimidated. He'd expressed no surprise at my mention of the article, which seemed to confirm that he already knew about it. I felt this was to my benefit.

"Would you please hear me out? This won't take a minute."

He stared at me for a moment, assessing, then made a tetching sound. "I read your article. It was filled with ignorant half-truths and speculation. It was sensationalist rubbish. It was written with no heart."

I looked at him with some surprise. Was he actually defending what he'd done? I found myself saying, "What did you expect? I could hardly have asked for an interview to get your side of the story." I swallowed. "People smuggling is illegal. I just reported what I was told. It was my job."

He looked at me for a long moment. "So what makes you think I knew anything of this?"

"Because it was your brother who told me about your involvement."

He showed no reaction to this, and I hesitated. "But you know that already."

"How do I know this?"

"Because you were there when I talked to your brother. I have the pictures to prove it."

"Pictures?"

"The pictures I took of your brother in Luton. You must have seen me take them. You were there, watching."

He was now looking at me with curiosity. "What makes you say this?"

"Because you are in the pictures yourself."

My words hung in that white space for a moment. Janni said nothing.

Finally I said, "Surely you must have seen them?"

"I have seen no pictures."

"I thought perhaps your brother had showed you them."

"He has not." He seemed to reflect for a moment. "But I think I understand something now." He nodded to himself. "He told me he had evidence of some kind."

I reached into my inside pocket and wordlessly handed him an envelope. He opened it and tipped out the colour prints I'd prepared. He pored over them for a full minute.

"So. You know I was there on that day. Very well." He looked up at me. "I knew my brother's little game. I wanted to see how far he would go with his interference." He looked back down at the pictures. "And now he thinks he can hold these pictures against me. I see what he is doing."

"But if you knew he was talking to me back then, why didn't you stop him?"

He shrugged. "I wanted to let him show me his true colours. It was already finished for us. Our work was done. Also your police were getting too interested in us. It was time to quit. After your visit, there was no more of this."

"But my article didn't actually stop the trade?"

I now saw anger in his eyes. "Trade? You think we do this kind of thing in exchange for money?" He held the pictures up and rapped them with the back of his hand. "You think we are immoral men like those bastard people traffickers in southern Europe and Africa with their economic migrants and their exploitation? Is that it?"

"I don't know why you do it. You tell me."

He slapped them down on the desk. "Why should I tell you anything?"

Chapter 30

I looked cautiously at Janni. Despite his bluster, I had a sense that there had been a subtle power shift in this conversation. He wasn't apparently threatening me after all, but maybe he thought I was threatening *him*.

He seemed to consider for a moment, then sat back, raised his arms and interlaced his fingers behind his head. "We are not speaking on the record here. Is this agreed? This is not for an article in the press. You will never report this. Do I have your word on this?"

"You do."

"Very well." He considered for a moment. "You British like to think democracy changed things in the east. The truth is that it did not. In many countries there is still corruption, persecution and suffering. Good men are hounded out of their livelihoods, put in prison, even executed. For them life is hard."

He lowered his hands again. "We ran haulage trucks to Turkey, Albania, Armenia, Azerbaijan, Turkmenistan – other places too. It gave us easy passage to those countries where there are men who wish to leave, but cannot." He let the implications hang in the air.

"What's wrong with the proper channels?"

He tetched contemptuously. "You can try that if you like."

I said nothing for a moment, then, "Your brother …"

"My brother is a fool. In your article you made him out to be an honest man, trying to put an end to an illegal trade. You were wrong. He thought that by threatening me he could claim a greater share of my business." He paused. "*My* business, not his. But it did not turn out as he hoped."

"So what happened?"

He suddenly laughed explosively. "You know what happened, Mr Stanhope. A police investigation, arrests, interference. In the end we lost our company. That's how much good his treachery did him."

"But you don't blame my article for that?"

He frowned at me. "So you wish for my absolution, is that it?"

I shrugged. "I just wondered what you thought."

He looked at me, considering. "Your article did no favours to our cause, but it said nothing that the rest of your country was not saying by then. Our time was already running out." He looked back at me. "Is this what you wish to hear?"

I shrugged again and sat silent for a moment, then said, "And now …?"

He sat up straighter, suddenly businesslike. "Now we have Ray Noble Rental. It is a new beginning. I have finished with these things. I tried my best."

Abruptly he leaned forward. "But my foolish brother wants to threaten all this. Is that why are you here, Mr Stanhope? You wish to support him?"

"No! On the contrary, I thought I could help you. I told you that when I came in."

He waited, and for a moment neither of us spoke. Then I reached forward and pushed the photographs towards him. "You might as well keep these. No one is interested in them."

He raised his eyebrows, clearly surprised. "How do you know this?"

I shrugged. "I have connections. I've been told that no action will result from these pictures. They have no value." I hesitated. "You might want to tell your brother."

He glanced down at them. "But there are copies, digital versions. What of those?"

"Same thing. No one cares about them."

He looked me in the eye. "So this is an act of generosity?"

"If you like."

He nodded slightly, and I said, "I have to ask. When I saw you in that restaurant in Amsterdam …"

"What? You are determined to make an enemy of me?"

"No, no, not at all. I just wondered if you had any comment about it."

He was glaring again now, but I could see his mind whirring. "You think this is some illegal trade? Perhaps I am dealing in drugs now, or uncut diamonds? In a public place? How foolish do you think I am?"

"Not foolish at all."

"No I am not." He reflected for a moment. "I am not obliged to explain this to you, but I will do so anyway. That man owed me a lot of money for work I did for him many years ago – legitimate transport work. He is an honourable man, and now he can pay me. But he does not want his money to go through his country's tax regime, through official channels – and nor do I."

"I see."

He stared at me. "Yes, it is not correct procedure. It comes with risk. So go and report me if you wish to be small-minded – and if you think anyone will take any notice of you. Or act like an adult person and put it out of your mind."

I looked at him for a long moment, then said, "Fair enough."

He continued to look at me, then said, "Very well, we have established our positions now." He paused. "But I think you had some other agenda in your mind when you decided to come here to see me."

I decided honesty was the best policy. I said, "People have been trying to steal something from me – breaking into my house, assaulting me. To begin with I thought it might have something to do with these pictures."

He sat back. "Preposterous! How could you imagine I would be involved in such a thing?"

"Well, you recognised my name when I met you in London, with Rick Ashton. I wondered if Tommy had told you it, and you made the connection with the article."

"This is true." He was nodding thoughtfully. "But I would not have threatened you in the way that you describe. If I had wanted to, I would have contacted you directly. But I did not."

"I can see that now, but the line between principled law-breaking and other kinds of law-breaking is thin. I couldn't rule anything out."

He said nothing for a moment, then, "If you write articles like yours, you upset people. You should know that. You should not be surprised if they come back to bite you. But not me."

"I got it wrong. I know that now."

"So why did you come here today?"

I shrugged. "It seemed like unfinished business. I felt you should know where things stand."

He picked up the envelope again and turned it on its end, resting his hands on the desk. He let it drop on the desktop several times between his fingers, looking at me. "It seems to me that if I were searching for photographs, I would not break into your house. What would be the point?"

"How do you mean?"

"With digital photographs, you can make multiple copies. You can upload them to the cloud. You can email them to your second cousin. Trying to destroy them would be like trying to catch water in a sieve."

I nodded. "Yes, but I thought maybe you just wanted to see them – to find out whether they were incriminating or not. Or to see if your brother was visible in some of them – to balance the score, as it were."

"That is not how I work, Mr Stanhope."

"As I say, I can see that now."

We looked at each other for a long moment, then Janni said, "I think that perhaps we have both misjudged each other."

"Maybe so."

He stood up and pushed back his chair. He tapped the envelope one last time. "It seems I am obliged to you for these."

I stood up in turn. "For what it's worth, I've moved on too."

He looked at me emotionlessly. "I am pleased to hear this."

Back on the motorway, I replayed the conversation with Janni in my head repeatedly, but try as I might, I couldn't spot any flaws in what he'd said. I was certain now that he'd had nothing to do with the break-ins at my house, or the kidnap attempt.

But someone was behind them.

2011

There was defeat in her father's eyes. Last time she'd visited Rockhampton his jobbing business had seemed to be thriving, and his comfortable single-storey house had been tidy and well-maintained. Now the pickup looked battered, the garden was neglected and the kitchen was a mess.

"I thought you said business was booming," she said over the washing up.

He glared at her from the kitchen door. "You must know the job never paid for our lives here. I had other money too. But it ran out."

Other money – she knew what that meant: robbery money. It was the thing never spoken of, the thing that hovered just out of sight, always present but banished from conversation. Her mother had gone to her grave without acknowledging it.

She said nothing. He said, "There should have been more, Sash – much more. I left most of it behind. I couldn't risk it on the flight out here. It got buried under six feet of concrete."

It was the closest by far that he'd ever come to admitting to his part in the robbery. His desperation saddened her. She looked at his bronzed features – still good looking, she thought, but haunted and resentful. His eyes were reddened by too many cans of lager, too many shots of Jim Beam.

She'd never intended to reveal what she'd done with those bags. It was a secret so distant that it now seemed almost a dream. But what if they were still there, where she'd so carefully hidden them? Would he know how to turn the contents into cash? Of course he would: once a thief, always a thief.

It was stolen property, not his. He had no right to it. But contemplating his compromised life here, she felt a sudden wave of warmth towards him. She could change his life, and no one else need know.

Speaking only to herself, she said, "What if it didn't get buried? What if it got moved?"

Chapter 31

The next morning Ashley phoned me.

"Mr Stanhope!"

"Ms Renwick."

She laughed. "So you're keeping safe on the mean streets?"

"Well, so far so good." I could have elaborated on the constant stress I was experiencing, but I decided not to.

"I'm glad to hear it." An apprehensive pause. "The thing is, do you find yourself over in Bristol very often?"

"It's been known."

"OK, well here's what it is. We've got one of these regional logistics shows coming up in Bristol next week, and we're taking a small stand – all very low key. So I thought if you happened to be anywhere in the area …"

I did some fast thinking. Would any of the magazines want a review of this show? It seemed a long shot. Unconvinced, I said, "I suppose I might be able to come and report on it."

"Honestly, I wouldn't bother. You won't see anything you haven't seen before. You must have reported these shows to death by now."

I could tell she had a plan, so I said, "OK, so what did you have in mind?"

"Well, I'll be travelling up on the Tuesday morning, and setting up the stand in the afternoon. I thought maybe if you were around, we could meet in Bristol. We could have the lunch that we missed last time."

"Let's do it."

* * *

I couldn't find any takers for a report on the logistics world of Bristol. This time I would have to pay for my own trip. Well, too bad; it was an offer I wasn't about to turn down. Come the day, I caught the train from Paddington; no point in driving if (as I hoped) a long session in a pub might be in prospect. Just after midday I was walking through the centre of Bristol in bright sunshine.

The city's uneasy architectural mix of Victorian, 1960s and modern always seemed jarring, but the pub Ashley had selected was in a reassuringly traditional Victorian block. It was thronging with lunchtime customers when I walked in, but Ashley had found a table, and was seated opposite a dark-haired man.

"Michael!" Her face broke into a smile. "I don't think you've met my brother Patrick."

Patrick rose to shake my hand – a slim, athletic-looking figure in his thirties, wearing jeans and a T-shirt. "I've heard a lot about you."

"Likewise."

I sat down between them and smiled at Ashley. She too was in jeans with a black T-shirt, but there was no Latimer logo in sight today. She had pulled her hair back into a short ponytail, giving me my first sight of her face without its usual framing of hair. Her fine features readily withstood the extra exposure.

"Patrick gave me a lift from Truro this morning. He's going to a convention in Cheltenham."

"I'm in computer software," he said. "They like to bring us together for the occasional bonding session. So what brings you to Bristol?"

I felt caught out. What was I doing here? Chasing his sister – that's what I was doing. I cleared my throat. "Ah – various things." I looked at Ashley. "I might dip into Ashley's show tomorrow."

Patrick went over to the bar to buy drinks and place our food order, and Ashley leaned towards me over the table. In a low voice she said, "I'm sorry about this. I didn't know Patrick would be here. I could hardly turn him down when he offered the lift."

"It's fine. I'm pleased to be here."

"You're not really staying over, are you? I told you the show's not up to much."

I shook my head. "Cover story."

When Patrick came back I said to him, "So you knew Trina Markham at the Fairmile."

"Well, yes, vaguely. I thought she was a cracking girl, but she didn't seem to rate me, to be honest. She had a great laugh."

I'd completely forgotten that. My version of Trina was a silent-film version. Instantly I heard it again in my head – that slightly husky, resonant chuckle. "My god, you're right!"

I asked him if he thought he would be able to unearth any more photographs from that period. "I don't think so, but I'll keep my eye out. There's a load of stuff stashed in my parents' loft that I still haven't checked."

We chatted for a while, then Ashley slipped away to the ladies' room. Patrick leaned forward.

"So what's happening with you and Ash then, if you don't mind me asking?"

"Nothing's happening. We're colleagues."

"Er, d'you want to try that again? You didn't have her jabbering at you all the way from Truro just now. You'd think Christmas had come early."

I wanted to smile at hearing this, but it also put me on the defensive. "Well, there's still nothing happening."

"OK, whatever."

I shrugged.

He said, "The thing is, I'm sure you know she's engaged to a bloke called Jack Forbes. He's a good friend of mine, and I don't want to see him messed around. Or Ashley, obviously."

"Patrick, I don't want to mess anyone around. I know you've never met me before, but I'm not one of the bad guys. Honestly."

"Well, you're here, aren't you?" He took a sip of his beer. "Ash had a bad time after Kieron, but Jack was there for her, and he helped her put her life back together. They helped each other."

I probably looked blank at this, because he added, "You don't know about Kieron, do you?"

"Guilty as charged."

"Well, let's just say he was the love of her life, and then all of a sudden he wasn't. Long time ago now. Jack always had a thing for her, and after Kieron it came together for them."

This was all going too fast for me. I could only muster, "I don't really know what to say."

He looked at me for a moment, assessing. "You seem a decent guy, Mike, and Ash knows her own mind. It's not for me to tell her how to live her life. But you need to decide where you stand. If Jack is on the way out and he doesn't find out about it pretty soon, I may find myself having to put him in the picture. And if you mess Ash around, you'll find you have me to reckon with."

Ashley returned at that point and sat down, looking brightly at the two of us. She turned to Patrick and said pointedly, "Didn't you have to be at Cheltenham pretty soon?"

He shot us both a pained look. "Bonding on the bloody lawn for afternoon tea, followed by bonding over dinner tonight, followed by bonding in a classroom all day tomorrow. Yippee." He stood up and held out his hand. "Very good to meet you, Mike."

"Aren't you staying for lunch?"

"Get something when I arrive."

* * *

"So was Patrick giving you the third degree while I was out of the room?" She raised her hands behind her head, worked the elastic tie free of her ponytail and shook her hair out. It was like a spontaneous celebration of our liberation from scrutiny.

I laughed. "Sort of. He's a good guy."

"Yup. But he likes to think he needs to look out for me."

"He was telling me about Kieron."

"Kieron. Right. I seem to remember that name vaguely." She gave me a dry smile. "I might tell you about him some time."

"That's assuming we're still in touch with each other."

She smiled again, then she sat forward. "Guess what, I've read your book!"

"My god. What did you think?"

"Really interesting. And I can see now why you're looking for Trina Markham. She obviously made a really big impression on you."

"Well, I probably exaggerated it for the story."

"Hm. I wonder."

A waitress arrived with two plates of chicken Caesar salad. As we picked our way through the meal, Ashley said, "I've got a theory about your break-ins and those people who tried to kidnap you. You'll probably think it's daft though."

"No, please tell me."

"Well, now that I've read your book, I can see that it's a really good account of what might have happened after that robbery. You make it sound as if you've talked to the people involved, and you really do know what happened to that missing loot."

"OK."

"But you didn't actually talk to any of them, did you? I mean, I got the impression you made everything up." She gave me a questioning look.

"Correct."

She nodded. "I thought so. But what if someone who's read your book believes that you did talk to them, and you actually know where the loot is? What if they think they could persuade you to tell them?"

I sat thinking about this. The idea wasn't actually new to me – it had been flashing in and out of my consciousness for several weeks, and seemed to have acquired new significance since I'd factored Janni Noble out of the equation. Yet it had seemed so insubstantial, so unlikely, that I hadn't yet allowed it to coalesce in the front of my brain. Now that Ashley had articulated the thought, it suddenly seemed to take on new substance.

"I wonder if that's really possible."

"Well why not? The question is who would be interested. Would it just be some nutter who believes the people in EastEnders are real, or would it be people who actually know about the robbery, and think you're on to something?"

I found myself smiling as she said this – chiefly at the way she pronounced "nutter" with a slightly self-mocking West Country twang. I hadn't noticed it before.

"I doubt if some nutter would raid my house, and then pay a bunch of heavies to kidnap me."

She frowned. "Maybe you're right. So if what I'm saying is true, probably it must be people who have inside knowledge of the robbery, or knowledge of the gang who committed it."

"But how do I work out who's read the book?"

"Can't you ask the publishers?"

"I could, but I don't think they'd tell me. Their position is that they're really just a retailer, and the people who buy it are their customers, not mine." My mind was racing. "In any case, other people have read the book as well. A couple of dozen literary agents, for a start. I'd never track them all down. They don't even speak to mere mortals like me."

"It's worth thinking about, though, isn't it? It could explain everything."

* * *

We finished our meal and chatted through another round of drinks, but finally Ashley started checking her watch. "I need to get out to the exhibition centre and make sure they haven't erected the stand upside down."

I wanted to say something definitive, to make our unacknowledged relationship into a reality. I said, "I may as well admit I've got nothing else to do here in Bristol. I just came over here for this lunch."

A faint smile spread over her face. "A hundred miles is long way to come for a chicken salad, Mr Stanhope. I hope you feel it was worth it."

"What do you think?"

She gave me a wry look. "On the whole, I think probably yes." She stared down at her beer mat for a moment, fiddling with it, then looked up. "I'm glad you did come."

We smiled at each other. The moment could have passed, but I realised with sudden fright that I wasn't about to let it. Almost as if someone else was speaking, I heard myself saying, "I suppose you realise I can't stop thinking about you? Every sodding minute of the day?"

We gave each other a wide-eyed look and she laughed nervously. "Well don't make it sound like some form of mediaeval torture."

She scooped up her overnight bag and we left the pub without saying any more. A moment later we were in the street, standing close to each other in the sunshine. Ashley looked over her shoulder, talking vaguely about taxis. As she turned back to me I reached out and pulled her tentatively towards me. I was worried that she might resist, but she didn't.

I said, "I'm going to kiss you now."

She gave me a slightly dazed look. "If you say so."

It was light, it was insubstantial, it was momentous. I pulled back and we looked at each other, smiling, then I put my hands on her shoulders. "I can't believe this."

She crinkled her eyes against the sun. "Now all we have to do is work out what happens next."

Chapter 32

I fell into the train in a trance. I couldn't remember when I'd last felt like this, if ever. I was euphoric, I was empowered, yet I was also bereft. It was as if a drug had been dangled in front of me, then snatched away. I needed my next fix, and soon.

It came that evening, though it didn't entirely do the trick. At about ten o'clock Ashley rang me from her hotel room.

"I've just been to the icebreaker dinner. God, I've had enough logistics talk to last me a lifetime."

I chuckled. "I'm glad I wasn't there."

"I wish you had been!"

We chatted about our lunchtime get-together, and she renewed her advice for me to work out who might have read my book. "I bet you there's some lunatic out there who thinks you're his meal ticket to riches beyond his dreams."

Tentatively I said, "Pity you don't have a show in Bristol every week."

She had nothing to say to that, and there was a pause. Then she said quietly, "I'm a bit out of my depth here, in case you hadn't noticed."

"I know."

"Jack said to me last night that he hoped I'd have a really nice day today. Well, I did, but not in the way he meant. That makes me feel awful." She sighed. "He'll probably say the same thing again when I ring him in a minute. I'm not sure I can hack this."

I wasn't sure how to reply. I said, "Well do you want to hack it?"

"Ha! Do you need to ask that?"

I thought I'd better not say anything.

There was another pause, then she said, "How often do you get to visit Cornwall, Mike?"

"Normally about once in ten years."

"Well, there you go. I get up to London maybe two or three times a year at the most. Sometimes not even that."

I took a deep breath. "These are details."

"No they're not details. These things matter."

Silence.

I said, "All I can say is I wish you were here now."

I heard her draw breath to say something, then she seemed to think the better of it. "Well, I'm not." She hesitated. "I think I need time to get my head together, to be honest."

"OK."

There was a longer pause, then she said, "God, I'm sorry to sound such a drip, Mike. This isn't me. Today was absolutely brilliant. It was fantastic that you came. I just need to ask you to bear with me."

"I think I can do that."

But I wondered how good I would be at it.

* * *

I was at my desk next morning, still thinking about Ashley in a disconnected way, when the phone rang.

"Mike, it's Sandy."

From would-be girlfriend to former wife in one quick switch: the juxtaposition was not lost on me. I wrenched myself to attention; she sounded upset.

"I'm sorry, Mike, I don't know why on earth I'm ringing you. It's just that we've had a break-in, and everything's such a mess."

"My god – what happened?"

"We were away last night. We stopped over in a hotel for Alan's company dinner in Aylesbury. When I got back this morning, someone had broken in through the patio windows and thrown everything all over the place. I don't even know what's missing yet …" She broke off with a half-sob.

"Is Alan there now?"

"No, he went straight off from the hotel to a meeting in Wales this morning. He's on his way back."

"Is there a lot of damage?"

"Well, come to think of it, I suppose not." I could visualise her staring around. "They've just chucked stuff all over the place. Papers, books, CDs ... oh, and my big bowl is broken! Fuck it! Bloody fuck it."

I kept quiet a moment. I knew there was nothing I could contribute. Then I said, "Have you had the police round?"

"They say they're on their way. But what can they do?"

I was about to draw a parallel with my own break-in, hoping to work up a bit of shared indignation, but at the last moment something held me back. What if it was my intruders who had now turned their attention on her? She wouldn't thank me if she thought I'd somehow brought this on her.

I decided to avoid suggesting any connection. Instead I said, "What have they taken? Is there anything missing?"

"I don't know. I can't see anything obvious, but it's such a mess."

"What can I do?"

"Oh, nothing, Mike. I don't even know why I rang you. I suppose I just needed to hear a friendly voice on the phone." She gave an ironic laugh. "It's funny how the mind works in a crisis."

"You'll need someone to help you clear up after the police have gone."

"I've got Marion from next door coming round. Anyway, Alan will be back in a couple of hours. I'm fine, honestly."

"Well, if you're sure." I paused to marshal my words. "Look, when you've got yourself on top of this, get back to me and let me know what's happened. I'm always here to listen."

"Thanks, Mike, I appreciate it."

* * *

I stared into space for a while, wondering about all this. Was it really possible that someone could be searching for information that they thought I had about the security van robbery? It seemed wildly implausible, and yet it did fit in with the facts. I'd been comprehensively burgled, then actually kidnapped, and now my former wife had also been burgled. Coincidence, possibly, but there could be a logic to it.

The more I thought about this, the more I found myself actually hoping it was true. If it was, it seemed to discount another possibility that had been quietly nagging at me. What if the break-ins at my house had been an attempt to warn me off the search for the Markham family?

It seemed pretty unlikely, given that my search had been so tentative and low-key, but I'd felt I shouldn't completely dismiss it. However, there seemed no logic at all in the idea that the perpetrators would go to the extent of burgling my ex-wife. So to my mind, if there was a connection between my break-ins and hers, the link was surely to my book, not to the Markhams.

I felt it was time to run the idea past someone who was qualified to take a view. I reached for the phone.

Dave wasn't answering, which didn't surprise me, but in the afternoon he rang me back. He asked if I'd seen any further sign of my would-be kidnappers.

"Thankfully no. But I'm still watching my back the whole time. I hardly dare to go out after dark these days."

"Glad to hear it. You can't be too careful."

"But I don't want to live the rest of my life like this."

"It'll all come out in the wash, trust me."

"I hope so."

We continued in this vein for a while, then I said, "Did I mention that I'd written a novel?"

"No you didn't. What about?" Straight to the point.

"Well, it's about a robbery actually. In a way."

"And you didn't think to talk to me about it first? I'm deeply offended. I could have had a credit as a consultant."

"Huh." Actually it had never occurred to me to talk to him. We'd been out of touch for a good while when I wrote the book, and it would have seemed inappropriate.

"I bet it's full of procedural mistakes. Writers never know anything about the police unless they're on the force themselves. Do you even know anything about ranks?"

I reeled them off. "DC, DS, DI, detective chief inspector, detective superintendent." I hesitated. "Detective chief superintendent."

"You got all that from the internet."

"Why shouldn't I?"

He chuckled.

I said, "I don't know why I brought this up with you."

"Yes, why did you?"

I laughed. "Actually, I wondered if you'd mind reading it. You can get it online." I hesitated. "I'll pay you back."

"Blimey, mate, you must be desperate if you're having to ring round and beg people to read it – and you're paying them to do it."

"Yeah yeah." I paused. "I could just send you the file if you prefer."

"Don't worry, I'm sure I can afford it. The question is, why do I think you're after more than just one more reluctant fan?"

"Well, I could explain it to you, but quite honestly it would be easier if you just read the book first. Then you'll know what I'm talking about, and you can draw your own conclusions."

"OK, you've got me intrigued. But don't blame me if I bring you a list of mistakes at the end."

"Fine, gratefully received." I paused a moment. "You do read novels, do you? Mysteries and thrillers, I mean. That kind of thing?"

"I've been known to."

"Well then, just give it a go." I paused. "And if you could manage to do it pretty soon, that would be really helpful."

"You don't ask much, do you?"

Chapter 33

The following day my office phone rang and a woman's voice said, "Mr Stanhope? I have a call for you. Please hold."

Such a formal opening usually heralded a call from someone eminent, or at least someone with pretensions to eminence. I picked up a pen and waited, intrigued.

"Michael Stanhope?" An over-loud, confident voice.

"Speaking."

"Mr Stanhope, this is Janni Noble. I have something I wanted to tell you."

I felt my eyes widen. This was a surprise.

I waited, but he seemed to hesitate. Finally he said, "Mr Stanhope, since our recent meeting I have a sense that …" He broke off. "I feel that I have misjudged you somewhat. You could say I am in your debt, in a manner of speaking."

"I hardly think so," I said.

"I do not thank you for the article you wrote, but – well, I can see that it was your job, and the truth is that it made no difference to us."

I said nothing, and he cleared his throat. "So. A matter has arisen that is causing me some annoyance, and I felt it incumbent upon me to report it to someone." He paused again. "I was not sure to whom I might pass this information, but it seemed to me that you might be an appropriate person."

"I'm pleased that you have changed your opinion of me."

He said nothing to that, so I added, "Just to be clear though, I can't make a commitment to using your information in any particular way, or in fact at all. This can't be a trade."

"This is understood. Of course."

"OK, fine. Well what is it?"

I could almost hear his thoughts whirring as he marshalled them into order. "You are familiar with the Vantage Express Group, I believe, and acquainted with its managing director, Mr Richard Ashton?"

"Yes, I was with him when I met you in London earlier this year."

"So. Mr Ashton's company has rented a significant number of vehicles from us. Around eighty-five, I believe." He seemed to be checking something, perhaps on his computer monitor. "Many of these are on long-term hire, some are on spot hire."

"I see." This was entirely unsurprising. Organisations in the logistics world regularly hired parts of their vehicle fleets, especially when they worked in a seasonal business like parcel deliveries, where the vehicle requirement fluctuated widely over the year.

"Eight months ago Mr Ashton approached me to ask for a deferral of payment for this business. I agreed, of course."

"Right."

"This was conditional upon full payment within a given time span. It is normal."

"OK." I wondered where this was going.

"When the payment date came, Mr Ashton asked me for a further deferral, on the promise of full repayment at the end of that time, plus immediate payment of all fees accrued in the meantime."

"OK."

"That time came, and now he is telling me he still cannot pay. He wants me to reduce my charge to a much lower figure, and he tells me I will have to wait another three or four months for the money." His voice was rising as he said this, and I could feel the anger behind it.

"So where does this leave you?"

"This is not how we do business here. This is not honest trading. Mr Ashton thinks his business is so important that I will be grateful to have it. Frankly he is expecting me to help him keep his own company afloat – and he thinks I should be thanking him for it."

I listened to this with fascination. I had a sense that moral indignation was a bigger factor in Janni's mind than the actual debt. I said, "So if you end up getting nothing from Vantage, will this seriously compromise your company?"

"It will not." He sounded nettled. "We are a substantial company, and we have many customers. No, it is a matter of principle."

"But there is a lot of money at stake here."

"Indeed there is! Mr Ashton owes us more than a quarter of a million pounds."

"Why don't you just withdraw your equipment?"

He clicked his tongue impatiently. "Ah, when to take this action? That is the sixty-four thousand dollar question, is it not? We do not wish to forfeit this money. I do not wish to give Mr Ashton grounds to sue us when he is the one who is in breach of terms."

"So what are you expecting me to do?"

"I do not wish to see others in this position. Mr Ashton's company should not be allowed to trade if it is insolvent."

"You don't know that, though. You're just speculating."

"You are the journalist, Mr Stanhope. You find out."

* * *

I tossed my pen down on the desk. What was I to make of this? Suddenly Janni Noble was my friend, and was feeding me a news lead. What a strange turnabout. Should I be grateful? I couldn't decide.

On the positive side, I was beginning to change my opinion of him. I could accept that he was an honest businessman, at least within his own moral framework, and in a way his good faith was flattering. But I liked Rick Ashton, and had no wish to do his company harm. I could never understand the relish with which some journalists would automatically go in for the kill. Where was the glory in kicking a man when he was down?

I could of course ignore what Janni had told me. Rumours of late payments were already circulating, feeding the speculation that Vantage needed new funding, so this was nothing new. But this was more than a rumour – it was apparently a fact. I had to pursue it, even if just to find out if it was true. When I knew that, I could decide what to do with the information.

I rang Rick Ashton's office, but he was unavailable. It would have been a miracle to get hold of him at the first attempt. So what next? I could approach him through his public relations firm, but that convoluted process could take days to run its course. I decided to stick to the direct method, and dialled his office again.

This time I was passed down a different route from the switchboard, and ended up speaking directly to Ashton's personal assistant, a woman I knew slightly.

"Rick's out at a lunch with customers," she told me. "He's back later, but he's got a load of appointments stacked up."

"Can you tell him this is pretty urgent? Tell him I have some uncorroborated information about Vantage, and I need to run it past him."

She gave a laugh. "Very cloak and dagger. OK, I'll see what he says."

* * *

It worked. An hour later my phone rang and a confident Australian voice announced, "Michael, Rick Ashton here. What can I do for you, mate?"

"Rick, thank you for calling me back."

"So, shoot."

"I was talking to one of your suppliers."

"Oh, yes?" Immediately a slightly dubious tone. "And who might that be?"

"Can we just say this is a significant supplier?"

"OK, OK. And your point is …?"

"This supplier says Vantage is over eight months behind with a major payment. Well over. He thinks he's being given the run-around, and he's not happy."

Ashton said nothing at all for a long moment. Finally he said, "Nobody pays on time these days. I don't quite get the problem here. What's the big deal?"

"I get the impression that this supplier might be on the point of taking action to recover the debt. But he thinks this will trigger a cash flow crisis at Vantage, and you might not be able to survive it."

"And you actually expect me to comment on that? Come on, Michael."

I pondered this for a moment. "I hear what you're saying. I can't force you to comment, obviously. I'm just thinking what a conscientious journalist would do."

"Go on – enlighten me."

"Well, a conscientious journalist would probably find out the names of some of Vantage's other major suppliers, and try to discover whether they were experiencing late payments too. A picture might build up. The conclusion might end up looking inescapable. And that journalist might feel compelled to write a story about it."

He seemed to reflect on this for a moment. "So you're telling me that you're not that conscientious journalist, right?"

"I could be. It would stand me in good stead to turn in a story like this. I need the kudos, to be frank."

"Bully for you mate." But he was obviously considering this. "But it sounds as if you think there's an alternative scenario? What might that be?"

"I presume you're still negotiating new funding, are you? Maybe you're nearly there with it? It would be nice to have an inside track on that." I paused, then added, "But if you end up having to blow the full-time whistle instead, it would be nice to have an early tip on that."

"So win or lose, you want to be the fly on the wall, is that what you're saying?"

"Kind of, I suppose."

Another silence, then, "Blackmail doesn't sit well with you, Michael. I thought you were better than that."

I sat back. I wasn't used to having this kind of exchange, especially with someone as powerful as Rick Ashton. I didn't know the rules. I said, "I think that's unfair. I didn't need to be telling you all this. I could just have asked for a comment and left it at that. I don't *want* to cause you a headache."

He actually had the grace to chuckle ironically. "Well you are doing, mate." He sighed. "Leave this with me for a bit, will you? I promise I'll play it down the line with you if you play fair with me."

2011

The hotel in Polperro had gone upmarket. That much had been clear from its web site. Everything was now pitched at foreign tourists, business conferences, conventions. A single night's stay cost three times what Sasha had expected, and ate into her limited travel budget. Never mind, it still existed; that was what mattered. And now she was actually here in person.

She wandered round the public areas and up the staircases, savouring snatches of memory from all those years ago. The aura was quite different now, but the general layout had stayed the same.

Most remarkable was the glazed extension, obliterating the outside entrance to the cellar – and presumably also the cellar itself. When had this been built? Before or after her father's friend had tried to recover the stuff he'd hidden? If it was before, she had done him a favour. Left where he'd put them, those bags would have been buried beyond reach, or else dug up. Either way, there would have been nothing here to retrieve.

But was there anything now? Initially she was wary; she scouted the gardens without heading straight for the spot. The area next to the hotel was quite different now – a new lawn, a patio, an outside bar. But through the rustic arch, the rose garden looked much as she remembered it.

She allowed her gaze to float over to the far corner. Yes! The little raised pond was still there, though its fountain was now silent and the stonework of the base looked scruffy and neglected. Behind it, the alcove set into the high stone wall seemed unchanged. She ambled over to it, trying to look inconspicuous. Fortunately it was a dull day and there were no other guests in sight.

She stooped, pretending to admire some wild flowers, and peered at the stone slab that served as a seat. It seemed much more substantial than she remembered it. How could she ever have shifted it as a twelve-year-old, in darkness? She shuddered at the memory.

Experimentally she shoved it. Surprisingly, the corner moved several inches back, to the accompaniment of a heavy scraping sound. She glanced around furtively. Still no one in sight. She shoved it again and it moved further, revealing the edge of a hollow area underneath.

She peered over the edge. Nothing visible. She thrust a hand through the aperture, and immediately encountered folds of stiff fabric: the canvas of one of those bags. They had survived! Now all she needed to do was pick her moment to pull them out, then choose what to keep and what to discard.

And there was the small matter of smuggling what she kept back to Australia.

Chapter 34

Next morning Rick Ashton called me again.

"Michael, have you got a minute?" His tone was unexpectedly friendly.

"Of course. Fire away."

"I'm not calling about this cash flow business. I'm looking into it, and I'll get back to you whenever. This is something else."

I said cautiously, "OK."

"It's about your book, mate. I presume you don't have a real-world publisher for it, do you? I mean, it's just a digital book, right?"

My mind was already racing. I was following his drift, but I was also looking for the hidden agenda. Chief executives of national parcel companies didn't phone me at ten in the morning to discuss my literary aspirations.

"That's correct."

"I thought so. Well, you probably know that Vantage Express is part-owned by Hunt Leinster Holdings, right? And they also own Hunt Topham Media, the book publishers."

"OK."

"Well I was talking to Annette Braddock there a couple of days ago, and I told her about your book." He broke off. "I hope you don't mind."

I smiled to myself at this. "Of course not."

"Well, the bottom line is, she gave it a once-over, and she says there might be room for it somewhere in their portfolio. What do you think of that?"

"You mean they would consider publishing it as a real book? In print?"

"Something like that, mate. Don't ask me the detail. It wouldn't be under one of their main imprints, I don't think, but they have a division that specialises in new talent. Topham Tyro? She thought you might fit in there."

I couldn't stop a smile spreading across my face. New authors simply didn't get direct approaches from publishers. Getting published was a long hard slog through a seemingly endless obstacle course, and very few made it all the way. I knew this all too well from my own limited experience. If Rick was right, this would be a massive leg-up – something I'd never expected in my wildest dreams.

Yet the coincidence of this offer was too obvious to ignore. Yesterday I'd told Rick I was on to a story that could do real harm to his business. Today he was offering me what had to be an inducement not to run with it. Moreover, he was making the offer pretty blatantly; there could be no pretence that it had come out of the blue.

I said, "I'm thinking there must be a catch here."

"No catch, mate, but you'll need to phone her this morning. She's off to a conference in New York this afternoon, and won't be reachable for some time."

I got the point. I had to take the bait immediately, or else it would probably be withdrawn. I said, "About the cash flow thing ..."

"What about it, mate?"

"You'll still be getting back to me about that, will you?"

"Of course I will, mate. Of course."

* * *

I sat staring at the phone number I'd written down. It could be my entry ticket to a new phase in my life.

It could also be a marker of the moment I finally decided to abandon my principles, such as they were.

I felt uneasy enough already about the information snippet I'd been given by Janni Noble. No sooner had it come to my attention than I'd passed it on to Rick Ashton to fend off. Technically speaking I was merely asking for his comment, but in reality I'd hoped he could tell me something that would make it go away. Now he appeared to be offering me a bribe to ensure that this would indeed happen – and I seemed ready to accept it. What kind of reporter did that make me?

I pushed my chair back and stared round the room. Was this my life now? Was I destined forever to be a medium-grade jobbing journalist –

ducking significant stories in favour of slight ones? And if so, what should I do about it? Knuckle down and play it straight down the line, or swallow my scruples and grab an opportunity – even a faint, insubstantial opportunity – to switch to a parallel track?

I shook my head. I was probably blowing this up into a much bigger deal than it really was. For a start, there was no guarantee that Rick Ashton was right in what he'd said. He'd presumably put the most positive construction he could on his conversation with this woman. His writ with her might not run nearly as far as he thought.

For another thing, talking to the woman wouldn't actually prevent me from pursuing the Vantage story at the same time, though Rick might be less than helpful if I did. It didn't have to be an either-or situation.

Perhaps the clincher was that Vantage might be about to confirm new funding tomorrow, which would mean Ashton could pay back Janni Noble the next day, and my news story would have run out of steam before it even started.

I sat back abruptly. Why was I letting my imagination run away with me like this? Surely a bribe was a bribe? No amount of rationalising would change it into something else. If everything was as above board as Ashton wanted me to believe, would he have taken such trouble to tempt me to drop my story?

I wanted to talk this through with someone, and I realised with a jolt that the first person to come into my mind was Ashley. I reprimanded myself sharply. I was hypothesising a familiarity between us that simply didn't exist. Perhaps with a large dose of luck it eventually might, but at present I shouldn't even be thinking of burdening her with my life choices.

By way of evasion I logged on to my digital publisher's web site, and spent long minutes trawling through their terms and conditions. I wanted to know whether I was legally entitled to withdraw my book from sale and have it published in print by another company.

After half an hour I was little the wiser; the answer seemed to be maybe yes, maybe no. Well, if these Hunt Topham people knew that my book was already online, and were willing to talk to me in spite of that, they must have experience of dealing with this situation.

The morning continued to tick away.

Chapter 35

But not for long. At eleven forty-five I picked up my mobile and tapped in the number Rick Ashton had given me. I'd decided I simply had to take this opportunity to the next level, and at least find out where I stood. The train was leaving the metaphorical station, and if I didn't jump on board I would never even get to the first stop.

It was a mobile number, and it was answered immediately. "Annette Braddock." Clipped, businesslike: a woman in her forties or early fifties, perhaps.

"My name is Mike Stanhope. Rick Ashton of Vantage Express suggested I give you a call."

There was a tiny moment while she worked out who I was. "Mike, yes. Your book. We thought it might fit into our newcomers' portfolio."

"That's very exciting."

I had the impression of her rummaging, perhaps in a notebook, perhaps just in her head. In the background I could hear an airport announcement. "We might need you to take another look at some aspects – work with our editorial team. Standard stuff."

Slowly I said, "But in principle you're saying you would be interested in publishing it?"

"Well, to be fair I only had a chance to skip through it. It has some good things going for it, but it's rough at the edges, and you don't have a head of steam behind you, which is a drawback. No significant social media presence, nothing like that. So let's see what my team comes up with before we get ahead of ourselves."

I sat back, running my free hand through my hair. "I realise this probably isn't a good time to talk, but could I just ask you a question?"

"Fire away."

"I feel I should be honest. I'm just thinking, why this book? You must see thousands like it. Why do I deserve a fast track?"

She gave a short laugh. "You don't sound exactly over-keen to sell yourself to me."

Quickly I said, "I assure you there's nothing I'd like more than to get into print. I'm just trying to understand what's happening here."

I could hear her thinking again. "OK, you seem like a straight guy, Mike. I didn't know what to expect from my conversation with Richard."

"Well thank you for that."

Clearly measuring her words, she said, "There are hundreds of plausible books out there. Potential sellers, I mean. Thousands. The fact is that indifferent books sometimes get published, and good ones sometimes don't. It's not just about merit, it's also about the entire package. About marketability." She put the word in slightly ironic verbal quotes. "At the end of the day, sometimes it's just about being in the right place at the right time."

"Fair enough."

"I suppose you don't have an agent?"

"Correct."

"OK, we might need to look at that." She paused a moment. "I tell you what, Mike. Call my team leader Zoe. She'll talk this through with you, and discuss what might need to be done. I'm out of action for a couple of weeks, but I'll keep a watching brief."

She gave me a phone number and hung up.

* * *

I needed a second opinion on all this, and I knew where I'd get a blast of common sense. I called Joanna.

She was all for it. I knew she would be. "What does it matter if this man Ashton has his own agenda? He's not the publisher. If you get a book deal, it'll be on your own merit."

"Hopefully, but that's still a big if. And whether I get it or not, well, my integrity as a journalist is shot."

"Only in your own mind, Mike. After all, nobody knows about this news story except you and me and Mr Ashton."

"And the man who fed it to me."

"He sounds big enough to stand on his own two feet. You don't owe him any favours."

I could always count on Joanna to make me feel better, but her words also set me thinking. Getting a book deal was far from a foregone conclusion, but having reached this point, I'd been assuming the outcome would depend ultimately on the book itself. But what if Ashton had the power of veto further down the track? Clearly he'd had no problem getting hold of Annette Braddock and floating the idea of taking up my book in the first place. Maybe he would be just as capable of intervening later and stopping it dead. Did I want to be in his thrall indefinitely?

* * *

Zoe, Annette Braddock's team leader, seemed to know all about me when I called her, and she already had a plan, which included meeting her in the flesh at their offices in Hertford. I wondered briefly if this was in order to gauge my marketability at first hand. Her explanation was that this would "get some personal synergy going."

I said, "Annette seemed to think you might want some rewriting done."

"That's pretty standard. Authors get too close to their own work. They can't see the wood for the trees. You get scenes meandering off into blind alleys, factual inaccuracies, continuity glitches, pointless purple prose, that kind of thing. Someone usually has to knock things into shape and get rid of the redundant bits."

"So who actually does this rewriting?"

"Oh, you do it, to start with. You." She seemed to think this needed stressing. "First of all we discuss it with you in outline, then you have another crack at it."

"God, it sounds a bit like having your homework rejected."

She laughed. "It's not always that bad. And once everyone's happy with it, we put our own edit team on to it to get rid of any rough edges."

"I thought I'd already done that."

She let that one ride.

"You do realise it's already been online ...?"

"Think of this as a second edition. A better one."

Chapter 36

I stared at my inbox, seeing emails about articles I had to write, press releases I didn't want to read, spam that I hadn't managed to intercept. It all looked so mundane, so endlessly tedious. How much more beguiling to be working with a real live book publisher on my first novel. Fleetingly I imagined book signings, foreign tours, receptions.

I stood up abruptly. Where was all this coming from? Did I seriously see myself as Booker Prize material? Hardly. I shoved my chair irritably towards the desk, which it struck harder than I expected. Coffee sloshed over the edge of my mug, sketching an arc of brown drips on some notes I'd been scribbling next to it.

Out loud I muttered, "You disappoint me, Mr Stanhope. Your integrity deficit is a disgrace to your profession, and your ambition outstrips your ability by a massive margin."

I sat back down, frowning. It wasn't going to happen, was it? Now or ever. Even published authors were lucky to reach celebrity status. Most had to keep their day job going for years after signing a book deal – perhaps for the rest of their lives. And I wasn't even past the first post.

Ah, but that day job – how long could I keep it up? There was the rub. I'd stumbled into business journalism, more or less; it had never been my goal. After university I'd worked as a dogsbody at a large magazine publishing company, and gradually I'd found myself given minor editorial jobs. When my boss realised I was reasonably literate, those jobs had become more frequent and more demanding, and when I proved I was up to them I'd been invited to join the editorial team permanently. I was the living proof that courses and qualifications weren't always a prerequisite for a journalistic career.

But I'd never actually set out on this path – it had just unfolded in front of me. Not only that, but for many years I'd felt a compulsion to justify my place on it. I felt a need to question everything I wrote about, to produce investigative articles even when there was nothing to investigate.

This continued even when I found myself steered into the relatively uncontroversial world of logistics and transport, which somehow became my speciality. People started to regard me as the go-to man for probing pieces, and oddly, the more of these articles I wrote, the angrier I became: angry with the world I was writing about, yet at the same time angry with myself for having to write about it.

But finally my anger ran out: a development that coincided pretty much with Sandy's announcement that she'd run out of patience with me. Since then I'd felt rudderless and incapable of doing much more than go through the motions.

* * *

But that was then and this was now. Lately two things seemed to be nudging my life in a new and more positive direction – my quest to track down the Markham family, and now Ashley Renwick.

I wasn't sure where my involvement with Ashley was heading. She was engaged – I couldn't ignore that fact; yet it seemed clear that she was as drawn to me as I was to her. All I could hope was that somehow this might shake out to a favourable outcome.

As for the Markhams, I felt ambivalent about my search. Yes, it would be intriguing to find out why they had disappeared – but not if it would be detrimental to them.

Abruptly my mind jumped back to the time when we'd all been on holiday at the Fairmile. It was a warm day at the end of our first week. I'd wandered round the corner of a building, my thoughts entirely elsewhere, and more or less bumped straight into Trina. To this day I still had an intense memory of the sunshine on the grey stone wall, and our exclamations of shock.

She said sorry and I said sorry, and I think she said something like "I'm always wandering around with my head in the clouds." I probably stammered, "No, I ought to look where I'm going." I was no doubt reeling at being peremptorily flung into such close quarters with her. We were *actually having a conversation*.

Without that unintended encounter, we would never have gone on to share a ball game on one of the lawns, or to sit afterwards at a metal table drinking lemonade provided by her mother. That sun-splashed memory had lived with me for years, and I'd sought vainly to re-create it with other girls in other environments. Somehow nothing had ever matched up, and the more I'd tried to make it happen, the more elusive it had become.

There was a bittersweet quality to the memory, though. When I'd eventually stood up to return to my parents, she'd pulled out a scrap of paper and a pencil from a small purse. "Give me your address. I'll write to you when we all get home."

I'd been surprised and flattered by this unexpectedly forthright gesture, but too nonplussed to ask for her own address in exchange. So it was a one-way street; and the letter had never come.

She'd left the following day, along with her family, and I'd never seen any of them again. It now seemed clear to me that my search for her family was inextricably bound up with that yearning for the unattainable.

* * *

My computer pinged, announcing the arrival of an incoming email. Without much interest I glanced at the inbox, but then I quickly sat up. It was a one-line message.

"My name is Trina Markham. I understand you are looking for me."

PART TWO

Chapter 37

Could it really be this easy? After all these months of searching, had Trina Markham really reached out to me of her own accord?

I examined the email more closely. It was from someone called tpowell9775, and had been sent from a free mass-market email address. Well, that was fair enough – Trina could have married someone called Powell.

How should I reply? I had to think carefully. Assuming this was the real Trina, I needed to say something friendly and reassuring to her. After all, at the end of the day I had no valid reason to be looking for her or her family in the first place, other than sheer curiosity. In my own mind I might have elevated the whole exercise into a piece of legitimate journalistic research, but she wasn't to know that. So I had to sound plausible and undemanding.

But was this in fact the real Trina? I'd spent years asking questions that people didn't quite want to answer, and I'd got used to evasion. It had made me sceptical. So in case this wasn't her, I had to avoid revealing too much that an impostor wouldn't know.

Finally I opened an email window and started writing.

Thanks so much for getting in touch.

You're quite right, I've been trying to track you down. I hope you don't mind. It was just a whim really. I had such a great time all those years ago at the Fairmile Hotel in Falmouth. I was trying to catch up with the people I met there, and I remember you very clearly, though you might not remember me so well. I was the shy bloke who used to wander around looking lost.

After all these years, I just thought it would be nice to get back in touch. If you felt like it you could let me know a bit about your life since then, and I could do the same with mine. We might have other friends in common. It's one of those things one could never do without the internet, so I'm just taking advantage of that.

I spent two summer holidays at the Fairmile with my parents, Tony and Janet Stanhope. I think we coincided with your family in my first year, which was probably 1989 or 1990. Sadly my parents have since died, but I went back to look at the place earlier this year. It has changed somewhat!

I don't want to intrude into your life if you'd rather I didn't, so please don't feel under any pressure. If you'd prefer not to take this any further, that's absolutely no problem – just say so, or don't even bother to reply to this. I'd hate you think I'm an internet stalker or something, which I assure you I'm not!

Thank you again for taking the trouble to write. Do let me know what you think, and I'll respond accordingly.

Throwing in the bit about internet stalking made me feel slightly uneasy, but it was an objection I felt I should meet head on. However, once I'd written it, I realised it was unsettlingly close to the truth. I *was* stalking Trina in a way, though I'd never thought of it like that until now. There was a fine line between reconnecting with old friends and hassling people who didn't want to be hassled, whatever high-minded journalistic imperative you used in order to justify it. Under the circumstances, you could argue that my pursuit of these people had crossed that line long ago.

Then again, she was the one who had contacted *me*, so she must at least be willing to enter into some kind of dialogue with me. No one had forced her to get in touch.

If, indeed, it was her.

My mouse hovered over the send button for what seemed like minutes, then I clicked it.

Gone. Sent.

* * *

Joanna was over the moon about the email.

"It must be her! Who else would bother to contact you like that?"

John was more wary. "You never know what's going to come at you out of the internet. Look at the endless stream of spam we all get."

We were walking along the street from their house, heading for an

182   PETER ROWLANDS

Indian restaurant. As usual these days I was glancing warily around for possible abductors, but saw no evidence of anything out of the ordinary. Hopefully there was strength in numbers.

I said, "John's right. Look at the hoax calls that the police always get when they put out appeals for missing people. This could be the equivalent of that."

Joanna said, "Well I think you're both being negative old miseries!"

After we'd arrived at the restaurant Joanna started again on the same tack. "So you haven't heard from her again since you sent your reply?"

"No, but it's only been a couple of days. I think I should give her a bit more time to decide what she wants to say."

She seemed ready to keep on picking over this, so I decided to move the conversation on. Turning to John, I said, "Did Jo tell you I might have an opportunity to get my book published in print?"

"I think she said something about it." He glanced quickly at Joanna, who nodded enthusiastically. "Sounds brilliant. You must be very pleased."

"Well, it's only a possibility at the moment. Someone I know is trying to pull a few strings for me, but I don't know if it's going to work out yet."

He could obviously hear the hesitation in my voice, and said, "I wouldn't worry about string-pulling. That's what keeps the world ticking over."

"Maybe."

"So how did this come about?"

"Well, someone I know through work has business connections with a publishing house, and thought he might be able to get them to take an interest."

"And have they?"

"I'm supposed to fix a meeting with them next week. I'll probably know if it's going to lead anywhere after that."

"Well, if it does lead somewhere, just be thankful. We'll certainly be keeping our fingers crossed."

The meal arrived, and I was spared the third degree for a while. Joanna suddenly said, "Mike, you're looking much more cheerful these days. Should we be presuming your love life is looking up?"

Was I more cheerful? If so, presumably I had Ashley to thank, but we hadn't been in touch since the day I went to Bristol, and I had no clear idea what was supposed to happen next. How long should I wait before contacting her again?

"I wouldn't exactly call it my love life."

"We're talking about your girl in Truro, are we?"

"Yes, her. But she's not really my girl."

"Well, it's obvious you want her in *your* life. What's she like?"

I hesitated. The urge to start talking about Ashley was almost irresistible, but I knew I would probably sound like a love-struck teenager. Cautiously I said, "She's very pretty."

"Of *course* she's pretty." Joanna gave me an admonishing frown.

I raised my eyebrows. I wasn't sure how to respond to that. "Well, she's slim and dark-haired …" I was floundering. "Small-chested."

She groaned. "Too much information. Tell us something actually useful."

I took a deep breath. "OK, well she's very wry. Great sense of humour. And there's a quiet confidence about her. She seems good at her job, and she knows her own mind." I paused. "Except in affairs of the heart, I suppose. She doesn't seem to know what to do about her engagement – whether she's really committed to it."

"No wonder, if she's thinking of ditching her fiancé for you." Joanna's eyes twinkled. "What on earth does she see in you, anyway?"

I shrugged. "You'd have to ask her that." I thought for a moment about Jack. "The fiancé seems a solid, reliable sort."

Joanna gave a short laugh, and John also looked amused. "So you think you offer her a bit of the wild side?"

I didn't see that in myself, but I merely scowled. "No comment."

"So what next?"

"Well she says she wants time to get her head together."

"No she doesn't." Joanna gave me a brisk smile and tore her chapati decisively in half. "Is that what she told you?"

"In so many words."

"Well, you shouldn't take what she says at face value. What she means is that it's your turn to make the running. She's fed up with having to push things forward herself."

I smiled at her, admiring her splendidly positive and pragmatic take on the world. Her advice was to do exactly the opposite of what Ashley had said. Where was the logic in that?

"I appreciate the support, but please let me deal with this in my own way."

She frowned at me. "Well all right – but don't leave it too long. She'll think you've lost interest."

Chapter 38

When I logged on to my email system next morning, the first thing I found was a message from tpowell9775.

Hi Mike

Thank you for your email. It's good of you to explain why you have been trying to make contact with me.

I remember the Fairmile Hotel well. It was in a very pretty location, and made a good base for heading out to see the other wonders of Cornwall with my parents.

I got to know a few of the other children there, but not many of them were the same age as me. I think I have a faint memory of you, but please don't hold me to it! I haven't kept in touch with any of the others.

I'm a very private person, and to be honest I'm not really into the idea of connecting with past acquaintances over the internet like this. I felt I should contact you because I could tell that you must have gone to a lot of trouble to find me, but I would prefer not to get into an extended correspondence with you, if you don't mind. I hope you won't be upset by this request. I bear you no ill will, and would be saying the same to anyone else in the same circumstances.

Trina

PS If you can remove some of the Facebook trails and other stuff about me, that would be great.

Well, that was telling me. I'd wondered for months what kind of reception I would get if I ever made contact with Trina. Now I knew, and the answer was extraordinarily disappointing: a curt, emotionless brush-off with no facts in it whatever, rounded off by what sounded like a mild rebuke.

There was no sense here of Trina's feelings at the time, no detail of her subsequent life, no clue about how she'd manage to slip completely off everyone's radar for twenty-five years. There was no explanation, even, of how exactly she knew I was looking for her – just a strong hint that any attempt to follow up would be unwelcome.

I stood up and walked over to the window, and stared out into the street. What on earth was I to make of this? I'd been prepared for some suggestion that the sender wasn't really Trina, but the negative tone of this message seemed strangely convincing. A hoaxer would surely have tried to extend the exchange, not shut it down when it had scarcely even begun? A hoaxer wouldn't have sounded so downbeat.

Yet if this was really her, wouldn't there have been just a little more of a spark of interest, of surprise? Somehow the tone of this message conjured up someone who was already in the habit of waving away unwelcome interest – who was primed to do it almost by rote, whatever the circumstances.

As for removing the Facebook mentions, that seemed like a lost cause. I could contact some of the people who had picked up on my original pleas for information about Trina and ask them to delete their posts on this subject, but it seemed to me that my requests would be likely to arouse more curiosity than just letting things be. Besides, the basics of my search for Trina could have been copied and reported elsewhere by now. Once you put things out there on the internet, there was really no taking them back.

* * *

I sat down again. I was finding it hard to believe that all my research, all my efforts could have been swiped away with this single, dismissive message. Was this really the end of it?

It struck me now that I seemed to have forgotten my earlier decision to let this whole thing drop. Trina's message had raised more questions than it answered, and it had made me realise I'd only ever put my search on the back burner, not truly abandoned it.

Well, too bad. I started thinking through other strategies I could adopt. Could I find out more about tpowell9775? Idly I opened the properties tab of the email and scanned through the technical details. To my untutored eye it looked just like other messages that I'd examined over the years, usually when checking for spam. There was no obvious indication of relay servers or fake return paths – just a message from tpowell9775 directly to me.

But this was hardly what you'd call a forensic examination. What else could I do? I reached over to a shelf and pulled down my *Writers' resource goodies* pamphlet. It had various suggestions, such as checking the IP address in the email for the country of origin. I did this as best I could, and concluded that it was probably in the UK.

I then lopped off the "9775" and tried just searching for "tpowell". In some social media sites this produced no finds at all; in others there were too many to contemplate. A straight web search on the name ran to hundreds of thousands of finds.

The pamphlet listed various web sites specialising in tracking down email addresses, but I wasn't sure if they would work, and I was reluctant to pay good money to find out. In any case I wasn't prepared to go that far. I wasn't a detective agency, and I didn't have any justification for trying to act like one.

At the back of my mind I still had the thought that Trina's family might have had to disappear into witness protection. Who was I to compromise something like that? Then again, would she have been rash enough to contact me under her real name if that was the case? The answer was that I simply didn't know.

No, if I really wanted to follow this up, the first port of call should be simply to send her another email. She could ignore it if she wanted to, but she might just volunteer a little more information.

But not now. I needed to think more carefully about this first. I closed her message and tried to focus on work.

It wasn't easy.

2011

Stepping off the train at St Pancras was always inspiring: that massive arched roof, the restored redbrick neo-gothic hotel, the bustling shopping mall. Such a contrast to the down-at-heel station of twenty years before.

I was in no hurry. I was early for an appointment. I ambled along the concourse. Then as I neared the Eurostar departure gates my eye was drawn to a woman standing on her own, rummaging through a handful of papers – perhaps searching for her ticket. Some of them slipped from her grasp and fluttered to the ground, and she crouched briefly, gathering them up.

She had straight shoulder-length dark hair and wore a light-coloured jacket and skirt. She was striking but not exceptional.

But I knew her. Against all logic, and after a gap of well over twenty years, I felt sure it was her. She'd been a young teenager when I last saw her. How could I possibly remember her now? But there was something in the way she was standing, the way she held her head – it was hard to pin it down, but the combined effect was unmistakable.

"Sasha?"

She immediately looked up, then just as quickly down again. She continued to leaf through her papers.

"Sasha?" What was the matter with me? If she didn't want to acknowledge me, what was the point? But I couldn't help myself.

This time she half-looked up. "Sorry, were you speaking to me?" Australian: those few words were enough to confirm it.

"I thought you were someone I knew from long ago."

Humourless smile. "I don't think so."

I was embarrassed. "Sorry. I must have got it wrong."

"No problem." She finally found the item she was looking for, and stood up straighter, obviously relieved. Our eyes met then, but she quickly looked away. "I've got to go. I'm late for my train." She grabbed the handle of her

suitcase, and without another look at me she walked off briskly towards the check-in area, trundling the case behind her.

As she disappeared into the crowd I noticed a scrap of paper on the ground where she'd been standing – an item she must have missed. I scooped it up and glanced briefly at it. It was a ticket counterfoil for an earlier journey, but the name on it wasn't Sasha's. Confirmation, then. I cast around for the nearest litter bin.

Chapter 39

Hertford was a pleasant county town twenty-five miles north of London, with a ring road running so close to the centre that it almost seemed to slice through it. Yet this didn't altogether detract from the prosperous period feel of the place. Genuine Victorian office blocks sat cheek by jowl with modern equivalents, yet there was an underlying consistency in the result. It worked. I couldn't remember ever coming here before; Hertford sat between the north-south A1 and A10, and wasn't really on anyone's route to anywhere.

Hunt Topham, the publisher Rick Ashton had referred me to, was based in a large redbrick block that was built to resemble its Victorian counterparts, and the department I wanted occupied part of the second floor.

Zoe Sanders welcomed me when I arrived and led me through an open plan office to a glass-walled meeting room, where she introduced me to a woman of about twenty-five. "Melanie will be your liaison on this project," she told me. It seemed I was gradually being passed further and further down the food chain.

It intrigued me to find that a publishing house's head office was so similar to the logistics company offices I was familiar with. Apart from a few wall posters featuring the front covers of well-known best sellers, there was little here to indicate any literary or academic bent. This was a business like any other. I felt unnerved. I was potential product. Did I measure up?

The two women were friendly and positive, but altogether non-committal. I was initially surprised that they both appeared to have read my book; they chatted comfortably about the plot and characters, and indeed showed more insight into it than anyone else I'd ever discussed it with. But they weren't entirely happy with it.

"There are one or two inconsistencies," Zoe said, tapping her pen on a chart. "Some bits need tightening up."

By the time Melanie went off to top up the coffee jug I was sweating – partly because of the sun beaming in through the picture window, but more because I felt matters were racing away from me. When I'd published my book online I'd been the sole author, editor and arbiter of every scrap of material in it. Here, I felt I was being judged and found wanting. We'd progressed no further so far than to talk general principles, but already I felt out of control.

It turned out that the whole meeting was really nothing more than a "getting to know you" exercise. As we broke up, Zoe said, "When Annette is back we'll get you to come in again, and assuming we can talk terms, we'll start looking at the contract aspect."

I stepped out into the Hertford sunshine with something like relief. These people might possibly change my life, but it wasn't going to be any walk in the park.

* * *

Back in my own office, I decided I'd better nudge Rick Ashton. Days had passed since I first contacted him about the late payments to Noble, and he hadn't come back to me so far with any new information. Did he know I'd made contact with Hunt Topham? Did he assume that because of this he no longer had any obligation to me?

If so, he was wrong. I'd spent half the previous Friday morning ringing around truck makers and other suppliers whom I knew to be working with Vantage, trying to discover whether they too were dealing with late payments. It was a delicate task, since I had to avoid stirring up rumours by the mere act of asking questions. I limited my calls to people I felt I could trust. I could only hope my judgement was sound.

The story I was getting was that others were in a similar position to Janni Noble, though possibly not facing quite such blatant delaying tactics. A picture was emerging, but it wasn't altogether clear.

I wondered why the largest shareholder, Hunt Leinster, wasn't prepared to support the company through this crisis, but perhaps the answer was obvious. From what I read, it was currently embroiled in a battle for media dominance in Canada, and had no spare resources for an ailing UK subsidiary. If Vantage was failing, it would be just as likely to cut the company loose as to supply any aid.

I opened a new email window. "Rick – I wondered if you had any comment yet on our conversation last week? I hate to hassle you, but I don't want to go to press without being able to quote your side of the story."

This was merely bluff, since I hadn't in fact placed the story anywhere yet, though I had little doubt that I'd be able to if necessary.

He surprised me once again by calling me back less than an hour later.

"Michael, what's this? I thought we were on the same side here."

"I think we are, but I can't let this run on indefinitely. I need to be able to say something."

"All I can say is I hope you and your publishers have good libel insurance." There was unmistakable anger in his voice. "If you come up with anything prejudicial to our company's good standing without proper evidence, we'll come down on you like a ton of bricks."

I said nothing for a moment. This was a hard-edge Rick Ashton I'd never encountered before, though I knew of course that he had to be tough to have reached his current status.

I said, "You know that's not my way, Rick. I don't want to make waves unnecessarily."

"Don't then." He almost spat this out.

I waited another moment. I wondered briefly if he was about to disconnect, but he didn't. Finally I said, "Maybe we should start this conversation again."

"Maybe we should. Hello Michael. How are you today?" It was sarcastic, but at least it was propitiating.

"I'm good. I'm hoping we can iron out this issue of late payments."

"Fine. Let's do that. I'm looking into it. I told you that. I'll get back to you when I have something to report."

"Thank you."

He paused again, then asked, "How did you get on with Annette?"

"Well, nothing is agreed yet, but as it happens I've just been up to their offices in Hertford this morning for a preliminary discussion."

"Promising, I hope?"

"Reasonably."

"You can never be sure how these things will pan out."

* * *

We disconnected, and I sighed. If I'd wondered in passing whether Ashton's referral to Hunt Topham was meant to be linked to the late payment story, I need wonder no more. He'd just made the connection plain enough.

What I didn't know was whether he really had the influence he implied to dictate policy at Hunt Topham, which was theoretically a completely separate and independently-run company. It could just be bluster.

I couldn't rule it out. Rick no doubt reported to Tony McGann, the head of Hunt Leinster Holdings, the parent company, and McGann would presumably prefer not to see one of his part-owned subsidiaries collapse with debts it couldn't pay. No doubt he could exert his influence at Hunt Topham if he chose, and this might well be an instance where he did choose.

Yet as I sat at my desk working through this logic, I couldn't resist smiling ironically to myself. What was I doing, worrying that Rick Ashton would block publication of my book? From my session with the publishers this morning, it seemed clear that if anything was going to stop it from being published it was much more likely to be their spontaneous conclusion that it simply wasn't good enough.

Chapter 40

Ten days had passed since my trip to Bristol, and I hadn't been in touch with Ashley since then. Joanna's warning was ringing in my ears; I didn't want to hassle Ashley, and contacting her again too soon might seem like exactly that. But I didn't want her to think I'd lost interest either. How much time for reflection was enough time?

I reached for my phone, flicking mentally through possible reasons to ring her. I couldn't think of any that sounded plausible. What would I be suggesting if I did? I couldn't think of an answer to that either.

I scrolled indecisively through my contact list, hovering over Latimer Logistics. And then I pressed the call button anyway.

She was there, and I was quickly put through to her.

"Mike. Good to hear from you."

Her tone was cool – not unfriendly, certainly not over-enthusiastic. Immediately I regretted making the call. This must be too soon.

I said, "How are you?"

"I'm good. You?"

"OK."

A pause this early in the conversation was bad news. Hesitantly I said, "I wondered if Patrick had come up with any more photographs of the Fairmile Hotel – photos taken when we were all there. Sorry to ring you out of the blue about this."

"Oh. Right. No, I don't think so. We haven't talked about it lately. D'you want me to ask him again?"

That was a good question. I'd managed to forget his protective attitude to Ashley. He might not want to give me any more help. I said, "Do you think he'll look?"

"He will if I ask him."

There was another pause, then she said, "What made you bring it up again now?"

"Well, believe it or not, I've had an email from Trina. Or at least, someone who says she's Trina. So I'm floundering around, wondering what to say in my reply."

"That's amazing!" For the first time in the conversation she sounded almost animated. "Where is she? What's she been doing all these years?"

"Well that's the thing. She hasn't really said. In fact she makes it sound as if she doesn't want to be in touch with me at all. So I'm trying to approach it delicately."

"Right, well let me talk to Patrick tonight."

A much longer pause, then I said, "I couldn't decide whether to ring you."

"It's fine." She didn't say whether she meant the time-lag was fine or this phone call was fine. "Look, I'm in the middle of something here …"

"It's OK, we can pick this up another time."

And that was that.

* * *

That afternoon Sandy rang me. "Mike, how are you doing?"

"More to the point, how are you? Did you manage to clear up OK after your break-in?"

"Yes, we're back to normal now, pretty much. Alan was great."

"Did they take much?"

"Well, that's partly why I'm ringing. You remember when you came round wanting your photos back? I just wondered what you actually took. Was it loads of CDs?"

"No, no, not at all. Just two. I didn't want to deprive you of the pictures you took yourself, I just wanted some of mine that got muddled up with them."

"That's what I thought. Well that's really strange."

"What is?"

"The people who broke in took loads of CDs from that cupboard. About twenty, I should think. All the pictures we took when we were together, and some other stuff as well. Data CDs – notes about my work, that kind of thing. I didn't notice at first because it was all such a mess."

"Weird. And what a pain for you." But I was thinking this fitted in rather too well with my break-ins. There was a similar pattern of someone looking for something.

I made some appropriately sympathetic comments, and we chatted more generally for a while. She said, "We really must fix to get together some time. I meant it when I said I'd like to do that."

"Let's consider it a plan."

Chapter 41

A call came at me from left field the following day, and for a moment I didn't know how to respond. A vaguely familiar voice announced, "Bob Latimer here, from Latimer Logistics. How are you doing, Mike?"

We'd never spoken on the phone before. He wasn't on my list of likely suspects to ring for industry comment, though I felt we'd got on well when I interviewed him for the article earlier in the year.

"Mike, we really liked the article you wrote about us in the spring. You understood exactly what we're about at Latimer Logistics, and you picked up a lot of detail in the course of a fairly short conversation. It did us a lot of good."

Cautiously I said, "I'm glad to hear it."

"The thing is, I wondered if you would be available to write some more material about us – articles, press releases, brochure copy, that kind of thing. We could really do with someone who knows the industry as well as you, and also knows the press. Is that something you could do?"

Many of my fellow-freelances did exactly this – wrote editorial and press releases for organisations in the industry. It was comparatively easy work, and paid much more than press articles did. I'd always meant to try jumping on that bandwagon myself, but somehow hadn't made the leap so far.

Playing for time, I asked, "Don't you have a public relations firm doing this kind of thing?"

"In the past, yes, but we never seem to get decent value for money. We dumped our last people a year ago, and since then Sally Meadows has been doing her best for us. But she doesn't really have the time."

Sally, his personal assistant, periodically sent me bland press releases about long-service awards and the company's charitable donations. They weren't exactly front page material.

What was concerning me was that if I took up this proposal I would be bound to encounter Ashley. She was the company's assistant head of marketing, which surely wasn't a million miles from press relations. What was her opinion of this proposal? Had she been involved in it in some way? From her distant response when I'd phoned her yesterday it seemed unlikely, so would she welcome it if it was suddenly landed on her?

The upside, of course, was that it would presumably give me a ready-made excuse to see her, perhaps on a regular basis. Yesterday I'd been racking my brains about how to engineer something like this; now, as if by magic, it was being offered to me on a plate. If I'd sat down to invent this scenario I couldn't have come up with a neater idea. But would she buy into it? It was a big assumption.

I said, "In principle the answer is yes, it's a great idea and I'd love to get involved. But do you mind if I ask whether you've run it past Ashley Renwick?"

"Ashley? No, I only thought of it a minute ago, and I thought I'd sound you out straight way."

"I understand." I was floundering. I didn't want to head him off; I had a sense that this was a once-only offer. But I couldn't accept it without her knowledge.

I said, "I get the sense that Ashley is really on the ball with this kind of thing. It would be great to know she's on board with it."

I could almost feel him reviewing the various aspects of this. Happily the pieces seemed to fall in the right places, and he said brightly, "Tell you what, I'll talk to her now, and maybe you could have a think about what you would charge us?"

* * *

I quickly rang a colleague who did similar work to mine. I asked what he charged for this kind of public relations writing, and he willingly gave me a run-down of his usual rates. I was amazed how high they were. Then I rang Bob Latimer back.

"Ashley says she's fine with this," he told me. I could almost hear her speaking that precise phrase, and I wondered briefly what it meant. It was hardly effusive, but what did I expect? She couldn't dismiss a perfectly reasonable idea proposed by her boss, so she was hardly going to overrule it. All I could do was wonder what she actually thought.

Well, too bad. This was another of those opportunities that had to be grasped while it was there. I quoted Bob some sample fees for various kinds of work, and he made a note of them without apparently paying much attention.

"So when can you come and see us? Could you make it later this week?"

* * *

So on the Friday morning of that week I found myself on the train to St Austell. It would have been convenient to have had my car with me at the other end, but I didn't fancy that long drive again, and in truth I had doubts that the car presented me in a very good light. I double-locked my front and back doors before I left, and made sure I had all my computer hardware with me.

I was picked up at St Austell by the company's driver, and quickly found myself in the board room with Bob Latimer, along with his sales director and his head of operations. Bob picked up a phone on a side table. "Ashley, would you like to join us for a minute?" Ashley would, and a minute later she walked hesitantly into the room.

Absurdly, I felt I must be blushing at the sight of her. Our eyes briefly met, and I saw not hostility in them, just a kind of uncertainty. Bob waved her over to a chair on the other side of the table, and she sat down. She was wearing an aquamarine top with matching beads, and had a slide in her hair in a slightly darker blue. The effect was striking, yet at the same time on her it seemed understated.

Bob introduced me to everyone and outlined his ideas about getting me involved with press promotion and publicity. Ashley asked how their press releases would be circulated, and I suggested I might be able to help with that, hoping it was true.

In due course it was time for an extended tour of the premises. Ashley prepared to return to her office and Bob went off to find some high-visibility jackets for the rest of us. At the boardroom door I said to her quietly, "You do realise all this wasn't my idea?"

Her eyes widened. "What do you mean by that?"

Quickly I said, "I mean, it's an amazing idea, but it wasn't just some plot of mine to ingratiate myself."

Bob returned at that point with an armful of orange tunics. She edged away, commenting with a smile, "That's what *you* say, Mr Stanhope."

* * *

I was shown round the same warehouse I'd seen last time, then another warehouse, then yet another, then the operations room, then the IT department, and finally the open-plan sales and marketing office. Ashley had a cubicle at one end, and gave me a little wave as I stood chatting with Bob and his colleagues near the door.

Then we returned to the board room and started to assemble a programme of press releases that would extend over the next few months. Some of it involved me speaking to, or even visiting, some of Latimer's customers. It would be quite a lot of work.

I asked about working on brochures. "We'll need to bring Ashley's team in on that. Let's talk about it next time you're here."

That was fine with me.

It was only when the meeting ended that it dawned on me I'd made no arrangement to see her at the end of the proceedings, and wasn't sure how to make it happen. I was debating texting her to see if she had any thoughts when I realised Bob was speaking to me.

"Do you have any plans for this evening, Mike?"

I didn't. I'd booked myself into the same hotel in Truro as last time, and had been hoping that somehow Ashley and I would get together between now and the end of the evening.

"Perhaps you'd like to join Brian and me over dinner?"

It was an offer I couldn't decline, and half an hour later we arrived at a roadside restaurant a few miles outside St Austell.

While we were there I found a moment to text Ashley: "Been hijacked by the brass and forced to eat fillet steak at gunpoint. Staying over like last time."

When we parted company at the end of the evening, Brian drove me to Truro, where he lived. From Ashley I'd heard nothing. Mindful that she might be with Jack, I resisted the temptation to phone or text her again. I checked into the hotel and fell into an uneasy sleep.

Chapter 42

There was no text message from Ashley when I woke next morning, nor any voicemail. I was unsure what to do. It was a Saturday, but I had no sense of whether this made a meeting with Ashley more or less likely than if it had been a weekday. I'd only booked myself into the hotel for one night, so my options appeared to be sightseeing in Truro or an early train ride back to London.

Then as I walked back from breakfast through the hotel foyer a figure entered from the street: Ashley, in jeans and a blue T-shirt. "Mr Stanhope! Surprise surprise."

I felt myself beaming foolishly at her. "Hello."

"I wondered if I could buy you a coffee."

"Don't mind if you do."

I went upstairs to grab my belongings, then hurried back down and checked out of the hotel. In the street, Ashley nodded to the right.

"This way."

"Where are we going?"

"Follow me and you'll see."

We set off at a brisk pace through pretty pedestrianised shopping streets with abundant hanging baskets brimming with pastel-coloured flowers. The cathedral loomed across a small square and she gestured towards it without slowing down. "Did anybody tell you that's a modern fake? Gothic revival. It's only just over a hundred years old."

It looked five times that age to me, but I nodded. "Are you planning to set up in business as a tour guide?"

We gradually moved out of the shopping area and into narrow streets of period terraced houses, and finally she stopped by a small blue Subaru car. "My flat is along there and round the corner, but I'm not taking you to it."

"Whatever you say."

She paused as she opened the driver's door, and suddenly gave me a brilliant smile. "I can't believe you're here, getting into my car!"

"You'd better believe it."

We made our way on to a main road out of the town, but before long we turned into a rambling suburb and drew up in front of a smart house of indeterminate age. It was finished in local stone, and the browns and greys did their best to convey a solid, dependable feel.

"The family home," she said as we approached the front door.

"Very nice."

"We had a much bigger place when we lived down in Falmouth."

She unlocked the door. "Don't get too excited, I'm not taking you to meet the folks."

"I've already met them."

"And once is enough, believe me."

She beckoned me through to a lounge at the back of the house. "Patrick told me he left the photos somewhere here." She cast around. "Aha!" She picked up an envelope from the sideboard. It had "Ashley" written on it and underlined.

We moved out into a sun porch and sat at a heavy teak table, looking through the pictures. There were about ten in total, and several of them had clearly been taken on the same day as the one Ashley had emailed to me. Some shots featured the diminutive version of Ashley on her own; in others she was with a young version of Patrick, standing a head taller than her. There was one other picture that included both Trina and me, but it looked like an earlier attempt at the one she'd already sent me.

Finally there was a shot from a different photo session. Trina was in it, wearing the same white top and blue shorts, but it was a posed shot featuring several adults. I said, "That's your father, isn't it?"

She looked closely. "Yes, and those are probably Trina's parents."

"How about this couple?"

She shrugged. "Other guests?"

I asked her if I could keep the pictures. She said, "I'll scan them and email them to you."

I looked up and glanced around the house. "Where are your folks?"

"Shopping. I checked. It usually takes them hours."

I hesitated. "And Jack …?"

"Playing football in Plymouth. But look, we don't live in each other's pockets."

We glanced awkwardly at each other, and at that moment a man and a woman loomed at the glass side door and the woman thrust a key into the lock.

Ashley gave me a wide-eyed look. "Aarrgh! They've come back early."

* * *

Her mother came in first, carrying two shopping bags. "Ashley! I didn't know we were expecting you today." She bustled off to the kitchen. Her father followed, carrying two more bags. He nodded to the two of us as he headed after her.

Presently her mother reappeared. She gave me a sideways glance and raised her eyebrows fractionally.

"This is Mike," Ashley said. "You met him at Dad's birthday party."

She reached out to give me a perfunctory handshake. Ashley offered nothing to explain my presence.

I studied Mary Renwick. She was well built but not conspicuously overweight, with an older and slightly looser version of Ashley's neat features, and dark hair streaked with grey. She stood erect and confident.

"Where's Jack?" she asked Ashley.

"Plymouth."

"Ah, of course." She turned to me again, but addressing Ashley said, "Are you staying for lunch?"

"No, I promised Mike some sightseeing around Cornwall."

"Coffee then." It was a statement, not a question.

She went off to make it and her husband wandered through. He seemed relatively indifferent to my presence, but leaned over our bundle of photographs for a moment.

"Where on earth did you dig these up?"

"Patrick found them when he was over on Tuesday.

He picked up the one featuring Desmond Markham and turned to me. "He's the chap you were asking about, isn't he?"

Surprised that he even remembered me, let alone our conversation, I nodded.

He said, "I'd forgotten all about this picture." He studied it for a moment, then looked up at me. "Have you had any luck tracking down these people?"

"Well, up to a point. I found out they lived in the Manchester area, and he was in property. But they seem to have vanished overnight – probably the same year I met them. It's a bit of a mystery, actually."

"Well well. Intriguing." He scratched his head. "I suppose you'll keep on looking for them, will you?"

"Probably."

"Good, good. You never know what you might turn up, do you?"

"I suppose not."

He nodded and started to wander away, but I said, "Do you mind me asking who these other people are?"

He looked again. "No idea. Friends of the Markhams, probably." He dropped the picture back on the pile.

Coffee proved a slightly stilted affair. Gordon had disappeared to the greenhouse, but Mary continued to make fishing remarks about why I was there, and Ashley continued to fend them off. I picked up a strong sense of mother-daughter friction, probably stretching back many years.

Finally Ashley stood up. "Well, we've got places to go and sights to see."

* * *

As we closed the car doors she turned to me. "I wish I really could give you a sightseeing tour."

"Rain check?"

She nodded. "So what time is your train?"

I shrugged. "No particular time. Whenever it leaves."

She glanced at her watch. "OK, great."

She drove back to the main road, then headed off at a brisk pace into a grey sky. The signs said we were going in the direction of Redruth.

We continued for a while without saying much. I had a feeling she had an agenda, and felt the safest approach was to let it run its course. Eventually she pulled in at a road house – a sort of combined diner and pub.

"Bit early for lunch," she commented as we walked over from the car, "and this isn't exactly Cornwall's finest, but what the heck?"

We found a table for two by the window, and she looked thoughtfully at me for a moment.

"OK, let me tell you about Kieron."

Chapter 43

She sat facing me over her coffee and smiled. "There's nothing much to tell, actually, but I suppose in a way I have Kieron to thank for everything that's happened to me since then."

I waited while she collected her thoughts.

"He turned up one day to check over some of Latimer's trucks. He was from a firm in Leeds who were putting a tracking system in our fleet. This is years ago. Latimer's had a place outside Truro then, and I worked there in admin. Next thing I know, he's left that firm and joined Patrick's firm here in Truro, and before I know it I'm living with him in his cottage." She raised her eyes heavenward. "Silly me."

I nodded without comment.

"I left my job at Latimer's and went to work on the counter at a craft centre – more or less for nothing. It was my Bohemian phase." She put verbal quote marks round the phrase.

"Then one day Patrick tells me he's found out Kieron is screwing some girl in Penryn. Plus, he's still seeing his girlfriend in Leeds when he goes up there. So that, in nutshell, was that." She sat back. "It was all horribly predictable, and I suppose it was pretty trivial in the scheme of things. But we all have our story, don't we?" She smiled ironically.

"Then what happened?"

"Well, you know, life. I moved on, Latimer's took me back, my parents got over themselves –" another fleeting heavenward glance – "and then there was Jack. He was a school friend of Patrick's, and suddenly we clicked."

Cautiously I said, "But do you actually want to marry him?"

She examined her coffee cup for a long moment without answering, prodding the sugar sachet that had come with it. "Ah, now there's a question." She raised her head and gave me a long, quizzical look.

We ordered more coffees, and then she leaned forward over the table. "So what's your story Mike?"

Ha. What was my story? I started to reflect, then suddenly it seemed incredibly simple.

"You could say it all started here, really. At Falmouth, I mean. I used to see that girl, Trina, and I wanted to get to know her, but I didn't know how to. I felt as if there was an invisible barrier blocking my way. And once I recognised it, it seemed immovable. Same thing happened every time I met someone I liked. I couldn't break it down. Years passed, and all my friends got themselves paired up, but I never did. Pathetic or what?"

She waited, so I added, "When I finally met Sandy, my wife, I just felt grateful that she was willing to give me the time of day. I smiled ironically. "Talk about marry in haste. Or live together in haste, anyway."

She scrutinised me for a moment. "Well, obviously you're nothing to write home about in the looks department, and as for your personality, well … should we just call it a personality deficit?" She paused theatrically. "I think I see the problem, Mr Stanhope."

We sat staring at each other for a moment, then we simultaneously broke into suppressed laughter. I said, "Maybe I should fetch out the violins."

From coffees we graduated to a hamburger lunch, chatting in a more relaxed way about our life histories. I asked her if she had ambitions beyond Latimer's.

"Probably not. I'm very settled there, and they're a great crew. Bob Latimer took me under his wing when I transferred over there from Truro, and they've promoted me repeatedly. It might not be that long before I'm running the marketing department."

"Do you like the logistics world?"

"Do I like it? It's more or less in the blood now. It's hard to imagine working in any other business."

"Well, it's a big part of our lives that we have in common."

She looked a little uneasy at this – reminding me that the one thing absent from the conversation was any sense of where we now stood with each other. We were behaving like a long-established couple, yet we were barely a couple at all.

Finally, as more coffees arrived, I sat back and looked at her. "I wasn't sure if you would want me to come on this trip. I didn't know what to think."

"Probably that I was being a pain."

"Of course not."

"I probably was. Anyway, I'm glad you did come."

I searched for the right words. "I've never been in this position before – that's all. I don't know the rules."

She stared at her coffee again, toying with the teaspoon. "Nor do I."

Finally we paid and left the restaurant. The sky had turned leaden, and heavy drops of rain were already falling on us by the time we reached the car. We sat without speaking for a moment, staring through the windscreen as the flat landscape collapsed into a distorted blur.

I reached out and took her hand, and that electrical connection instantly sparked between us. We stayed like that for a long moment.

* * *

We said little as she drove me back to Truro. As we approached the station I said, "The way things are shaping up with Latimer's, I'll probably be down here again in a few weeks' time."

"Good." She said it with emphasis.

"I don't know …" I tailed off. I wasn't sure what I didn't know.

She said, "I've got some thinking to do. I need to work things out."

"OK."

I probably sounded disconsolate, because she immediately said, "I will, I will." And as I prepared to get out of the car she leaned over and kissed me briefly on the lips. "See you soon, yes?"

2012

It became almost a hobby, tracking Sasha down. The more I looked, the less I found, and the whole thing turned into a challenge: if the woman I'd seen wasn't her, what in fact had happened to her?

The people at Polperro would tell me nothing. If they still had records, they weren't sharing them with me. The internet was worse than useless. It gave no clue that she had ever existed. It was months before I even discovered her surname: Hawkins. I soon learned this was a common name. Too many Hawkins, and none of them was mine.

Still, I launched a Facebook page and subscribed to various missing persons web sites. It brought no success, but I soon had several live threads in progress on forums and in chat rooms. I might not be getting any closer finding Sasha, but the search was almost becoming an end in itself.

It was only later that year that I started thinking laterally. I rummaged through news reports for the summer we'd first encountered each other, searching on "Hawkins" and looking for notable events – events that might prompt someone to disappear.

That was when I found it: the Newbury security van heist. It happened the very week we were at Polperro. Coincidence, I thought at first. I checked the names of the perpetrators, most of whom had spent many years in prison. No Hawkins among them.

Then I looked among the back-stories and deep-level investigations – and suddenly I had my answer. Terry Hawkins, a former police officer, had been a known associate of Simon Bartleby, who was reckoned to have masterminded the robbery. And Hawkins had disappeared forever during the week of the robbery.

Chapter 44

Rick Ashton rang me first thing on Monday. "Michael, good news my friend. It looks as though our new funding is in place."

I asked for details, but he was evasive. "The bean counters are still firming up the details," he said. "We'll be putting out a press release, but maybe not for a few days, so I'd be glad if you said nothing yet. I just thought I'd give you a heads-up."

"I appreciate it."

Actually, though, I wondered if this was just another delaying tactic. How long was I supposed to wait before this news was made official? Still, he'd presented me with the story from the horse's mouth, so I had to take him at his word. At least it released me from pursuing the lead in other directions – for the time being, at any rate.

* * *

I reviewed the work I'd taken on for Latimer's. I had to write a string of press releases, some of which meant contacting Latimer customers to get quotes and testimonials from them. Others were more routine, involving announcements of new depots or extra staff.

Unexpectedly, the work struck me as a refreshing change. It meant defining news from scratch – expressing it the way I wanted it expressed. In some ways it reminded me of creative writing, though of course the underlying stories had been fed to me. I wasn't allowed to make them up.

By lunchtime I had several themes going, and felt moderately pleased with my progress. It was the first time in an age that I'd actually felt enthused by what I was doing. Was this my true calling then? Not so much probing journalist as jobbing feature-writer? Or was it just that the whole endeavour was indirectly connected to Ashley Renwick?

I felt I'd earned a break. I reopened the email from Trina Markham, if that's who she was, and read it through several times more.

I quickly realised that my doubts about its authenticity had increased since the previous week. Phrases that had seemed merely evasive the first time round now struck me as downright contrived.

The hotel "was in a very pretty location, and made a good base for heading out to see the other wonders of Cornwall," I read. That sounded more like text from a travel guide than something written from lived experience. "I got to know a few of the other children there." Plausible, but it seemed oddly unemotional and barren of detail.

But what did this mean? Was the message not from Trina at all? If not, who would want to deter me from looking for her? And if it really was from her, why did it sound like a message written by numbers?

I did a web search on "Trina Powell" and "Catrina Powell", which I'd neglected to do last week. There were plenty of finds for both, and I trawled idly through a few of them. Several could possibly be the person who'd sent this email – except that the most likely ones seemed about as far away from a "private person" as you could get. There were photographs, discographies, profiles, comments, blogs. If people were prepared to share this much of their lives online, it seemed a reasonable bet that they would be happy enough to pick over childhood memories. Yet my Trina evidently wasn't.

I studied the photographs with particular interest. Did any of them bear the faintest resemblance to the Trina of my childhood – of whom I now had several photographs? The answer seemed to be a fairly convincing no. But then, if she was a private person, her picture probably wouldn't be on show in the first place.

What about the woman I'd crossed paths with at Euston a couple of years ago? Did any of these pictures remind me of her? The problem was that I didn't really remember her properly any more. At any rate, none of the images brought her back to my consciousness.

I wondered what I could do to keep the search alive. If this really was Trina and she genuinely didn't want to communicate with me, it would be discourteous of me not to take her at her word. But I was becoming increasingly convinced that it wasn't.

I opened a new email window, but I hesitated before I wrote anything. My initial thought was to send an apparently bland message with some trap in it – a reference to some fake memory that a false Trina wouldn't pick up on. If she bothered to reply, I might get confirmation that she was an impostor.

Then I dismissed the idea. It was too devious; it was childish. Quite the opposite, I would throw in something to prove to her who *I* was. My thoughts crystallised as I wrote.

> *This is a message for Trina*
>
> *I was delighted to receive the reply to my email last week.*
>
> *I realise I've been asked not to get into extended correspondence with you, and I don't want to seem as though I'm ignoring this.*
>
> *I just wanted to say this. I really am Mike Stanhope, and hope you might vaguely remember me from your time at the Fairmile. Nobody else has asked me to contact you, and I have no hidden agenda. My most vivid memory is of nearly walking into you one day, and of talking nonsense at you instead of just saying hello. Your mother gave us some lemonade.*
>
> *I admit I have wondered why you seem to have disappeared for all these years, but I realise it's not my business. I just wanted you to know what a big impression you made on me at the time. Being honest, at the back of my mind I also wondered whether I even registered on your radar. But perhaps you have already answered that.*
>
> *As I said in my previous message, I don't want to be a nuisance. After this you needn't ever hear from me again.*
>
> *With the very best of intent,*
> *Mike*

I felt slightly uneasy about the claim that there was no hidden agenda. There was, wasn't there? My original thought was to make some kind of editorial mileage out of all this: hardly an innocent motive. But I told myself not to be concerned; I would respect Trina's wishes. Assuming this really was her.

Overall, I was rather pleased with my message: nothing too heavy or demanding, just a barely coded indication that I thought the original reply wasn't from Trina, and a modest show of frankness. Yes, I was surely a writer. People just didn't appreciate me.

Chapter 45

In the afternoon there was a knock at the front door, and my policeman friend Dave Matthews stood grinning at me.

"Can I have your autograph please?"

It was his second-ever visit to the house, and this time it seemed the call was only semi-official. I led him through the lounge and out on to the patio, and waved him towards a rickety garden chair. The late summer sun still had surprising warmth in it.

"So you read the book then?" I said as he sat down.

"Indeed I did. Very impressive."

I looked warily at him. "And the list of mistakes …?"

"Too numerous to mention." He smiled, affirming that that he meant no malice.

"But you managed to struggle through it anyway?"

"Well, I could see what you were getting at."

I brought two coffees out to the patio. Dave was looking round at the modest climbing roses on the patio walls, but turned to me as I drew up a chair. "So why exactly did you want me to read your book? Apart from the ego boost, that is."

"Ah. Well. You might think this is a ridiculously long shot, but I've been wondering about the security van robbery aspect."

"Right."

"You'll realise it's loosely based on the real robbery around that time?"

He smiled ironically. "I picked up that much, yes."

"So in my story, one of the thieves gets away, and keeps back a significant amount of the loot. He stashes it somewhere for a rainy day."

"Right."

"Well, I have no idea if that's what happened in real life, but some people think it might be. So here's what I'm thinking. What if someone in the real world, someone connected to the real robbery, has read my book, and thinks I actually know where the stash is? Or at least, that I know where to find the people who could tell them? What if that's what's behind all these break-ins? What if they're trying to find out what I know?"

Dave looked at me for a moment. There was deep scepticism in his gaze.

"Well, I thought it was at least worth considering."

He gave one of his resonant laughs. "Life meets art, you mean?"

"There's a kind of logic to it, don't you think?"

He sat for a moment without replying, squinting against the sun as he reviewed this notion. Finally he said, "So how did these hypothetical people find out about your book?"

"I don't know. It's not exactly on the best seller list, but it's not a secret either. It's out there on the internet. You wouldn't necessarily find it unless you went looking for it, but let's just assume for a moment that someone did."

"OK, so what makes these people think this fictional story, which has completely different characters, locations and plot from the real events, has anything whatever to do with their own miserable lives?"

"I don't know. That's the weak point of this hypothesis. But just suppose there's just enough plausible detail to make them think I based it on reality?"

He shook his head. "I honestly don't know what to think about you, Stanhope. You get this idea that Janni Noble is responsible for your break-ins, so I go rummaging around looking into his life for you, and now you change tack completely and come up with this even more far-fetched scenario. What do you want me to say?"

I stretched, pushing my chair back. The metallic feet rasped on the concrete. "I'm sorry about Janni Noble, Dave. I got the wrong end of the stick about that. I should have thought it through properly before I raised it with you."

"Amateur detectives." He smiled dryly.

"I think this explanation really is much more plausible than the other one was. It just needs an imaginative leap."

"Ha! In my world we don't generally operate on the basis of imaginative leaps." He reflected a moment. "Not usually, anyway."

We sat in silence for a while, then I asked diffidently, "Do you think there really was a stash of loot that was never recovered?"

"Don't ask me, mate …" He broke off. "Ha! I get this. You're expecting me to go and find out for you. What am I, your unpaid researcher?"

"But it wouldn't be just for my benefit would it? If this really is true, the implications would go way beyond my book."

"So Stanhope cracks a case that defied the massed resources of the Met and the regional forces. Is that what you're saying? You've been reading too many thrillers, mate. Or rather writing them."

"I haven't cracked anything. I'm just thinking out loud, is all."

He seemed to consider for a moment. "OK, I'll grant you there's a slender thread of logic in what you say." I started to speak, but he waved a hand in admonition. "A very slender thread."

"So what are you thinking?"

"What am I thinking? Nothing, at this point. You're the one who set all this in motion. What happens next according to you?"

I laughed. "I have no idea. All I know is that if this is true, the people who are looking for the money presumably won't stop. They'll keep hassling me until they find out what I know. Which doesn't make me particularly happy, I can tell you." A new thought struck me. "Did I tell you my ex-wife also had a break-in? Not long after mine?"

"Coincidence."

"Or part of a pattern. I certainly wouldn't want to inflict any more of this kind of thing on her."

He gave me an assessing look. "So, what, you and I lay some kind of trap for them? Catch them red-handed? Is that the plan? I can definitely see that. Is it a scene for your next book?"

I sipped my coffee and considered. "All I'm thinking is, do you reckon you could find out if there really might be a stash from that robbery that was never recovered? At least that would be a starting point, wouldn't it? If there isn't, then this whole idea is a false trail."

He gave me a sardonic smile. "So you get what you wanted from me after all."

I lifted my arms in exasperation. "Give me a break!"

Chapter 46

Days stretched into a week, and there was still no news of Rick Ashton's new investment. How long was I supposed to wait before contacting him again? I kept giving myself one more day.

There had been no contact from Hunt Topham about the supposed book deal either. Possibly they were waiting for Annette to return from the US and take the lead, or more uncharitably, they were waiting to find out if I was still on Rick Ashton's Christmas card list.

As for my kidnappers, I'd seen no further sign of them. I wanted to believe this meant they'd given up on whatever mission they had, but I couldn't convince myself of this. Clearly they wanted something from me, and there was nothing to indicate that they'd found it yet. How long did I have to wait before I could feel safe again in my own home? I had no idea, but I had a strong suspicion it must be a lot longer than this.

My book had sold one more online copy. I wasn't rushing to celebrate. I'd had another review, too: "Well enough written, but it's hard to decide if it's a thriller or a bit of reportage. Underwhelming." Well, at least it was frank.

By now I should have been promoting it for all it was worth with tweets, blogs, social media postings – all means at my disposal. That had been my original plan, but I'd been slow off the mark. With the possible book deal now pending, I felt the whole project was in limbo.

Then Dave Matthews rang.

"I don't know why I go to all this trouble for you, but you might find some of this interesting."

"Drinks are on me for the foreseeable future then."

"Well, wait till you hear and you can judge for yourself. The first thing is yes, seemingly some of the haul from this robbery was never recovered. A lot of it was found at the farm where the arrests were made, but definitely not all of it.

"The press had a field day speculating about the value of the unrecovered stuff. You presumably know about that. The owners and insurers weren't saying much, even to the police, but from what I'm picking up, it was probably at least two million, so I think you can take that as fact. It may well have been quite a lot more. Some of it had no value except to the owners, but the thinking is that there will have been diamonds and jewellery amongst it. So the two million is probably just a bottom-end estimate."

"Well, it's a useful start."

"Next, I can confirm that one of the suspects disappeared. A man named Liam Stone. But you probably know that already."

"Yes, and there were reports that he was arrested in Australia, but got away."

"Well, someone who might have been Stone was arrested a few years later. Andrew Franklin. But nothing was proved, and the next thing anyone knew, he'd dropped back off the radar, never to be seen again."

"What about Stone's family?"

"His wife and daughter? I can't tell you anything about them."

Something about this turn of phrase made me prick up my ears. "You mean there's nothing to tell, or you're not allowed to tell me anything?"

"Read my lips, mate. I can't tell you anything about them." He paused meaningfully. "Don't forget, somebody blew the whistle on the robbers. It was never revealed who that was."

I decided to think this over later.

"Anything else?"

"The people in the robbery got varying prison sentences, but most of them are out now."

I sat for a moment thinking this through. Dave said, "Will that do you for now?"

"Well, I'm thinking that none of this contradicts my theory about who might be giving me grief. In fact it would fit in with all this."

"Yes it would," he said noncommittally, "but there's nothing whatever here to suggest that you're right."

"So what's your thinking?"

"No thinking at all at the moment. I'm just giving you some facts."

I thanked him and disconnected.

His evasiveness about the wife and daughter intrigued me. Was he implying that he knew what had happened to them, but couldn't share it? If so, that might suggest that they'd gone into witness protection – which would be logical if in fact it was Stone's wife who had tipped off the police about the robbery.

As to why she might have given him away, I could only speculate. Maybe their relationship had already been failing, and the robbery was the last straw.

Did Dave have enough professional clout to have found out about something as sensitive as this? I had no idea. If it was true, it would be rather different from my story, where the whole family emigrated together. Whether it had any significance for me, I couldn't decide.

* * *

Later the same day I had a call from Ashley. I'd made no attempt to contact her since I'd last seen her, so I was uncertain where our relationship was now supposed to be. But her opening gambit was on a rather different topic.

"Mike, this first press release you've written for us."

It hadn't occurred to me that she would be involved directly in the work I was doing for Bob Latimer. I wondered how it might affect the dynamic between us.

"What about it?"

"Well, it doesn't play very well from the point of view of web search optimisation. The repetition would probably mark us down."

Cautiously I said, "It's how I would expect to find it written. I get loads of stuff like this sent to me by other PR people all the time."

"Tell you what, I'll mark it up with the things I think need looking at from the web point of view, and I'll send it over to you."

"You mean you're giving me back my homework and telling me to have another shot at it?"

She laughed. "We're not getting sensitive about this are we, Mr Stanhope?"

"Huh!"

We chatted for a while longer, then in a lower voice she said, "I feel I should tell you something's come up with Jack."

Suddenly I was nervous. "What?"

"Well, he's broken his ankle quite badly. The poor guy was trying to beat the opposition single-handed at football on Sunday, and he fell awkwardly."

I waited. I could feel a punch line looming.

"The thing is, I've moved into his house full-time to help him with the basics. I'll probably be there for at least a month – maybe more."

Up to now I'd been assiduously resisting the thought of Ashley sleeping with Jack. I knew it must happen, but I seemed to take comfort from the fact that she still lived a relatively independent life. Suddenly, I had to confront the notion of her being with him all the time. It made their relationship much more real.

I said, "What do you want me to say?"

"Nothing. I just thought I should put you in the picture."

Wildly I said, "Don't get too settled there. You might never leave."

"Give me a bit of credit, Mike, for god's sake." An unfamiliar burst of impatience.

"Sorry, I shouldn't have said that."

She was silent for a moment, then said, "Maybe this is a chance for reflection."

"I don't want to reflect." I could hear the petulance in my voice. I needed to end this call as quickly as I could.

"I can see that. But I have to."

2012

It was lucky that I was such a hoarder. Football programmes from my childhood, raffle tickets from a dance, funicular rides on a holiday in Austria – I could pin them all down to the exact day: my life charted in ephemera.

It was months after I saw that woman at St Pancras that I connected her with the robbery. I'd accepted she wasn't Sasha, the girl from my childhood, but that was simply because she'd said she wasn't. How short-sighted was that? More to the point, I'd picked up a used ticket that she'd dropped, and the name on it wasn't hers. That seemed to confirm it. But what if she was using some other name?

I could scarcely believe my stupidity. I'd simply thrown that ticket away. But what if I hadn't?

Superfluous junk tended to get cycled through my "system". It was chucked in a box, then later shuffled and squirreled away in a cupboard. There was no order, no filing system – just junk. Finding that ticket took me two hours. But I found it.

Sarah Trent. A nice name. And "Sarah" was quite like "Sasha", wasn't it? If you wanted to change your identity, it would make good sense to pick a name quite like your real one. Less risk of giving yourself away if you answered to the old name without thinking.

Mind you, Hawkins didn't sound much like Trent, did it? But maybe she'd married and changed her surname.

All I had to do now was track down Sarah Trent.

Chapter 47

"It was all going so well," I told Joanna. "Then suddenly a broken ankle."

She smiled sympathetically and flopped down on her sofa. "You should have more faith. Or are you having second thoughts about it all?"

I'd been babysitting for the two of them. They seldom required this of me; Joanna probably doubted my competence in a child-related crisis. In practice, though, Jeremy had always proved himself splendidly self-reliant. On the rare occasions when I'd been called upon, all I'd had to do was chat to him about football for a while, watch a bit of television with him, then pour myself a glass of wine or two while he went to bed (or more probably went off to play computer games).

I said, "No, Ashley is fantastic. If I can make something happen with her, I will. It's not beyond the bounds of possibility."

"You seem to have come a long way since last time you talked about her." Joanna kicked off her shoes. "I thought things had been heading in the right direction since then."

"It looked promising – but now this."

John wandered in offering coffees, then wandered out again. Joanna said, "This thing with Ashley, I hope you don't mind me asking, but you and she, you're not actually, you know …"

"No, we're not actually." I smiled at her in silent exclamation. "In fact come to think of it, we've hardly done more than shake hands, to be honest."

"How splendidly old fashioned."

I didn't know whether conversations like this were legitimate or helpful, and in my past life I would have been far too precious to get drawn into them. These days I couldn't be bothered to worry. I simply hoped Ashley had some equivalent friend she could talk to. We hadn't yet reached the stage of mutual introductions – and perhaps, I thought disconsolately, we never would.

"What about the Markham family? Have you made any more progress with them?"

"Aha! Yes I have. Trina replied to my follow-up email."

She was impressed. "You should have told us straight away."

"Well, I had my doubts about whether it was really from her. I've sent her another message, and I'm waiting to see what she comes back with."

She nodded, then asked, "Standing back from this, do you feel now that you've been looking for this entire family, or is it really only Trina who interests you?"

It was a good question. After starting off by concentrating my search on the girl herself, I'd gradually persuaded myself I was more intrigued by the investigative puzzle as a whole. To some extent this had actually become the reality. Yet the more I'd relived that fleeting encounter with the girl herself, the more I'd realised just how much of an impact she'd had on me. Now that I'd had some personal contact with her, it was clear that she was once again the main focus of the search.

"I suppose if I'm honest, I'm more interested I her."

"So do you actually want this to be her? What will you do if it is? Do you want to meet her?"

I didn't answer that straight away. Finally I said, "In some ways that would be interesting, but I've started wondering whether I really do want to turn my memories into real life. I think it's a big question."

"Do you really mean that? After all this trouble and effort?"

I shrugged. "The trouble with the internet is that it doesn't let you forget. It prevents you from having your own version of the past. The real version is always there to contradict you. Sometimes it might be best not to dip into it."

Joanna, however, merely smiled mischievously. "But surely you must wonder in the back of your mind what became of that girl?"

I shrugged. "Maybe the back of my mind is where she belongs."

"You don't believe that. You should meet her. I think you'll regret it if you don't."

"Maybe."

Abruptly she changed tack. "Don't give up on Ashley. She sounds really good for you."

"I wasn't planning to."

"It's just … sometimes it's hard to change course mid-flight. She needs to work out how to do it."

"What makes you so wise?"

Ignoring that, she added, "And don't start worrying about her boyfriend. If he's not the man for her, it's not going to happen."

"If only life were that simple."

John came through and we finished our coffees, then I said my goodbyes and headed off home on foot.

But I didn't get there.

Chapter 48

You'd think after the last time that I would have been wise to it, but it's hard to keep your guard up all the time. Besides, this time it was very different.

Two streets away from my house, I was just coming level with the back of a parked Transit van when a figure appeared from the far side of it.

"Got a light, mate?" It was a youngish man in dark jeans and a sweater. I stopped dead, startled.

Before I had the chance to speak, two things happened at once. A second figure emerged from my left, perhaps from someone's front garden, and the rear doors of the van burst open. The two men closed in and grabbed me roughly by the arms, shoving me towards the back of the van, and I was flung on to the bare metal floor. Someone lifted my legs and shoved me all the way inside, and behind me I heard both men scramble in after me and the doors slam shut.

I tried to stand up, but a foot shoved me down again. "Just stay put, mate." Someone started the van's engine, reversed, pulled out and drove off calmly up the street.

I yelled "What the FUCK now?" but this prompted a savage kick in my side. It was shocking and humiliating, and tears sprung to my eyes.

"Shut up and speak when you're spoken to."

I shut up and waited.

The driver negotiated his way through a succession of side streets. I quickly lost all sense of where we were heading. I risked a glance at my captors, who were visible in the dim glow of a single interior light. Two of them were standing, holding themselves steady by the interior ribs of the van walls. A third was sitting on a wooden crate. As last time, they were hatted or hooded and nondescript.

I said, "Can I say something?"

"No."

"Can I sit up?"

I braced myself for another kick, but none came. There was no reply for a moment. "Go on then." So I struggled round into a sitting position, and managed to shuffle to the side of the van so that I could lean back against the wall. I massaged my ribs where I'd taken the kick. They were sore, but hopefully nothing worse. My shins were also smarting. I'd scraped them on the sill when I was first shoved inside, and I had a strong sense that they were bleeding.

Presently one of the men squatted down opposite me. The third remained standing, perhaps ready to administer the next kick if called upon. None of them spoke, which was more unnerving than if they had. They were coolly disciplined.

The journey seemed interminable. At times we sped up, evidently on major roads. At other times we stood still at junctions or traffic lights. I had an idea that we were crossing London rather than heading out towards the country. The pattern of our progress didn't seem to vary much.

In fact, we were probably on the move no more than forty or fifty minutes. Then we came to a stop and the driver put the van into reverse. I had the impression that we might be entering a driveway or a building. We came to a stop and the engine was switched off.

One of the men opened the back doors jumped down to the ground and another instructed me, "Out." I stood up stiffly and was hustled to the back of the van. I clambered clumsily to the ground, watched closely by all three.

We seemed to be in a small yard, but there wasn't enough light to see any detail. They shoved me in the direction of a wooden door, then down two flights of stone steps, along a corridor and round a corner.

They opened a door leading off the corridor and led me across a small room into another larger one. It had a scuffed bare board floor and there was little furniture apart from a couple of old upright chairs and a small wooden table with an old-fashioned desk lamp on it. One of the men pulled one of the chairs out and placed it about fifteen feet from the table. "Sit." I sat.

"Give me your phone."

Reluctantly I handed it to him. I had a feeling that this time I wasn't going to get it back.

He said, "Wait here," then followed the others out, closing the door behind him. I heard a heavy bolt being slid home on the other side.

* * *

A minute passed, then another. I fancied I heard the distant sound of a vehicle starting up – possibly the Transit van – but it was so muted that it might have been nothing.

I stood up and walked over to the door, which indeed proved to be bolted on the outside. I looked around. There was another door in the opposite wall, and a third beyond the desk. They were both locked or bolted and all were solidly built. I wasn't going to be breaking them open in a hurry. The only windows were high up and set back in the walls, and appeared to be covered over with plywood boards. The place was lit by two bare bulbs hanging from the ceiling.

I went back to the chair and sat down again, examining my surroundings more closely. It was a modest-sized space, perhaps thirty feet by twenty, and the walls were panelled in dark oak. It had the air of a disused Victorian board room or meeting room. On some walls there were lighter rectangles where a painting or mirror might once have hung. There was a Victorian fireplace in the centre of one wall, complete with mantelpiece and ornate surround.

I rubbed my shins, preferring not to check for blood. I sat there for a long time, unable to think what the hell to do next.

I checked my watch. It was coming up to one thirty in the morning: just two hours since I'd left John and Joanna. Was I supposed to stay here all night? Then what?

Two more hours passed before I found out. I spent most of that time pacing impatiently round the room, rattling the door handles and searching in vain for some other way to escape. I was tempted to start yelling, but I had the feeling that if this was likely to summon up rescue, my captors wouldn't have left me alone here.

In the end I sat down again and waited. And waited. Finally I heard steps approaching, and a key rattled in the door beyond the table. I stood up spontaneously, as if being on my feet would somehow arm me against whatever was about to ensue.

The door opened slightly, and I heard light switches flicking on and off. The main lights in the room went out and the desk lamp came on, casting a pool of light in my direction. Then a figure came in from beyond it and the door closed.

"Please don't get up, Mr Stanhope. Just stay where you are." It was the voice of a man in his fifties or sixties – a world-weary smoker's voice, with a thin patina of culture barely disguising the east London accent.

I sat down again cautiously as he drew out the other chair and sat down on the far side of the table, staring at me. He was directly behind the lamp, where I could barely see his features.

"I'm sure you know what this is about, Mr Stanhope, so shall we talk?"

Chapter 49

"I ought to apologise for the theatricals," he said. "This is all a bit too much like a spy movie, isn't it?"

I shrugged, saying nothing.

"The thing is, the lads checked all this out for me this morning, and found that if I sit here, you can't see me properly."

"So what?"

"Think about it, Mr Stanhope. We can have a nice friendly chat, and then you can go home and we can all live happily ever after. You don't know me – I'm just a ship passing in the night."

"Whereas?"

"You don't want me to spell it out, do you? Just be advised to stay exactly where you are. Over there you're safe and so am I. If you get to know me, it's an entirely different case. So don't be tempted to leap up and charge over here with all guns blazing." He laughed dryly. "Come to think of it, you don't actually have a gun – but I do. That's another thing you might want to think about."

I started to speak, but had to clear my throat first. "I hear you."

"Excellent."

There was a pause, then he said, "You've been talking to our friend Mr Stone, I believe."

Despite the circumstances, I felt a surge of adrenaline. He must mean Liam Stone, the vanished diamond robber. In that single question he appeared to have confirmed everything I'd been speculating over.

Mustering up what I hoped was a convincing show of incredulity, I said, "*What?*"

"I'm asking you about Mr Stone. He's no friend of mine, to be strictly accurate, but I'd very much like to get in touch with him. You can help me."

"You think so?"

He coughed briefly, then said, "The others were all for doing this the hard way, checking your files and all that bollocks. I told them we were wasting too much time. We don't have months to check through every bleeding letter and email you've sent your bank manager since nineteen ninety eight. I said let's just have a friendly little chat with the man himself." He paused. "So here we are."

Here was confirmation, if any were needed, that these were the people behind all the break-ins. At the moment this news brought me little consolation.

I waited a moment. I needed to give my next remark as much weight as I could summon. There was no mileage in making it sound like a throw-away line. I cleared my throat again.

"Look, I think there's a fundamental misunderstanding here. An absolutely basic mistake. If you'd come to me months ago and explained what you want, you could have saved yourself a lot of hassle and me a lot of grief."

"I don't think so, Mr Stanhope."

"Hear me out, please. The simple fact is that I don't know Liam Stone, I've never met him, he's never been in touch with me, and I know nothing about his life or his current whereabouts. Absolutely literally nothing whatsoever. You've read this all wrong. It's a total misunderstanding."

"Oh, I can't agree, Mr Stanhope. You know a lot about him, and in particular you know how to contact him. I would like you to share this information with me. In fact I won't be satisfied until you do."

I said nothing for a moment. I turned my head and stared at the shadowy shape of the Victorian fireplace as I tried to round up some coherent thought. Finally I looked back towards him and said, "Look, can I ask where you're getting this from? Should I assume it's my book?"

"That's correct."

"Right! Well you need to understand something. That book is total fiction. I made it up. I *invented* it. I'm a writer, for god's sake! That's what writers do. It isn't a true story about real people. I don't know anything about real people. It's fiction!"

He said nothing, but through the light beam I could see him uncross and re-cross his legs and adjust his position on his chair. "Give me some credit, Mr Stanhope. Your story is about an actual robbery that happened in the real world, a famous robbery. The whole world knows about it. You're hardly going to tell me you made it up."

"No, no." I could hear the urgent impatience in my voice. "I didn't invent everything, I just invented the back stories – the bits about what happened afterwards." I took a deep breath. "I took a real event, and hypothesised the detail. It's a well-established technique. Writers do it all the time."

"I've no doubt they do, but not in this case. You had inside knowledge, and I want you to share it with me."

I found myself almost laughing with frustration. "This is ridiculous! You're wasting your time and effort here. If I did know how to contact this man I might be tempted to tell you, but the fact is that I don't, so I can't. Please don't take offence when I say this, but read my lips: *I don't know him.*"

There was a long moment's silence. Briefly I thought I might have convinced him, but then he said slowly, "You seem determined to make this difficult for yourself, Mr Stanhope. Frankly I don't understand your misplaced loyalty. When I said we were having a friendly chat, I don't think you weren't following my meaning. It can only be friendly if you tell me what I need to know." He paused. "Am I making myself clear?"

I resisted answering. My mind was racing as I searched for ways to break out of this loop. I said, "Can I ask which parts of my book have convinced you that I know these people?"

The question seemed to puzzle him, which I thought was probably good. He said, "Which parts? What are you getting at?"

"Well look, I've told you I invented a lot of the details in the book. If you can tell me which of those details you think are true, I might be able to tell you where they actually came from. Then you might see how I came to make them up."

He said nothing. I said, "Please! Just humour me."

"But if I pick out details, that just gives you the chance to think up some plausible explanation for them."

"Oh for god's sake! One of us is getting the wrong end of the stick here, and it's not me. We're going round and round in circles. If you really want to find those jewels or whatever they are, you might as well let me go home and try some other approach."

He seemed to consider for a while. "All right, what about that hotel? You didn't make that up, did you?"

"Yes! I based that on my own life. I stayed in a hotel in Falmouth when I was about twelve years old. I switched it to Polperro for the book."

"Ha! But we happen to know that Liam and Martina were booked into a hotel on the south coast. He told me that himself. It was all part of his game plan to get them away." He paused reflectively. "And it worked, didn't it?"

I stared over at him in disbelief. By pure luck I'd apparently guessed this part of the story correctly. Quietly I said, "I don't know anything about that. If it's true, it's a complete coincidence. What I put in the book came straight out of my head."

"Yeah, yeah, you said that before. You're beginning to sound like a cracked record. I suppose you invented Australia too."

"Yes!" I stopped myself and reflected. "I realise Stone apparently did go there, but I didn't know that when I wrote the book."

"You made it up."

"Exactly."

He gave a rasping cough and cleared his throat noisily. "If you want to take all night over this, that's up to you. But you're going to tell me how to contact him one way or the other, so you might as well get on with it and stop wasting everybody's time."

Chapter 50

The man stood up, pushing his chair back.

I said, "You're leaving then?"

"I need a decent night's sleep. I can do without these midnight shenanigans." He started to turn.

"So what next? You expect me to sit here indefinitely?"

"My colleagues will be back to talk to you." He adopted a more confidential tone. "I strongly advise you to tell them what they need to know."

More than a little desperately I shouted, "I can't tell them anything any more than I can tell you! How many times do I have to say it?" I stood up abruptly and took a step towards him. "For god's sake, can we just stop this nonsense and go home?"

"Sit down!" His sudden vehemence cut through the space. "I can fire this gun in here and no one will bat an eyelid. Please don't think I won't."

Beyond the pool of light I could see his arm thrust forward, pointing a handgun at me. It wasn't a bluff.

I sat down slowly and risked saying, "If I really did know what you're asking, it wouldn't do you much good shooting me before I told you."

He lowered his arm. "Leave me to worry about that." He turned again to the door.

As he pulled it open I said, "Can I ask you something?"

He half-turned back. "What would that be?"

"How did you know about my book?

He paused and gave a chuckle. "My nephew read it. Thought it might appeal to me. Very helpful of him, I must say." He seemed to reflect. "I've got a question for you, too. How did you get on to Liam Stone in the first place? I thought we'd looked everywhere for him."

"I keep telling you I didn't get on to him. If you couldn't find him, what the hell makes you think I could?"

"That's what we're going to find out."

* * *

A good hour passed. I spent much of it roaming around the room again in a state of increasing alarm. The man had left the desk lamp switched on and the top lights off, so the place was still illuminated by an eerie glow. I pointed the lampshade downwards so that it wouldn't shine in my face.

I rattled the doors and poked at the wood panelling, hoping in vain to find a cupboard or even some hidden exit. I was also on the lookout for weapons, though I found it hard to imagine using one against another human being. In any case, apart from the meagre furniture and the lamp, nothing suggested itself.

Eventually I sat down on the chair again, then abandoned it and sat on the floor next to the fireplace, leaning on the wall with my legs stretched in front of me. The air was cold and slightly dank, but they'd left me with my jacket. In any case, that was the least of my problems. I could hardly feel relaxed knowing I was soon likely to be facing the thugs who had brought me here.

Footsteps insinuated themselves into my consciousness. They grew louder and I heard the outer door being thrust open, followed by the door I'd come in by. My three original captors entered, and one of them came over to me.

"Get up and sit on that chair."

"Or what?"

"Grow up. Do it."

I rose stiffly to my feet and walked to the chair.

"Sit."

I sat. He contemplated me – a man probably in his late twenties, with a jacket collar folded up over his unshaven chin and a beanie hat pulled down over his forehead. Once again, I was struck by how difficult I would find it to identify him later.

Without warning he raised his right arm and slapped me ferociously across the face. The effect was shattering. I felt as if my neck must be dislocated, my head knocked clean off my shoulders. Stinging, smarting, shocking pain – all that in one swift blow. I fell with the chair to the ground, jarring my elbow and shoulder as I landed, and lay there with my head ringing. I felt I was going to die.

Distantly I heard the man saying to me, "You need to understand this is not a joke."

I could hear them muttering among themselves while I fought to rejoin the normal world. I could still move my neck. Nothing seemed to be broken. But what hope did I have if they were going to repeat this? What could I possibly tell them to make them stop?

"Get up."

I managed to gasp, "What, so you can do the same thing again?"

"Just get up."

I rose on to my knees and stayed there for a long moment. My head was still ringing. I stood up gingerly and looked at the three of them.

"Sit."

I sat.

"You need to give us some information. You know what the man wants. Just tell it to us, then you can go on your merry way. All right?"

It was about the longest statement I'd heard any of them make so far, but you could still hardly call it a meaningful dialogue.

"I hear what you're saying."

"We're going to leave you for a little while to think about it. When we get back, we'll be staying till we get a result." They started to move towards the door, then in sudden inspiration I said, "Toilet."

"What?"

I drew a deep breath and cleared my throat. "There must be a toilet here. Can I go to it? You won't enjoy talking to me in here if I have to piss and crap all over the place."

They seemed to think about this for a moment, then the speaker said, "Get up."

He shoved me towards the door, through the outer room and into the corridor. A little way down there was another door into a tiny toilet. He pushed open the door with exaggerated courtesy and switched the light on. "Hurry up."

I shoved the door shut behind me and looked desperately around. There was just a single high window in one wall – a vent really, and far too small to climb through. No weapons suggested themselves. I looked at the WC. It was relatively modern – which is to say maybe forty years old, not Victorian – but there was hardly any water in the bowl, just a disreputable brown residue at the bottom.

I leaned forward against the wall above it, breathing deeply and trying to get on top of the immense throbbing in my head. Then I realised I was looking at my own face in a small mirror. It was red and raw, and there was drying blood on one eyebrow. I looked down instead, and found myself staring at the white porcelain lid of the cistern. On a whim I lowered my hands and tried moving it. It wasn't screwed down. I straightened my back and lifted it off.

There was no water in the cistern. The ballcock lay limply on the bottom at the end of its metal arm. Was there a weapon amidst all this?

A voice from somewhere down the corridor shouted, "Hurry up in there." I lifted my head and called, "Just a minute."

Normally you'd need tools to dismember a piece of engineering like this. I had no tools and no time. I put the cistern lid down on the toilet seat, grabbed the metal shaft with both hands and wrenched it with all my might. It came away from the inlet valve as if it had never been attached, cutting into my fingers painfully, and I was left holding a strip of metal about a foot long, with a plastic ball the size of a grapefruit on one end.

I waited for a second, wondering if this manoeuvre had been heard outside. Apparently not. But how was I to smuggle a ball on a stick out of the room? Or was I going to rampage out of the toilet like a deranged Mr Punch, smiting my captors on the head with it? Even in my panicked state I recognised the absurdity of this.

I could see only one solution. I leaned my back against the door, placed the ball under my foot, then jumped on it as hard as I could with both heels, faking an explosive bout of coughing as I did so. The ball shattered, leaving only tattered shards still attached. I hastily replaced the cistern lid, stuffed the metal strip up the sleeve of my jacket and opened the door. My captors led me back to the big room, and I made it with my new toy intact. And then they were gone.

Chapter 51

I eased my hard-won trophy out from my sleeve and considered it. It was a thin metal tube, with the remnants of its previous fixings at either end. Not really a weapon, more a device. But for what?

My first and only thought was the heavy planked door we'd come in by. During our to-ings and fro-ings I'd been vaguely aware of seeing various holes and other marks in its surface. I pointed the lamp over towards it and went to examine it more closely.

It had clearly been altered, patched and repaired repeatedly over its long life. There were screw holes and marks where latches and other fittings had been attached and then removed. At some point, someone had evidently made the strange decision to attach a bolt outside rather than inside the room.

There was one larger hole in particular that interested me. It was at the right height for a doorknob, and presumably had once housed one. I put my eye to it, and could see two slits of light from the adjoining room, one above the other. I was hoping against hope that between them was the bolt.

Experimentally I poked my metal strip through into the hole and tried applying a levering action. If my logic was right, in theory this would prise the bolt open. Nothing seemed to happen, but when I jabbed the metal strip in and out, I could hear a rattling sound on the other side, suggesting that whatever was obstructing it was loose. Hopefully that was the bolt. I just had to get some purchase on it.

I tried the other end of the strip where the ballcock had been, but it was too wide to fit through the aperture. Then I tried pulling the door towards me and pushing it away, hoping to gauge the point where the bolt would not be pressing on either the door or the catch on the outside wall. After some trial and error I got a sense of the right point, and worked out how to wedge the door in that position with my foot. And then I resumed levering. What worked in my favour was that it didn't seem to be a round bolt, more of an ancient flat thing, possibly made of wrought iron. This meant it seemed to present a reasonable area for me to work on.

I kept poking and levering for an age without sensing any useful result, but then suddenly I felt a definite movement at the other end. When I checked, the door was still resolutely closed, but I felt encouraged. Feverishly I continued, constantly aware that the three men could return at any time.

For a while there was no result, then I detected another of those sudden movements as I caught a sweet spot. More incremental movements; more time; then abruptly I felt the bolt shoot the whole way open, just as if it had never really wanted to be closed in the first place. Scarcely daring to believe it, I was able to push the door outwards.

Without waiting even a second I barged through the outer room and into the corridor. And then I heard voices. My captors were on their way back.

Wildly I looked around. I had no idea where the corridor led in the other direction: presumably further into the building. I had no intention of finding out. Keeping as quiet as I possibly could, I ducked into the toilet again and eased the door nearly shut behind me. The three men passed me, and I heard their exclamations as they entered the outer room and saw the open inner door.

Timing was now everything. I waited an agonising moment for them to go into the main room. It must be evident to them that I'd escaped, but I sensed that they would feel the need to make sure. When I was certain they'd gone in as far as they were going to go, I slipped round the toilet door and headed off as fast as I dared in the direction they had come from.

I was just rounding the corner of the corridor when I heard a shout behind me. "Hey! He's here!"

I bolted along the rest of the corridor and stumbled up the steps at the end: two flights, and my head was now throbbing violently. It was only the thought of capture that kept me on my feet.

At the top was a wooden door, which mercifully was partly open. I burst past it and into the small yard where we'd arrived. It was very dark, and at first I couldn't see any way out. What I didn't need now was to come up against locked gates.

As I got my bearings I could hear feet on the stone steps, only moments behind me. I stepped away from the door, getting a clearer view of the yard, and now saw a car parked in the middle. And beyond it, wondrously, was an open gateway with street lights beyond it.

I was tempted to sprint for it, but I worried that I might not make it. Then all this would have been for nothing. Instead, I ducked down beyond the car.

The door was flung open with a bang as the first of the three emerged, followed quickly by the other two. Like me, no doubt, they needed to get used to the dark. I could hear them hesitating, presumably unsure whether I'd made it to the gateway or hung back and hidden.

"Check the street!" one of them instructed, and I heard two sets of footsteps running across the yard. I glanced around, trying to gauge whether there was any other exit. All I could see was a shadowy brick wall opposite the one we'd emerged from, with a hint of windows and perhaps closed doors.

Now I could hear the one who'd hung back approaching the car. He would surely walk all the way round it and find me cowering here. I had to move. I launched myself towards what turned out to be a wooden door, and pushed on it as quietly as I could. Thankfully it opened inwards, but it gave out a rasping creak as it did so. I shoved my way inside.

I could hear the man outside immediately following the sound, but instead of lunging further into the building I crammed myself behind the door. As he hurried in after me I squeezed round it and back out into the yard.

What happened next was pure instinct. I pulled the door nearly shut behind me and hovered outside, waiting. The instant I judged that the man was about to pull it open, I gave it a massive shove with my foot. I heard a muffled cry from within, followed by a string of expletives.

I grabbed the edge of the door, pulled it slightly towards me, then rammed it inward a second time. This time it didn't connect so well, but there was another cry from within.

It was enough. I sprinted the few yards back to the car and ducked down again on the far side of it. I heard a single set of footsteps running back from the gateway to the door. There was muttering as the two of them exchanged notes.

I glanced around. I couldn't expect to separate them so easily again, so what now? The yard appeared to be lit only by hazy moonlight, and the wall opposite the door was in the shade. Maybe that was my best hope. I half-crawled over to it, then stood up cautiously and started to edge my way along it in the direction of the gateway.

The two men were standing at the doorway where I'd hidden, still muttering, but didn't seem to have spotted me. I kept on edging towards the exit. In the back of my mind I remembered the kidnapping in Streatham. At the first sign of danger my captors had given up and fled. They were hired hands; they weren't committed to their task. I was hoping the same would apply now.

I was nearly at the gateway when I saw the third man. He was facing me only a few yards away, in the middle of the entrance, but had not apparently seen me yet. However, I couldn't pass him without revealing myself.

There was a shout from across the yard. "Anything out there?"

He turned and looked over towards the voice, and in that moment I lunged forward and rammed into him as hard as I could. My head actually knocked against his in the impact, but not very hard.

I had no advantage except surprise, but it helped me slightly. I felt sure I had no chance of winning a fight with him, but all I wanted was a few seconds' grace. While he was still recoiling I shoved him again as hard as I could with both hands, and he stumbled slightly.

I sprinted for it.

I was in a narrow street flanked by nondescript warehouses and ageing commercial premises. I could hear the man I'd rammed recovering immediately and heading after me. Had this all gone wrong at the last hurdle?

To my joy, I realised that there was a substantial road junction not far ahead. I could see traffic bustling past across the end and belisha beacons winking at me. Surely salvation must lie there? I just needed to reach it.

I was terrified of stumbling; it could make the difference between capture and freedom. I felt as if someone else's limbs were spiriting me along. The man I'd shoved was barely two paces behind me. Thankfully I was still ahead as I reached the junction, and I sensed rather than heard the pursuing footsteps slackening.

I stumbled out on to a broad pavement flanking the main road. I had no more energy. Slowing to walking pace I made my way over to the kerbside railing and leaned heavily against it, gasping to catch my breath. I glanced over my shoulder, worried that my pursuers might be preparing to grab me, but I saw no sign of them.

Then I realised why. About a hundred metres down the road was a police car, parked at an odd angle with its blue light flashing in the dark. Never had I seen a more reassuring sight. I dragged myself away from the railing and jogged towards it, then slowed to a walk. Two policemen in high-visibility jackets were in the process of breathalysing a man leaning against a parked car. One of them glanced at me but paid me no attention. I checked behind me, but my pursuers had melted away.

I'd escaped. I could hardly believe it. I felt exhausted and battered, but also euphoric.

Across the road I now saw the welcoming sign of an Underground station. No chance of any trains at this time of night, but it seemed a joyous assertion of normality. I reached into my jacket, and realised with relief that I still had my wallet. All I needed now was a taxi.

2012

There might be disbelief, angry resentment, recrimination, tears. Her father might fly into a rage. But somehow it had to be done; she had to hand over the pieces she had recovered, and explain to him what they were.

In the end she took him to the pub. He wouldn't be able to bawl her out there, to make a public spectacle of himself. Even he would see that. Glancing around first, she opened her purse. "Why don't you check out what I've got in here?"

He peered over at the two jewels, then looked up at her. "What the hell is this?"

"I've just been to fetch them from Polperro. I hid them."

He looked at her for several seconds, taking in what she'd just said. In the end, it was the tears that came first. "You HID them? Good god." He stared down again, then up. "Is there more?"

"Quite a bit more, yes."

"Jesus H Christ."

Back at his bungalow, she explained how it had all played out. He displayed some anger now, but not much; some recrimination, but it was quickly set aside. Chiefly he seemed amazed at her nerve. "I can't believe you went back for them all on your own."

She became businesslike. "They're all yours now, Dad. I don't want anything to do with them. I don't have the first idea how to turn them into cash, and I don't want to know."

He was rallying even as they spoke. She could already see a spark of his former vigour returning. "Yes, yes, that's fine. Leave it to me."

"You realise these will probably be on a watch list, even after all these years? You can't just wander into a jeweller's shop and sell them – especially in a tiny place like Rockhampton."

"I know, I know. I'll have to go down to Brisbane. I just need to get my bearings. I'll start with a couple of stones, and keep the rest back until I know the score."

"OK, so long as you understand the implications."

He nodded vigorously, then sat back in his chair and beamed at her. "Jesus, Sash!".

Chapter 52

Dave handed me a mug of coffee and sat down. For once he seemed genuinely concerned, and had throttled back his usual sarcasm.

I shrugged. "I'll live."

We were in an interview room at his police station. I'd rung his mobile first thing in the morning and explained what had happened. He'd listened without comment, then suggested I make my way over there. "Strictly speaking it's not our case, but let me deal with that."

He'd been disappointed initially that I hadn't reported my kidnapping to the police as soon as I'd escaped. "We would have had more of a head's start then."

I'd shaken my head. "Can you imagine how long it would have taken me to explain all this from scratch to someone I didn't know? By the time I got away from that place I'd had quite enough for one night."

He seemed to accept this. "All the same, the local station could have sent someone round straight away to take a look at the building."

"What, just on my say-so?"

He couldn't really answer that, so I added, "Trust me, they wouldn't have found anyone there, or anything incriminating. These people are professionals."

"And you know all about that, do you? I suppose you writers have an inside track on the criminal mind."

I gave him a reproachful look and he let it drop.

Once he'd got my report sorted out, I asked him, "Who do you think these people are?"

"From what you say, it's almost certainly someone connected to the original robbery. The older guy could be one of the gang, out of prison and looking for payback. He thinks you know where Stone is, and wants to try and get some of the loot back from him. Mind you, after all these years he's probably on a hiding to nothing."

I thought about this. "Yes, but in my novel the man who gets away doesn't cash in the haul until years later. If this guy thinks that's what really happened, he might think there's still enough of it around to make all this worthwhile."

Dave nodded his assent. "Of course, this doesn't have to be one of the people who were caught. There might have been more than one who got away. This could be someone completely off our radar, someone who's been biding their time, keeping on the lookout all these years for any clue about what happened to Stone."

"So what will you do?"

"We'll probably have a look at the likely suspects, and maybe check what sort of alibis they have." He hesitated. "I have to say, kidnapping and false imprisonment can be difficult to prove if the victim has escaped and can't reliably identify the perpetrators. Especially if there's no solid evidence."

"What about the rest of his crew?"

"The younger guys? They sound like some kind of 'gun for hire' mob. Somehow they've got themselves on your friend's payroll."

I asked him if he'd found out anything about the premises where I'd been held.

"It's an old candle factory. It's been scheduled for demolition for years, but there's been an ongoing dispute about a possible listing of some of the buildings. You were in the office complex, in a meeting room."

"Funny place to hold meetings – underground."

"They must have been a secretive lot, these candle makers."

* * *

I parked my car warily when I got back to Thornton Heath. The first kidnapping had been in broad daylight, so there was no knowing when these persistent people would make their next move. With relief, I found a space close to my house and hurried to the front door.

Dave had told me he'd renewed his request for my local police to keep their eye out for me, but this had clearly counted for little so far, and I was nervous. As soon as I was indoors I rang the joiner who'd repaired my front door, and arranged for him to come and fit extra bolts front and back. It was hard to believe I was being forced to adopt this fortress mentality, but the simple fact was that I needed to feel secure.

Having sorted that out, I sat at my computer trying to think about work. However, I couldn't stop my brain from playing back the night's events repeatedly. What the hell would have happened if I hadn't escaped? How much casual violence would those people have been prepared to inflict on me before accepting that I simply had nothing to tell them?

I wondered if I could have improvised some tale in order to get them off my back. Possibly, but I had a strong feeling it would only have bought me a respite, not release. And what kind of fury would I have unleashed when they'd realised I'd misled them?

As I thought through these events yet another time, I remembered the question I'd asked the ringleader as he left. Where had he heard about my book? From his nephew, he'd said. Was that significant? Was it a lapse on his part? Who could his nephew be?

I opened the publishing web site and checked my account. Twenty-three copies of my book had now been sold. I suspected that at least half of these were sales to my friends, and probably a lot of the others were recommendations by my friends to their friends. That just left a handful of sales to unknown people.

Who were these? I checked the small print, which confirmed that the publisher was not willing to provide me with that information, though presumably Dave Matthews and his team could demand it as part of their investigation – assuming they saw this as a genuine lead.

My mind flicked back to the last visit I'd paid to the Park Reading Group. Amelia had told me Harry had bought my book as soon as it was published. Could he be the nephew? He was probably the right sort of age and he came from the East End, though that seemed pretty thin evidence. Not much to go on, but something.

I didn't know Harry's surname, but presumably Eric, the reading group chairman, must have it somewhere. I scrolled through my contact list and dialled his number. No answer. I'd have to try again later.

Chapter 53

"Michael How do you fancy a day out in the country?"

Phone calls from the head of a national parcels company, previously a rarity, these days seemed a regular occurrence, but each one held its own agenda. What was it this time?

Cautiously I told Rick, "Sounds intriguing. What's the deal?"

"Martha and I are holding a little party. Just a few selected guests. Since you and I have been so much in touch lately, I thought you might enjoy it." He hesitated. "Annette Braddock will be there, so you could hook up with her again too."

Journalists simply didn't get invited to top men's private events – not unless they were also personal friends, which clearly I wasn't. Presumably Rick saw it as a way to keep me on side. His hint of further contact with Annette Braddock underlined this. Presumably she wasn't a close friend of his either, so he must have invited her specifically to orchestrate a meeting between us. I was tempted to decline, but I was too intrigued.

"Sounds fun. Where and when?"

Rick explained that he lived in rural Oxfordshire, and the party would take place there the following Saturday. He gave me his address. "Bring your wife or partner," he said fulsomely.

After the excitements of the last few of days I'd neglected to follow up either the Vantage Express story or my would-be book contract. Keeping safe and intact seemed higher priorities. But life went on, and one way or another this trip might move things forward.

* * *

I rang Eric at the reading group again, and this time he answered. I asked if he knew Harry's surname, and he told me it was Slater.

The name meant nothing to me, but I decided to check back on the security van story. Maybe one of the people involved was called Slater. I opened my browser and pored over facsimile news reports from the period, blogs about the theft, mentions in forums. The name Slater didn't come up in any of them. None of the convicted robbers had that name; nor did any named investigating officers, suspects or hangers-on.

All the same, I thought it might be a clue, so I rang Dave Matthews and ran it past him. It seemed he was maintaining his non-sarcastic tone. He just said, "Could be useful. Leave it with me."

Who else had read my book? Well, of course Amelia had. Could she be connected to all this? In theory yes, but it seemed unlikely.

And two dozen literary agencies had read it – or at least had read the synopsis and sample chapters I'd sent them. Or they claimed to have done. But it was plain that they wouldn't tell me the names of their readers. Even asking them all would be a task beyond anything I could attempt. I wondered if I should raise this aspect with Dave, but it seemed too fanciful to contemplate.

The trouble was that once you accepted the hypothesis about someone connecting my book to the real robbery, the ripples extended far and wide. And this was before even two dozen electronic copies had been sold.

*　*　*

Then Ashley rang me. "I can't speak for long. I just wanted to tell you that I've broken it off with Jack."

"What?"

"I've told him I don't want to marry him."

A jolt ran through me. What did I feel? Relief? Elation? Fear? Whatever it was, I was aware that nothing could be quite the same now.

"What did you tell him?"

"I just said I didn't think it was going to work. It was the safe option, not the right option." She was speaking in a low voice, perhaps aware of others in the office around her. "I just thought you should know."

"How did he react?"

"He said he already knew what I was going to say."

"How come?"

"Oh, he's been picking up the vibes for a year at least. We just haven't been facing up to it." She paused. "I haven't, anyway."

"I see."

She seemed to be considering something, then said, "I also think he knew you were on the scene. Patrick or my mum must have mentioned it."

"Charming."

"Living here is like living in a goldfish bowl. Did I not mention that?"

"I hope …" I hesitated, measuring my words. "I hope he realised nothing had actually happened between us?"

This immediately seemed to annoy her. "For god's sake Mike! That's hardly the point, is it?"

"No!" I cursed myself silently. "Of course it isn't."

There was a silence, then I said, "So how has this left things?"

"Well, I'm staying on at Jack's for a few weeks. I promised him I'd see him through this injury of his, and I don't see any reason not to. It's the least he deserves."

"And he's OK with that, is he?"

"I don't know. He says he is. Anyway, that's what I'm doing."

"I'd like to see you."

"Well, you're due over here at Latimers' in a few weeks' time. Shall we leave it at that?"

I should have been ecstatic, but instead I felt deflated. Somehow I'd managed to play this wrongly. Was I never going to learn how to handle relationships? In theory Ashley was now free to pursue her involvement with me, yet the first thing I'd done in this new phase of her life was irritate her.

I hadn't even found the opportunity to tell her about my latest kidnapping experience, which I knew would fascinate her. As for the pipe dream of taking her to Rick Ashton's party as my partner, it wasn't going to happen. Not that I'd seriously expected it.

Chapter 54

I walked cautiously to my car on Saturday morning, peering around in search of kidnappers in the late summer sun. None in sight; nothing out of the ordinary.

I'd spent the past few days in a frenzy of activity, trying to catch up with work I'd neglected. I'd dismissed phone calls and ignored the usual torrent of incoming emails. I'd learned from long experience that this was the only way to maintain any sense of control. At the end of the week I had completed an article and I was all set to write up another. I felt I'd earned myself a day out.

I navigated my way across south London to the M25, then headed north up to the M40. Rick Ashton lived in a small village north of Oxford, and the journey took well over two and a half hours.

His house was a rambling stone-built period property with a semi-circular driveway in front of it, surrounded by trees and fields. I was expecting to see a clutch of guests' cars, but in fact there was just a solitary Jaguar in front of the double garage – no doubt Rick's own car. Puzzled, I drew up next to it and scrunched my way over the gravel to the front door.

Rick answered the door in person, dressed in white shirtsleeves and clearly not in party mood. He looked surprised and faintly annoyed. "Michael – what are you doing here? Didn't you get my messages?"

"Oh god – you cancelled."

"Yes, I sent you a couple of emails and left you a voicemail as well. Don't you pay attention to any of this stuff?"

"I'm so sorry." I couldn't really see why I should be apologising – I was the one who'd just driven eighty pointless miles and used up half my Saturday in the process. But he looked so aggrieved that I couldn't stop myself.

He seemed to reflect for a moment, then said, "You'd better come in." He waved me up the step and patted me on the back as I passed, apparently trying to recover his usual avuncular style.

"Through here." He directed me into a large sitting room decorated in a comfortable period style. "Can I get you a drink or something?"

I shook my head. "Don't worry. I'm sorry to intrude." I looked at him for some cue, but saw nothing. I said, "Do you mind me asking what happened?"

"What happened?" He frowned, then seemed to reach a decision. "The bank's going to pull the plug on Monday, unless I can whistle up some funding mighty quick. I'm damned nearly out of options, mate. I've been on the phone all the morning with backers and advisors and the other directors – you know the kind of thing. I'm going off to a meeting in Birmingham in a minute."

He ran his fingers through his hair, then added, "I don't care what you write in your paper, but just do me a favour and leave it till Monday afternoon. By then we'll have a decision one way or the other." He thought some more. "I don't know if you realise this, but I've got a lot of my own money tied up in Vantage. If the company goes down, I'm fucked."

A phone rang in another room. "Bear with me, I need to take that." He hurried out.

I glanced around, waiting. I could vaguely hear Rick's voice, and the call showed no sign of ending. I sat down in a large winged armchair facing the window, and picked up a picture book from the coffee table next to it. Britain from the skies.

* * *

The doorbell jangled, and I heard Rick mutter his apologies on the phone and stride through to the front.

"Andy! What are you doing here?"

From the outside I heard the visitor saying, "I've had enough of all this, Rick. I want that tape."

"Come on, mate …"

"Don't 'come on mate' me. I've had enough of this bullshit." The visitor's voice grew louder as he strode into the hall: not a voice I recognised. It had a faintly Australian twang, but not as strong as Rick's. He came to a stop outside the room where I was sitting. "I don't know why this didn't occur to me before."

Rick said, "What didn't occur to you?" There was a pause, then he said, "Oh." In that single word I heard a whole world of enlightenment.

"Just get the tape, and then I'll get out of your hair."

I heard Rick shut the front door. "There's no need for this kind of thing, mate. Let's just talk like civilised people."

"Civilised people? You call it civilised to demand a million pounds from me?" I could feel the fury in the voice. "I call that fucking extortion on a grand scale. I've had enough of it."

"It's just a loan, mate. I told you that."

"And I told you I couldn't find the money for that kind of loan. You must live in cloud cuckoo land."

Rick said nothing for a moment, then, "I think we could have a more rational conversation if you would stop pointing that gun at me." He said this in a slightly louder voice than before, no doubt to ensure that I heard it.

"Just get the tape and I will."

I didn't know what to do. If I showed myself, I would find myself at gunpoint alongside Rick. If I tried to creep out I might be spotted – and in any case there didn't appear to be any other exit. Would the man back off if he realised there were two of us instead of one? Knowing nothing about him, I had no idea.

Before I'd reached any conclusion Rick said, "The tape isn't here."

"Why not?"

He hesitated. "My wife …"

"Your wife what?" A sharp burst of laugher. "You mean she really doesn't know about your little peccadilloes?"

"Of course not. I told you."

"Is she here now? I could put her in the picture."

"She's out for the day."

"Maybe I'll send her a copy of the tape."

There was a pause. I could imagine Rick looking aghast, but the voice said, "Don't worry, I won't. I just want it for myself, then we can call it quits."

Even under this threat, Rick clearly wasn't ready to give in. "Mate, I really need that money. Just for a week, if you like. It'll give my backers confidence."

"I don't care about your fucking backers, Rick. I've had enough of this. If the tape isn't here, where is it?"

Rick hesitated. "It's at my new office."

"And there are no copies?"

"I told you that. I don't even have a player to copy it to."

"Right, let's go and get it then."

In a slightly self-pitying voice Rick said, "I've got meetings set up, people to see. I really need to make this happen."

"Not my problem. If you get a move on, maybe you can do it later."

I heard the front door open and then slam shut. I crossed warily to the window, and in the driveway I saw the visitor usher Rick into the driving seat of a large black BMW car, then climb into the back seat. The engine started and the car circled round to the exit, then turned left on to the road and disappeared.

It was only then that I realised I hadn't made a note of the registration number.

Chapter 55

What the hell was I to make of all this? So much information to take in, and so much of it incomplete. And apparently I now had to contend with someone wielding a gun for the second time in a week. It was something I'd never expected to do even once in a lifetime.

What should I do? Call the police? Would Rick thank me if this tape of his came to light? He'd obviously wanted me to know what was happening, but what would he actually expect?

I hurried out of the house, slamming the front door behind me, and got into my car. Now what? I wondered about phoning Dave Matthews. At least he would trust me, though he knew nothing about Rick Ashton, so I'd have to explain that aspect to him from scratch.

Then it occurred to me that I hadn't yet got round to transferring my contact list to my cheap new phone, so I didn't have Dave's mobile number. I could call his police station, and they might or might not give it to me, depending on who answered. If they did, I would then have to hope he would pick up.

I could call 999, but what on earth would I say? A man in an unspecified black BMW is currently driving from somewhere to somewhere else at gunpoint? It sounded ridiculous.

I wondered wildly about following the BMW, but I'd already delayed too long. It could be at least a mile ahead of me by now, and I might head off in the wrong direction.

Where was Rick Ashton's office? I actually didn't know. His company's headquarters were in a small town somewhere north of London. Was it Hemel Hempstead? Beaconsfield? That was where he must theoretically be based. But I'd noticed him saying just now that the tape was in his *new* office. That seemed significant.

I decided to take a punt. I would go to the new Vantage hub outside Rugby. It wasn't a million miles from where I was now, and I knew Rick had an office there because we'd been shown it during the press visit.

I glanced at my fuel gauge as I pulled off. Probably just enough petrol to get me there. Then I wrangled my phone into my hands-free device. I might try contacting Dave Matthews on the way.

* * *

The route was oblique to say the least. I had to negotiate a series of meandering country lanes before emerging on anything like a decent road, and then I found myself having to drive right through the centre of Banbury. Happily the traffic was light, and finally I was able to make up some ground on the A423 towards Coventry.

I drove as fast as I dared, but managed to call up directory enquiries along the way. I got hold of the number for Dave's police station and spoke to a woman who knew me vaguely, and she proved willing to give me Dave's mobile number. But when I rang it my call was diverted to voicemail. I left what was probably a pretty incoherent message. And hoped for the best.

It was nearly an hour before I finally pulled up outside the new Vantage sortation hub, a giant facility in glass and gunmetal grey, trying without much success to hide itself against the sky. Tall grey metallic railings surrounded the site and a new concrete service road ran along the periphery, disappearing at the far end into a field. Grass was just beginning to shoot up in the unmade plot opposite, which had evidently been turned over during construction.

This was the place I'd visited as a journalist weeks before – the new beating heart of the Vantage operation, where parcels from all over the country were consolidated and sorted for onward delivery. But there was no host to shepherd me around today – I was on my own.

I pulled into the entrance bay and stopped at the barrier next to the security booth. A uniformed man leaned out.

I now had a decision to make. Did I sound the alarm to this man, hoping I had the patience and articulacy to convince him what I believed was happening? Or did I attempt to deal with matters on my own?

I tried to peer past the barrier, hoping to see if the black BMW was anywhere in sight. There was no sign of it, but in a place this size that probably meant little.

I made up my mind. I would press on by myself. It seemed simpler somehow. I said, "I'm due to join Rick Ashton's party. I'm a bit late."

He gave a slightly sceptical look at my ageing car, then glanced down at a board he was holding. "Name?"

"It's Stanhope, but you won't find me on your list. This was all a bit unplanned." I tried a confident smile, but wasn't sure it worked. Chancing my arm, I said, "I think Rick probably arrived a little while ago. I was following him, but I lost him in traffic."

The man looked dubious, but then a colleague leaned over his shoulder. "He's right, Mr Ashton got here about fifteen minutes ago."

Thank god for that. At least I was on the right track.

The man gave me a final look, then checked his watch, wrote something on his board and held it out to me. "Sign here."

I scribbled my name and put the car in gear, but he said, "Hang on a minute. There's no one in reception to give you a visitor's badge. You'd better have this." He reached round, pulled a plastic name badge from somewhere and painstakingly wrote down its serial number on his chart. "There you go. Park over there, then go to the main entrance across there." He pointed at the glass office block built on to the front of the premises.

I drove over to the virtually empty visitors' car park, left the car and trotted across an expanse of concrete acreage to the office, ignoring an indirect walking path marked in yellow paint. To either side, rows of big red and white Vantage trailers were backed up against loading bays, and one of them was just in the process of being pulled out by a Vantage truck. Beyond it another trailer was about to be hauled out by a blue and white vehicle bearing the logo of Ray Noble Rental.

Chapter 56

There was no one in the palatial reception area. Distantly I now remembered that a large contingent of the company's head-office staff was due to move in here, but not until later in the year. However, I vaguely remembered the geography of the place from my previous visit. I hurried across to a curving marbled staircase and bounded up two steps at a time, then along a corridor, through an empty open-plan office and into a smaller corridor at the far end.

By this time I'd slowed to a cautious walk. I didn't want to barge blindly into Rick and his assailant. I still had no idea what to do if I found them. I wasn't even sure I'd come the right way. I moved as silently as I could, listening for any sound of conversation.

Then not far away I heard Rick's voice raised in protest. "Don't ask me, mate, I thought I had the key on this key ring."

"That's the biggest load of crap I've ever heard. Look again."

They were in an office at the end of the corridor, beyond a half-closed door. I tiptoed up to it and hovered outside.

And then my mobile phone rang.

The door was snatched open and I was facing a man in his fifties, neatly dressed in a tan casual jacket, blue shirt and cream trousers. He had receding curly hair and a permanently bronzed look.

"Why don't you join us?" He was holding an automatic pistol loosely by his side, and he moved it into plain view without raising it.

I stepped into the room. It was a typical modern office, but the whole of the opposite wall was made up of a picture window overlooking the main sortation hall. There was a glass door in the centre, giving on to a small balcony, and below it the high-level sorting conveyor stretched away into the far distance.

"Michael!" Rick said. "What a surprise."

Swallowing, I said, "There'll be a bigger surprise when the police get here. That's them on the phone." On cue, the phone stopped ringing.

The man waved me over to where Rick stood. "One of you please open that fucking door NOW!"

I'd been imagining a safe, but actually the object of their attention was just a grey pressed-metal office cupboard. The man indicated a steel letter opener on the desk. "Use that."

Rick glanced at him, then picked it up, thrust the end into the cupboard at the edge of the door and jerked it vigorously sideways. The door swung open. He reached inside and pulled out a padded envelope from a shelf. "Will this make you happy?"

The man stepped forward to take it, but at that moment my phone started ringing again. The man glanced over to me, and while he was distracted Rick turned abruptly, snatched the glass door open and stepped out on to the balcony. He leaned over the rail, held up the envelope tauntingly, then lobbed it out towards the main carousel.

All three of us watched its progress, which seemed to take much longer than it actually did. Then the man was jolted into action. He lunged through the glass doorway, pausing briefly to check where the envelope had landed, then turned to his right and launched himself on to a short metal staircase that led down to the carousel system. As I joined Rick on the balcony I saw the man stumbling on to an elevated walkway that led off beside the conveyor.

I glanced along the conveyor to see what had become of the envelope. Numerous other much larger parcels were being trundled away from us, and I could see the envelope among them, leaning against a much bigger cardboard box.

The man could see it too, and he hurried along the walkway until he was adjacent to it. He glanced around, obviously trying to gauge how he could retrieve it. The walkway was separated from the conveyor by a waist-high railing and by the deep metal rim of the conveyor itself. As he looked, the envelope moved further on. He followed it.

At regular intervals, chutes led off the main conveyor and down to the load assembly area to our left. Individual parcels were being diverted off the conveyor and on to these chutes by swinging arms that shot out from the side in response to some unseen command, then swung back again. This was how consignments were allocated to their various destinations.

The man started clambering over the railing. As he did so his gun slipped from his hand and clattered on to the metal walkway. He glanced uncertainly back at it, then seemed to come to a decision. He turned and completed his manoeuvre without recovering it. He jumped over the rim of the conveyor and landed awkwardly on the moving surface. The envelope was a few yards ahead of him.

Abruptly I felt the need to do something. Rick Ashton might now be out of immediate danger, but he was about to lose a tape that he clearly considered valuable. However, he was simply staring after the man with a look of shock on his face. I hesitated for a moment, then turned and lunged down the steps towards the walkway.

Later I wondered what had possessed me to chase someone with a plainly violent disposition. At the time I was simply thinking to myself that the man no longer had the gun, so he couldn't be a threat: a somewhat narrow view.

It wasn't hard to catch up with him. I was able to run along the walkway while he was still wobbling precariously on the conveyor, trying to reach the envelope. Within a few seconds I was parallel with him. He glanced over at me and called, "Fuck off, mate! Stay out of things that don't concern you."

I ignored him, clambered over the railing and jumped on to the conveyor, landing in a crouch. By now it had moved on, leaving me a few yards behind him. I rose to my feet and stepped cautiously after him.

His eyes darted between me and the envelope, now just a few feet ahead of him. He looked poised to lunge for it, but was hesitating, presumably uncertain what I would do while he was looking away. He shouted, "I warned you, mate. There's no call to make this your fight." He bunched his fists in preparation to take a jab at me.

At that moment a swinging arm shot out and deflected the envelope on to a side chute, along with the larger parcel it was leaning on. The man saw my eyes widen as I looked past him at it, and he swivelled round, watching with new alarm as the envelope slithered away down the metal chute.

He hesitated a moment, glancing back at me, then clambered on to the chute after it. He slid down, arriving awkwardly at the end of it like someone reaching the bottom of a helter-skelter. His arms flailed as he staggered to his feet, gathering up the envelope as he did so.

I couldn't slide down after him until he moved away; I would be a literally sitting target for his fists when I reached the bottom. It appeared that he'd achieved his objective, but then the carousel abruptly stopped moving, and in the sudden silence an urgent voice rang out. "Armed police! Stay where you are!"

I raised my eyes and quickly identified the speaker, crouched behind a trolley stacked high with boxes. He was holding an automatic weapon with both hands. Further away I now saw another, and a third.

The man looked around wildly, then straightened in defeat. He could see that the game was up.

Chapter 57

A long period of explanations followed. Rick and I were interviewed separately and at length by detectives in two meeting rooms at the sortation centre. I told them a more or less straight story, but held back when it came to describing the conversation I'd overheard at Rick's house. I told them about the tape, but didn't mention the implication of some sort of sexual content. They would find out soon enough if they examined it, but I thought that was up to them.

One of the detectives was reproving. "Did it not strike you as foolish in the extreme to set off on your own after an armed man?" It wasn't a mild enquiry, it was a heavily weighted reprimand.

"In hindsight, yes. I just acted on instinct, I suppose."

"Next time you need to think more carefully first."

Gradually I was able to piece together the sequence of events. It appeared that Dave Matthews had picked up my voicemail message, understood the gist of it, and been able to galvanise an armed response unit in double quick time. I had a lot to thank him for.

His good word was perhaps helping me slightly with these detectives, but they didn't know him, and didn't seem inclined to do me any special favours.

Finally, after what seemed like hours, the detectives had finished with us for the time being, and I was taken to a small office where Rick was already on the phone. He waved me towards a chair and I sat down.

He disconnected and banged his phone down on the desk. "Christ! What's the matter with these morons?" He looked at me and smiled briefly. "Michael, I think I owe you a vote of thanks."

"An explanation would be good, too."

"I don't know about you, but I could do with a drink."

* * *

Twenty minutes later I pulled in at a pub not far from the sortation centre. Rick ordered two double whiskies.

We sat in an alcove away from potential eavesdroppers, and he looked at me cautiously, perhaps wondering how much he would have to tell me. Finally he said, "This is in complete confidence, right? I mean not just off the record, but this conversation isn't happening at all. Are we agreed on that?"

I nodded, and he looked at me carefully. "All right," he said finally. "You won't want to hear this, but I suppose you have a right." He stared in front of him for a moment. "Do you know who that man was? You should."

"You called him Andy. That's all I know."

"That's right – Andy Davidson." He downed half his whisky and squinted theatrically. "But his real name is Liam Stone."

"*What?*" I stared at him in amazement. This was the name of the alleged robber who had escaped capture – the one whose whereabouts my captors had been prepared to pummel out of me last week. Somehow, Rick Ashton knew him, and now I'd actually met him. How on earth could this be?

"I don't believe you."

He shrugged. "Well, it's true. Coincidence or what?" He spoke dryly. It was plain that the coincidence no longer impressed him.

I stared at him, almost speechless. The people who'd kidnapped me evidently had some connection to the security van heist, and now, through a completely different chain of events, Rick was telling me he knew someone else who also had a connection to it. To call this a coincidence barely did it justice.

Eventually I managed to say, "Astounding, that's what I'd call it."

"Just one of those weird things, mate."

I looked at him for a moment longer without speaking. Finally I said, "You'd better explain."

He ran a hand through his hair. "I don't know where to start, mate." He stared into the middle distance for a moment, then shrugged. "You've probably gathered that I'm not a very nice person."

I shook my head. "You don't need to make any apologies to me."

He shrugged. "I think you'll change your mind when you've heard me out."

I said nothing.

Continuing to stare bleakly into his memory, he began, "Well, I met Andy in Queensland, years ago now. He was calling himself Andy Franklin then. I was still working in Sydney in those days, and my wife and I were having a holiday – the Great Barrier Reef, all that good stuff.

"She took ill in Brisbane – some kind of stomach bug. She was hospitalised, but she insisted that I go on up to Cairns on my own. That's where we were due to stay next.

"I met Andy there. He was running a bar. Believe it or not, he can be a nice guy. We hit it off." He glanced at me. "I hope I don't have to spell it out?"

I shrugged.

"We had three amazing days, and on the last day we were totally off our heads. Anyway, he can't keep his mouth shut, and he starts telling me about this 'big thing' he's done in his past. Turns out that he claims he was in on a big jewellery heist in the UK, and he hopped it with half the loot."

He turned to me. "I thought it was a load of crap, to be honest. I got it that he had some kind of past he was escaping from, but I thought the stuff about the heist was just a load of horseshit to impress me. The next day he didn't even remember anything about it."

He stared around the bar, perhaps realising he was on a roll now, and wondering how to rein it in. If so, he quickly seemed to give up on the idea, and turned to me with an air of renewed complicity.

"So the years pass, and here I am in GB, and then one day I meet him out of the blue. I didn't even think it was him at first. He's not a beach bum any more – he's Andy Davidson, a man of substance with a Cotswold stone cottage at Chipping Norton. Pillar of the community.

"So after a while we started … seeing each other again. And that's when I ran into problems at the company. We lost a big chunk of business overnight, and suddenly we were cash-strapped. Our parent company made it clear they weren't going to help, and other investors were worried about market competition, so I asked Andy if he would be willing to stump up a loan, or even put in some investment himself – just to encourage the others. He seemed to be rolling in it, so I thought he might help, and to begin with he was fine with it. But then he started to get cold feet."

"So …?"

"Well, your book."

"How do you mean?"

"Well, I read it, and I started putting two and two together. I did a load of web research, and realised the time frame fitted. It was him, Stone. No question."

Once again I felt nonplussed. Just as my book had apparently deceived my kidnappers into believing it, it had apparently also deceived Rick Ashton. And in this case it seemed to have pointed him towards the truth.

I couldn't think of anything to say. There was no point in explaining that the book was mostly conjecture; that wasn't the point.

He shifted his glass around on the table, staring pensively at it. "It didn't bother me that he was Liam Stone. What difference did it make? Water under the bridge. As far as I was concerned he was Andy, not Stone." He left a meaningful pause. "But I thought I could help persuade him about the loan if I mentioned the tape."

"The tape?"

"I made a video of us back in Cairns. In secret. I rigged the camera." He paused, then continued awkwardly, "I've done it once or twice, actually." He looked up sheepishly. "I said you wouldn't want to hear this."

Again I just shrugged.

"Well, it was while the tape was running that he came up with all this stuff about the heist. Mate, I recorded this man making his confession."

"It would probably never stand up in a court of law."

"But do you think he's going to risk that? At the very least, it opens up a trail. He doesn't want any of it."

"So today was the last straw."

"Apparently. I didn't have him pegged as a violent man, but it seems I read him wrong all these years. I should never have pushed him."

I stared at him. "But it was OK to blackmail this man just because he was a thief? It's a strange kind of logic."

"It wasn't blackmail, for Christ's sake! We were mates. He was baling on me when I really needed his help, that's all. And it was a loan – seed money. I wasn't trying to take it from him permanently."

"But it was stolen money in the first place. You would have been funding your business out of a robbery."

He shook his head vigorously. "No no no. I didn't know that when I asked for it. I only guessed later, and I might have been wrong. The robbery was years ago. His present wealth might be perfectly legit for all I know. I don't know the ins and outs of his investment portfolio."

"I suppose that's one way of looking at it."

Rick went to the bar to buy himself another round, and I sat in silence, running all this information round in my head. He amazed me. He seemed to occupy a world I could only imagine. His resourcefulness apparently knew no bounds, but it seemed to give him leave to swipe aside the moral flaws in his philosophy. But who was I to judge? In a sense I was his friend too, though I wouldn't have cared to put that to the test.

As for the coincidence of his knowing Liam Stone in the first place, that seemed to defy belief, and it was taking me a while to come to terms with it. I still found the discovery astonishing, but at least I was beginning to understand it. The more you learn about the circumstances of a coincidence, the less extraordinary it can seem.

When he came back I said, "I wasn't sure what to do today, after the two of you drove off. Maybe I did the wrong thing."

"How do you mean?"

"Well, that tape … presumably the police have it now. Your involvement with Stone will come out. I wasn't planning on that."

He beamed at me. "You mean the tape of my daughter at her riding school nine years ago?"

I stared at him. "That wasn't the right tape?"

"Give me a bit of credit here, I'm not that stupid."

"But what if he'd checked what was on it?"

"How? There's no VHS player at the parcel hub. How many people have one at all these days?"

I shook my head in wonder. "But he would have found out eventually. He would have come after you again."

He shrugged. "You have to take a risk sometimes. I probably would have thought of something else. He might have calmed down by then."

I said, "Did you tell the police who he was?"

"No way. They may find out on their own, but that's not my affair."

"So how did you account for him driving you here at gunpoint?"

"I just said he'd flipped. He knew I had a compromising tape with him on it, and suddenly he wanted it." He gave me an ironic smile. "I'm not out of the woods yet, I know that, but my solicitor will know what to do."

I shook my head in wonder. Would I ever have this kind of presence of mind in such a crisis?

I said, "If he's put on trial, he might bring you into the frame, just out of spite."

"But what does he have to gain? He'd have to admit he's gay. Nothing wrong with that, but I can't see him wanting it to come out like that. No, I think he'll keep quiet."

"And you're not going to give up the real tape?"

"You must be joking. First chance I get, it's going in the furnace."

"But what if there's no other evidence, and he gets off?"

He shrugged. "So be it."

* * *

As we prepared to leave I asked, "What happened about the refinancing?"

"I don't know. I've missed a meeting in Brum with some possible backers, but I didn't have high hopes for it, to be honest." We stood up. "I've got to talk to the other directors again. I still have a couple of irons in the fire. While there's life there's hope, eh?"

On a sudden whim I asked, "What about Janni Noble? Have you talked to him?"

"Noble? Christ, no. He wants my guts for garters. I owe him more than half a year's contract hire fees. Why would he want to do me any favours?"

"He's ambitious and well connected. I'd have thought he's just the kind of person who could put his hands on the capital you need. For a start, he might turn some of that debt into equity."

Rick was looking deeply sceptical, so I added, "Best of all, he's an honourable man. He would never have swallowed the debt so long otherwise."

"How come you know so much about him?"

"Long story."

He looked at me a moment, assessing, then said, "I'll give it some thought." He glanced at his watch. "I've got to go."

On an impulse I asked, "Can Vantage really get through this, or is it fucked?"

Without any hesitation he said, "Of course it can survive. It's basically a sound business. Why should I have to watch the receivers move in and let someone else reap the benefits?"

2012

Finding Sarah Trent proved much easier than I expected. She was a nurse in Brisbane, Australia, and had a Facebook page, just like the normal person she was making herself out to be. The beguiling face that I'd seen at St Pancras shone out at me from my screen, defying me not to believe she was the girl I'd known back in Polperro.

There was no single source of information about her life, but from snippets on various web sites I discovered that she'd married someone called Trent, but he had since died. She seemed to have been working in Brisbane for at least ten years, and now appeared to live alone in an apartment in the city.

I decided not to make direct contact yet. If she really was connected to that robbery, hearing from someone in her former life would presumably alarm her – and might even send her off into hiding. I had no wish to cause that to happen.

Yet the desire to meet her was overwhelming. After all this effort, I couldn't imagine abandoning the chase at the last hurdle – especially if the hurdle was purely one of my own making.

I decided the only reliable way to make contact with her was in person. That way she couldn't avoid me … and she would see that I meant her no harm.

I started researching the prices of flights to Brisbane.

Chapter 58

Should I phone Janni Noble? I stared at my phone on Monday morning. If Rick contacted him and actually managed to persuade him to invest, it would be at least partly my doing. Surely I owed it to Noble to give him some sense of what Rick was capable of? Or should I just consider him an adult who could form his own judgements?

Remarkably, before I'd had the chance to resolve this in my mind, Noble rang me. It was only ten past nine. Once again his secretary asked me to hold the line, then his voice boomed out from the phone.

"Mr Stanhope. I wish to speak in confidence. Is this clearly understood?"

"Yes, fine."

"So. Yesterday I received a call from our mutual friend Mr Richard Ashton. He seems to think I should invest in his parcel company. My people are looking into this."

"I see."

He seemed to reflect for a moment. "I ask him for his financial credentials, his credit references, his bona fides, all those things that I would need to give to my investors, my lawyers, my accountants. He gives me all this ... and then he tells me I should speak to you."

"Oh. So what do you want me to say?"

He laughed humourlessly. "I thought you would be telling me this."

I decided frankness was the only way to respond. I said, "Rick is in trouble, but he says his firm is sound. For some reason his bail-out options have fallen through. I suggested he might consider speaking to you."

"*You* suggested this?"

"It was just a passing thought."

"And Richard Ashton is prepared to listen to you?"

"Apparently."

"So do you believe him when he says his company is sound?"

That was an interesting one. I had virtually no real knowledge of the company's financial status, only anecdotal information from Rick himself. How far could I trust him? Clearly he was willing to play a devious game when it suited his interests, yet beyond that I still felt there was a fundamental honesty about him.

I said, "I'm no expert, so you can't take my word for it, but speaking personally, I think yes."

There was a silence, then he said, "I feel there is something more that you wish to say."

Marvelling at his astuteness, I said, "I just think … Rick Ashton is a very driven man. He would probably go a lot further that most people to keep his company afloat. You know what he's like yourself."

"Go on."

"Well, I just think if I were investing with him, I would want to keep him on a very short leash. That's all."

"Very well. That is all I wished to know. Thank you, Mr Stanhope." And he was gone.

* * *

As I thought through all this, I suddenly found myself wondering what impact these developments might have on my supposed book deal with Hunt Topham. In theory Rick Ashton no longer needed to buy my press silence over his debt crisis. Either the company would go bust today or it would be rescued. There was little I could write in the press now to influence the outcome.

On the other hand, now that I knew so much more about Rick's affairs – public and private – arguably his obligation to me was even greater. If his company survived, perhaps his instinct would be to thrust me into the arms of Hunt Topham for all he was worth. But if he did, would it be a favour I could live with?

There was a knock at the front door. Dave Matthews stood there with his usual ironic grin.

"You certainly lead an exciting life, Mr Stanhope."

I ushered him in and he filled me in on Saturday's events from his end. He'd been playing squash when I phoned him, but had picked up my voicemail at the end of the game. He'd understood everything I'd said in it, and had persuaded the local force in the midlands to deploy the armed response unit.

"The biggest chance I took was that you were right about the location. If your friends had gone off to Beaconsfield or somewhere else, I would have been up to my neck in the proverbial."

"I'm glad you did."

He asked me what I knew about the gunman. I thought I'd better show ignorance, but he said, "What I'm getting from the local force is that he might be Liam Stone, the man who was implicated in your robbery, but never caught." He beamed at me with a look of triumph on his face. "What kind of coincidence is that?"

Adopting what I hoped was a look of amazement, I said, "You have to be joking!"

He wasn't a policeman for nothing. I could tell he was wondering what I already knew. However, he simply said, "Well, to be honest they're not sure. If it's him, he's covered his tracks pretty well." He paused. "But my god, Mike, you certainly know how to live an interesting life."

"You can say that again. You realise that's the man I was supposed to give up when I was kidnapped the week before last?"

"That fact hadn't escaped me, yes."

"Well, if the police could go public now with the fact that he's been arrested, that would get these people off my back, wouldn't it? They would realise they couldn't get at him any longer. Or at any rate, they wouldn't need any help from me."

"I can see where you're coming from, but we can't jump the gun on this. It might not be him, and if it is him, it might suit our interests to keep quiet about it for a while."

"And meanwhile I'm at risk of having three kinds of shit beaten out of me by his former friends!"

"I don't think that's going to happen. They know we'll be on the lookout for them now. If they have any sense they'll be keeping their heads down from now on."

"I hope you're right." A thought struck me. "Were you able to follow up that name I gave you? Harry Slater – the guy from my reading group? He might be the link to these people."

"Nothing yet. We're still looking into it."

* * *

In mid-afternoon an email from Rick pinged into my inbox. I opened it quickly to find a single paragraph in front of me. "Sorted! See attached. This is going out on the wire services in an hour. If you want to run it as an exclusive, you'd better get your skates on." There was also a PS: "Thanks."

I opened the attachment and found a curt press release drafted by Rick's PR firm.

Vantage Express secures new funding
Parcel company Vantage Express has announced new funding that has secured its future.
An undisclosed multi-million pound sum has been committed to the company by a consortium of investors in the North West. The deal has still to be ratified, but following successful completion, it will leave the consortium in overall control. The previous majority shareholder, Hunt Leinster Holdings, will retain a substantial minority shareholding.
Under the deal, maverick CEO Rick Ashton will retain his current position, and his team will be reinforced by the appointment of several new board members.

Hastily I copied the text into my word processor and started rewriting it and embellishing the fairly stark details. Then I made a couple of brief phone calls to corroborate a couple of points. Thirty minutes later I made a phone call.

"Jason, I've got a news story you might want to run with."

Chapter 59

The next morning Ashley rang me. We hadn't been in touch since the previous week.

"Mike, I wasn't very friendly when I rang you the other day."

She sounded upbeat. Cautiously I said, "I don't blame you. I have a habit of putting my foot in it."

"It was a big thing for me. I'm still getting my head round it."

"I realise that."

She laughed. "Will you stop being so bloody understanding, please?"

"Right."

She laughed again, then fell silent for a moment. "Well listen … what if we were to meet up?"

"Definitely!"

"OK, well this is what I was thinking. Jack has to go into hospital in a couple of days' time, to get his fracture re-set or something. It sounds horrible, poor guy, and I should really be there to support him."

"But?"

"But what if I came to London for the day? And stayed over, I mean. I can take a day's leave, but I would have to come back again the next day …"

"Yes!"

She laughed. "Well I do like a positive reaction."

I was doing some fast thinking. Absurdly, I said, "My house is a dump. You'll hate it. You'll wonder who on earth would want to live in it. *I* wonder that, most days. You'll realise the kind of person I really am."

"I see."

"Maybe you could keep your eyes closed?"

"Do you want me to come or not?"

"Yes!"

"All right then."

We agreed that I would meet her at Paddington station. This was unnecessary, but in the back of my mind I felt I wanted to see her on neutral ground first, then introduce her gradually to my living environment. I felt somehow that it would be less of a shock that way.

I disconnected with a sense of awe. Having left our relationship dangling in mid-air, she had brought it back down to earth with emphasis. "Staying over" meant spending the night with me – there was no other way to read it. My pulse was going into overdrive at the very thought of it.

Many of my male acquaintances seemed able to fall into bed with women at the drop of a hat. I never knew how true their claims were, but I suspected there had to be a fair amount of substance in them. I could never identify with this. Even after I'd overcome my adolescent shyness, every instance still seemed a significant event in my life, and never more so than now. I'd been dreaming about sleeping with Ashley for months. Now, in the space of one short phone call, she'd implied that it was about to happen.

* * *

If that phone call was a jolt to the system, the next was an even bigger one. An hour later I lifted the handset to hear an unfamiliar woman's voice asking, "Is that Michael Stanhope?"

"Mike, yes."

"My name is Christina Marsden." She hesitated. "You would know me as Catrina Markham. Trina."

What on earth was I to make of this? After all that had been happening to me lately, my search for Trina had slipped down my list of priorities. I now had to ask myself if the real Trina would really ring me up like this.

"Seriously?"

She gave what seemed a sad little laugh. "Seriously. And I do remember you, vaguely. Not what you looked like, I have to say, but your presence. I remember wondering why it took you so long to speak to me."

I stood there in silence for a moment. I could almost hear the blood pounding in my ears. A little wildly I said, "I was shy."

"I thought as much." Another of those little laughs. "Well here I am now."

I said, "It really is you, isn't it?"

"Yes it really is."

Her voice was slightly low, unaccented, and infused with a downbeat sense of humour. I realised that any doubt about her identity had vanished in the first few seconds.

"I don't know what to say. Thank you for ringing."

"My pleasure. I read your email. I could see that we weren't going to get anywhere with the written word. We needed to speak."

"You're not T Powell, though?"

"No, that's Tish. She fields these things for me if they ever come up. There's no direct connection between us, so it's like a sandbox – a layer of protection."

"But you're ringing me now."

"Yes I am."

She was being deliberately cryptic, but perhaps it was her coping mechanism. I said, "So what do we talk about?"

"Well, you've been going to a lot of trouble to find me."

"I know. I hope you're not offended."

She took a second to consider this. "Not really. I should probably be flattered."

"Well, that's something."

"Under the circumstances it might not have been the best thing to happen, but ... well, circumstances can alter."

"I don't really follow."

"No, I realise that." She seemed to be thinking again. "Look, I'm assuming you would you like to meet up. Am I right?"

"Of course! That would be brilliant."

"I'm not sure about brilliant." Another pause. "How about this Friday, in Chesterfield? Would you mind making the trip – if you're free, that is?"

It was an unlikely curved ball. Chesterfield was a market town about a hundred and fifty miles north of London: several hours' drive from my house. Being asked to make such a long trip at such short notice was completely outside my experience. And on Friday morning I was hoping Ashley would still be with me after her overnight visit.

Cautiously I said, "Is this a once-only offer? It's just that I'm not sure how quickly I could get there."

"Late lunch? About 2pm?"

"OK, fine, let's do it. Where exactly?"

"There's a market square with a telephone box on one corner. Anyone will tell you how to find it."

I scribbled down the details, then said, "This seems a bit like something from a spy movie."

"Yes it does."

"How will we know each other?"

"Oh, I know what you look like. I looked up your LinkedIn profile."

"Ah, right. What about you?"

"Average height. Longish dark hair. Probably a suede jacket. You'll find me."

"So I'll see you on Friday."

And that was it. Months of intermittent research and travel had finally come down to this – an arrangement to meet. I didn't know whether to feel delighted, overawed or simply stunned.

Chapter 60

Part of my brain wanted to fall into a miasma of anticipation over Ashley's impending visit. Another part was preoccupied by the wonder of having apparently made contact with Trina. It was hard to believe that the two women had phoned me within an hour of each other.

Thinking about Trina seemed a useful distraction from dwelling too much on Ashley, so I tried to focus on her. If I was going all the way to Chesterfield to meet her, I'd better have something worthwhile and coherent to say.

Turning to my laptop. I pulled up the notes I'd made about my search for her and scrolled through them, making sure I'd got the sequence of events right. As I thought, she and her parents had been living relatively conventional lives in the public eye until the day they'd left Altrincham, then they had disappeared. But I had a nagging suspicion I was missing something.

I read and re-read the notes – her father's early history, his involvement in the property firm, its sudden collapse. Then something struck me. There had been three partners in that firm – Trina's father and mother, plus someone named Robert Stainer. Who was he? I'd never bothered to research him.

I rummaged around the search engines and found several people who might conceivably be the right Robert Stainer. Finally I settled on the one who seemed the best fit. He had worked in the property market in Manchester, and popped up in the years after the Markhams' disappearance as a director of various other companies.

Was he still alive? I looked for present-day references, and sure enough there he was, a leading figure in the North West business community. I found a picture of him giving a speech at a charity event last year – a well-built man with greying curly hair, a little heavy-jowled now, but still bearing a hint of the good looks he probably had in the past. In this shot he was sporting a poppy on his lapel.

Whether his existence had any bearing on the Markhams' subsequent life I could only conjecture. There was no obvious reason to think so. I could ask Trina about him, but that would depend on whether the question seemed appropriate. I had to remind myself that this was supposed to be a private meeting, not a piece of research for an article. I'd long since abandoned that idea – hadn't I?

* * *

I started thinking about Ashley again. She would actually be coming here on Thursday, to this house. It was a strange thought. I gazed around me, trying to see the house through her eyes. What I saw was dowdy paintwork that Sandy and I had planned to update; old furniture that we'd intended to replace; and a film of dust over everything. Housework was not my forte.

I knew I couldn't fundamentally change the place, but I felt an urgent need to do something. I stood up started tidying the office in a desultory way, and gradually the task expanded. I found myself attacking the fat-spattered cooker, the stains in the sink, the hints of cobwebs over the stairs. I rounded up several empty wine bottles and a couple of whisky bottles and shoved them in the outside bin. Then I spent an age over dusting, vacuuming, polishing. Hours seemed to pass in a frenzied blur.

Finally I collapsed in an armchair and stared around me. What I now saw was clean dowdiness, which was hopefully one step up from grimy dowdiness.

The reality, it now struck me, was that whatever happened between Ashley and me, she was never going to live here. She might not ever even come here again after this one visit. Even if there were any chance of it, which seemed extremely remote, I wouldn't want her to. All I could do was avoid allowing this house to convey too depressing a picture of what I was about.

Maybe I should suggest that she stay in a hotel? No, that was ridiculous. What would it say about my attitude to her? Either that I wanted to shunt her off out of my sight, or that I was going to join her, and wanted to make absolutely sure that we spent the night together.

By the end of this convoluted train of thought I was actually laughing to myself. I was behaving like a nervous teenager. I needed to get a grip.

* * *

My mobile buzzed.

"Mike, it's Joanna. We're having a few people round for dinner on Thursday night. Are you up for it?"

"Ah. Well, believe it or not, Ashley is coming up from Cornwall on Thursday. I'm meeting her at Paddington around six."

"Really? That's brilliant!" I could hear her thinking. "Things must have moved on quite a bit then."

"Hopefully."

"Well, you can bring her along if you like." She said it cheekily, knowing the answer would be no.

"What, and subject the poor girl to your eagle eye the first time she sets foot in south London? I don't think so."

She laughed. "No, I can see that. But I want to meet her soon. Make sure you keep that in mind."

"Yes boss."

She seemed about to disconnect, so I quickly added, "You'd better hear the latest. Trina Markham actually phoned me this morning. And it really was her."

"My god! What did she say?"

"Not a lot, but I'm meeting her on Friday."

"Amazing." She paused, perhaps processing this information. "What, and you're taking Ashley along to meet her? I'd like to be a fly on the wall in that conversation."

"No! Ashley's going back to Cornwall. But it's not a secret. I'll tell her all about it."

"I think you'll need to."

"For god's sake, I'm not trying to get involved with Trina. It would be ridiculous. I don't even know her."

"Whatever. But you'd better be sure you make that clear to Ashley."

I laughed. "You should get a job as an agony aunt."

"I'm working on it."

2012

The heat and humidity of Brisbane hit me with a double shock.

Arriving after thirty-six hours and a stop-off in Singapore, I'd been protected from the climate by the air-conditioned airport environment, and then by the futuristic Airtrain, which had whisked me into the downtown area. Now I'd wandered out of my hotel and into the city streets to get my bearings. The temperature was something else.

Sasha, or rather Sarah, lived several miles outside the centre. I could probably get there by public transport, but the idea seemed over-complicated. I decided to hire a car.

Although the traffic here drove on the left, just as in Britain, everything else about the streets seemed foreign and slightly forbidding. I arrived at Sarah's address around 8pm, and pulled over to the kerb with relief.

She lived on the fourth floor of a crisp modern apartment block. I turned off the engine and wondered what to do. My plan, which was simply to turn up unannounced, had seemed straightforward enough back in Britain; now it felt ill-considered.

I sat there for ten minutes, unsure of my next move. Then, remarkably, I saw Sasha herself rounding the corner of the street, heading briskly towards her building.

There was no time to consider. I stepped out of the car and crossed the road, timing my movements to coincide with her arrival.

"Hi Sasha. We met in Polperro twenty-five years ago. I was just passing."

Chapter 61

Ashley strode purposefully towards me across the station concourse with a faint smile on her face. She was wearing jeans and a brown leather jacket, and was carrying a small overnight bag.

I took the bag. "Welcome to London."

"Thank you kindly, Mr Stanhope."

I led the way out of the station and along to a pub not far down the street. We took two stools at the bar and she looked at me challengingly.

"So what's this about your dump of a house?"

"Oh, I just meant it would seem a dump to someone who lives in a bijou flat in Cornwall."

"It's not *that* bijou. You think I'm made of money?"

"I was hoping so."

She laughed. "Dream on."

The inevitable awkwardness between us lifted as we talked. She updated me on her trip to drop Jack off at the hospital and her train journey, and then I recounted my recent experiences: the kidnapping, the stand-off at the parcel hub. By the end of it she was staring at me in amazement.

"My god, Mr Stanhope, you're a walking disaster area. What kind of world have you brought me into?"

"It's not usually like this, truly. It's usually pretty mundane."

"Why do I find that hard to believe?"

I looked at her reflectively. "You know what's most amazing to me about all this? I've only sold twenty-four copies of my book, yet one way or another it has already affected two different people who were involved in some way in that robbery. In both cases somebody believed the book was more or less true, and acted on it – and what they did rebounded on me. It has to be some kind of record."

"Be careful what you wish for, eh?"

"And some."

She told me Bob Latimer was pleased with the editorial work I'd been doing. "He said he wished he'd got you involved years ago. The last PR firm we had knew nothing about logistics. He had to do half their job for them. It's such a difference having someone who actually knows the business."

"Happy to oblige."

She looked at me mischievously. "Maybe you should get him to take you on full-time. Then you could come and live in Cornwall."

I looked into her eyes. She was being deliberately provocative, but there was a glimmer of earnestness somewhere there too.

"I can just see that."

"Well why not?"

I laughed. "Not really enough work in it for a full-time role."

"I'm sure you can work round that."

I shrugged.

She said, "My father sends his regards."

"You told him you were coming to see me?"

"Oh, we just happened to be speaking last night." She smiled cheerfully. "He's not my mum. He doesn't pass judgement."

"I'm glad to hear it."

"He said he hopes your never-ending search for the Markhams is progressing well."

"Well, I might have some progress to report soon on that score."

"Aha! Tell me more."

*   *   *

We left the pub and walked a few doors down the street to an Italian restaurant. Dining out in Paddington wasn't exactly my idea of showing Ashley the London high life, but there was a natural flow to the evening, and I felt simply grateful to go along with it.

Once we were sitting down, I told her Trina Markham had contacted me and I was due to see her tomorrow.

"And you really think it's her this time?"

"I'm more or less certain. It's just an instinct really."

"What will you say to her?"

"To be honest I have no idea. All I know is that for some reason she's willing to meet me. In fact she actually volunteered it. I just feel I need to follow it through."

"So are you going to fall in love with her all over again?"

She was smiling at me, but I felt there was also a hint of uncertainty in her look. Perhaps Joanna hadn't been as far off the mark as I'd thought.

"What, are you jealous or something?"

"Ha! Get over yourself."

A couple of hours later we paid and left, and I led her along to the station taxi rank.

"Won't this cost a fortune?" she asked.

"It's worth it."

Partly, I'd opted for a taxi because I couldn't stand the thought of the convoluted journey by tube, mainline train and even a bus. Partly, I didn't want to arrive at my house late in the evening on foot. I had no idea if my kidnappers were still likely to be on the rampage, and had no desire to find out.

The cosy intimacy of the taxi might have thrown a pall of awkwardness over us, but in fact as we climbed in we were rocked with hysterical laughter about something one of us had said, and that set the tone for the lengthy journey to south London.

* * *

As I opened my rickety gate my senses vaguely registered light from the street lamp being reflected off the doorstep. It wasn't raining, so how was this possible? Then as I pushed the key into the lock I realised water was trickling out from under the front door.

"Oh god," I said. "Something's wrong."

The hallway floor was soaking wet, and I was immediately aware of hissing water pipes – the sound you get when someone has just flushed a toilet or run a bath. I reached for the light switch, then stopped myself at the last moment. It could cause an electrical short.

I turned to Ashley, who was just behind me. "There's a water leak. Don't switch any lights on."

"Oh my god."

I stepped forward, and almost tripped on some indeterminate object in the middle of the floor. Kicking it aside, I made my way up the sodden staircase to the landing. Water was dripping through the ceiling in several places and coming down in a constant trickle round the edges of the loft hatch.

By feel more than sight I managed to prod the hatch open and wrestle the loft ladder down, and I climbed half-way up. I could hear the cold water cistern in full flow, but could see nothing. I retreated into my office and groped for the torch that I kept on the mantelpiece. Thankfully, the batteries were charged.

I climbed back up to the loft and went over to the cistern, pulling the plastic cover away. The tank was full, and water was gushing in through the inlet valve. I shone the torch around the outside, looking for the overflow pipe that should have channelled excess water out on to the patio. It wasn't there – there was just a hole, through which water was streaming in a steady torrent.

I reached inside the tank with one hand, groping for some means to stop the flow, but I couldn't think of anything. I climbed back down the ladder and descended to the kitchen. I needed to find the main stop cock for the house and turn it off. I quickly located it under the sink and turned it vigorously to the left. Immediately the hissing sound stopped.

Now I had to turn off the electrics for the house. I opened the fuse box in the hall and switched everything I could find to the off position.

Ashley was still hovering by the front door. I pointed the torch at her briefly. "I told you this house was a dump."

I hurried back upstairs and into my office. I wanted to recover my laptop, which nowadays I kept under the suspended files in the bottom drawer of my locked filing cabinet. Ashley tentatively followed me. The laptop was intact, and with relief I put it down on the desk and shone the torch around the room. "This wasn't exactly what I planned."

"What on earth caused this?" She was illuminated by the street lamp in a weak yellowish light.

"I have absolutely no idea. I suppose these things happen, but – "

At that moment there was a creaking noise above us and a section of plasterboard ceiling slumped down, releasing a torrent of water that cascaded directly over Ashley. It was as if someone had tipped a bucket of water on her head. She shrieked briefly and jumped sideways.

I stared at her, aghast. She said nothing for a moment, then gave a hysterical laugh. "Well I was hoping for a welcome, Mr Stanhope, but you needn't have gone to all this trouble."

Chapter 62

We stood in the lounge, taking stock. Most of the clothes in my built-in wardrobe were damp, and so was the bed. The only dry garments were a few random items that happened to be lying around loose, plus the contents of an overnight case that I usually kept packed. I had hardly anything suitable to offer Ashley, whose teeth were now chattering, and I was still wary of switching on any lights.

I looked at my watch. It was 11.30 – late enough, but not hopelessly late. I said, "I've got some friends who live just a few streets away. Could you stand meeting them? They would probably lend us some dry clothes, and they might even give us a bed for the night."

"Would they mind?"

I smiled inwardly. I could already imagine Joanna's delight at having Ashley delivered so soon for her inspection. "I'm sure they wouldn't."

"Well, whatever you think."

I phoned their house and Joanna picked up. I said, "How's your dinner party?"

"Mike! Did you miss me that much?"

I explained briefly what had happened. She said their guests had just left and they were about to go to bed. "But you must come over. Now. Understood? No excuses."

We returned to the hall, and I found myself kicking the object that I'd encountered on the way in. I shone the torch down. It was the ball valve assembly from the cistern, complete with the red ballcock. Suddenly this all started to make sense.

I kicked it away angrily and turned to the front door, and then saw a large piece of paper pinned crudely to the back of the door. Scrawled on it in large red letters were the words "Regards, A. Plumber".

* * *

John and Joanna were practical and down-to-earth. Joanna was clearly fascinated to meet Ashley, but managed to keep her enthusiasm in check. She led Ashley away to deliver some dry clothes to her.

"You're having a time of it," John commented.

"You could say that."

"And this was definitely malicious damage?"

"No question. How else would the ballcock find its way from the loft to the ground floor?"

He laughed grimly. "You should phone the police."

"I will." But it wasn't going to be tonight, and I couldn't be sure of fitting it in tomorrow either. I wasn't going to cry off the meeting with Trina.

The two women came back downstairs. Ashley was wearing a red and yellow woollen pullover that I'd seen often on Joanna. She grinned at me encouragingly, and Joanna commented, "We're a reasonable match for size."

Joanna provided hot drinks all round, and we sat chatting for a while. She and John asked Ashley about Cornwall, and expressed their liking for the South West in general. Presently, though, I was aware of Joanna giving John a visual signal that probably translated into something like "They need some space".

"We only have one guest room," she said. "I assume that's OK with you."

Ashley immediately said, "It's fine Joanna. Thank you."

As we dispersed into the hall Joanna caught my eye. Her look said, "She'll do nicely!"

* * *

Ashley smiled up at me. "I'm not into night-time garb."

"Me neither."

I stripped off quickly and slid under the duvet beside her. The pine bed frame creaked slightly. I was more than a little nervous. I leaned on my elbow and looked at her.

"Hello."

"Hello yourself."

"This wasn't exactly how I planned things."

She glanced quickly around the room, then looked back at me and gave me a wry smile. "Friends' house. Clean sheets. Thin walls. Young son. I think there are rules."

"Shall we play it by ear then?"

She nodded, and I shuffled tentatively towards her. She slid into my arms, and I relaxed into the soft pressure of her body. I muttered, "I might as well tell you I've been dreaming about this for months."

It should have been a sublime moment, but as I spoke the bed creaked again. Ashley stifled a slightly hysterical giggle and lifted her head. "You mean to tell me you've been dreaming about lying feet from your best friends and their little boy in a bed that creaks as soon as you draw breath? Sounds a bit kinky to be honest."

"I must have forgotten to mention my exhibitionist fetish."

She laughed again, and I gave an ironic scowl. The tension was broken, and I flopped on to my back and stared at the ceiling. "What's to be done?"

There was a moment's silence, then I felt her reach over and run her hand cautiously up and down my chest. She said, "I've been thinking about this too."

"Huh!"

She seemed unperturbed. Almost in a whisper she said: "Of *course* I have. Why do you think I'm here?"

I leaned up on my elbow again, looked into her eyes, then leaned forward and kissed her. When I pulled back she wasn't smiling; her features were relaxed and her eyes were closed. I shuffled to rebalance, took her head in both my hands and kissed her again – eagerly, gratefully, exultantly.

After a while she opened her eyes and in slightly cracked voice asked, "How good are you at keeping really really REALLY quiet?"

"Very good. Excellent. How about you?"

"Let's find out."

* * *

By the time we got up in the morning John had left for work and Joanna had already headed off to deliver Jeremy to school. We sat in the kitchen facing each other across the breakfast bar. Autumn sunshine cast us both in soft lights and shades. Ashley was wearing Joanna's red pullover again.

I said, "I wish you could stay longer."

"What, in your sopping house? No thank you."

"You know what I mean."

"As a matter of fact I do know what you mean."

She leaned on the bar with both elbows and gave me a hazy smile. Then she sat back and stretched. "Jack should be discharged this afternoon, and I promised I'd be there tonight."

"I know."

I looked at my watch. "I need to make a phone call."

Thankfully, Dave Matthews answered his mobile immediately for once. I said, "Dave, I've got a big favour to ask."

"What, another? When do I get one in return?"

I explained about the water damage as succinctly as I could. "I don't know if there's any evidence to find. Probably not. But I think at least someone should look. I might need it for the insurance, too."

"So what's your problem?"

"I need to be somewhere else this morning. It's really urgent. I can't be at the house to wait for the police to come round. No way."

"So the favour is …?"

"Could you possibly organise it anyway? I'll sign a statement or whatever later. They can get the keys from Joanna." I gave him the address.

He hesitated for a moment, and I wondered if for once I'd pushed his good nature too far. However, he finally said, "Mate, you owe me so many favours you're off the chart."

When Joanna returned I explained my arrangement with Dave, and we prepared to leave. She asked me, "Where are you staying tonight?"

"I don't know. I'm not sure if my house will be habitable."

"Come here. Stay as long as you like." She turned to Ashley. "And you must come again too. I mean it."

Ashley smiled warmly at her. "You've been really good. I can't thank you enough."

I drove Ashley all the way to Paddington. It was a long slow trek, but it meant we could stay together longer. Periodically I kept reaching out to touch her, as if to reassure myself that she was really there. Finally she said, "I'm not going to vanish or turn into a pumpkin, honestly."

As she got out of the car at Paddington she said, "Give Trina my regards. Tell her I remember her too."

And I was on my own, heading north up Finchley Road towards the M1.

Chapter 63

Something was nagging at me as soon as I hit the M1. All I wanted to do was daydream about the previous night, but my brain wouldn't let me. I worried away at the problem as I drove through the drab grey morning, and was still trying to track it down when I reached Toddington services; still trying at Watford Gap, forty miles further on.

It was at some point after the M6 turnoff that it came to me. When Trina had phoned me I'd scribbled down the details of our meeting in red pen on the back of a printed sheet of A4 paper – probably an estate agent's flyer. It had been lying on my desk ever since, and I clearly remembered seeing it before I set off yesterday afternoon to meet Ashley. Yet last night it wasn't there – definitely.

The people who had sabotaged my water system were the same people who had held me captive in that meeting room – that much was obvious. Their break-in had seemed just a childish act of revenge for my escape – but suppose they were still looking for information about Liam Stone? Would they have taken those scribbled notes? Why would they have seen any significance in them?

I thought back over recent events. At one point they'd stolen my computer; therefore they could have read my recent files and emails. I'd never bothered to password-protect it – an omission I'd rectified with my new one. If they had, they would almost certainly have seen stuff about Trina and my search for her. Would they have concluded that she was Liam Stone's daughter?

My thoughts raced as I tried to follow the logic. The fictional daughter wasn't called Trina, but they might still have made the connection. They'd already decided that the rest of the book was substantially true, so why not this?

What had I actually written down about our meeting? I couldn't remember exactly, but I had an idea it included the time, the place, even what she would be wearing. I hadn't really needed to make a note of any of this – it was simply a habit borne of all the interviews I'd conducted over the years. Without notes, you had no evidence of what you'd been told.

I broke into a sweat as I thought through the implications. If these people believed Trina was Stone's daughter, in their eyes she would be a target – and it would be my fault. Her years of carefully cultivated anonymity could be swiped away at a stroke. And all through a bizarre misunderstanding.

Suddenly I felt powerless, captive on this motorway while Trina was possibly stepping into danger. I had to contact her, to warn her. I took out my phone, but immediately realised the battery was flat. I'd intended to put it on charge when I got home last night, but in the fuss I'd completely forgotten about it.

I fumbled in the glove compartment for my in-car charger, then remembered I'd taken it indoors the last time the car was serviced. Then it occurred to me that this was academic. She'd rung me on my landline, so I wouldn't have her number anyway. How incredibly stupid of me not to have asked for it explicitly. Yet again, I was losing my grip.

What should I do? I was in an even weaker position than I'd felt when Rick Ashton headed off to Rugby with Liam Stone. This time there was no crime to report – just a vague suspicion that one might be committed at some indeterminate time in the future. And if I did call the police and they actually paid any heed to me, how would Trina feel if they descended on her, even if it was merely in a benign attempt to protect her?

No, the only thing I could do was meet her as planned and try to ensure she was safe when I got there. Subconsciously I pressed harder on the accelerator.

* * *

The exit for Chesterfield was seventy miles further on. That final long stretch of motorway seemed to take an age. Then I had about four miles of feeder road to contend with, and finally I was on a sort of bypass, looking for signs to a car park.

With just under half an hour to spare I was speed-walking through the streets of Chesterfield, looking out for the market square. I kept glimpsing the town's famous twisted spire, peeking through alleys or towering above other buildings.

At several points I stopped to ask the way, but I was misdirected twice – or more likely I misunderstood what I'd been told. Everywhere I seemed to see black and white mock-Tudor facades – apparently a feature of the town. They all looked frustratingly similar to one another.

Eventually I emerged into the square. It was filled with canopied market stalls in uniform ranks, and was bustling with late lunchtime shoppers. There was a phone box on the corner as Trina had said, and I cast around, looking for her and at the same time looking for any sort of threat.

I could see neither, so I leaned on a wall, catching my breath and continuing to watch. For a while nothing happened.

And still nothing. The minutes ticked past. Two o'clock approached. Then it occurred to me that there might be phone boxes at other corners of the square. There was none in view, but I couldn't see across to the opposite corner. Cursing my stupidity, I made my way hastily round the square. Another pair of phone boxes came into view.

And there she was: the woman I'd encountered at Euston all that time ago. No question – she was Trina. After all my speculation, it turned out I'd got it right.

She was dressed as promised in a brownish jacket and darker skirt, and was glancing at her watch. I approached her diffidently.

"Hello?"

She looked up and smiled. "Mike."

Chapter 64

She led the way to a modern-looking restaurant and bar. I glanced around warily in case I'd been right about my stalkers from the south. I could still see no apparent threat.

"Chesterfield's finest," she commented as we sat down facing each other. She took off her jacket and hung it over her chair back. She was wearing a high-necked dark yellow jumper and a necklace of wooden beads.

Comparisons were pointless, but nonetheless I found myself reflecting that her hair was a little darker than Ashley's and a little longer, and she also looked older: my age, in fact. But she had a similar type of face – my type, clearly. There was a slightly haunted grace about her. I was aware of a faint but distinctive scent.

She smiled briefly. "So. Here we are."

I smiled back. "I can't actually believe it's you."

"Well it is." She was smiling cautiously, probably assessing me.

I waited a moment, then said, "I saw you at Euston station. Two or three years ago. I thought it was you then, but I wasn't sure."

"I remember."

"Really? Did you think it was me?"

"No, not at the time. I didn't remember you *that* well. I didn't make the connection. But when I realised you were looking for me, I started to wonder."

"I must seem like an obsessive. I'm amazed you were willing to meet me at all."

"As you see, I picked a public place." Another brief smile.

"I don't blame you."

A waitress arrived with menus and we both ordered food.

"So," Trina said when we were alone again. "What shall we talk about?"

I smiled. "The Fairmile Hotel?"

"Ah, the glorious Fairmile. I understand it is no more."

"Correct. It's now a housing estate. A shame."

"It was nice," she said reflectively. "We used to have holidays in all sorts of places back then, foreign holidays mostly, but somehow the Fairmile seemed special." She smiled faintly at me. "You should have spoken to me sooner. We could have done stuff together."

"Ah, but I didn't know how to do ordinary stuff. I was a thwarted romantic. I had a crush on you. The trouble was, I couldn't imagine you feeling like that." I shrugged.

Another faint smile. "You'll never know if you don't ask."

I hesitated, then said lightly, "You were going to write to me, but you never did."

She raised her eyebrows. "Was I? It probably wasn't the best of timing." She gave me a dry smile. "I'm sorry if I left you traumatised."

"I think I got over it."

We looked at each other in silence for a moment. Finally she said, "OK, so we've covered the Fairmile Hotel. What else should we talk about then?"

I looked carefully at her. I had a sense that she had her piece to say, but was holding back. Playing for time, I said somewhat fatuously, "Good question."

"Well, we could talk about why you've been so keen to find me. Juvenile crush aside, I did notice that you're a journalist. Did you see a story in this, Mike?"

Immediately I felt put on the spot. What she said was at least partially true, but I didn't want it to be. To deflect the idea I said hastily, "No, no, I would be more inclined to call it a kind of therapy."

Therapy? What the hell did that sound like? Floundering, I added, "I was divorced, I was depressed. The Fairmile Hotel seemed to conjure up a happier time from my past, but it was a bittersweet memory. I thought I might be able to shake some kind of sense out of it. And the harder you were to track down, the more of a challenge it became."

"Therapy," she repeated. "A challenge. Right." She pulled a plastic cigarette lighter from her bag and started tapping it absently on the table, evidently thinking. "And why do you suppose it was such a challenge?"

"Well, for some reason you obviously didn't want to be found. That is, your family didn't."

"Precisely. It was a challenge because my father intended it to be. He made it as hard as he could for anybody to find us. He needed us to disappear." Her look had hardened. "But you were determined to find us anyway. You treated our lives like some kind of game – a puzzle to solve."

Ah, now we were getting to it: her real opinion of my efforts. Well, I'd put myself up for hearing about it, so now I'd better listen. I said, "You're upset with me. I'm sorry. I can't blame you."

She sighed. "It's OK, Mike, I didn't bring you all the way here to lecture you. I just find it ironic to think that we've avoided being found all these years by the people we were hiding from, and now along comes Mike, just looking for a bit of 'therapy'."

"I don't know what to say."

She put her lighter down on the table, twirled it around and watched it come to rest. Then she looked up again. "It's no real surprise, to be honest. When we went to ground, there was no internet, no Facebook, no way to find missing people online. All that came later. In the last few years it dawned on me that in the end some persistent person was bound to start digging into our past. It just happened to be you."

"I can stop it," I said awkwardly. "I mean I can take down some of the internet stuff and drop the whole thing. Not all of it, but some."

"It might be too late, but thank you for the thought."

I said nothing. Neither of us spoke for a moment, then she said, "You know, in some ways it's the trivial things that bother me the most. Suppose my identity was blown. My passport would probably be cancelled. My credit cards might stop working. I could lose the mortgage on my flat. I might have a fight on my hands to keep my pension rights. I would suddenly be a non-person. Can you imagine the months of hassle it would all cause – years even?"

"Surely it wouldn't be as bad as that? You can't be the first person ever to be put in this position. There must be procedures to deal with it."

"And you know this for sure, do you?"

"No."

"No you don't. And what about the publicity if it got into the press? You'll gather that my father was hiding something. Suppose it all came out. My face would be all over the papers. Suddenly I would be public property. And all this is before we start talking about interrogation by the police, things like that. Jesus."

I stared at her, humiliated and unsure what to say next. Weakly, I commented, "You were only a child when all this happened. Surely you can't be blamed for it now? Presumably you just did what you were told?"

"That's what I would argue, but if you were in my shoes, would you want to put it to the test?"

"No I wouldn't."

She looked at me again without speaking for a moment, then smiled briskly and said, "Cheer up, it hasn't happened yet."

I cleared my throat. "So why exactly did you decide to meet me then?"

"Ah, partly it was out of curiosity to see who this persistent person was."

"You could have got that from my Facebook page."

"I did. But I thought a one-to-one would be more effective."

"But you could just have kept your head down."

"Perhaps, but I felt the only way to calm all this down was to talk to you in person. And having got you here, I knew I couldn't just paper over my history. Filling you in is part of the compact between us, isn't it?"

I shrugged. "I'm not pressuring you. Truly."

She looked at me. "I might be wrong here, but I feel I can trust you. I know I'm stupidly quick to form opinions, so I can only hope my judgement is sound."

"I can't really comment on that."

"You don't have to." She resumed tapping the table with her lighter. "I suppose partly I was tempted by the idea of talking to someone external to everything – but someone with a past connection to our lives." She smiled slightly. "As you can imagine, there aren't many such people in my life. In fact you seem uniquely equipped for the role – and you put yourself up for it."

She stopped there, but I sensed that there was more. I gave her an encouraging look, and after a moment she said, "There's also another thing. Basically, somebody has died, and somebody else might die. In a way these things take away some of the pressure. Not the hassle factor, just the original pressure."

She straightened her back and looked directly at me. "And for some reason, you seem to be the man to hear the story."

Chapter 65

The waitress arrived with our meals, and when she'd left us Trina turned to me.

"It all started when my father was looking for an investment opportunity. He got to know a property developer in the North West."

"Would that be Robert Stainer?"

"Ha! You know about Robbie bloody Stainer, do you? You've done your homework then."

I nodded, thinking I should probably have kept quiet. However, after a moment she continued.

"Robbie Stainer was a really charismatic guy. People just liked to work with him. *I* liked him. Anyway, he was running a property company that went belly-up, and my father helped bail him out. They started again as equal partners."

I nodded.

"I think the original company failed because the other directors were suspicious of Robbie, but my father didn't know that at the time. All he knew was that Robbie seemed to have access to almost unlimited investment funds. The new company started doing well right from the get-go. My father must have thought he'd tapped into the money tree."

She paused, staring into her memory. To prompt her, I said, "You moved to Altrincham."

She raised her eyebrows. "You do know a lot about us."

"It just came up when I was trying to work out what happened to you."

There was another of those pauses while she assimilated what I'd said, but then she resumed again. "For a while everything was brilliant. They were involved in loads of projects – development schemes around Greater Manchester and Merseyside, you name it. They always had the money to invest.

"Then it dawned on my naive father that all this was too good to be true. It was tainted money. Robbie and his cronies were involved in all kinds of money-laundering scams – protection rackets, tax fraud in the West Indies, even drug money. Don't ask me, I don't know the half of it."

I nodded encouragingly.

"The trouble was, all this money was pouring through my dad's company, and the financial regulators were starting to ask questions."

"Couldn't your father have blown the whistle?"

"There might have been a time when he could have, but by this stage he was in it too deep. If he'd done that, the risk was that the company's assets might have been frozen or even seized. He could have lost everything. He might even have been put on trial. And if not, he would have had to answer to Stainer and his gangland friends. He simply wasn't into court cases and witness protection. He didn't trust that kind of thing."

I waited.

"He was really stupid in some ways, my father, but quite shrewd in others. He knew how to divert some of these funds into offshore trusts, numbered bank accounts, that kind of thing. Regulation wasn't as tough then as it is now.

"So overnight, he shunted a big chunk of the company's assets into some of these accounts. Not everything, just what he felt entitled to for the work he'd done. And basically we just vanished. New names, new everything. Bye bye Catrina, hello Christina." She laughed dryly. "He was even clever enough to go to London for the documents we needed, to avoid getting tangled up with Stainer's crew. He was very thorough."

"So he knew a few shady people himself."

"I didn't say he was whiter than white."

I sat for a while, taking all this in. I said, "But you didn't flee the country – you just moved across the Pennines. Surely your father was worried that he would come across Stainer somewhere eventually?"

"Oh no, we lived in Edinburgh for the first few years. And my father kept his head down. With all that money, he didn't need to work any more. I won't say he was a recluse, he just kept himself to himself. He was never much of a party animal in the first place. Nor was my mum. We just lived quiet, comfortable lives. I went to school up there and became a wee Scot." She said that in a Scottish accent, then gave me an ironic smile. "And my father grew a beard."

"You don't sound Scottish now."

"Hanging on to the vestiges of my old life, wouldn't you say?"

"But you must have been constantly worried about Stainer all the same."

"Speaking for myself, no. I just got on with my new life. I think my mother worried for the first few years, but time passed, they put on weight, they looked different, and our new life took root."

"But now you do live somewhere round here?"

"My father lives in a village a few miles away." She gestured vaguely behind her. "My parents moved down here ten years ago. I was already working in Doncaster, so it meant we saw more of each other." She paused. "It's just my dad now. My mother died two years later."

I said, "But Robert Stainer is still at liberty. Did the authorities never catch up with him?"

"You're out of date there, Mike. He died suddenly of a heart attack three months ago. It was in the press."

So the man immediately behind Desmond Markham's flight was no longer a threat to Trina and her father. That presumably helped explain her openness. I said, "I see."

"But no, he was never prosecuted for anything. He was a slippery bastard, and he always had the right contacts in the right places. The firm went bust when my father bailed out, but somehow Robbie himself came out of it smelling of roses. Of course, at the time he was able to point the finger at my dad. 'Not my problem, guv. My partner hopped it with the dosh.' I assume that was what he claimed, anyway."

"What about the people he was involved with? Do you think they still have your father in their sights?"

"I very much doubt it. If they'd been that aggrieved, they would have gone after Robbie himself. The fact that he survived tells me he was able to keep them off his back. I told you, he was Mr Escapologist." She shrugged. "Besides, even if they found us – and hopefully they won't – there would be no point in them thinking they could get their money back. There isn't any – just my father's house and a few savings."

We sat in silence for a long time. Finally I said, "How come you know about all this?"

"Oh, bits and pieces from my father. He was very cagey to begin with, but he couldn't hide everything, and once he knew I was going to buy into the whole name change thing and not make a fuss, he started to confide in me. In the end I think he told me more than he told my mother."

I nodded. We seemed to have covered everything. She tapped her lighter on the table again a few times, then said, "So tell me something about your life, Mike."

I shrugged. "Pretty mundane compared with yours. I write articles about logistics and transport. Not a life's calling, it's just the way things fell. I got into a steady relationship when I was quite young, and in the end we got married, but then we split up after a few years. We weren't compatible. No family. What about you?"

"Long-term partner. No kids."

"Does your partner know about your history?"

"Bits of it. Not as much as I've just told you. He doesn't like to ask."

The waitress arrived with our bill, then I said, "You told me two things had happened to make you think it was OK to ring me and use your own name. One of them was presumably Stainer's death, so what was the other one?"

"Ah, yes. Well, my father is ill. In fact he's dying. Might as well tell it like it is. That's why I've dragged you all the way to Chesterfield. He's in hospital up in Sheffield. I don't want to be away from the area for too long at the moment."

"I'm sorry to hear it."

She nodded her acknowledgement.

"Anyway, the point is, my father is the one who's been on the run from the police and Robbie all these years, not me. And pretty soon he won't be around to do any more running."

I said nothing, and she pushed her chair back. "Don't get me wrong,

Mike, I'm not about to go public with all this. I just think I've done enough creeping around."

Thinking back to our phone conversation, I said, "What about Tish? Your friend? Couldn't you confide in her?"

"Ah, Tish. Yes, she's the one person I've kept in touch with from my old life. She knows the score. But she doesn't know where I live, or anything else about my life. We felt it was safer that way. I just contact her very occasionally when something comes up – you and your Facebook stuff, for instance. We have a communication system that's very hard to trace – or so I'm told. There's no obvious electronic trail. We have a sort of code that we use when we want to get in touch."

"Wow. And that actually works?"

"Well, it seems to. She has deniability. She doesn't know anything, so she can't give anything away. If someone starts to show undue interest in me online, she'll simply try to discourage it – to make out that she thinks I might have emigrated, or even died." Trina shrugged. "That's the theory, anyway. It's never been properly stress-tested, so I don't know how robust it really is."

"But when she contacted me she actually pretended to be you."

"Ah, yes. That was a new strategy. You were so persistent that we thought we'd better try something different." She smiled dryly. "It didn't work, did it? You saw through it."

I looked at her in wonder. "It's hard to believe people can actually live their lives like this."

"It's easier than you think. Emergencies like that are the exceptions. Mostly you just get on with the daily grind."

"What do you do in life?"

"I'm in sales and marketing. That's why I have to go to London sometimes."

"Ha! My … my girlfriend is in marketing." I liked that term – girlfriend. "She's Ashley Renwick. You met her at the Fairmile. She sends her regards."

She looked at me quizzically.

"She lived near the hotel, and used to play there sometimes. She would have been about six or seven when you were there."

"I think I remember her. Precocious little brat."

I laughed. "You were her heroine. She remembers you clearly."

"So how come she's your girlfriend? Did you keep in touch with her or something?"

"No, hardly. I only got to know her in the last few months. In a way it was through looking for you."

"Looks as if I have a lot to answer for."

Chapter 66

We left at around four o'clock, and exchanged phone numbers and email addresses before we parted company. "I won't give you my street address," she said dryly. "Got to draw the line somewhere."

Outside the restaurant I found myself looking around again uneasily for my captors from London. I'd managed to forget the possibility that they might have made their way here, but that didn't make it any less real. I couldn't see anything out of the ordinary.

Should I alert Trina to the danger? It was too late really. I should have mentioned it while we were in the restaurant, but I hadn't wanted to interrupt the flow. It would seem absurd to raise it as an afterthought.

A weak sun was now shining. We walked together for a little way, then she said, "My car is this way, but I think you said yours was up this street?"

I wasn't sure what sort of parting gesture would be appropriate, but she solved the problem for me. We shook hands briefly, and she said, "Now we've done this, let's keep in touch." I watched as she walked briskly away: a poised, dignified woman with a strange past.

It took me much less time to find my car than it had to get here from it, and I was soon driving around looking for signs back to the M1. I made my way on to a main road out of the town and drew to a halt at the end of a traffic queue.

I glanced idly to my left across a large open-air car park, and immediately spotted Trina about thirty yards away, presumably heading towards her car. As I watched, a white Transit van slowly passed her, apparently in search of a parking space. It stopped a little way ahead of her, and a figure opened the passenger door and jumped down.

Immediately I recognised him as one of my assailants from London. It wasn't his face that I knew, just his stance, his way of moving. He was even wearing the same grey hoodie outfit. Aghast, I realised they must be going to grab Trina. I was about to witness a kidnapping in broad daylight in the middle of a busy car park. These people were incredible.

I had involuntarily pulled away as my traffic queue started moving. I jammed on my brakes, and immediately there was a sharp bang and my car jerked forward. The car behind had shunted into me. Fuck.

Thankfully the impact hadn't caused my air bag to deploy. I yanked the handbrake on and plunged out of the car. From the corner of my eye I could see an outraged face through the windscreen of the car behind me. Ignoring him, I ran round my car and over to the roadside, and vaulted over the corrugated crash barrier.

Beyond it there was a rough grass verge, then a wire fence bordering the car park. I glanced to either side and realised there were several jagged holes in it. I lunged through one of them and started weaving my way among parked cars towards the van.

Its rear doors were now open and Trina had almost reached them. The man I'd seen was standing near the back of the van, clearly ready to make his move. At the top of my voice I shouted, "Trina!" Then, "Tina!"

She stopped and looked round. The man looked round too. I was closing in on them, and I shouted "Trina! Look out! Run!"

She didn't need telling twice. She immediately ducked to her right and took off between parked cars. The hooded figure now turned to me.

I felt a blind fury surge through me. How much of this incessant hassle was I supposed to put up with? Without breaking my pace I strode up to the man, almost spluttering as I spoke. "When will you fucking leave me and my friends alone? When?"

I could see his muscles tense in readiness to throw a punch at me, but I was beyond caring. Oblivious to the danger, I kept on moving towards him and thrust him backwards with both arms against the van. He nearly lost his footing, and I thrust at him again before he had time to recover. This time he stumbled to his knees, looking at me in surprise.

He was up in a second and ready to hit me, but then a car hooted impatiently behind us. He hesitated, then seemed to come to a decision. He turned and ran to the van's passenger door, and dragged it open. The van's engine revved and it drew vigorously away while he was still climbing in. I watched as the rear doors slammed shut.

I fumbled my mobile phone out of my pocket, then remembered that the battery was flat. Explaining all this to Trina would have to wait until later.

* * *

Much later, as it turned out. By the time I got back to my car a police cruiser had already pulled in front of it, blue light flashing. The irate driver of the car behind mine was standing with two policemen in high-visibility yellow jackets, remonstrating angrily.

The policemen reminded me that it was illegal to flee the scene of an accident. I pointed out that I hadn't fled. Here I was. OK, so what on earth did I think I was doing then? I said I thought I'd seen a woman being assaulted in the car park, and felt I had to go to the rescue. They said this was no excuse for endangering other motorists, and in fact causing an accident. I said I understood.

They came close to arresting me, but eventually seemed to decide that the circumstances didn't warrant it. However, they warned me I would probably be summonsed for an offence of some kind – possibly driving without due care and attention.

To give them credit, they also asked about the woman I thought was being attacked, and made a note of what I told them. I said she'd run away and the attackers had escaped. "Maybe someone got it on CCTV."

I gave them my details and then exchanged insurance information with the other driver, and he was eventually able to drive away unaided. I wasn't so lucky. The impact from his car had put a major dent in the back of mine, and body panels were pressing against the wheels.

I then realised I'd let my motoring club membership lapse, so I had no recovery insurance. Great. One of the policemen organised a breakdown truck to tow my car away, and when it arrived I accompanied the crew to a garage on the outskirts of Chesterfield.

They told me there was nothing they could do with the car until the following day at the earliest, so I decided I might as well leave it there and go back to London. I walked all the way into town and made my way to the railway station.

I found a public phone box and dialled the number Trina had given me. The call went to voicemail with an anonymous announcement. I didn't leave a message.

2012

Fury is the best way to describe Sasha's immediate reaction to my sudden appearance on her doorstep: fury at me, at herself, at her situation. I could see it all in her eyes in that fleeting moment of first contact.

It was followed quickly by surprise, bafflement, and finally resignation. Which is how come we were sitting in her kitchen ten minutes later, and she was handing me a cold drink.

"I don't normally invite total strangers into my home." She spoke with an Australian accent.

"I should hope not."

"If you hadn't mentioned Polperro I would have been calling the police by now."

"I can understand that."

She looked at me carefully. "I know about you. You've been running a Facebook campaign in the UK, trying to find me." She shrugged. "And now you have. So what do you want?"

I said, "Nothing. I just thought it would be amazing to meet you again, after all these years." It had seemed such an imperative, yet now it sounded so weak.

She gave me a hard look. "And you've come all the way from England just for that?"

I nodded mutely.

"Jesus. You must be some kind of moron." She looked me up and down. "Well you've met me. Will that do?"

"If that's what you want."

"Clearly you've joined the dots. You know why I'm here in Australia, and what happened to my family."

"Some of it, yes."

She looked around her. "Well, this is my life now. I'm Sarah, and I don't have anything to do with any of that any more. And I'd have preferred it if you hadn't come interfering."

"I'm sorry."

"Are you thinking of going to the police or the press? If you do, you'll ruin my life. You do understand that, do you?"

"Don't worry, I won't."

"I hope you mean that."

Chapter 67

It was after eleven in the evening when I finally got back to London from Chesterfield. Joanna was agog for information about my meeting with Trina, but I managed to fend her off and slip away to the spare room – now strangely vacant without Ashley in it. I put my mobile on charge and immediately rang her. I knew she might be with Jack, and she might have gone to bed. Too bad.

In fact she was about to leave her parents' house. "My mum bought some things for Jack, so I'm taking them over to him."

I gave her a run-down on my lunch with Trina, and she listened with fascination, stopping me frequently to ask for more details. Finally she said, "Just a minute," and I could hear her moving to a different room.

"So *are* you in love with her all over again?"

I smiled to myself. "I was never in love with her in the first place, just smitten."

"That's what you say now."

"Don't worry, you'll be the first to know."

"Ha."

I said, "She remembered you. She thought you were a precocious brat."

"I think I'm liking this woman less every minute."

We chatted on for a while. I said, "I'm due down at Latimer's again for a catch-up meeting in a couple of weeks' time … but it's too far ahead."

"Yes it is." She paused to reflect. "What's to be done?"

"I don't know. I could come to Cornwall, but I don't see how we could meet. You can hardly ask Jack for a night off."

She chuckled at this, then said, "This is terrible, thinking of running around behind his back." But she didn't sound as if she thought it was so terrible. "I'll only be there for another two or three weeks, then I'll get my life back."

"Maybe you could make up some event in London that you have to attend?"

"Probably best not to be caught in a lie."

"You're right." I took a deep breath. "Aarrggh!"

* * *

Next morning I sat in Joanna's lounge with my laptop open on her coffee table. My first call was to the garage in Chesterfield where my car had been taken. I was told there would be no chance of looking at it until next week, and it was unlikely to be Monday.

Next I organised a plumber to repair the cold water tank at my house and a joiner to repair the window. Then I called Dave Matthews, who didn't answer, but rang me back an hour later.

"Dave, I wondered what happened about my house?"

"I went round there myself, as it happens. Charming lady, your friend Joanna."

"Ah, it was you she was talking about. So what did you find?"

"Nothing much, frankly. They broke in through your kitchen window, and they must have taken tools to extract the ball valve from your cistern. All very neat. No damage to the house that I could see, except water damage. It's starting to dry, but you'll probably need a few new ceilings, and maybe some new carpet. Oh, and you need to get that back window repaired."

"In hand. Thanks, anyway. I owe you yet again, needless to say."

"All part of the service."

Ignoring the irony, I said, "Did you get any joy with that surname, Slater? Did it tie in with any of the likely suspects behind all this harassment?"

"Afraid not. No apparent connection with any of them. Also, the people from the original robbery all seem to have solid alibis for the night you were kidnapped. We haven't been able to link it to anyone specific."

I sensed a small hesitation. "But?"

"Well, if my money were on it, I would be looking at a guy named Derek Flynn. Devious bastard. His wife evidently alibi'd him, but what value is that?" He paused. "Mind you, most of them used that kind of alibi. What can you expect when these are middle-aged men, and you're asking them about something that happened in the middle of the night?"

* * *

I wondered about Harry Slater from the reading group. Maybe I'd got this wrong. Just because he came from somewhere east of London, he didn't necessarily have to have gangland connections. I was being over-simplistic.

But who else could have passed on the lead to my book? That man had definitely talked about "my nephew". Who could that be?

I rang Eric, the reading group chairman, and today he answered at my first attempt. I asked if he could give me contact details for Amelia, and he readily provided them. Amelia's surname, it turned out, was Henderson, and she lived in Wandsworth.

At the end of the conversation Eric threw in, "I hope you're not canvassing my members to start up a rival reading group or something?"

"Don't worry – not a chance. This is just something private."

"I'm glad to hear it."

I rang Amelia's number, and she picked up straight away.

"Mike! What a nice surprise."

"Look, I hope you won't mind me asking this, but I'm trying to track down people who have read my book. It's a long story, and I promise I'll tell about it one of these days, but for now I just wondered if you happened to know anyone else who might have read it?"

"To be honest, no. You did say you didn't want anyone at the reading group to know about it, so I took you at your word."

"And I'm really grateful. I wasn't suggesting that you'd dobbed me in to the group. I just wondered if you'd mentioned it to someone in the outside world."

"No, not really." She paused. "Apart from my son Alec, that is."

"Your son?"

"Yes. He's fifteen. You wouldn't think he would be interested in anything I'm interested in, but he actually likes mystery novels. He read your book on his tablet, through my account. So it was free – sorry!"

I hastily processed this information. It would hardly be politic to ask Amelia if any of her relatives were jewellery thieves, but there was one thing I could ask.

"Do you know if he happened to tell anyone else about the book? A friend, possibly?"

"No, but I can ask him. He's at school, but he'll be back later."

"That would be excellent, thanks."

"He said he liked your book, by the way. It was quite interesting."

Damned with faint praise.

Chapter 68

My house looked much worse to me than Dave Matthews had implied. Carpets in the upstairs rooms were still sodden, there were tide marks of receding water on several rugs, and chunks of ceiling were dangling by a thread in two places. Perhaps most dispiriting was the pall of dampness – already with overtones of mould after just one day.

I risked turning on the electricity, which seemed to work normally. Both tradesmen turned up during the afternoon to carry out the repairs, and both charged a massive premium for an emergency call-out on a Saturday. At least by the end of the afternoon I had a house I could live in again – if you discounted the sodden bedclothes and the depressing aura hanging over everything.

I hadn't yet tried to contact Trina, to explain to her what had happened when she was attacked yesterday. I couldn't think of anything acceptable to say. The kidnap attempt had come about because of me – that was the long and short of it. It might well have resulted from an ongoing misunderstanding, but what consolation was that? As far as she was concerned, the reason was irrelevant. It would surely confirm that she should never have trusted me in the first place.

I was tempted to report the attack to Dave Matthews, simply to reinforce the message that something needed to be done to stop these people. But I couldn't, because it would mean breaking faith with Trina in an even bigger way. Once Dave knew the score, he would surely have to report what I'd told him, and that would be the end of Trina's new identity.

I went back to John and Joanna's, marvelling at the contrast between my own increasingly soulless home environment and the warmth and vitality of theirs.

"Can I live here all the time?" I asked Joanna.

"Course you can – but Ashley might have something to say about that."

"You liked her then?"

"Need you ask? She's an absolute gem! I don't know how you managed to hypnotise her into liking you, but you should consider yourself very lucky."

"I do."

She leaned forward confidentially. "If you want to know, she thinks you have kind eyes." She gave an ironic smile. "I didn't put her right on that."

My phone buzzed in the middle of supper, just as Jeremy was building up to the climax of a story about his day at school. I saw that it was Amelia's number, and excused myself to the kitchen.

"Mike, I don't know if this is any use, but I asked Alec if he'd told anybody about your book, and he said he'd mentioned it to one of his best friends, a boy named Danny Watson." She hesitated. "But you're not going to try to contact him or anything, are you? I don't think that would be a very good idea."

"God, no, nothing like that." I felt I needed to offer her some alternative explanation. "I'm just trying to get a feel for the ripples of interest, to work out how the word gets around."

"OK, well I'm glad if I've helped."

* * *

Up in my bedroom that evening I opened a browser window on my laptop and started searching the reports on the security van robbery for anyone named Henderson, Amelia's surname. No luck. Then I tried the same thing with Watson, her son's friend's surname. Still no luck. Maybe it was another blind alley.

Idly I started searching on various permutations of Watson, Danny and Wandsworth. There were thousands of finds of all kinds, and it seemed a pointless exercise, but for want of a better idea I kept on following links.

Suddenly I had a small breakthrough: I tracked down the correct Danny Watson. There was a picture of him with a boy called Alec Henderson, who had to be Amelia's son. This encouraged me, and I kept on trawling. And that's when I found it – a page for Danny Watson's parents: Rory Watson and Gillian Flynn.

Derek Flynn was one of the security van robbers – the one Dave had felt was a good candidate for having organised all these assaults on me. So if Gillian Flynn was related to him, that would make Danny his nephew – or great-nephew, or at any rate some kind of nephew. It was too much of a coincidence not to be true.

I checked my watch: 9.30. Not too late to ring Dave and run this past him. I caught him at home, apparently having just finished eating. He was impressed by my success in identifying Danny Watson, but dubious about the usefulness of the information.

"It confirms to you and me that Flynn must be the man behind all this, but it's extremely tenuous evidence, given that the man has an alibi for the night in question."

"But can't someone start looking harder at his friends and associates? I mean, he must have links with the gang who actually pulled me off the street. Isn't this part of an evidence trail?"

"Well, I can run it past the people in Essex, and see if they're willing to follow it up, but I had a hard enough job getting their support in checking alibis. I'm probably not their favourite person at the moment."

"Where does this bloke actually live then?"

"A place called Warley."

"Maybe I should go and see him myself."

"That would be a very stupid thing to do. Forget it, Mike. These are very nasty people."

"You think I don't know?"

Neither of us spoke for a moment. I was wondering what I might say if I actually did speak to Derek Flynn. Finally I said, "Could I ask you one more favour?"

He sighed deeply. "Yeah, OK, what is it?"

"Could you find out what happened to Liam Stone, the man who turned up in Oxfordshire with a gun? I mean, have the police confirmed his identity, and are they going to prosecute him?"

"Dare I ask why you need to know?"

I reflected for a moment. "Call it a moral issue."

"You've lost me there, I'm afraid."

"I'll explain next time I see you. All I need is to know what happened to him."

"OK, if I find out anything I'll get back to you tomorrow. But don't hold your breath."

Chapter 69

It was two days before Dave got back to me with news of Liam Stone. He rang me on Monday morning as I was debating whether to go home to work or stay in Joanna's sunny sitting room.

"Stone, if that's his real name, has been released on bail."

"What?"

"It's an option in this kind of case. The police weren't helped by the fact that they couldn't find the gun he was allegedly using."

"You've got to be kidding me! It wasn't alleged. I saw it!"

"Well, be that as it may, it's disappeared. Also, it seems your Mr Ashton doesn't want to press charges. That doesn't mean this man gets off scot free, but it does make the police case more complicated."

"But don't they want to find out if he really is the missing robber?"

Dave sighed patiently. "It's not as simple as that. For a start, it sounds as if he's covered his bases really carefully. To all intents and purposes he really is Andrew Davidson, not Liam Stone."

"Surely they can dig through all that?"

"Eventually they probably can, but it's taking time. Also, you have to remember that even if he's found to be Liam Stone, there may not be any solid proof that he was actually implicated in the robbery in the first place. There's anecdotal evidence, suspicion, hearsay, but it was all a very long time ago."

"Huh."

"Look, I haven't seen the case files. I don't know what they're thinking up there. I'm only telling you what I know."

* * *

I sat back on Joanna's sofa and tried to think through my situation. Point one: It very much looked as though the person behind my kidnapping and break-ins was convicted robber Derek Flynn – yet the police didn't seem to think they had enough evidence to pull him in.

Point two: All along, Derek Flynn had believed I knew how to contact the escaped robber Liam Stone. Initially he'd been mistaken, but quite miraculously, I now did know.

Point three: If I were to find out how to track down Derek Flynn, and I told him where to find Liam Stone, theoretically that should get him permanently off my back.

Point four: But if I did that, it would be a bare-faced betrayal of Liam Stone.

The moral implications of this were dizzying. Did I owe any loyalty towards Stone? Of course not. But did I have any right to sabotage his life even further than he'd already sabotaged it himself with the gun escapade? That would be the likely outcome of giving him away to Flynn. I wasn't so sure.

My first priority, surely, was to myself. Why should I be flung from pillar to post in the furtherance of some long-standing gangland dispute? And why should it affect people like Trina, who simply happened to have strayed into the crossfire?

Yet at the back of all this, I was aware that my book had sparked this whole thing off. Indirectly, and quite unintentionally, I was responsible.

I wondered what kind of life Liam Stone had led. Was it as bleak, as compromised, as that of the escaped robber in my story? It didn't sound like it. He'd lived life to the full in Australia, then come back to Britain and become a prosperous member of society. Why should I feel sorry for him? Then again, what if I set Flynn on to him, and my actions resulted in him being seriously injured or even killed?

* * *

I decided the first thing to do was see if I could find some way of contacting Derek Flynn. There was no phone number listed for him in Warley, and I wasn't sure where to look next. However, I'd only been trawling the net for a couple of minutes when I found some photographs taken at the time he was released from prison. I felt sure they held a clue.

They were part of a press interview he did, along with his still glamorous wife, and the two of them were shown standing in front of their own house – a substantial modern property with distinctive period-style lanterns on the front. I knew they now lived in Warley, so assuming they were still in that same house, presumably I could find it on Streetview or some other mapping web site.

I painstakingly worked my way through the streets of the town on screen, and finally, after many wrong turns, there it was. Those lanterns were unmistakable. So in theory I could go there. But what would I say? That rather depended on my next phone call.

Getting hold of Rick Ashton was as convoluted a process as ever, but finally he picked up the phone to me.

"Rick, thank you for the heads-up on the funding."

"Least I could do, mate."

"Look, could we meet up? There's something personal that I need to discuss with you, and I don't think it's really something for the phone."

He seemed to consider briefly, but then perhaps recognised that he had to say yes. "Tell you what, I'm working at our old offices in Hemel Hempstead today. Do you want to come over here this afternoon?"

As ever, getting from south London to somewhere out to the north took far longer than it should have, but there were direct trains from Euston to Hemel, and after an unexpectedly long walk across a common I finally found myself approaching Rick's offices. He'd told me they were near what he called "the magic roundabout", which had presumably once functioned as a normal roundabout, but now had mini-roundabouts at every exit. For once I was glad to be on foot.

Chapter 70

Rick had an office on the fifth floor, with a striking view across the town and surrounding countryside. He smiled almost warmly as I walked in.

"Michael my boy, good to see you."

I asked how things were going under the new regime. "Not bad at all," he said briskly. "Not sure how long they'll put up with having me in charge, but I'll always land on my feet."

"You mean you might not survive here?"

"We'll see. Early days yet."

"You're finding it hard to work with Janni Noble?"

He laughed dryly. "No, on the contrary, he seems very straight. Doesn't want to interfere. Tough cookie though. I think I misjudged him."

"At least your own investment is safe, is it?"

"Seems to be." He straightened. "So what was it you wanted to talk to me about?"

I looked round to check that the door was shut. "It's about Liam Stone."

"Oh yes?"

"That is, Andy Davidson."

He waited expectantly.

"I understand you're not pressing charges."

He shrugged expansively. "Well I couldn't, could I? You spelled it out yourself the other day. In some ways I was no better than him. Who would I be to cast the first stone, if you'll pardon the pun?"

"And ... no gun?"

"Surprising, that, isn't it?"

I thought back to the day in question. After we'd returned from the pub I'd left Ashton on his own at the parcel centre. He said he would get a lift home from one of his staff. He must somehow have managed to grab the gun and hide it while the police were moving in, and then later hidden it or disposed of it.

I said, "Fair enough. Anyway, that's not exactly what I wanted to talk to you about."

"What then?"

"Well, are you still in contact with Stone? I mean, could you get a message to him?"

"I presume so. I imagine he's still living at home in Chipping Norton. Needless to say, I haven't checked."

I sat thinking for a moment. Rick knew little or nothing of what had been happening in my life, and I was unsure how much to explain. Finally I said, "You know how you worked out Liam Stone's identity from my book?"

He nodded.

"Well, I need to put you right on something. That book was never a true story. The actual robbery was more or less true, but I made everything else up. I certainly never talked to Stone, which you presumably realise, and I didn't contact anyone else either. It was pure fiction. I just happened to hit on a few truths by pure chance."

He simply stared at me.

I added, "So when you worked out Stone's identity from the book, it was just a lucky guess."

"My god." He stared out of the window for a moment, then turned back to me. "All I can say is you were remarkably lucky with your guesswork. I took that book as being basically true. That's what gave me the confidence to confront Andy. And it did the trick. He never denied who he really was."

"What can I say?"

He gave a single explosive laugh. "Bugger me!"

I waited a moment to get his full attention again, then said, "The next thing you need to know is that you weren't the only one to take the book seriously. Amazing as it may seem, some of the other people involved in that robbery, people who were convicted and put away for it, also got hold the book, and they believed it too. They concluded that I must know how to get hold of Stone. They have a grudge against him. They think he skipped out with part of their share of the proceeds. And they've been giving me all kinds of grief, trying to make me tell them where he is. They're quite violent people."

"Struth."

"You can say that again. You don't know the half of it."

"So what are you thinking now?"

"Well, to begin with I didn't know where to find Stone. I couldn't have told these people anything because I didn't know anything. But now I do know … thanks to you. It's an amazing coincidence that you got to know him, but there it is. You did. In a way you've squared the circle for me. So now I could tell these people exactly where he is."

He was watching me carefully, reading the implications. "But if you did, presumably they would go and beat three kinds of shit out of him, trying to steal back money they think he owes them."

"That's about it, yes."

"Jesus." He gave me a long look. "So what *do* you plan to do?"

I shrugged. "My problem is that the police might never find enough evidence to prosecute him. He might just walk away. But if that happens, I'm still exposed to these people who are after him."

"So …?"

"So basically, I need them to find out where he is and who he is. That seems the only way to convince them to stop hassling me. How I do it is irrelevant in a way. I could leak it to the press, I could find a way to put it on the internet, or I could actually tell these people face to face."

"But does he deserve that? He's not a bad guy at heart."

"Ha! More to the point, do *I* deserve it? He's the one who made wrong choices in his life. All I did was write a book – a work of fiction."

He stared at me, perhaps unable to find a reply to this. Finally he said, "But my god, Andy will love you if he finds out you gave him up to these people."

"Well, I'm not exactly planning to put myself in front of him. The less he knows about me the better."

Rick nodded slowly as realisation dawned. "OK, I'm getting this. You want me to get hold of him, and basically warn him off. You want him to know that the net is closing in."

"Precisely."

I could see him thinking fast. "So wait a minute, how am I supposed to know all this?"

"You could tell him anything you like. You could say the police have hinted that they're going to prosecute, or you've had an anonymous phone call saying the baddies are after him. You can make it up as you go along." I paused. "Tell him I'll wait forty-eight hours after he gets the message before I go public."

"OK OK." He paused. "And why am I doing all this for you?"

I gave him a long look. "I'm not answering that."

The words didn't seem like mine, nor the implied threat behind them. Circumstances seemed to have hardened me. I no longer had the patience to finesse this kind of negotiation.

"So you're prepared to ruin this man's life, to make him a fugitive again?"

I sighed. "Give me a break, Rick. He made himself a fugitive. He's had a good few years on the run – and if he's clever, he'll find a way to give himself a good few more. Do you think he deserves more than that?"

"Point taken." He picked up a pen from his desk, clicked it reflectively a few times, then put it down decisively. "OK, leave it with me. I'll see what I can do."

It was as if we'd been doing a magazine interview, and my allocated time was up. But as I opened the door, he said, "So are we even after this?"

I looked back. "I'll let you know."

2012

I bought her flowers. It was our undoing.

Our conversation yesterday evening had more or less petered out. In the end Sasha seemed not resentful or hostile, just disappointed. If there had been any magic between us as adolescents, I picked up no hint of it now. It was plain that all she saw in me was a threat. I represented evidence that her new identity, painstakingly built up over two thirds of a lifetime, had finally been unpicked. I was her harbinger of doom.

We'd parted on reasonably amicable terms. I told her I would make a holiday of my trip – travel on up the Gold Coast, check out the Great Barrier Reef. But today I'd felt things between us were still unresolved. I bought flowers and headed back to her flat that evening, hoping to make my peace.

Her voice when I pressed the entry buzzer was much more guarded than yesterday. "This really isn't a good time. I thought you were heading off up north?"

"I bought you some flowers. I've got them here."

There was a pause. "That's good of you. You'd better bring them on up."

But when I reached her apartment, she merely held the door ajar.

"Thank you for the flowers. Do you mind if I just take them? It's not a good time."

I held them out. "Good will gesture." I tried a friendly smile.

And then things came unstuck. I heard footsteps behind me, and abruptly I was thrust heavily against the door. It swung inwards, hurling Sasha backwards. I was shoved again, and I half-turned to see two men looming behind me. One of them was pointing a handgun with a silencer at me.

A man's voice from inside the flat called, "What's going on, Sash?"

The man with the gun said, "Let's tell him, Sash." He pronounced her name with malevolent irony. He hustled us through to the main room, where a bronzed man in his late fifties was staring at us aghast.

The gunman said, "Mr Hawkins, we have some unfinished business to tidy up."

Chapter 71

Dusk was falling as I drew up outside Derek Flynn's house in Warley. Lights were on in several rooms, which I took as an encouraging sign.

I parked obliquely opposite and got out, then took out my phone and lined up a selfie with the house clearly in view in the background. I emailed a copy to Ashley and another to Joanna.

Rick Ashton had come through with a terse email the day after I saw him. "Message passed on and understood at 11.20am today. Are we done?" I'd sent a one-liner acknowledgement without answering the question.

That evening I'd phoned Ashley and told her about my plan to visit Flynn. She was initially horrified, but I convinced her that my idea would work if we kept to the plan. The arrangement was that unless I contacted her at the end of the evening, she would get in touch with Dave Matthews and raise all kinds of hell with him. I didn't doubt that she could do it.

I'd waited another day in order to give Stone the promised 48 hours' notice, then borrowed Joanna's car. Getting to Warley involved a drive round the south-east corner of the M25 and through the Dartford tunnel, then out eastwards.

I walked nervously up to the front door and pressed the bell push. A resonant gong sounded somewhere inside, and as I stood there one of the ornate lanterns on the front wall flickered into life, followed by its twin.

The door was opened by a well-preserved blond woman in her mid-fifties. "Can I help you?"

"Is Derek Flynn available please?"

"Who wants to know?" Her tone was neutral: not exactly tough, not friendly either.

"Michael Stanhope."

"Is he expecting you?"

"No, but he'll know who I am."

She started to turn, but then a man came into view behind her. He looked about sixty, and was sparely built with receding fair hair. He was wearing khaki chinos and an open-necked white shirt.

"You say I know you? I don't think so."

The voice was less freighted with menace than it had been that night in the underground meeting room, and the Essex accent less pronounced, but it was definitely him.

"Indeed you do, and I have something to tell you that you might want to know."

I started to enter, but his wife blocked my way. He said, "It's all right, Marcie, let Mr Stanhope come in."

I took a step into the hallway, and as I did so Flynn slipped a phone out of his shirt pocket and started tapping at the screen.

I said, "I wouldn't make that phone call if I were you."

He broke off. "I beg your pardon?" He was looking up at me with disbelief. "You're telling me who I can and can't phone in my own house?" There was menace now in that smile.

"You want to call up your merry men to come and kick the living shit out me. Well don't. There's no need."

He turned to his wife and shrugged – a gesture saying "I don't know what this man is talking about." His wife, however, merely shut the front door loudly, wheeled round and headed off to some interior room.

Flynn lowered his phone, looked indecisively at me for a moment, then said, "OK, you might as well come in."

I followed him into a large, well furnished lounge. A giant TV screen was flickering on the wall, showing a football match. He picked up a handset and silenced it.

"So what's this about then?"

"You know perfectly well what it's about. You've been taking a lot of time and trouble trying to get me to tell you something. Well, I've come to put you out of your misery."

"Oh you have, have you? That's very generous of you, I must say. So what's this fascinating information that you think I want from you?"

"You want to find Liam Stone. Well, I know where he is, or rather where he was. If you ask me nicely I'll tell you."

"If I – if I ask you nicely?" His face broke into a malevolent grin. "Do you realise who I am?"

"Clearly, otherwise I wouldn't be here."

He gave me a long, steady stare, then chuckled slightly. He turned and sat down in the middle of a long cream-coloured sofa. He thrust his legs out and put his hands behind his head. "Tell me more."

There was an easy chair opposite him and I was tempted to sit down, but I decided that on the whole I felt better standing. I said, "Just so you know, people know where I am at this precise moment. People who will come knocking in double-quick time if I don't walk safely out of here."

He nodded. "I was getting that impression." He looked me over. "I suppose you're wearing a wire as well?"

I raised my arms. "No I'm not. You're welcome to pat me down if you want to."

"Pat you down? You're watching too much TV, young man."

"Whatever."

He waited a moment, perhaps inwardly debating the truth of what I'd just told him. Then he said, "So what makes you think I want to contact this Liam Stone?"

I stared at him in frustration. "Look, do you want this information or don't you?"

He seemed to consider this for a moment, then said, "OK, suppose I did want to contact him, how would I go about it?"

I said, "OK, well here's the thing, and you need to hear this first. For most of the time that you've been hassling me and giving me grief, I didn't actually know where Stone was. Not a bloody clue."

I couldn't read his reaction, but he was staring intently at me. I went on, "If you'd been courteous enough to listen to me, you would have realised I was telling you the truth. I made that bloody book up. The whole bloody lot. Some of it turned out to be quite close to the truth, but that was sheer bloody luck. I never actually had any dealings with Stone or anybody else involved in that robbery. Never! That wasn't part of my plan."

I was practically shouting now. I paused for a moment, staring down at him. I could feel the blood pulsing through my temples. "If you want to know the truth, I was too bloody lazy. A decent novelist would at least have made an effort."

He leaned forward, and in a low voice said, "You've got a fucking nerve, standing in my house shouting at me." I could see him struggling to gain control of his anger, and I did my best not to flinch from his gaze.

"Ha! And you've got a nerve having me assaulted and beaten up in order to tell you something I didn't bloody know. What the hell kind of world do you live in?" I could hear my voice rising again. "And then you send people to kidnap a friend of mine in Chesterfield – someone who has absolutely nothing whatsoever to do with any of this. Stone's wife and daughter went into witness protection years ago – I happen to know that. If you're looking for them, I suggest it's a lost cause. Even if you found them, they wouldn't be able to tell you where Stone is. They wouldn't have the faintest idea."

He watched me for a moment without speaking, apparently processing all this, then took a deep breath and settled slowly back on the sofa. "You told me a minute ago that you did know how to find Stone."

"As it happens I do, but it's completely by coincidence. I only found out a couple of weeks ago. After we met."

"Did we meet? I don't seem to remember that."

"Well I do."

There was a silence. Finally he said, "So you found out how to get hold of Liam?"

"Yes. He's been living in England for the past few years under the name of Andy Davidson. He has a house at Chipping Norton in Oxfordshire. You can Google him. He's a solid citizen, but it's him."

"Is that so? How come we didn't find this out, I wonder?"

I lifted my hands in frustration. "There's no point in blaming me just because he's good at keeping his head down."

"But how do I know this isn't a load of bullshit?"

"For Christ's sake, do you think I would come here inviting trouble for myself just to give you a load of bullshit? Give me some credit."

"So if I go to this man's house tonight, will I find him there? Will he say, 'Hello Mr Flynn, would you like a nice cup of tea?'"

"I've no idea whether you'll find him or not. I've told you all I know."

"And dare I ask how you came by this information?"

"Yes you can. Indirectly I got it from the police. They already know who he is, or they think they do. But they're not sure. I hope you're happy with that."

"Oh, great, so they'll be sitting waiting for me to turn up, will they? Very nice."

"No, so far as I know they won't. I haven't set this up with them. I'm speaking to you completely on my own behalf. I'm fed up with you hassling me and fucking about with my life, and I want it to stop. So I'm telling you what I know in good faith – which is a hell of a lot more than you've ever shown me. If Stone has skipped it, I can't help you. It's down to you to find him. I've told you everything I know."

He gave me another long hard look, then rose slowly to his feet. "In that case you'll probably want to be on your way."

"First I want to hear from you that you're done with me and my friends. Forever. Whatever happens, there's nothing more I'll be able to tell you about this. Case closed. Can we agree on that?"

I looked carefully at him, and he gave the faintest nod of acknowledgement as he ushered me to the front door. He gave me a final expressionless stare on the doorstep.

"Drive safely."

Chapter 72

"I think it worked!"

I'd rung Ashley as soon as I got back to John and Joanna's.

"Really?"

"He's obviously a really tough bastard. You hear about people like him and see them on TV, but you never expect to meet them in real life. He was very difficult to read, but I think he got the point."

"I don't know how you had the nerve to confront him in his own home."

"Nor do I!"

"Do you think he'll go after this man Stone?"

"I'm sure he will, but I don't know what good it will do him. Stone will presumably be long gone."

"Do you feel guilty, prompting him to skip bail?"

That was an interesting question. It opened up yet another moral dimension to this puzzle. I said, "In a way I do, but in another way I feel guilty about handing him over to these other people in the first place. At least this way I'm being even-handed."

"It's a no-win situation. You've done what you had to."

"I hope so."

"At least maybe you'll be able to get your life back now. You can have a bit of normality again. You certainly deserve it."

* * *

Normality, it soon dawned on me, posed its own set of challenges. I sat in Joanna's living room the next morning, confronting the mundane issues that had come up in recent days.

My house was a mess, and would presumably cost thousands to repair – and I had all the hassle of insurance to deal with. My car was in

Chesterfield, and the repair bill for that would probably also be far higher than I was expecting. I would lose my no-claims insurance bonus over the back-end shunt, and I might even be prosecuted.

Then there was my freelance life. An email from Jason Bright sat in my inbox, offering me two feature articles to write in the next fortnight. I was apparently back on track with him, yet the prospect of actually doing the work depressed me.

The upside, of course, was Ashley. She trumped all the hassle by a massive margin, and the very thought of her made me smile. But I wasn't deceiving myself. I knew our emerging relationship would inevitably mean negotiation, decisions. We still lived nearly three hundred miles apart, and she had a happy and settled existence where she was. How could we orchestrate some arrangement that would allow us to live in the same place full-time?

Meanwhile, what was I to think about Trina? I'd sent her two emails since we'd met, trying to reassure her that the events in that car park had nothing to do with her secret past. She hadn't replied to either of them. A single phone call had been diverted to her anonymous voicemail.

At least after last night's events I could tell her with confidence that she wouldn't be pursued or hassled again by Flynn's people. I wasn't sure whether that would persuade her to restore contact with me, or in fact whether this had ever been on her agenda in the first place. But at least I could try. I wrote:

Trina – I hope you received my previous emails, but even if you ignored them, please read this one.

I simply want to reassure you that you won't be hassled again by those people you ran into in the car park in Chesterfield. As I said in my last, they weren't after you personally, and didn't even know who you were. In fact I happen to know that they thought you were someone else. Now they know different. I've made sure of that.

You might think it strange that I should be tangled up with people who would do anything like this. I think so too! The story of how it came about is pretty weird, but I'd love to tell it to you some time, and I sincerely hope you'll give me the chance.

The bottom line is that I didn't betray your trust or give away your identity to anyone, and so far as I'm aware, you're no more at risk now than you were before I met you last week.

It seemed the best I could offer for now. I clicked Send.

Five minutes later the garage at Chesterfield rang me to say my car was ready for collection at a body shop round the corner. Could I pick it up as soon as possible? They said their premises were surrounded by streets with double yellow lines, so they couldn't park it outside, and they had limited room to store it inside the body shop.

Tomorrow was a Saturday, but they said they would be open if I could turn up by one o'clock. I thought I might as well get the job done, so I said yes. Then I logged on to a ticket web site and bought a one-way train ticket to Chesterfield.

Then Ashley rang.

"Mike, you know you were saying that two or three weeks was too long to wait before we meet up?"

Immediately I felt a surge of anticipation. "I do."

"Well, what if I were to come to London again – for the weekend, I mean?"

"Really?" A smile surged through my entire body. "But what about Jack?"

"Well, to be honest he can do most things for himself now. But more to the point, he's going to stay with my parents for a few days."

"Really?"

"He's always been a favourite with my mum. They've kept inviting him over ever since his injury. They know the score between him and me. I think my mum wants to reassure him that they're not going to cut him off just because I have."

"I can see I might have a mountain to climb with her."

"Don't worry about it."

I was doing some fast thinking. "Look, I've just arranged to go up to Chesterfield tomorrow to collect my car. I've already bought the train ticket."

"I could come with you."

"Really? You'd be willing to spend all that time in a train from Truro, then head off on another train the very next day?"

"If you'd like me to."

"Absolutely! In fact I'll pay for your ticket."

"Mr Stanhope, your generosity knows no bounds."

I thought some more, then said, "What if we stay somewhere in Derbyshire tomorrow night? A country hotel or something? Make a proper weekend of it. Could you stay over Sunday night and go back to Cornwall on Monday?"

"Not really, but – yes, sod it! Just book it."

* * *

I did some internet trawling and found a country hotel in the Peak District that seemed to fit the bill. I phoned them and made a booking for the following night. Then I logged on to the ticket web site and bought a ticket to Chesterfield for Ashley.

At lunchtime Joanna bustled in, and I told her Ashley was coming to London again. "I'm sorry for the imposition. We could always stay over at my house."

"Don't you dare. Do you want to drive the girl away before she's even got to know you properly?"

"Well, I was hoping you would say that."

"Do you want to bring her to dinner with us?"

I started to protest, then realised I was being over-protective, and maybe also slightly selfish. Ashley could hold her own perfectly well against Joanna, and I'd have her to myself later on. I said, "That would be great, but she may not be here till mid-evening."

"Not a problem."

I wondered briefly about trying to contact Trina again. After all, I was about to take a trip back into her territory. It would be an ideal opportunity for us to meet up so that I could clear the air. I could even introduce her to Ashley.

I quickly dismissed the whole idea. She didn't want to meet Ashley, and Ashley probably wouldn't want to meet her, except perhaps out of curiosity.

Chapter 73

I borrowed Joanna's car again to pick up Ashley from Paddington. It wasn't strictly necessary, and the long drive to the station through the late Friday evening rush hour took forever. I just had to do it. Her smile as she approached me from the barrier was reward enough.

As we headed up on to the Westway flyover I said, "We're due to have dinner with Joanna and John tonight. I hope you don't mind. She wouldn't take no for an answer."

"They're lovely people. It'll be great."

We shot down the dual carriageway past the giant Westfield shopping centre, then crept round Shepherd's Bush Green. Ashley commented, "It's amazing the way you know all these streets. There's so *much* of it. I don't think I could ever get used to it."

I wondered if there was a message for me here.

She continued to examine the environment with evident wonder, then turned to me and commented, "Do you think Joanna fancies you?"

"Joanna? No!" I reflected for a moment. "Really?"

"She treats you like a second husband. She talks to you more than she talks to John."

"She's been a good friend to me. I couldn't have got through the last couple of years without her. But it's all completely platonic. For a start, she's your biggest fan. She's over the moon that you've turned up in my life."

I glanced over at her, and she gave me a mischievous grin. "Maybe I'm helping her live out her secret fantasies vicariously."

"West Country girls aren't supposed to know long words like vicarious."

She reached over and rapped me on the arm. "Watch out, Mr Stanhope. I might ask to be put back on a train back to Cornwall if you're not careful."

"You'd better not."

We continued for a while in amicable silence, then she said, "I must tell you a rather strange thing."

"What's that?"

"Well, I gave Jack a lift to my parents' house at lunchtime. They weren't there, but I was looking for something in my father's study, and I happened to glance at his desk. And there were loads of notes on a pad about Trina Markham and her mother and father. Stuff about Altrincham, and her father's company, and even the word Chesterfield." She gave me a perplexed look. "How could he possibly know about that? You only found out where she lived the other day."

I turned to look at her, baffled. This didn't make any sense. Had her father known where she was all this time? How could he have? Trina had given me the clear impression that she and her family had made a clean break with their past lives, so how could Gordon Renwick have kept track of them? And why would he want to? He'd told me on more than one occasion that he barely even knew them.

I said, "That's bizarre. I can't think what it can possibly mean."

"I suppose I can ask him next time I see him, but I'm not sure I should. He would realise I'd been peeking around among his notes."

I shrugged. "Maybe we'll think of a way for you to bring it up innocently."

* * *

Jeremy had somehow managed to force his parents to let him wait up to greet us, so we had a shy exchange as he hovered round Ashley. Clearly she had made a big impression on him.

Then John served up the casserole and we sat putting the world to rights. Ashley held her own valiantly against Joanna's oblique scrutiny, and I silently applauded her. It must have been easy for her to see through Joanna's transparent plot to tease out her commitment to Cornwall and her life there, but she took it in good part. The occasional private glances between us were enough to fend off any kind of inquisition.

Finally bedtime was declared, and we were able to slip away. Up in the spare room I opened my computer while Ashley was in the bathroom, and called up the scans of those photos Patrick had found of the Fairmile Hotel.

I stared at the group photograph of Trina with various adults. They included Gordon Renwick, Desmond Markham, a woman who was presumably Shirley Markham, and another couple I didn't recognise.

I looked more closely. The unknown man looked vaguely familiar from somewhere. On an impulse I did a web search for Robert Stainer. I wanted to find a picture of what he'd looked like when he was younger.

It didn't take long. There was a lot of information about him on a variety of web sites, and many photographs. And there he was – a good-looking younger man, just as Trina had said: the same man in the photograph at the Fairmile.

In itself this told me nothing. He and his friend Desmond had holidayed there together. So what? Well, I now realised that the answer lay in the picture itself. That warm smile on the face of Gordon Renwick told the story. He was looking not at the camera but at Desmond Markham and his wife and Robert Stainer. It was the smile of friends sharing a private joke. Whatever Gordon might have told us, it seemed clear to me from this picture that they knew each other well.

I wanted to ask Ashley about this, but when she walked in I forgot any thoughts of conversation. We had another agenda, and it wouldn't wait.

Chapter 74

I sat in the lounge next morning staring into space. I was wishing we could just forget about going to Chesterfield and stay here – preferably in bed.

My phone burst abruptly into life in my hand, shaking me out of my trance.

"Mike." Not a regular caller, but the voice struck a distant chord. "It's Jack here. Jack Forbes. Ashley's ..." He was presumably going to say fiancé, but at the last minute checked himself. "I was trying to get hold of Ashley."

"She's in the shower. She probably didn't hear you."

"Oh, right. Well, Mary gave me your number. I hope you don't mind? I think Ash must have left it with her."

"Of course not."

"The thing is, could you give her a message?" He seemed to be unsure exactly what he wanted to say. "Could you just tell her that her father has gone charging off in his car, and Mary's a bit concerned?"

"How do you mean exactly?"

"Well, if Ash gets back to me, I'll probably be able to explain it better to her."

"OK, I'll get her to call you." I nearly asked him about his ankle, but stopped myself just in time. We weren't about to become best buddies.

I recounted this to Ashley, who fetched out her phone and called him straight back. I listened as she talked to him with growing concern. Finally she disconnected and turned to me.

"This is completely bizarre. According to Jack, my father got up at about six o'clock this morning, which he *never* does, and announced to my mother that he was driving up to Sheffield. Mum didn't seem to know what to do, so Jack thought he ought to contact me."

"Did your father say why he was going there?"

"No, but the point is that he never ever does anything like that. He always plans everything beforehand, and keeps my mum in the picture. They do things together."

"What's in Sheffield?"

"Nothing, as far as I know. I doubt if they've ever even been there, and I've never heard of them knowing anyone there."

"So what do you think your mum will expect you to do about this?"

"To be honest, I don't know." She was already opening her contact list. "I'd better phone her and see."

She talked to her mother for a couple of minutes, then I waved my hand to interrupt her. "Ask her about Desmond Markham. Ask what she knows about him."

She looked at me for a moment, then said into the phone, "Mike says I should ask you about Desmond Markham. Did you know him?"

She listened for a moment, then said, "OK, OK. I'll speak to you later." She clicked to end the call. "She says there's nothing to say about him."

We went through to the kitchen to get some breakfast. Joanna wandered in, and we all stepped round each other in that strange dance of friends thrown unexpectedly into a shared space. My mind was whirring the whole time.

Finally we were seated at the breakfast bar, and I said to Ashley, "You know I told you about Robert Stainer, the man who forced Trina's father to go into hiding?"

She nodded.

"Well, he was at the Fairmile at the same time as Trina and her family. He was the other man in that picture you found for me. And I think your father knew them both."

"He said he didn't."

"I know. But suppose he did. What would that mean?"

She shook her head. "I've no idea. What are you getting at?"

"I don't know, I don't know. I'm just trying to think it through." I put my mug down. "I'm certain this has to do with Desmond Markham and Robert Stainer. Your father was making notes about Markham, wasn't he? That more or less proves he knew him. I just don't quite get the significance."

Joanna said, "Can somebody tell me what all this is about?"

I looked at Ashley, who replied, "Apparently my father has gone chasing off to Sheffield in his car, and nobody knows why."

"Is that unusual?"

"On a Saturday morning at six a.m. it's completely unheard-of. And apparently he's not answering his phone."

Joanna yawned. "It's a hell of a long trip."

I said to Ashley, "We know your father is aware that Trina is living near Chesterfield."

"Or we're guessing that." She was becoming faintly defensive.

"OK, we're guessing. Anyway, it so happens that Trina's father is in hospital in Sheffield. Could he know that too?"

"You tell me."

I shrugged. "It could be, although I don't see how. But then, I don't see how he knew about Chesterfield either."

Suddenly I felt we needed to be nearer this apparent centre of activity. We were due to catch a train to Chesterfield, and I felt the need to get going.

Before we left, I decided I should try once more to contact Trina. If all this involved her father, she needed to know. I rang the number she'd given me, which went to voicemail again, and said, "Trina, this is urgent. I felt you should know that a man named Gordon Renwick might be on his way to visit your father in hospital later on today. He's my girlfriend's father, from Truro. I don't know why he would be going there or what he would want, and I truly don't know how he knows anything about you or your whereabouts. We certainly didn't tell him. Anyway, I just thought you should be aware of the situation."

I paused, then added, "If you want to ring me and talk about this, you have my number. I'll be on the train to Chesterfield this morning to pick up my car from being repaired, and I could meet you later on if you like."

Ashley smiled briefly at me as I disconnected. "So I'm your girlfriend, am I?"

I smiled back. "I hope so."

2012

"You have some belongings of ours. All you need to do is hand them over."

The two men had barged their way into the main room of Sasha's apartment, and were standing just inside the doorway, both pointing guns at the rest of us.

The speaker had an Australian accent and looked to be in his mid-thirties: too young to have been involved in the original security van robbery. I guessed they were both local muscle, hired by someone in the UK. They were dressed incongruously in fashionable-looking dark waistcoats and open-neck white shirts, a bit like waiters.

"The fuck I will." Hawkins, in a check shirt and jeans, glared defiantly at them. "I'm calling the police now." He reached for a phone on a bookshelf behind him.

Without even a moment's delay, the second of the two intruders levelled his gun and fired. The silencer reduced the sound to a muted thump. I watched in disbelief as the shot hit Hawkins in the leg. He yelled out in agony and collapsed to the floor, groaning.

Sasha shouted, "Jesus Christ!" She crouched next to her father, looking up at the two men in horror. Then she turned to him. "Just give them what they want!"

Wincing, he said, "If I do, they'll kill us all."

As for me, my head was exploding with a rage beyond anything I'd ever known in my life. I had caused this scene myself through my pointless, relentless search for these people. Me. It was my fault. I was so incensed that my thoughts seemed to have been swept up in a blinding, incoherent vortex. All I knew was that there was no time for hesitation here, no room for negotiation. I had to act.

In front of the sofa was a glass coffee table, and on it was a marble figurine, about ten inches tall. In a single motion I seized it, lunged towards the nearest of the intruders and swung it at him with all my might, crying out with anger as I did so.

The figurine struck him solidly on the arm before he had a chance to react, but his partner, still holding his own gun in front of him, merely shifted his stance slightly and fired at me. I felt a searing pain in my left arm and cried out, spontaneously shrinking to my knees.

I was aware of a shriek from Sasha, and conscious that all eyes had turned to me. And in that moment there was another gunshot, not silenced this time. In that small apartment it sounded as loud as an explosion. I jerked my head round and saw that Hawkins had pulled out a handgun from somewhere and fired from his position on the floor.

The man who had shot me collapsed, evidently out of the reckoning, but the one I'd struck raised his own arm reflexively and fired at Hawkins twice. To my horror, I saw both shots hit him in the chest.

This time Sasha came to the rescue. She grabbed a small silver clock from the shelf and flung it at the man's head, and remarkably it found its target. He recoiled, and before he'd recovered I managed to launch myself to my feet. I raised the figurine again and smashed it as hard as I could against his head.

He crumpled to the floor, and when it was clear he wasn't going to get up again Sasha crouched down again over her father, picked up the phone and shakily called for an ambulance. While she was speaking to them her father called out in a weak voice, and I shuffled over to him. "Mate, you'd better listen up. There's something I need to say."

Chapter 75

Journey time from St Pancras to Chesterfield was just under two hours. Once we found seats on the train Ashley phoned her mother again. There was no further news about her father.

I asked, "When your mother told you she had nothing to say about Desmond Markham, do you think she meant she didn't know him, or she did know him but she wasn't prepared to talk about it?"

"Difficult to tell."

"If you asked her again, do you think she might say more?"

"Knowing her, I think the answer is no."

I considered this for a while. "What if Patrick asked her in person? Do you think she might open up to him?"

"Possibly. She treats him more like a grown-up than she does me."

"Is it worth asking?"

She nodded, already thumbing her way to his number on her phone. Fortunately he answered immediately.

"Patrick, it's Ash. Did you hear about Dad and this sudden trip up north this morning?"

She nodded, listened for a while, then started throwing in snippets about our curiosity over Desmond Markham and Robert Stainer. Finally she disconnected.

"He's going to drive over there later on and speak to her. He'll let us know what he finds out."

For a while we allowed ourselves to forget this strange turn of events. We chatted about past train journeys, or just sat in silence, abandoning ourselves to knowing smiles.

As we pulled out of Derby Ashley's phone jangled – a burst of heavy metal rock music. She glanced at me. "That's Patrick's ringtone."

She listened for a while, responding with the occasional question, then disconnected.

"He's not really getting the full picture, but basically yes, my parents did know the Markhams. They were quite friendly for a while. They also knew this guy Robert Stainer. She thought he was charming, but too good to be true."

"So why didn't they tell us this when I was looking for the Markhams?"

"My mother probably wasn't paying any attention to what you were doing. As for my father, well, it's beginning to look as though he *was* paying attention, but not letting on to us."

"Why not?"

"My mum said my dad had some kind of financial involvement with Desmond Markham. She was a bit vague about that, but maybe it has something to do with all this."

"What does your dad do for a living?" As I asked the question, I marvelled at my failure to raise it before, or to take any interest.

"He's an investment advisor. He's semi-retired now, but he still has a few clients."

"So he might have advised Desmond Markham?"

"I suppose so." She reflected for a moment. "Or Desmond Markham might have advised *him*."

* * *

At Chesterfield we took a taxi to the body shop where my car was waiting. The repair work had not magically made it look any younger than it had before – just put it back to its previous condition. What did I expect? I paid the exorbitant bill and drove us out of the building and round the corner, where I pulled up on a double yellow line and turned to Ashley.

"So what do we do now?" My unspoken question was whether or not we should head for Sheffield and try to find out what Ashley's father was up to.

Ashley shrugged. "Is my dad's trip really any of our business? In all honesty, do we have any right to interfere?"

I stared for a moment down the empty street of ageing industrial premises. It offered me no answer. I said, "I can't help feeling it *is* our business. I think we've somehow nudged your father into tracking down Desmond Markham, and he must have gone looking for him this morning. We made it happen."

"Well no need to include me in this! You're the one who was so desperate to find Trina Markham and her parents."

"Sorry – you're right. I'm the one who instigated this. I know that. The point is, if I'm right, I feel as if I owe them a kind of moral duty of care. I need to take responsibility."

She took a moment to consider this, then said, "But we don't know where exactly Desmond Markham is in Sheffield. You said he was in a hospital. There could be lots of hospitals. Do you even know his new name?"

What had Trina told me? Was her new surname Marsden? I should have been listening more carefully. As for his first name, I had no idea what that might be.

We finally hit on a compromise. We would drive up to Sheffield, which was only twelve miles away, and see if we had any further inspiration when we got there. If not, we would call it a day and head off to the place where we were staying.

* * *

We weren't going to leave it at that, of course. As we made our way through the Sheffield suburbs we started planning our next move. Using her mobile browser, Ashley found that there were two main hospitals in the city, plus numerous specialist facilities and private clinics.

"Should I ring some of them? Who should I ask for?"

"You could try Marsden, initial D."

She tried four or five. Some said they had no patient named D Marsden; others refused to look on the basis of the slender information she was providing.

I said, "Maybe this is a lost cause."

"Wait wait – how about this? St Anthony's private hospital and hospice. That sounds about right, doesn't it?"

"OK, why not give it a try?"

She rang their number, and yes! Dennis Marsden had been a patient there for several weeks. We looked at each other in triumph.

Using her phone as an ad hoc satnav, Ashley directed me round the city centre and out to the west in the direction of Hallam Head, which turned out to be a comfortably middle-class area. The private hospital was a low-rise modern building set in its own grounds amongst well-heeled housing, with an imposing view across the dales.

As we pulled into the car park, Ashley shouted, "There! It's my dad's car."

We hurried into reception area and asked to see Dennis Marsden. Surprisingly, no obstacles were put in our way; we were simply pointed down a long corridor and round a corner. Ashley's low heels clattered on the shiny floor. As we approached the room number we'd been given we could hear raised voices.

"That doesn't excuse what you did." I recognised this as Gordon Renwick. "You've got away with it all these years, but now it's time to pay."

Ashley and I exchanged glances and instinctively hushed our footsteps as we approached the door. Renwick continued, "Don't you think you've let your daughter down for long enough?"

That comment intrigued me. I put my arm up to halt Ashley, and indicated that we should hang back. As we stood outside the door a weak voice, presumably Markham's, replied, "She's had a good life. She hasn't wanted for anything, has she? What else could I offer?"

Clearly this incensed Renwick. Spitting out the words, he said, "You have the nerve to ask me that? After all that you did?"

There was a pause, then Markham said quietly, "Well I hate to rain on your parade, Gordon, but standing there threatening me isn't going to change anything."

"Oh, believe me, it does. You can't imagine how often I've imagined this moment. Give me my moment of glory."

"And you think this would make Ashley proud?"

At the mention of her name, Ashley glanced at me again, then pushed past me and thrust the door open.

"Would someone mind telling me what the fuck's going on here?"

Chapter 76

It was a surprisingly large, predominantly grey room whose main feature was a bed backed against one wall. In it, propped up by pillows and flanked by various bits of technical paraphernalia, lay a gaunt-looking Desmond Markham. He had unkempt greying hair and a small moustache. A tube dangled from a gantry above his head and was attached to his arm.

Gordon Renwick was standing on the far side of the bed, looming threateningly over Markham. As we walked in he had the vestiges of crazed determination on his face, but this was quickly replaced by a look of annoyance as he glanced at Ashley.

"Darling, what on earth are you doing here?"

"I might ask you the same question."

Gordon said nothing, and into the silence Markham said, "Would someone like to introduce us?"

Renwick glanced back at Markham. "This is my daughter Ashley."

Markham looked at her appraisingly. "I'm very pleased to meet you, Ashley." He shuffled in a weak attempt to sit up straighter. "Delighted in fact. It's a privilege I never expected." He continued to gaze at her, and I could see a hint of a smile playing on his lips. "You're even prettier than the pictures I've seen of you online."

Ashley glanced from Markham to her father and back. "Why would you be looking at pictures of me online?"

He gazed at her a moment longer, then turned to Renwick. "Are you going to tell her, or shall I?"

At this Renwick stiffened and seemed ready to lunge at Markham. In an almost hysterical tone he said, "Nobody needs to tell anyone anything. Do they, Des?"

Markham merely relaxed into his pillow. "That might have been true until you came barging in here threatening to attack me.

Now all bets are off."

"I'm warning you …"

"Warning me what? That you're going to hit me? Go ahead – put me out of my misery. I'll be dead soon enough without any help from you." He turned to Ashley and me in appeal. "Could someone tell this man to start behaving in a civilised manner please?"

Gordon stepped a half-pace closer to Markham and raised his arms, clearly planning to throw a punch at him. Ashley shouted, "Dad, for god's sake stop this! Have you gone raving mad? This man is dying. Whatever he's done to you in the past, attacking him isn't going to put it right now."

"Ha! But it'll make me feel so much better."

"For how long? Five minutes? Then what?"

He turned to look at her, and there was a longer silence.

Markham cleared his throat. Quietly he said, "I'm your father, Ashley, not Gordon. That's what he's been struggling to avoid telling you. I never had any intention of bringing this up with you, but now he's forced the issue. I'm sorry."

"*What?*" She stared at him in astonishment.

To his credit he looked almost repentant. "There's never a right time to tell someone something like this." He shrugged weakly. "I wish there was. But I'll probably never get another chance. I don't know what else to say."

She simply repeated, "You're my father? You?" She turned to Gordon in bewilderment. "Is this true, Dad?"

He took a small step back and gave her a pained look. "I'm afraid it is." He turned back to Markham. "You bastard."

Ashley looked desperately backward and forward between the two of them. "For god's sake! Does somebody want to explain, please?"

Renwick stepped forward again towards Markham, grabbing the suspended tube as he did so and tensing his arm as if in readiness to snatch it away. He paused at the last moment with the tube still stretched taut, staring fixedly at Markham, and said, "This man stormed his way into our lives, robbed us of our savings, robbed me of my wife, then sailed off into the fucking sunset, never to be seen again. This man is a despicable, cowardly worm who doesn't deserve to live a single day longer."

Now he yanked at the tube. Markham's eyes darted between Gordon and the tube, filled with alarm.

I'd been watching this unfolding scene in amazement. I wanted to intervene, but couldn't think of anything constructive to say or do. I could try wading in and physically restraining Gordon, but what damage might he do to Markham by the time I scuffled round the bed to his side?

Thinking fast, I said, "Gordon, can I say something?"

I felt all eyes on me. Markham said, "Who are you?"

I said, "I'm with Ashley." I drew a deep breath. "She's my girlfriend."

Markham said, "I hope you deserve her."

Ashley said briskly, "He does." She turned to me. "What was it you wanted to say?"

Quickly I said, "Gordon, all this is between us. Everyone in this room is family, more or less. We can stop this now and all go home. But any second now a nurse or a doctor might walk through that door. If that happens, things will immediately get out of hand. The police will be called. You'll probably be arrested."

Gordon looked over at me without lowering his arm. At least he was listening.

I went on, "Is this really what you want for Ashley? You've just turned her world upside down by coming here and raking all this up. Do you want to do the same thing all over again by killing someone? You could go to prison. Do want to leave her with the aftermath of that? If you do, you must be even stupider than you appear to be."

He seemed to be wavering, but then Markham said, "Listen to the man, Gordon. He's speaking good sense."

Gordon turned back to him, angry again. "And what would you know about that, you miserable fuck?" He tugged at the tube again.

At that point I heard the door being pushed open behind us and someone new stepping into the room. I glanced round, dreading to see a nurse or doctor. In fact it was Trina, dressed in a light jacket and jeans.

She glanced around at the tableau in front of her. "Has everybody here gone mad?"

Chapter 77

Markham said, "Trina, welcome to the party. I was just having a visit from my old friend Gordon, from Falmouth." He turned to Gordon. "This is Trina, my daughter." He smiled ironically. "My *other* daughter."

Gordon looked over at Trina without speaking. Wordlessly she strode round the bed to him. "Would you kindly stop intimidating my father?" She reached out and pulled his arm gently but firmly away from the tube, which he released without resistance. "And you might like to give my father a bit more space."

He looked at her as if bemused, then stepped back past her to the foot of the bed. He paused there a moment, then reached into the side pocket of his jacket and pulled out a heavy object: an old fashioned-looking handgun.

A wave of concern seemed to surge through the room. However, he simply looked down at the gun as if wondering what it was, then turned, perhaps seeking a horizontal surface to put it on. In that spare environment nothing seemed to suggest itself, so I stepped forward. "Shall I take that?"

He surprised me by saying, "Thank you Michael." He handed it to me as if it was the most natural thing in the world. "I think I need to sit down." He glanced behind him and sat down heavily in the armchair. I could feel the collective sigh of relief.

Trina glanced around her. "Jesus!" She turned to me. "You see? This is what I get when I answer an email."

I lifted my arms in resignation. "I'm sorry."

At that moment a nurse in a blue uniform really did bustle in, and demanded privacy while she attended to Markham.

Trina said, "I'll stay."

I said, "We'll wait outside." I turned to Renwick. "Are you coming?"

He nodded and stood up stiffly, and the three of us trouped out.

* * *

We found a lounge area along the corridor, and sat down in a cluster of modern multi-coloured armchairs. Ashley was looking distraught. She immediately turned to Gordon and said, "So that man is my father? Is that what you're telling me? And you've been keeping this a secret from me all these years? I don't bloody believe this."

Gordon seemed thoroughly shaken, and was barely able to respond. He was shivering slightly. He looked at her mutely for a long moment, then managed to say, "I should have told you years ago, but there seemed no point." He swallowed. "He was gone forever – disappeared. I never thought we would see him again. I hoped he might be dead."

She glared at him. "I don't know what the hell to say." She stared at him for a long moment. "You should have given me the chance to meet him – to get to know him. At least it would have been my choice."

He looked at her bleakly. "But I didn't know how to find him. He'd vanished off the face of the earth. What would have been the point?" He swallowed. "We wouldn't have found him even now if it hadn't been for Michael."

She sat there computing this. I could see that she wanted to remonstrate further with him, but she could also see the logic of what he was saying. Finally she said, "Good thing Mike made the effort, then." She switched her gaze to me. "I bet you didn't expect this outcome when you started all this, did you?"

I gave her what I hoped was a sympathetic smile and said nothing.

"Well what the fuck." She dropped her hands in her lap and stared across the room, evidently lost in thought. Gordon and I both kept quiet for our different reasons.

Finally she shuffled round to face Gordon. "OK, so tell me how all this came about. At least you owe me that."

He stared into space, still shivering. "I can't ..." He tailed off and looked down at his feet. He lifted his hands and placed them carefully on the arms of the chair, as if considering some complex manoeuvre, but said nothing and simply shook his head.

Ashley turned to me. Was she slightly moist-eyed, or was it a trick of the light? Either way, her look still hovered somewhere between anger and anguish. "I want to know what the hell actually happened to make this possible. Is he going to tell me?"

I shook my head. "I don't know."

She turned back to Gordon. "So come on – you might as well spell it out. Desmond Markham was part of our lives at one time. Mum knew him, obviously." She broke off. "Was she ever going to tell me about this?"

He shook his head slowly. "I don't know. Probably not."

"I think I'm getting that." She nodded several times. "But *you* can tell me, so let's have it." She paused. "Please."

He lifted his head and looked at her for a moment. "All right." He cleared his throat. "All right. But I don't think … Mike doesn't want to listen to all this."

She said, "Yes he does."

He glanced briefly at me and shrugged. "Well, so be it." He paused and seemed to think for a moment. Then, speaking in a defeated monotone, he began, "I met Des Markham in Plymouth, at a finance convention. Your mother was with me. I had to spend most of my time in the conference hall, but he wasn't all that interested, so the two of them spent a lot of time together. They became friends."

He shook his head in apparent disbelief. "I liked him. We arranged that he would come and visit us in Falmouth. A few weeks later he did – and he offered me an amazing investment opportunity. It was too good to turn down, so I went for it. Money of my own that I'd saved, money I'd inherited from my father – everything." He stopped.

"Then what happened?"

He gave her a pained look. "Well, you were born, and we were happy. Your mother never said anything, and the years passed. We even suggested that the Markhams should come and have a holiday at the Fairmile, and we got to know his wife and his business partner."

I said, "Robert Stainer."

"Yes, Robbie Stainer. Mary never really liked him, but I didn't have a view."

Ashley was silent for a moment. "So there you were, living happily ever after. What changed?"

"Ah, well, I suddenly heard that Desmond's company had folded, and when I chased him up, he'd vanished. Didn't answer his phone, didn't answer letters – simply vanished off the face of the earth. Along with all my investment money."

I said, "But the police must have got involved, surely?"

"Oh yes, there was some kind of fraud investigation, but I never got the details. All I knew was that my money was gone. Robbie Stainer sympathised, but he said there was nothing he could do, and my solicitor told me he was right. He'd built an intricate wall of protection around himself."

"So when did you find out Desmond Markham was my real father?"

"Ha!" He spoke with more animation. "That was quite soon after all this happened. When Des cleared off with my money I was left with debts. We couldn't keep the place at Falmouth. I had to sell up to get myself out of a hole. We moved to somewhere smaller." He drew a deep sigh. "Mary wasn't very forgiving. She blamed me for my poor judgement, and one day she told me about her and Desmond. I think she saw it as a kind of punishment, and in a way I just took it."

Ashley received this with astonishment. "How unbelievably mean-spirited! She was the one who slept with this odious man, not you. And then he robbed you! How was that your fault?"

He gave a humourless laugh. "That's what I thought too. But I also felt responsible for failing to provide properly for her and you kids. I felt I'd let her down."

Ashley said, "God, I knew she could be a vindictive cow, but I never thought she would go to that length."

Gordon gave a small shrug.

"And there was no question that Desmond was my father? Mum was absolutely certain?"

He nodded. "I'm afraid so. She told me she'd lied about the date when she first found out she was pregnant, to make it fit in with the times we were together …" He broke off. "You don't really want me to go into all this, do you? There really wasn't any doubt."

Ashley shook her head. "It's all right, I get the picture."

He looked at her for a moment without speaking. "There's no point in being resentful. The fact is that we got through it all. Mary and I eventually agreed to put it behind us. We settled in at Truro, and you and Patrick did all right for yourselves. After a while my business picked up a bit. We had a good life."

He shuffled round in his chair to face Ashley more squarely, and fixed her with an earnest stare. "I never thought of you as anything but my own daughter. Never!" He looked at her for affirmation. "You must believe that. You're not complaining, are you?"

I saw a look of compassion slide fleetingly across her face. "No, of course not. But this is a hell of a lot to take in."

We sat in silence for a while, then Ashley turned to her father again. "So how come you took it into your head to drive all the way here today?"

He shook his head. "I don't know, darling. I think it just dawned on me that after all these years, I finally had the chance to come and confront Des. And he was dying, so I didn't have much time. Suddenly I couldn't bear the thought of missing the opportunity to remind him what he'd done to us."

"So do you feel better now that you've done it?"

"No! No I bloody don't. None of this would ever have come out if I hadn't come. I would have saved you all this melodrama. Stupidist thing I've ever done in my life." He looked down. "But I couldn't see that without coming here. Somehow it was inevitable."

I realised I was still holding Renwick's gun, and I glanced down at it. It was a heavy revolver, and looked old. I said, "How come the gun?"

He looked at it reflectively. "I inherited that thing from my father. God knows where he got it. Totally illegal, but it got to the point where I felt embarrassed to hand it in, so I just kept it."

"If I give it to you, will you put the safety catch on, rather than shooting us all?"

He shrugged ironically. "Give it here."

I flashed a look at Ashley, who nodded slightly, so I handed it to him. He fiddled with it, then handed it back to me. "Will that do you?"

Ashley said, "Would you have actually shot Mr Markham?"

He waited a moment before answering that. "I certainly felt like it."

Footsteps sounded in the corridor, and we looked round to see Trina approaching us. I gestured to an empty chair.

"Join us?"

Chapter 78

Trina took a seat and turned to Ashley. "So you're my sister then? Does that mean I have to start sending you Christmas cards?"

Ashley looked at her in wonder. "This really is too much to take in." For a moment they sat without speaking, assessing each other.

I said to Trina, "Are you telling us you had no idea that your father was also Ashley's father?"

"Not a clue, until ten minutes ago. That man is one twisted individual. Fancy living all these years knowing this, and never saying anything."

"You're taking it very well."

"Huh! With the life we've led, you get used to surprises." She glanced at Ashley. "Mind you, I thought we'd probably had all the surprises we were going to get. This one is something else."

Ashley said, "He told me he'd seen pictures of me online. He knew what I looked like."

"I suppose that was as far as he dared to go."

Trina turned to Gordon Renwick, who was watching this exchange impassively. "I'm not surprised that you went after him with a gun. Under the circumstances I probably would have done the same."

"It's no excuse though. I can't tell you how sorry I am to have caused all this fuss. It was a kind of madness."

Ashley said, "I'd better ring Mum and tell her everything's all right." Then she broke off, looking dismayed. "What the hell am I talking about? How can I even speak to her?"

I started to reach over to her, then stopped myself. I said, "Nothing has really changed. She's still the same person." It sounded weak, but it was the best I could come up with.

Gordon said, "I'll call her myself in a little while. It's my job really."

Nobody spoke for a while, then Ashley looked at me, forcing a smile.

"Mr Stanhope, was I hallucinating, or did you come up with that 'girlfriend' thing again in there?"

"Can I apologise here and now?"

"Apology accepted – just so long as we've got this strange propensity under control."

Trina said, "Ashley, I think I'm going to like you."

"Well, I hope the feeling will be mutual."

For a moment no one spoke, then Trina gave Ashley another assessing look. "Do you think you would be up to seeing my father again? He asked me to ask you."

Ashley glanced at Gordon, who attempted an encouraging smile. She said, "OK, I think I can handle that." She stood up. "Should I go in on my own?"

"Up to you. Whatever you can deal with."

She nodded and walked off resolutely towards his room.

I said to Trina, "Clearly I owe you one giant apology for causing all this trouble. I don't know what to say."

"You weren't to know about Gordon's interest in all this. None of us knew that."

"It's good of you to say that." I turned to Gordon himself. "How come you knew about Sheffield?"

He seemed to be recovering minute by minute, and now said, "Ever since you started trying to find the Markhams I've kept my eyes and ears open."

"You've been very surreptitious about it."

"I thought if I showed too much interest, Ashley would be suspicious. I could see you were a pretty tenacious person, so I just left you to get on with it."

"You see more in me than I do."

He shrugged. "I have to admit I was also checking some of her emails." He looked slightly sheepish. "I didn't read any love letters."

"Probably because I didn't write any." I thought for a minute. "How come you had access to her email account?"

He actually chuckled at this. "Oh, I knew how to log in. Patrick set up all our email addresses for us. He's a software engineer. One time he showed me how it all worked. He even told me the default passwords, and Ashley never changed hers." He gave a tolerant sigh. "Patrick and Ashley probably think I'm an old duffer who couldn't copy a file without having someone to hold my hand. The arrogance of youth."

"So you just pieced everything together?"

"More or less. Last night everything suddenly gelled in my mind, and when I woke up this morning I felt I had to come here immediately and confront Des Markham in person."

"How did you know which hospital to come to?"

"I just phoned around. I picked up his new name from you and Ashley."

"That's what we did." To Trina I said, "Did you come here this afternoon because you got my message, or were you coming anyway?"

"I got your message." She hesitated. "I didn't mean to cut you off after that weird thing in the car park. I just needed some time to get my head round it."

"You're probably being kinder to me than I deserve."

She smiled slightly. "Don't push your luck."

We all sat in silence for a while. Finally I said to her, "Those people who tried to snatch you in the car park – they were after me because of a book I wrote."

"A book?"

"A mystery novel. I published it online. It was based on a real-life robbery in the nineteen eighties, but it was completely fictionalised. The problem was that those people read it and thought it was true. They thought some of the loot was never recovered, and I might know how to find it – or at least, I might be able to lead them to someone who did. And they thought you might be a real life character that I re-created in the story."

She stared at me. "This is too far-fetched for words."

"It's true. Trust me."

"Unbelievable." She shook her head. "That whole sequence of events sounds like fiction if you ask me."

I smiled briefly. "I'll tell you all about it one of these days."

Gordon said, "Trina, can I reiterate my apologies? I can't forgive your father for what he did to us, but I can see that he's in a bad way. I wouldn't wish that on my worst enemy. And I can hardly blame you for what he did to us in the past. It wasn't any of your affair."

"Well thank you saying for that."

* * *

Ashley came back. "OK, we've done the father-daughter thing. We're good buddies now." She was being upbeat about it, but I could still see the shock in her eyes.

She sat down and turned to Trina. "How long has he got?"

"We're thinking maybe a week or two at the most."

"So I get a new dad, and then within a fortnight he's gone again."

"At least you got to meet him." Trina looked at her a moment, her eyes burning. "He's actually a nice guy. He's been a good father to me, anyway." She gave a mirthless laugh. "That is, if you exclude the bit about him snatching me away from my life and my friends, and making me change my name."

"I can see that his heart is in the right place," Ashley said. "He's just a weak man who found himself in the wrong place at the wrong time."

"You seem to have got the measure of him pretty well."

Trina said she wanted to spend some more time with him, so the rest of us prepared to leave. As we stood up she said, "Look, are we all agreed that you won't tell anyone else about our true identities? If you blow the gaffe, it will blight my father's last few days."

She looked earnestly from one of us to the next, then added, "As for me, I'm happy with my identity now. If you blow the whistle on me you could cause me untold grief for years to come."

We each assured her that we would keep her secret, and we left her at the door to Markham's room.

As we emerged from the hospital into a grey afternoon, Ashley turned to her father. "Are you all right now?"

"I'm fine." He straightened his back to underline the point. "I can't tell you how sorry I am about all this. I don't know what the hell came over me. It feels like a bad dream, but I've woken up now."

Ashley looked indecisively from her father to me, then said to him, "Do you want to follow us in your car? We could all go somewhere and talk." She laughed ironically. "God knows, there's plenty to talk about."

"If you don't mind, darling, I think I would rather just head straight home. We can talk more when we're all back in Truro." He looked at me. "Is that all right, Mike?"

"Of course."

She said, "But are you fit to drive all that way? It'll take you hours."

He sighed philosophically. "Mike put his finger on it earlier. This could all have ended up very differently. I could have killed a man. I could be in a police cell now. I honestly don't know what came over me. Frankly I'm amazed that I'm able to walk away from this. I've got a lot to be thankful for. I'm not going to squander it by driving into a tree."

"What will you tell Mum?"

"Ah, that's a good question." He considered for a moment. "Probably I'll tell her mostly the truth. She'll just have to deal with it." He looked carefully at Ashley. "Don't judge your mother too harshly over this. She's a good person and she made a mistake. Think of the happy life you've had all these years. Simply knowing what happened doesn't cancel any of it out."

"You're very forgiving."

"I've had thirty years to forgive. It wasn't hard." He glanced over his shoulder at the hospital. "It was Markham I hated, not Mary."

I said, "You'd better take this." I carefully handed him the gun. "But no repetition of today?"

"Absolutely not."

So we waved him away in his Volvo, and then I turned to Ashley.

"What now?"

"I wish I could just go home and curl up."

"Really? Did you want to go with him?"

"No way!" She looked at me indignantly. "Can you imagine me having a five-hour conversation with him after all this?" She gave a mock shiver. "I just need some time to unpick my life. This is very big thing for me. I need to understand who my parents really are. Neither of them is the person I thought they were."

"I wish I could help you, but I can see that it's something you have to work through by yourself."

I saw that gleam in her eye. "There you go again, Mr Stanhope, being too bloody understanding. I think you should be dragging me away somewhere where I can forget all this for a while. Preferably somewhere with a bit of life and lot of beer on tap."

"Truly?"

She shrugged. "Why not?"

"Well, I happen to know a delightful country inn somewhere in the Peak District. Shall we give that a try?"

Chapter 79

The inn lived up to its promise. We sat in the cosy bar for most of the evening, talking of past experiences and happier times, not of the day's revelations. Then we made our way upstairs and collapsed into a night of lovemaking that was free from the awkwardness of the previous occasion. We had moved on.

Next day, despite the dull and slightly chilly weather, we went for a modest walk on the dales. "Might as well do this properly," Ashley said cheerfully.

We found that she could travel straight back from Derby to St Austell by train, making just one change at Exeter, so I dropped her off at the station on the Monday morning. "I might as well show up for work this afternoon," she said. "Remind them I haven't completely abandoned them."

Driving out of Derby towards the M1, I felt an acute sense of being alone. These repeated separations were becoming a real trial.

* * *

I reached Joanna and John's around lunchtime, just as Joanna was arriving back from a morning's work. I told her, "I'm going to move back into my house. It's been wonderful here, but I need to get on with my life." She protested, but I could see that she understood.

She asked me about the weekend, but I was wary about telling her the whole story. Maybe some time I would, but not today. I wanted to see how things would settle first. I was also wary of introducing Trina into the conversation. Joanna knew enough about her for now, and I was reluctant to share her secret identity with anyone else. My interest in her had already caused enough trouble.

My house seemed bleak and unwelcoming, but at least it was drying out slowly, and the smell of mould was fading. I switched on lights and heaters in all the rooms and turned on the radio to give the place a sense of life. It worked to an extent. Then I phoned a builder to arrange for a quotation for the repairs to the water damage.

I sat at my desk and allowed my mind to wander over the events of the last few months. If you took my search for Trina and my book together, they had affected an extraordinary number of lives: Ashley and her family, Trina and hers, Rick Ashton, Liam Stone, Derek Flynn … the list ran on.

In several cases the outcome had been truly life-changing. Things would never be quite the same now for Ashley and her parents, or indeed for Trina, who now had a half-sister she'd known nothing about.

One thing that surprised me was the fact that I'd found so few internet references to Desmond Markham's disappearance, and none to the financial irregularities that accompanied it. I opened my browser now and casually tried a couple of new searches, using different keywords that included the word "fraud". Within minutes I came up with a link I'd never seen before to a facsimile of a news story from long ago: "No trace of HGRC boss as company crashes".

Well well. The information had been there all along. I just hadn't looked carefully enough, or in the right places. It was only a short piece, but it might have pointed me in the right direction much earlier in my search. Well, too bad. For better or worse, I'd arrived at the true story in the end.

The search had changed my own life a well as other people's. Without it, I would probably never have got to know Ashley. And assuming we stayed together, as I fervently hoped we would, Trina would become a *de facto* member of my own extended family. It was an extraordinary thing to contemplate.

Should I be feeling guilty about any of this? I wasn't sure. I found it hard to feel apologetic about my book. Surely it couldn't be wrong to invent a story and publish it? But when it came to my search for the Markhams I was on shakier ground. Curiosity might be a fine thing, but could it be justified when it had so many unintended consequences?

As for Liam Stone, I felt especially uneasy about the way I'd given him up to Derek Flynn. Who was I to play god over these people? I had to keep consoling myself with the thought that Stone was a self-confessed thief. If you applied a skewed kind of logic to the situation, he had betrayed Flynn and the rest of the gang by fleeing with part of their haul from the robbery, so in a sense I was merely helping to even out the score. I might have disrupted Stone's new life, but I wasn't actually helping to get him arrested.

But how did one strike a moral balance in a situation that was already bereft of any normal moral framework? I'd set myself a profound puzzle here, and would probably have to live with my doubts.

Perhaps the greatest dividend for me personally in this whole affair, apart from Ashley herself, was the fact that it had dragged my life up from the low point it had reached. I hadn't realised just how bad things had become, but I could now see how much I owed people like Joanna, Dave Matthews and even my ex-wife Sandy for keeping me from falling apart completely. Now I felt I'd justified their efforts. I'd picked myself up, and this strange saga was largely the reason.

* * *

Dave phoned me at tea time. "I thought you might like a status update."

"Definitely."

"Well, the police are still considering whether to charge Liam Stone, or at least Andy Davidson, with a firearms offence. No gun, no proper witnesses, and your mate Rick Ashton doesn't want to pursue it. And they're still not completely sure who he is."

"But they still might prosecute him."

"In theory yes. They also have your statement, don't forget. But I'm getting unofficial word that in the meantime he may have skipped bail and disappeared. So it might never happen."

Ha! So it looked as though he'd taken heed of the message Rick had passed him. I couldn't help feeling a sense of relief.

"What about Derek Flynn?"

"We've got nothing on him to link him unequivocally with your kidnapping. But you might be interested to know that we've got CCTV footage of your lady friend Joanna's car in Warley one night recently, near his house. Would you care to explain that?"

I hesitated. "Am I allowed to plead 'no comment'?"

He gave his characteristic dry laugh. "I warned you not to go round there, but you won't be told."

Picking my words with care, I said, "I think it might have solved a few problems."

"I'll have to take your word for that."

"Shall we say I don't think I'll be getting any more break-ins?"

"Good thing, because we still don't have anything concrete on the crew who snatched you. We know who they are, but there's no evidence."

"I suppose I'll have to put that episode down to life's experience."

"I think you might."

There was a pause. I was wondering how I could possibly show my gratitude to this surprisingly consistent and undemanding friend. Thinking on my feet, I said, "Dave."

"What?"

"I'd like to introduce you to my new girlfriend. Ashley. You'll love her."

"I hope not, for your sake."

I ignored this. "She lives in Cornwall, but I'll get her to come to London. Can we all meet up for a meal?"

"So long as you're paying."

* * *

I checked my watch. It was coming up to five: just about early enough to make my next call, which was to Annette Braddock, the publisher at Hunt Topham Media. I still had her mobile number, so I rang her direct. The call went to voicemail, but twenty minutes later she called me back.

"Mike, you wanted to know about your book?"

"Yes, if possible."

"Not good news, I'm afraid. We reviewed it again at the team meeting on Friday, and basically we decided we couldn't run with it."

Fighting my disappointment, I said, "Dare I ask why not?"

"Of course. Just a few too many rough edges, a few too many inconsistencies in the plot. And the overall package doesn't quite have the wow factor that we look for – the indefinable thing that gives books by unknown writers a flying start."

"I see."

"It's well written, Mike. Don't get me wrong. It's a very readable book. It has some good things going for it."

"Well thank you for that."

"Can I say this? You've made this connection now, so feel free to get back to me in the future if you want to pursue your writing career. I would say get yourself an agent – you can quote me as a reference if you like – and let them advise you. Then by the time we talk again, hopefully you'll have something we can all work with."

"I appreciate it."

So my embryonic career as a novelist was limited for the time being to my massive online audience of twenty-four – no, twenty-seven, as I found when I logged into my account on the publishing web site. Maybe it was what I was secretly expecting. If I ever did go back to Annette to offer her a new book, at least I would feel I was presenting it on its own merits, not under some strange deal that might or might not have been orchestrated from above.

I happened to glance down at the back page of a logistics magazine that had been waiting for me amongst my mail. A small article caught my eye: "Rick Ashton appointed chairman of Vantage Express".

Marvelling at this coincidence, I read quickly through the text of the piece. Did this change of role amount to promotion or a sideways shunt? The article wasn't saying. Either way, it meant Rick wouldn't be lost for a job in the near future. Presumably he must have impressed Janni Noble and his fellow-investors sufficiently for them to keep him on.

I smiled to myself. After everything, I still liked him.

2012

Hawkins was dead, the man I'd hit was in a coma, Sasha was inconsolable, and the Australian police were relentless. The other assailant was also dead, shot by Hawkins.

I spent the night in a Brisbane hospital, where I was told my injury should heal without any problem, then next day the police held me for long hours in an interview room. Eventually I was allowed back to my hotel, but they took possession of my passport.

All told, I had to stay on in Brisbane for ten days before I was told I could leave. No charge would be brought against me for my actions, which the police had finally accepted were undertaken in self defence.

I never saw Sasha again, but the police told me she had spoken up for me. I learned afterwards that no charges were to be brought against her either. But her new identity was wrecked, and she now had to rebuild her life without her father.

I wondered through all this whether to reveal what Hawkins had told me in his dying moments. In the end I said nothing. One day I might contact Sasha and tell her what he'd done with the rest of the jewel stash. For the moment, I felt she would be more comfortable in ignorance.

During my final interview with the police I was told that the man I'd hit had regained consciousness. They'd asked him how I'd been tracked down, and he seemed to know more than I'd have expected.

The officer told me, "Some of the original robbers found out about your Facebook campaign to find these people, and put a Trojan on your computer to track your activity. They thought they would let you do their work for them. When they realised you were heading off to Oz, they called up their local mob to follow you when you got here."

Just as I suspected, I'd caused this mayhem myself.

He told me the British police were going after the robbers who were suspected of orchestrating all this. I would be interviewed when I got back, and would need to hand over my computer for examination. This affair seemed to have no end.

And what had I learned? Not to meddle in things that didn't concern me? Not to yearn after the unattainable? All the above. Two men had died, and Sasha's life had been changed forever. I would have all this on my conscience for the rest of my life. I felt empty – robbed of an obsession and weighed down with guilt.

But as I sat in the plane during the long flight back, an idea gradually formed in my mind. This story would make an ideal subject for a novel. I'd always been drawn to the notion of trying my luck as an author, so why not now? Then at least something positive might come of all this.

However, my own story would end up much more happily. I wasn't having any of this death and destruction. I wanted to present a kinder world, with a more responsible leading character than I had been. I would have to change some of the details, of course. For a start, I would switch the hotel scenes away from Polperro. Where would I set them? Somewhere in the same area. Falmouth, perhaps ...

Chapter 80

Ashley raised her beer glass to me. "Welcome to your new home, Mr Stanhope."

We were sitting on high stools at the bar of the hotel in Truro where we'd first got to know each other. I'd just driven down from London on a Saturday morning at the end of November, and we'd arranged to meet up for a very late lunch.

I smiled back at her. "It's still hard to take all this in."

"You'd better get used to it."

It was my second visit to Cornwall in a month, and this time I wasn't returning to London. A few weeks ago I'd met up with Ashley in Truro to check out a flat to rent, and today I was moving in. I hadn't transferred my worldly goods here yet – just enough to get by with. As soon as the seemingly endless repairs to my house were completed I would put it on the market, and then I would move out any of the stuff that I wanted to keep.

I said, "I only wish I felt I could afford it here."

"Wait till you sell your house. You'll be rolling in it then."

It had all happened surprisingly quickly. I'd started asking myself why I needed to live in London, and soon realised that the answers didn't stack up. Theoretically I could run my freelance life from anywhere at all, so what was keeping me there?

The answer, of course, was a lifetime's associations, plus friends like Joanna and Dave; but all this didn't add up to a convincing case. Work was more of an issue. Admittedly, I could write desk-bound articles anywhere, but travelling from Cornwall to the rest of the country to do interviews would be a challenge. In the end I'd decided it was something I'd have to live with.

On the plus side, I'd negotiated an increase in my work load for Latimer Logistics, with a commensurate rise in my fee. Bob Latimer had even offered me use of a desk in a little room adjoining that of Sally Meadows, his PA. He clearly had a soft spot for Ashley, whom he seemed to hold in high esteem. Whatever she wanted seemed to suit him fine.

I wasn't so happy with the way this left my journalistic life. Promotional PR for Latimer Logistics and ring-around articles for Jason Bright didn't seem to add up to a satisfying career mix. But what the hell? I was with Ashley, I had enough of an income to live on, and if I decided to keep on trying to write novels there was nothing to stop me. What more did I want?

As if reading my mind, Ashley said, "Dave Matthews reckons you should be a diplomat or a high-level negotiator of some kind."

She'd come on another visit to London a few weeks ago, and I'd organised the promised dinner with Dave, who was clearly captivated by her.

"How so?"

"Well, he knows all about the way you dealt with that man in Essex. He seems to have picked up a bit about other stuff you've been involved with, too. He says you could talk the birds out of the trees."

"I don't think so."

"I only tell it as I hear it."

"Pity I couldn't talk my way into a book contract, then."

"Maybe you weren't completely committed to it. Maybe it's not your destiny."

"We'll see about that."

"You may not have much time for novel writing. Bob Latimer reckons you'll be an exec at his company before you know it."

"What? I hardly think so."

"He didn't tell me that himself. I just overheard him chatting to Brian in the office one day. They like your interpersonal skills." She turned to me with an ironic grin. "Personally I can't say I've seen much evidence of them."

"Huh!" Taking a permanent job with a logistics company definitely wasn't part of my plan, but I couldn't help feeling flattered. Eventually I might have some choices to make.

We smiled amiably at each other. We'd agreed that I would get my own place here for the time being, rather than move straight in with her. That would have meant making too many life changes too quickly for both of us. She'd also pointed out that her tiny flat was barely big enough for one person, let alone two. Having spent several nights in it, I was more than ready to concur. But our thinking was to look for somewhere together over the next few months.

I asked how her parents were doing.

"Dad's all right. He's a great one for the quiet life. If it were up to him, he'd just let everything go back to normal."

"But your mum won't let him?"

"He spelled it out himself when we were up in Sheffield. She can be unforgiving. She thinks that if he hadn't gone chasing up there that morning, I would never have found out about Desmond Markham, and nothing would have changed. As usual she blames him."

"But nothing does need to change. You've come to terms with the situation yourself. Why can't she just accept that?"

She shook her head. "She's a proud woman, my mum. She'll get used to all this in the end, but it's going to take time."

I wondered where this left me. Mary Renwick still seemed resentful about my relationship with Ashley. On the two occasions when we'd met in recent weeks she'd barely spoken to me. I said, "Will that include me, do you think?"

Ashley looked pensively at me. "She knows that you instigated the search to find the Markhams. In her book, that means you take a share of the blame."

"Huh."

"All I can say is, if she's going to make me choose between her and you, it's a no-brainer. She needs to grow up and see that for herself."

"I should be flattered."

"I'll keep on working at her."

Neither of us spoke for a moment, then I said cautiously, "You probably blame me yourself in a corner of your mind. If I hadn't gone looking for Trina, none of it would have happened."

She gave me a reproving look. "Mr Stanhope, that's not worthy of you. Do you think I'd be sitting here now if that's what I thought?"

"I suppose not."

"No supposing about it." She took a sip of beer. "Apart from anything else, you've given me a new half-sister. How good is that?"

"I'm glad you like her."

"I think she's great. We're going to get on well."

"She thought you were a brat."

She laughed. "I think we've got past that."

Since Sheffield, Ashley had become Trina's first point of contact instead of me. She'd made a brief visit to Chesterfield on her own, wanting to meet her real father again while she still had the chance. Then shortly afterwards we'd driven up there together for his funeral. She and Trina now seemed to be in regular touch.

Ashley said, "Guess what? She's coming down here for a few days in the new year, with her partner Martin."

"Your mum will love that."

She shrugged. "That's up to her. They're staying over in St Ives, so she doesn't have to see them if she doesn't want to. Patrick wants to meet Trina, so that will be nice." She chuckled. "She keeps telling me I must call her Tina and not Trina."

I looked reflectively at her. "Isn't it strange? I fancied her, and then years later I fancied you, and it turns out that you're sisters. I still can't get my head round that."

She gave me a scolding look. "But you don't fancy her now. We're agreed on that, are we?"

I grinned at her. "Definitively."

She seemed to hesitate for a moment, then said, "In that case, I can tell you that she really likes you." An unaccustomed blush passed across her face. "She thinks I've made a good choice."

"I won't argue with that."

* * *

A voice behind us said, "Hello Ash, Mike. How are you doing?"

It was Jack Forbes, who must have been seated at one of the tables round the corner. A slim girl with short-cropped blond hair and a gold nose stud was hovering at his side. "This is Paula."

He and Ashley chatted briefly. He said his shop was closed for the day. "It's an electrical fault. The bean counters at head office are having a fit, losing all this Christmas trade, but we're not complaining."

The two of them went on their way, and Ashley turned to me with a grin of complicity. "She's a girl from his shop. She's really nice. Looks as if their electrical fault has brought them together."

The afternoon wore on. Christmas shoppers wandered in for their quick one on the way home, mostly carrying bulging shopping bags. The place started to fill up.

Ashley turned to me with a smile. "My place or yours?"

"Yours is nearer, and mine's a mess."

"Done deal."

We stepped out into the street. The daylight was fading, and lights in shops and on the street gave the scene a festive air. Shoppers bustled past. I said, "I think I like Truro."

"That's what I want to hear."

We headed off, and she took my hand as we merged into the crowd.

If you liked Alternative Outcome, please review it!

Thank you for buying and reading *Alternative Outcome*! If you enjoyed it, could I ask you to do me the great favour of writing a review on the Amazon/Kindle web site? Positive reviews play an enormous part in spreading the word to new readers.

UK book page:
www.amazon.co.uk/dp/B01CK1XVHK

US book page:
www.amazon.com/dp/B01CK1XVHK

Also by Peter Rowlands

Deficit of Diligence (Mike Stanhope Book 2)

Mike Stanhope is out of his depth. It seemed such a simple assignment: "Go north, keep an eye on the company we've acquired, report back." A chance, perhaps, to flex his untried executive muscle – or some free time to chase down a mysterious bequest.

Instead, Mike finds himself caught in a spiral of corporate chicanery, threats and kidnapping, topped off by the prospect of a murder charge. His work is soon hanging by a thread, and his hard-won relationship with his girlfriend is on the line. His familiar points of reference are disintegrating one by one.

Acknowledgements

In some respects (but only some), *Alternative Outcome* echoes my own experience of attempting to find a traditional publisher, and then embracing the wild west of e-publishing. Whether I'll fare any better than my leading character will be decided by people such as you.

E-publishing has brought fantastic new opportunities for writers like me, but it has also created competition on an unprecedented scale. In some ways it's probably just as hard now for novelists to find a readership as it ever was in the past. But at least there's nothing to stop anyone with a story to tell from getting a foot on the bottom rung.

I hasten to add that I have not met or encountered any traditional or online publishers or agents like those in this book. They are entirely my own invention; I created them somewhat with tongue in cheek to illustrate the long hard road that still confronts any would-be writer who is trying to find a voice.

If I had an editor to thank, this is where I'd be doing it, but we self-publishers tend to edit our own work, and simply hope we will apply as much rigour to it as people who have been paid to do the job.

However, there are a number of people to whom I'm greatly indebted for encouraging me to press on with writing this book, and for making comments and suggestions along the way, as well as picking up inconsistencies and mistakes.

In particular, my thanks go to Clive, Jonathan, Ros, Stewart and Sue for their enthusiasm for the project and their invaluable feedback. Special thanks go to Christine for her helpful thoughts on character and motivation, and to Mel for taking the book (and me) seriously. And of course above all my thanks go to Fleur for her unswerving support and encouragement, for her patience in reading and re-reading the many draft versions, and for indulging me with our endless conversations about it.

About the author

Peter Rowlands was born in Newcastle upon Tyne, but has lived almost all his adult life in London. Like the leading character in *Alternative Outcome*, he edited and contributed to transport and logistics magazines for many years. "But I'm not nearly as resourceful as Mike Stanhope, or as good with people." Chronologically, this is his second novel, but it is the first to be published.